PRAISE F

New York Public Library Best Books for Teens, 2017

Chicago Public Library Best Teen Fiction, 2017

Amelia Bloomer List, 2018

Amelia Elizabeth Walden Award finalist, 2018

"A masterfully fierce, stirring, and deeply
empowering story of hope and courage."
—AMBER SMITH, *New York Times*
bestselling author of *The Way I Used to Be*

"Empowering, brutally honest, and realistically complex."
—BUZZFEED

"A call-to-action to everyone
out there who wants to fight back."
—BUSTLE

★ "Scandal, justice, romance, sex positivity,
subversive anti-sexism—just try to put it down."
—KIRKUS REVIEWS, starred review

★ "Gritty and timely . . . A must-read."
—SCHOOL LIBRARY JOURNAL, starred review

★ "A thoughtful, literary portrayal of female sexuality."
—BOOKLIST, starred review

"A strong statement about rape, sexism, and girl power."
—VOYA

ALSO BY AMY REED

BEAUTIFUL

CLEAN

CRAZY

OVER YOU

damaged

OUR STORIES,
OUR VOICES
21 YA AUTHORS GET REAL ABOUT INJUSTICE,
EMPOWERMENT, AND GROWING UP FEMALE IN AMERICA

THE BOY
AND GIRL
WHO
BROKE
THE WORLD

THE NOWHERE GIRLS

AMY REED

SIMON PULSE

NEW YORK LONDON TORONTO SYDNEY NEW DELHI

SIMON PULSE

An imprint of Simon & Schuster Children's Publishing Division

1230 Avenue of the Americas, New York, New York 10020

First Simon Pulse paperback edition July 2019

Text copyright © 2017 by Amy Reed

Cover illustration copyright © 2019 by Ulla Puggaard

Also available in a Simon Pulse hardcover edition.

All rights reserved, including the right of reproduction in whole or in part in any form.

SIMON PULSE and colophon are registered trademarks of Simon & Schuster, Inc.

For information about special discounts for bulk purchases, please contact Simon & Schuster Special Sales at 1-866-506-1949 or business@simonandschuster.com.

The Simon & Schuster Speakers Bureau can bring authors to your live event. For more information or to book an event contact the Simon & Schuster Speakers Bureau at 1-866-248-3049 or visit our website at www.simonspeakers.com.

Cover designed by Heather Palisi

Interior designed by Greg Stadnyk

The text of this book was set in Garamond.

Manufactured in the United States of America

2 4 6 8 10 9 7 5 3 1

The Library of Congress has cataloged the hardcover edition as follows:

Names: Reed, Amy Lynn, author.

Title: The Nowhere Girls / by Amy Reed.

Description: First Simon Pulse hardcover edition. | New York : Simon Pulse, 2017. | Summary: "Three misfit girls come together to avenge the rape of a girl none of them knew and in the process start a movement that transforms the lives of everyone around them"—Provided by publisher.

Identifiers: LCCN 2016044338 (print) | LCCN 2017020892 (eBook) | ISBN 9781481481731 (hc) | ISBN 9781481481755 (eBook) |

Subjects: | CYAC: Rape—Fiction. | Conduct of life—Fiction. | Sex—Fiction. | High schools—Fiction. | Schools—Fiction. | Family life—Oregon—Fiction. | Oregon—Fiction.

Classification: LCC PZ7.R2462 (eBook) | LCC PZ7.R2462 Now 2017 (print) | DDC [Fic]—dc23

LC record available at https://lccn.loc.gov/2016044338

ISBN 9781481481748 (pbk)

For us.

You save yourself or you remain unsaved.

—Alice Sebold, *Lucky*

US.

Prescott, Oregon.

Population: 17,549. Elevation: 578 feet above sea level.

Twenty miles east of Eugene and the University of Oregon. One hundred thirty miles southeast of Portland. Halfway between a farm town and a suburb. Home of the Spartans (Go Spartans!).

Home of so many girls. Home of so many almost-women, waiting for their skin to fit.

The U-Haul truck opens its sliding door for the first time since Adeline, Kentucky, unleashing the stale air from the small southern town that used to be Grace Salter's home, back when her mother was still a dutiful Baptist church leader (though not technically a "pastor," because as a woman in a church belonging to the Southern Baptist Convention, she could not technically claim the official title, nor its significantly higher pay grade, even with her PhD in Ministry and more than a decade of service). Everything in Grace's life changed when Mom fell off that horse and bumped her head and suffered

the concussion and subsequent spiritual experience that, according to Mom's version of events, freed her mind and helped her hear the true voice of the Lord and, according to Grace's version of events, got them booted out of Adeline and ruined their lives.

Couches, beds, and dressers are in their approximate positions in the new house. Grace's mother starts unpacking the kitchen. Dad searches on his phone for pizza delivery. Grace climbs steep, creaking stairs to the room she has never seen before today, the room Mom and Dad only saw in photos their real estate agent sent them, the room she knows is meant to be hers because of the yellow wall paint and purple flower decals.

She sits on the stained twin mattress she's had since she was three and wants nothing more than to curl up and fall asleep, but she doesn't know where her sheets are. After five days of nonstop driving, fast food, and sharing motel rooms with her parents, she wants to shut the door and not come out for a long time, and she certainly doesn't want to sit on boxes of dishes while eating pizza off a paper towel.

She lies on her bed and looks at the bare ceiling. She studies a water-damaged corner. It is early September, still technically summer, but this is Oregon, known for its year-round wetness, something Grace learned during her disappointing Web searches. She wonders if she should try to find a bucket to put on the floor in anticipation of a leak. "Be prepared." Isn't that the Boy Scout motto? She wouldn't know; she had been a Girl Scout. Her troop learned how to do things like knit and make marzipan.

Grace turns her head to look out the window, but her eyes catch texture beneath the peeling white lip of the frame. Carved words,

like a prisoner's inside a cell, through layers of peeling yellow, then blue, then white, the fresh words sliced through decades of paint:

Kill me now.
I'm already dead.

Grace's breath catches in her throat as she stares at the words, as she reads the pain of a stranger who must have lived and breathed and slept in this room. Was their bed in this very same place? Did their body already carve out this position in space where Grace's body lies now?

How intimate these tiny words are. How alone a person must feel to cry out to someone they can't even see.

Across town, Erin DeLillo is watching Season Five, Episode Eleven, of *Star Trek: The Next Generation*. The title of this episode is "Hero Worship." It's about a traumatized, orphaned boy who becomes emotionally attached to Lieutenant Commander Data, an android. The boy admires Data's superior intelligence and speed, but perhaps even more, he wishes he shared Data's lack of ability to experience human emotions. If the boy were an android, he wouldn't be so sad and lonely. If he were an android, he wouldn't feel responsible for the careless mistake that tore his ship apart and killed his parents.

Data is an android who wants to be human. He is watching them from the outside. Like Data, Erin is often confounded by the behavior of humans.

But unlike Data, Erin is more than capable of feeling. She feels too

much. She is a raw nerve and the world is always trying to touch her.

Mom says, "It's a beautiful day! You should be outside!" She speaks in exclamation points. But Erin's skin is almost as pale as Data's and she burns easily. She doesn't like being hot or sweaty, or any other discomfort that reminds her she lives in her imperfectly human body, which is why she takes a minimum of two baths a day (but definitely not showers—they feel too stabby on her skin). Her mother knows this about Erin, and yet she keeps saying things she thinks normal moms of normal kids are supposed to say, as if Erin is capable of being a normal kid, as if that is something she would even aspire to be. Mostly, what Erin aspires to be is more like Data.

If they lived by the ocean, Erin might not have the same reluctance to go outside. She might even be willing to subject her skin to the stickiness of sunscreen if it meant she could spend the day turning over rocks and cataloging her findings, mostly invertebrates like mollusks, cnidarians, and polychaete worms, which, in Erin's opinion, are all highly underappreciated creatures. At their old house near Alki Beach in West Seattle, she could walk out her front door and spend entire days searching for various life-forms. But that was when they still lived in Seattle, before the events that led to Erin's decision that trying to be "normal" was way more trouble than it was worth, a decision her mother still refuses to accept.

The problem with humans is they're too enamored with themselves, and with mammals in general. As if big brains and live birth are necessarily signs of superiority. As if the hairy, air-breathing world is the only one that matters. There is a whole universe underwater to be explored. There are engineers building ships that can travel miles

beneath the surface. One day, Erin aims to design and drive one of those ships, armed with PhDs in both marine biology and engineering. She will find creatures that have never been found, will catalog them and give them names, will help tell the story of how each being came to be, where it fits within life's perfectly orchestrated web.

Erin is, unapologetically, a science geek. She knows this is an Asperger's stereotype, as are many other things about her—the difficulties expressing emotion, the social awkwardness, the sometimes inappropriate behavior. But what can she do? These are parts of who she is. It's everyone else who decided to make them a stereotype.

One thing Erin knows for sure is that no matter what you do, people will find a way to put you in a box. It's how we're programmed. Our default is laziness. We categorize things to make them easier to understand.

That's what makes science so satisfying. It is complicated and massive, but it is also so tidy, so organized. What Erin loves most about science is the order, the logic, the way every bit of information fits into a system, even if we can't see it yet. She has faith in that system the way some people have faith in God. Evolution and taxonomy are comforting. They are stable and right.

But there's the pesky problem of chance, which never ceases to trouble Erin, and which she has made it her life's goal to figure out. The whole reason there are humans, the whole reason there's anything more than the very first single-celled organism, is because of mutation, because of something unpredictable, surprising, and unplanned—the exact kind of thing Erin hates. It's what makes

chemists and physicists and mathematicians look down on biologists as inferior scientists. Too much relies on powers outside our control, outside the laws of reason and logic and predictability. It's what makes biology a science of stories, not equations.

The thing about evolution that Erin needs to get to the bottom of is how sometimes it's this unexpected and unplanned thing that is the most necessary. Freak accidents are what make evolution possible, what made one fish start breathing air, what made his progenies' flippers turn into feet. So often, the key to survival is mutation, change, and most of the time that change is nothing more than an accident.

Sometimes it's the freaks of nature who end up being the strongest.

In the small but steadily growing Mexican part of town, there is one extended family consisting of five adults, two teenagers, seven children under the age of fourteen, and one wilted matriarch with quickly advancing dementia and questionable citizenship status. This does not include the additional cousins, second cousins, and cousins-once-removed scattered across Prescott and several surrounding towns. Rosina Suarez is the only child to a single mother, a widow whose husband died only five months after they were married, six months before baby Rosina was born. Instead of a father, Rosina has an extended family of aunts and uncles and cousins who move in and out of her house as if it were their own. Her mother's two sisters-in-law, who live in the identical townhouse apartments to the left and right of Rosina's, have been blessed with living husbands and large families. Their children do not complain or talk back or wear dark clothing, do not paint their faces with

unflattering makeup or shave the sides of their heads or listen to loud music from the 1990s that consists mostly of girls' screaming.

Rosina's family is from the mountains of Oaxaca, with deep indigenous Zapotec roots, with short, sturdy bodies and smooth dark brown skin, round faces and flat noses. Rosina's father was a mestizo from Mexico City, more European than Indio, and Rosina is tall and thin like him, towering over her family, an alien among them in so many ways.

As the eldest and only daughter, Rosina's mother has inherited the duty to house and look after her grandmother, who has a tendency to wander off when no one's looking. And because Rosina is her family's eldest daughter, it is also her duty to look after the entire brood of cousins, in addition to her regular shifts at her uncle José's restaurant, La Cocina, the best Mexican restaurant in Prescott (some would say the entire extended Eugene metropolitan area), and the center of the family's economy. Rosina spends the two and a half hours between the end of school and the start of her shift at the restaurant at her other uncle's house watching her seven young cousins while Abuelita somehow takes a nap on a chair in the corner despite the screaming horde of children, and Rosina's eldest cousin, Erwin, who is a senior at Prescott High and, in Rosina's opinion, the biggest waste of breath in the state of Oregon, sits around playing video games and popping his zits, with periodic trips to the bathroom, which Rosina suspects are masturbation breaks. Rosina's second-oldest cousin is a boring girl with no interests who is almost thirteen and perfectly qualified to take her place as primary babysitter. But Rosina is, and always will be, the oldest girl, and it is, and always will be, her responsibility to be her mother's assistant and take care of the family.

How is Rosina ever going to form a band if she's busy every afternoon changing diapers and keeping the toddlers from sticking sharp knives in electrical sockets? She should be rocking, she should be screaming into a mic onstage, not singing lullabies to her unappreciative little shit cousins while they smear boogers on her favorite pair of black jeans, which she has to hang outside to dry because the dryer's broken again, where they're going to get faded and absorb the smell of so many neighbors' tortillas frying.

The front door opens. One of the babies squeals with delight at the appearance of his mother, returned from working the lunch shift at the restaurant. "I'm out of here, Tía," Rosina says, leaping up from the couch and out the door before her aunt can even close it behind her. Rosina steps over the scattered pieces of hand-me-down junk that pass as toys, jumps on her secondhand bike, and gets the hell out of there without noticing the spit-up on her leg and something brown on her shirt that is either smashed banana or baby poop.

A mile east is a neighborhood without an official name, but which most Prescott residents openly refer to as Trailer Town. It is home to double- and single-wide trailers and small houses tilting off their foundations, yards that have been overgrown for so long, the weeds are as tall as young trees. In one of these trailers, a popular boy is kissing the salty neck of a girl whose neck is used to being kissed. She is not his girlfriend. She is used to not being anybody's girlfriend.

The little electric fan inside the trailer is on full blast, but the heat of both their bodies inside the metal box is making the girl sleepy and

a little nauseous. She wonders if she had anything she was supposed to do today. She wonders if the boy would notice if she took a little nap. She resigns herself to the answer as she closes her eyes and waits for him to finish. None of these boys ever takes very long.

There was a time when, like so many girls, she was obsessed with princesses, a time when she believed in the power of beauty and grace and sweetness. She believed in princes. She believed in being saved.

She's not sure she believes in anything now.

In a very different neighborhood, a very different girl closes her eyes and lets go, feels the boy's head between her legs, painting pleasure on her body with his tongue, just like she taught him. She smiles, almost laughs with the joy of it, how it takes her by surprise, how it bubbles up and makes her weightless.

She has never questioned her entitlement to this. She has never questioned the power of her body. She has never questioned her right to pleasure.

There are a handful of hills in Prescott, and Prescott High School student body president, straight-A+ student, pre-pre-med at (fingers crossed!) Stanford University, lives on top of the tallest one. At the moment she is driving last year's Ford midlist floor model (her father owns the dealership—"Prescott Ford: Most Fords sold in the 541 area code!") into her family's three-car garage, after finishing her volunteer shift at the old people's home (though of course she would never call it that out loud). "Retirement community" is less

offensive, which is important; she doesn't like offending anyone. She would never in a million years tell anyone how old people actually kind of gross her out, how she has to fight off the inclination to vomit through most of her shift, how afterward she sometimes cries with desperate relief as she steps into the hot shower and washes the smell of them off her, a combination of mothballs and soft food. She picked this particular volunteer opportunity because she knew it would be the most challenging, because she knows this is the key to success—embracing challenge.

In her head, she counts up her volunteer hours. She files this number away with her other favorite numbers: her GPA (4.2), her number of AP classes (ten so far, and counting), and the countdown of school days until graduation (one hundred eighty. Ugh.). She vowed long ago to not end up like her mother, a Prescott native who almost made it out, but who skipped college to marry her high school sweetheart. Sure, her mom ended up rich, but she had a chance at something more. She could have been someone besides the wife of a car salesman and the head of her neighborhood book club. She gave up the opportunity to *be* someone just as her fingers were about to brush against it, just a second before she could have grabbed it and run and never looked back.

Two miles west, a girl searches the Internet for easy ways to lose twenty pounds.

A quarter of a mile east, someone checks for the third time that the bathroom door is locked. They look at themselves in the mirror and

try not to cringe, carefully apply the lipstick they stole from their mother's purse, stuff toilet paper in the bra they shoplifted from Walmart, cross their eyes so the blur will turn them into somebody else. "I am a girl," they whisper. "My name is not Adam."

On the other side of the highway, a girl has sex with her boyfriend for the second time ever. This time it doesn't hurt. This time she moves her hips. This time she starts to understand what all the fuss is about.

In the next town over, two best friends kiss. One says, "You have to promise to never tell." The other thinks, *I want to tell everyone.*

One girl watches TV. Another plays video games. Others work part-time jobs or catch up on their summer reading lists. Some wander aimlessly around the mall in Eugene, hoping to get noticed.

One girl looks at the sky, imagines riding the clouds to somewhere new. One digs in the earth, imagines an underground tunnel like a freeway.

In another state, an invisible girl named Lucy Moynihan tries to forget a story that will define her for the rest of her life, a story no one claimed to believe.

GRACE.

The problem is, even when she ruins your life, it's kind of hard to hate your mom when she's perfect. And not "perfect" with flippy air fingers and an ironic teen accent. Perfect as in practically a saint, like almost literally. Except, technically, you have to be Catholic to become a saint, which Grace's family is not. But what are they, exactly? Certainly not Baptists anymore. Are they *Congregationalists* now? Is that even a thing?

Grace's father said Prescott, Oregon, would be more in line with their family's values than Adeline, Kentucky. He has a special gift for putting a positive spin on things that suck. He's in marketing, after all. For instance, seeing a benefit in having to move away from the only home Grace has ever known because their (former) church pretty much drove them out of town. This, Dad interpreted as an opportunity to show fortitude and resilience. It was also a great motivation to improve their skills of clipping coupons, minimizing toilet paper usage, and finding new variations of rice and beans while Mom looked for a new job and Grace tried to get

through a day of school without crying in public. While her parents practiced their fortitude and resilience, Grace practiced pretending to not be too upset that every friend she had, most of them since preschool years, threw her to the curb because her mom fell off a horse and bumped her head and refound God to be a way more liberal guy than everyone in their church wanted Him to be.

Mom's first mistake in the church was being a woman, which happened way before she bumped her head. Many of the old white folks (in a congregation that was mostly old white folks) crossed their arms in front of their chests and frowned during her guest sermons, waiting for the real pastor to take over and do the real preaching. Even before the head bump, she was a little too chipper for their tastes, a little too into the love business. So they were primed and ready for all hell to break loose when she went and married those two gay guys who owned the dog salon. In her last sermon before she got the boot, in addition to reminding the congregation of the annoying fact that Jesus loved and accepted everyone without judgment, she alluded to his being a brown-skinned socialist. There was even a rumor around town that someone overheard her exclaim, "Fuck Leviticus!" while she was pruning roses in her yard.

So, just like that, after years of service, Grace's mom was out of her job as director of women's activities and guest speaker at Great Redeemer First Baptist megachurch, instantly reviled and hated by nearly seven thousand parishioners from Adeline and the neighboring three counties. Dad had just started his online marketing business and wasn't making any money yet. But worse than being suddenly poor was being suddenly friendless in a small town where everybody

was friends. No one would sit by Grace at lunch. Graffiti started showing up on her locker, the strangest of which was "Slut" and "Whore," since she was, and is, still very much a virgin. That's just what you call girls when you want to shame them. So Grace spent what remained of the school year eating lunch alone in the gym bathroom, talking to no one throughout the day except the occasional teacher, and her parents had no idea. Mom was too busy trying to find a new job and Dad was too busy trying to find clients; Grace knew her pain wasn't something they needed to talk about.

Grace isn't quite sure how to define what she's feeling right now, but she at least knows it's not sadness about leaving. Adeline made itself very clear that it no longer had anything to offer Grace and her family in terms of friendship or feeling welcome. And even before that, when Grace was comfortably lodged in her low but stable place in the social hierarchy, with a set cast of friends and acquaintances, with well-defined rules of behavior and speech—even then, with all that order—Grace suspected something was off. She knew her role well and she performed it brilliantly, but that's what it was: a performance. Some part of her always felt like she was lying.

Maybe she always secretly hated Christian music and the cheesy, horribly produced Christian-themed movies they always watched in Friday night youth group. Maybe she secretly hated her social life revolving around youth group. Maybe she hated sitting at the same lunch table every day, with the same bland girls she never really chose and never particularly liked, who could be both timid and insufferably hostile to anyone outside their circle, whose gossip cloaked itself in Christian righteousness. Maybe she secretly wanted

a boyfriend to make out with. Maybe she was curious about all sorts of things she was not supposed to be curious about.

Grace had always yearned for something else. Different town, different school, different people. And now that she finally has the opportunity to possibly get it, she realizes she's terrified. She realizes she has no idea what she actually wants.

What's worse? Lying about who you are, or not knowing who you are at all?

Right now, faced with the uncertainty of starting a new school year at a new school in a new town, Grace would give anything for the simplicity of her old life. It may not have been satisfying in any meaningful way, it may have not been true, but at least it was safe. It was predictable. It was home. And those things sound pretty good right now.

But instead, here she is—in this weird place that doesn't know if it's a small town or a suburb, stuck in this purgatory between an unsatisfactory past and an unknown future. School starts tomorrow, Sunday is Mom's first sermon at the new church, and nothing feels close to being okay. Nothing about this place feels like home.

Grace suspects she should be praying or something. She should be asking for guidance. She should be making room for God. But right now she has bigger things to worry about than God, like surviving junior year of high school.

Grace realizes what she's feeling is homesickness. But how can someone be homesick for a place that doesn't even exist anymore?

And how can someone start a new life when she doesn't even know who she is?

ROSINA.

Fuck cousin Erwin and his useless boy exis-
tence, fuck all the uncles of the world, fuck Mami and Tía Blanca
and Tía Mariela for thinking Rosina's their slave, fuck old-school
tradition for agreeing with them, fuck this bike and its crooked
wheel, fuck this town for its potholes and crumbly sidewalks, fuck
Oregon, fuck rain and rednecks and football players and people who
eat at La Cocina and don't tip and throw their greasy napkins on the
floor for Rosina to clean up.

But Abuelita's okay. Rosina both loves *and* likes her grandmother, which is no small thing for Rosina. Even though Abuelita
thinks Rosina is her dead daughter, Alicia, who never made it out
of their village in Mexico. Even though Abuelita wandered off
Tuesday night when no one was looking and made it all the way
to the slightly nicer and much whiter neighborhood nearly a mile
away, and that pretty cheerleader named Melissa who Rosina's been
crushing on since sixth grade had to bring her back. After crying for
an hour, after riding her bike through the neighborhood searching

for Abuelita, Rosina heard a knock and opened the front door, her face blotchy, her hair a mess, her nose wet with tears and snot, to a vision of beauty and kindness: Melissa the cheerleader holding Abuelita's hand, a warm smile on her face, her eyes radiant with sunlight. "Look who I found," the cheerleader said, and Abuelita kissed Melissa on the cheek, said, "Eres un ángel," walked inside the house, and Rosina was so embarrassed, she shut the door in Melissa's beautiful face after only barely managing to say thank you.

Rosina cringes at the memory. Never has a girl made her feel so un-Rosina-like. Never has she felt so bumbling. She thinks of the stupid expression "weak in the knees," how she always thought of it as some gooey romantic nonsense, but now she realizes she has experienced scientific proof that it's a real physical condition, and she hates herself for being such a cliché, for having such a crush, for being such a *girl* about it.

She pedals hard, hoping the burn in her legs will wipe away this unsettling feeling of wanting something, wanting someone, she knows she cannot have. Even on her bike, riding as fast as she can, Rosina still feels caged, trapped. She can't ride to Eugene. She certainly can't ride to Portland. All she can do is wander around the streets of this tired old town, looking for something new. Sometimes after a rain there are sidewalks full of half-drowned worms. Sometimes lost mail. The usual empty bottles and candy wrappers, receipts, a couple of crumpled-up shopping lists. Roadkill. The only new things in this town are trash.

Rosina races through the streets of Prescott, an eternal loner, the only brown girl in town who doesn't hang out with the other brown

girls, as if she's trying to stand out on purpose, her spiky black hair snaking through the air, earbuds in her ears, listening to those wild women that made music in towns and cities so close to here but practically a whole generation ago, those brave girls with boots and electric guitars, singing with voices made out of moss and rocks and rainstorms. Relics, artifacts. Everything worth anything happened a long time ago when new really meant new.

Why does she always end up on this street? There's nothing here but cookie-cutter houses that were new in the fifties, a few scraggly trees, small front lawns with browning grass. This street isn't on the way to anywhere Rosina wants to go. It's not on the way to anywhere.

But there it is. The house. Lucy Moynihan's house. Faded white paint peeling like on every other house. From the outside, it's nothing special. It housed a girl Rosina barely knew. It's been empty all summer. It shouldn't matter. It doesn't. So why does she keep coming back here? As if it's calling her. As if, even though Lucy's long gone, she's not done with this town quite yet.

But the house isn't empty now. Not anymore.

If Rosina hadn't already been staring, she probably never would have noticed the plain, chubby white girl reading on the front porch. There isn't much about the girl that makes her stand out from the side of the house. She is off-white against off-white. She has the kind of soft, undefined face you don't remember. But she's new, and that's something. That's more than something.

"Hey!" Rosina calls, screeching to a halt on her bike.

The girl jumps. Rosina thinks she hears a mouselike squeak.

"Who are you?" Rosina says as she kicks open her kickstand. "You just moved here?" she says as she walks up the cracked footpath. "This is your house now?"

"Um, hi?" the girl says, setting her book down, a mediocre fantasy novel. She brushes limp, dirty blond bangs out of her eyes, but they fall right back to where they were.

"I'm Rosina," Rosina says, thrusting her hand out for a shake.

"Grace."

Grace's hand is limp and slightly moist in Rosina's tight grip. "What year are you? You look like a sophomore."

"Junior."

"Me too."

"I'm going to Prescott High."

"Yeah, that's kind of the only option here." Rosina does nothing to hide the fact that she's sizing the new girl up. "Your accent is hilarious. You're like a cartoon character or something."

Grace opens her mouth, but nothing comes out.

"Sorry, that sounded rude, didn't it?" Rosina says.

"Um, kind of?"

"I actually sort of meant it as a compliment. You're different. I like different. Where are you from?"

"A small town in Kentucky called Adeline."

"Huh. Well, there are a lot of rednecks here, so you'll feel right at home. You know whose house you're moving into, right?" Rosina doesn't wait for an answer. "Do you know what 'pariah' means? This was the town pariah's house. Have you read that book *The Scarlet Letter*? She was kind of like that, except not."

"I never read it. It was banned from my school's library."

"Wow. Even we're not that backward here."

Rosina's quiet for a while. She kicks a clump of weeds growing through a crack in the sidewalk. "I guess she's a sophomore this year. Wherever she is."

"Who?" Grace says. "What'd she do?"

Rosina shrugs. "*She* didn't do anything. But it doesn't really matter what actually happened. It just matters that she talked about it." Rosina's eyes shift around but nothing holds her gaze. She wants something to lean on. She is the kind of person who likes to lean.

"What do people say happened?" Grace asks.

Rosina shrugs. She is trying to act cool, trying to act like there aren't feelings running deep beneath the surface. But it is hard to act cool when you're not leaning on something, when you were already pissed off before this unexpected conversation even started, when the late afternoon sun is in your eyes and you're standing in the shadow of the house of that poor girl who deserved better and you should have done something for her when you had the chance.

"The thing is," Rosina says, "people don't want to hear something that'll make their lives more difficult, even if it's the truth. People hate having to change the way they see things. So instead of admitting the world is ugly, they shit on the messenger for telling them about it."

Rosina spits on the sidewalk, sickened by the slow heat rising from the pit of her stomach and threatening to burn her down. What is it about this quiet girl on the porch that is making her mouth move and flames come out? Is it simply because she's asking questions? Because she actually seems to care?

"Who gives a crap about some girl getting raped?" Rosina says with bitter sarcasm. "She wasn't important. None of us is important. The girl is gone. We should all just forget her." Rosina looks at Grace like she just noticed she's there. "You really don't say much, do you?"

"You've kind of been doing all the talking."

Rosina smiles. "Well, New Girl, do you have anything interesting to say?"

"Oh," Grace says. "Um . . ."

"Time's up," Rosina says. "I'm out of here. See you at school, I guess."

"It was nice to meet you?" Grace says. Rosina tips an imaginary hat, then turns and lifts her leg over her bike.

"Wait!" Grace says. She seems as surprised as Rosina at the sudden volume of her voice. "What was her name?"

Rosina sighs. "Does it matter?"

"Um, yes?" Grace says softly. Then a little louder: "Yes, I think it does matter."

Rosina doesn't want to believe her. That would mean caring about something she can't do anything about. She doesn't want to say the girl's name out loud, because that would make her real, and what's the fucking point of that?

"Lucy," Rosina says as she hops onto her bike. "Lucy Moynihan." Then she rides away, as fast as her long legs can pedal.

ERIN.

"I practiced my routine for tomorrow morning," Erin tells her mother. "It will take me approximately one hour and fifteen minutes from the moment I wake up until I get to school. Margin of error is plus or minus three minutes. This schedule also assumes that I select and lay out my outfit the night before."

"That's nice, honey," Mom says. "But maybe it's not necessary to lay your clothes out since you wear the same thing every day." Mom is always trying to convince Erin to do things differently. There is always a better way than Erin's way.

"But it will add a cumulative one to two minutes to take each item out of its drawer."

Erin's wardrobe consists of three checkered flannels, four plain white T-shirts, two gray T-shirts, three pairs of baggy jeans, two pairs of baggy cords, one pair of black Converse All Stars, and one pair of blue Converse All Stars, everything with the tags cut off.

"Why don't you wear those new shirts I got you?" Mom says.

"They're too scratchy."

"I'll wash them a few more times. They'll soften up."

"I like my old shirts."

"Your old shirts have holes in them. They're stained."

"So?"

"You may not care about things like that, but other people notice," Mom says. "People will make judgments about you."

"That's their problem."

Erin knows that Mom thinks she's helping, that Mom thinks this is the key to happiness—belonging, finding a way to fit in. But Erin already tried that. She spent her whole childhood studying people, trying to figure out how to be a "normal girl." She became a mimic, an actor playing multiple parts—she had long hair, she wore clothes her mom said were cute, she even wore makeup for a short period in eighth grade. She sat on her hands to keep herself from rubbing them together when she got nervous. She bit her cheek until it bled to keep herself from rocking in public. Erin was a chameleon, changing herself to fit whatever group she happened to find herself in, constantly racing through the database in her head for appropriate things to wear, to not wear; to say, to not say; to feel, to not feel. But no matter how hard she tried, Erin was never quite appropriate. Her words were always either a little too early or a little too late, her voice always a little too loud or a little too quiet. The harder she tried to fit in, the worse she felt.

People know what boys with Asperger's look like, or at least they think they do. Boys rage and thrash and scream. They fight and throw themselves around. They punish the world for making them hurt.

But girl Aspies are different. Invisible. Undiagnosed. Because

unlike boys, girls turn inward. They hide. They adapt, even if it hurts. Because they are not screaming, people assume they do not suffer. The girl who cries herself to sleep every night doesn't cause trouble.

Until she speaks. Until her pain gets so big it boils over. Until she has no choice but to emerge from her almost two weeks of silence to tell the truth about what she did with the boy named Casper Pennington—her final and most drastic attempt to do what she thought the other girls were doing. The event that led them here.

Erin shaved her head soon after. She vowed to never again care what anyone thought of her. She vowed to stop caring, period.

Mom sighs. "I just want to help make life easier for you."

"My old shirts make life easier for me," Erin says flatly. If she didn't wear the same thing every day, she'd have to decide what to wear every single morning. How do people do that? How do they even leave the house?

"Fine," Mom says. "You win." As if it's a war. As if it's Erin against Mom and the Normal Police.

Mom serves Erin a lunch of avocado-and-grapefruit salad with a side of raw almond butter and celery. It looks more like art than food—weird vegan chipmunk art. She put Erin on a raw food diet last year because she read somewhere it's supposed to help with mood stabilization and digestion issues for people on the spectrum. As much as Erin hates to admit it, it does actually seem to be working. But now, no matter how much she eats, she's almost always hungry again in an hour.

Mom is standing at her usual station at the kitchen island behind her laptop. This is where she lives her online life in the world of

Asperger's parents—sending e-mails to the support group she leads, moderating her Facebook group, tweeting helpful tips and articles, posting raw, vegan, gluten-free recipes on her Pinterest page. She does all these things, is considered to be an expert on Asperger's by a growing number of virtual friends, but she still doesn't understand Erin at all.

Erin's dog, Spot, is sitting in his usual station next to her under the table. He is named after Data's pet cat, Spot, featured in several episodes of *Star Trek: The Next Generation*. Erin could not get a cat because she's allergic. This Spot is her second Spot. Spot number one was a guinea pig. Spot does not have spots. He is a golden retriever. Data's Spot didn't have spots either, so Erin isn't worried about these inconsistencies.

"Are you looking forward to your job in the school office?" Mom says. She has been trying to teach Erin small talk. They practice at mealtimes.

"It's not a 'job,' Mom. They're not paying me. It's essentially slave labor. In some ways, you and Dad are paying *them*, since public schools are funded by tax dollars, and I assume you both pay taxes. Dad does at least. You don't work."

"I work, honey," Mom says. "I just don't get paid money for the work I do."

"You could get advertisers for your blog," Erin says. "You could get paid for speaking at conferences and stuff."

"Thank you for your input," Mom says. "But I'm happy where I am."

"No, you're not," Erin says. Mom gives her the look that means

she said exactly the wrong thing, but Erin keeps talking. "If you made money, you could become financially independent."

"Why would I want to do that?"

She doesn't say it. As mean as she can be to her mom, as many inappropriate things that come out of her mouth, there is one thing she never says: *So you wouldn't have to stay married to Dad.*

Erin shrugs. "A monkey would be overqualified for my job in the office. They just needed to put me somewhere during PE." Erin got a doctor's note saying she has problems with group sports and touching people. The note does not specify her dislike of sweating, which is also a problem.

"The training went well this morning?"

"I have access to the whole school database. I can look up everyone's grades if I want to."

"But you wouldn't do that, would you?"

"It's against the rules." Everyone knows how Erin feels about rules. That's why they gave her the job, which includes access to sensitive information.

"What's your plan for the rest of the day?" Mom says.

"I will read for one hour. Then I will pick up Spot's poo in the backyard and dispose of it. Then I will wash my hands for a full minute. Then I will eat an apple and carrot sticks because this meal will only keep me satiated for approximately ninety minutes. After that, I will watch my episode because I have completed all my duties for the day."

Erin's old occupational therapist in Seattle taught her about delayed gratification, about how it's the key to success. Erin has

become very good at it. She does all the things she doesn't want to do before she does the things she wants to do. That way she is always motivated to keep doing things and she always gets everything done. She always has at least one list going of what needs to be done, in a precise order based on a combination of importance, time sensitivity, and enjoyability (or lack of). Making these lists is sometimes as much work as the tasks themselves. But what people don't understand is it's necessary; it's a matter of survival. Without Erin's elaborate lists and schedules, tasks would have no hope of ever getting done. Erin would forget. Things would get jumbled around in her head until they crumbled into misplaced pieces, burying Erin in anxiety. Without her lists, without her obsessive organization, there are no rules, no order. The world makes no sense. It flies apart and threatens to fly Erin away with it.

"Sounds like a plan," Mom says.

"I always have a plan."

"Yes, honey," Mom says. "I know."

Maybe Erin can't pick up on subtle tones all the time, but she's pretty sure Mom's voice means exasperated. Erin feels a wrenching in the place in her chest where pain always starts, the place from which anxiety radiates into the rest of her body. Right now, the pain place is saying Mom should be proud of Erin for the success of her lists, not annoyed and ashamed that she needs them.

Spot paws at Erin's leg because he can tell she's feeling agitated. Mom got him cheap because he failed out of helper dog school, but he's still very talented.

"There's a new family in my Tuesday night support group,"

Mom says, even though she knows Erin hates talking while she eats.

"That's nice," Erin says. What she wants to do is say nothing, but that is unfortunately not how conversations work.

"They have a ten-year-old daughter who was just diagnosed. She's very high functioning, like you. Very intelligent."

High-functioning, low-functioning. As if it's that simple. As if those two designations mean anything real.

Erin doesn't say anything. Her excuse is that she's chewing celery.

"I thought it might be nice if you two could have a playdate sometime."

"Mom, I'm sixteen years old. I do not have playdates."

"I know she'd really like to meet you."

"I don't care."

"Erin, look at me," she says. Erin does, but she aims her sight just below Mom's eyes, a special trick she developed to make people think she's looking them in the eye when really she's not. "Remember how we talked about empathy? Try to imagine how this girl feels, and how reassuring it would be to meet someone older with Asperger's who's doing well."

Erin rubs her hands together to help calm her anxiety, to help her think straight. She thinks about empathy, how people mistakenly believe Aspies don't have it, that it's something people like Erin need to be taught. But Erin has empathy, lots of it, so much it hurts sometimes, so much that other people's pain turns into her own pain and makes her completely incapable of doing anything useful for anyone. That's why it's easier to avoid it than to engage. It's easier to try to ignore it than try to comfort whoever's hurting, because

usually that backfires and makes things worse. What Erin wants to do with pain is fix it, make it go away, and sometimes that's not what other people want. And that makes absolutely no sense to Erin at all.

What makes sense is logic. When in doubt, Erin asks herself, "What would Data do?" She does her best to think like an android. She uses her excellent logic skills to deduce if meeting would be a beneficial situation for the ten-year-old.

"But, Mom," Erin finally says, having reached her conclusion, "I'm *not* doing well." Despite her lists, despite her adapting, every day is a struggle that leaves Erin exhausted in a way Mom will never understand.

Erin knows what Mom's face means. It is what people call a face "dropping," though it hasn't actually gone anywhere. It means very sad and disappointed. In the case of Erin's mom, it also means you just said something that's obvious but that she's working very hard to pretend isn't true.

"Why do you say that? You get great grades, your IQ is off the charts, you're thriving in a mainstream high school."

Erin thinks about that. "I have one friend. Everyone else calls me a freak. Even she calls me a freak sometimes. And my one attempt at having a boyfriend made us have to move to another state."

"Erin, we've talked about this. That's not why we moved. Your dad got offered a job here."

But Erin doesn't have to be a genius (even though she is) to know the real reason they moved. Whether or not her parents admit it, she knows no one willingly moves from a tenured position at the

University of Washington to the University of Oregon for a job that pays less money.

"Mom," Erin says, "you need a better hobby."

She recognizes the look on Mom's face. It's like the face dropping from before, but worse.

"Empathy, Erin," Mom says softly. Her eyes are wet.

Erin feels something grab and twist the pain place in her chest. That means she is supposed to say she's sorry.

"I need some space," Erin says instead. "I'll be in my room." Her mother exhausts her more than almost anyone else. It's not necessarily being around people that drains Erin's batteries, it's being around people who want her to act like someone she's not.

"Come on, Spot," Erin says. The dog follows Erin out of the kitchen, loyal even when Erin says things that make Mom sad. Erin never knows if Mom moves from her place at the island counter while she's gone, because every time she comes back, Mom's still there.

GRACE.

Grace keeps her head down as she navigates through the various groups crowding Prescott High School's front steps. Through her bangs, she sees fragments of faces and hairstyles and clothes, and her mind races to catalog those she should try to avoid. Maybe a different kind of person would be looking for people to actively befriend, but her strategy for finding friends is through the process of elimination. She has thought long and hard about her plan, which is to scratch out first-tier popular (and who is she kidding? Probably second-tier popular, too), last-tier losers, druggies, super-jocks, any conspicuous outliers, and then she'll take whoever's left. At her old school, Grace's friends defaulted to being the kids of the super-devout parents at Mom's church, the kids she grew up with through years of Sunday school and youth group. She put all her eggs in the wrong basket. She lost everyone she had when they unanimously decided to defriend her when their parents decided her mother was, more or less, possessed by Satan. She cannot let that happen again.

Grace takes a deep breath when she locates the main office. She

has accomplished her first task. She has made it through the front door. Now to acquire her class schedule. If she breaks the day down into small parts, it won't seem so scary.

Please God, she prays silently. *Give me strength. Guide me through this torment.*

She stands at the front desk for what seems like a very long time. An androgynous-looking girl with a shaved head sits on the other side, eyes glued to the screen of an ancient computer. Grace knows the girl can see her, even though she's acting like she doesn't.

"Um, hello?" Grace says.

The girl looks at her for a moment, then back at the computer screen. "I'm not supposed to be at the front desk," the girl says flatly. "The computer I'm supposed to use is in the back of the office, but it's broken."

"Oh, okay?" Grace says. The bald girl shifts from side to side, looking nervous, saying nothing. "Um," Grace continues. "I'm here to pick up my class schedule?"

"You were supposed to get it in the mail two weeks ago."

"Um, I just moved here? So I didn't really have an address two weeks ago? So they told me to come to the office to get it."

The girl finally looks up. "Who is *they*?"

A heavyset woman hurries out of an office in the back. "So sorry, honey," she says. "I had to run back here for just a second." She looks at the bald girl with what seems like a worried expression, then back at Grace. "Was Erin helping you?"

"Um, sort of?"

"The way you talk is called 'upspeak,'" the girl named Erin

says. "It sounds like you're asking a question even when you're not."

"Erin." The woman sighs. "Will you please focus on your task and let me help this young lady?"

"I was trying to be friendly," Erin says softly. She takes a deep breath and moves her hands together as if she's trying to rub lotion into them.

"Okay, Erin," the woman says. "Calm down."

"Never in the history of the world has telling someone to calm down actually helped them calm down," Erin says.

"How can I help you, dear?" the woman says to Grace, with a look in her eyes that says they're in on something together, which Grace suspects is supposed to be a mutual exasperation with Erin. But what Grace thinks is that Erin seems stressed out, so shouldn't this woman be trying to help her? If you work at a school, isn't it your job to help kids?

"My name's Grace Salter. I just moved here. I'm supposed to pick up my schedule."

"Of course," the woman says with far more friendliness in her voice than when she spoke to Erin. "Welcome to Prescott! I'm Mrs. Poole. I run the office here. How do you like Prescott so far?"

"It's okay, I guess?"

"We are exactly eighty-one point seven miles from the nearest beach," Erin says. "Which is not okay."

Mrs. Poole ignores Erin. She flips through a file on the desk and pulls out a paper. "Here we go. Grace Salter's class schedule. Home-room is American Literature with Mr. Baxter."

"Mr. Baxter is the football coach and only assigns books by dead straight white men," says Erin.

"Erin, that's enough!" says Mrs. Poole with a huff, then turns to Grace with a pitiful face. "She's going to be here every first period for the entire semester."

"I can hear you," Erin says.

"You know what?" Mrs. Poole says. "The bell is about to ring. Erin, will you show Grace to her first class? We don't want her to be late on her first day."

Erin stands up, and even though she's wearing an oversize flannel over a baggy white T-shirt and ill-fitting jeans, Grace can tell she has a model's body, and she wonders why she's trying so hard to hide it. Grace thinks if she had a body like that, she'd want everyone to know it.

"Let's go," Erin says, and walks out the door without checking to see if Grace is coming with her.

Grace wants to ask Erin why Mrs. Poole thought it was okay to be so mean to her, why she seemed to think it wouldn't hurt, but what Grace says instead is "Have you lived here long?" to the back of Erin's head.

"More than two years," she says.

"Where'd you live before?"

"Seattle."

"Oh, was it cool there? I heard it's cool."

"You have an accent."

"I'm from Kentucky."

"Here's Mr. Baxter's classroom." Erin stops in front of an open

door, her eyes tilted toward the ground. Grace realizes that except for that first glance up from the computer when she first entered the office, Erin hasn't looked her in the eyes once.

"Thanks."

Erin's eyes dart across the floor. After a long pause, she finally says, "You're welcome." Then she walks away.

Grace enters the noisy classroom and finds a seat in the back. She keeps her eyes on the floor and can't tell if anyone's looking at her. She doesn't know which would be worse—if they were looking, or if no one noticed her at all. The bell rings. The teacher is nowhere in sight.

"I heard Lucy Moynihan had a nervous breakdown after she left school," a dark-haired girl says next to Grace. "She just, like, lost it. She's in a mental institution in Idaho or something."

"That's not true," the girl's blond friend says. "Her family just moved to Portland because they were embarrassed and couldn't deal."

"Serves her right," the other girl says. "For all the trouble she caused. Like, couldn't she think of a better way to get attention?"

The two girls laugh. Grace wants them to stop. She doesn't know Lucy, doesn't know the whole story, but she knows in her heart that the girl who carved those words Grace found in her room was not just looking for attention.

But mixed in with her annoyance is also the hope that these girls are possible friend contenders. She can tell they're not popular, but they're also not the bottom rung. They're like her, the kind of girls no one notices. So what if they gossip? Grace may have to look past things like that. She's doesn't have a ton of other options.

Grace closes her eyes. She tells herself, *Say hello.* She prays for strength. She opens her mouth, but just then a tall, thick, clean-cut man enters the room carrying a pile of tattered textbooks.

"Yo, Coach Baxter," says a beefy dude in the front row.

"Aarons," says the teacher. "You ready to win on Friday?"

"Hell yes!" Then a few other guys in football jerseys high-five and whoop.

"Here, McCoy," he says to one of the football guys, dropping the pile of books on his desk. "Pass these out."

"Yes, Coach."

"All right," Mr. Baxter says, rifling through a stack of papers on his desk. "Attendance. Attendance. Where's my attendance sheet?"

The loudspeaker crackles. "Good morning, Prescott High School, and happy first day of school," says a female voice. "This is Principal Slatterly." Half the class moans. "I speak for the teachers and administration when I say we're glad to see you and hope you are returning from your summers well rested and ready to learn."

Her voice turns somber: "I want to emphasize that in addition to education, the mission of Prescott High is to instill in its students a respect for authority, discipline, and order. Without these things, your school, your community, society as a whole, would fall apart. We aim to nurture and grow constructive members of society, young men and women who want to contribute to, not disrupt and destroy, the spirit of the school community." She clears her throat, and her voice turns chipper once again. "Our varsity football team is looking stronger than ever this year, and we're looking forward to the pep rally Friday afternoon. Remember, students,

only you can take charge of your own future. Go Spartans!"

Half the class cheers while the rest stare blankly out the window. The blond gossiping girl smiles at Grace. Grace worries that her smile back is crooked. The girl says, "Are you new?"

"Yeah. Hi. I'm Grace."

"I'm Allison. Nice to meet you."

Her friend says, "I'm Connie." Grace feels the flutters of hope in her chest. All girls gossip, don't they? Even nice girls are a little bit mean.

"All right," Coach Baxter says from the front of the classroom. "This class is American Literature. Before we get started, there are some things I want you to know. I believe in the canon. I believe in reading great works of literature that have endured through the ages because they explore universal themes. I'm not going to waste our time with work that is popular because of passing fads and political correctness. My job is to give you a strong foundation in the classics, and that's exactly what I'm going to do. We will start with selections by Edgar Allen Poe, Ralph Waldo Emerson, and Henry David Thoreau. Then we'll read *Moby Dick*, by Herman Melville."

"Isn't that about a whale?" says a guy in the front row.

"It's about obsession and man's eternal struggle with himself and God," says Mr. Baxter. "Among other things. But yes, there is a whale. Is that all right with you, Clemons?"

"Yes, coach."

"Good. After *Moby Dick*, we'll move on to selections from American greats like Mark Twain, Henry James, Faulkner, Hemingway,

and Steinbeck. Then we're in for a real treat with F. Scott Fitzgerald's *The Great Gatsby*, which most intelligent people consider the greatest American novel. If we have time at the end of the semester, we'll hopefully be able to read selections from a few great living authors, including my personal favorite, Jonathan Franzen."

"Now," he says. "Open your textbooks at the beginning, and we'll go around the room taking turns reading. Page four: *What is a novel?* Who wants to start?"

Grace opens the textbook on her desk to a pencil-drawn doodle of a penis wearing sunglasses.

Grace gets lost trying to find her locker, so by the time she gets to the lunchroom it's nearly full. She looks around for Connie and Allison, the girls from her homeroom, but they must have a different lunch. She searches the room for other potential friends—not too pretty but not too ugly, somewhere in the middle of being nobodies and somebodies, the kind of friends she could dissolve into. For a moment she considers turning around and finding a hidden spot under a stairwell to eat.

But then a table catches her eye. In the corner of the lunchroom, near the hallway that leads to the library, is an island in the sea of high school hierarchy. Sitting there are Erin, the bald girl from the school office, and Rosina, the girl she met in front of her house yesterday, equally strange but in a different, louder, way. The two girls seem unaware of the world around them, as if they don't even know they're sitting in the middle of a high school cafeteria. How nice it would be to be that free, that unencumbered by the whims and weaknesses of other people.

Rosina looks up and catches Grace's eye. Erin turns her head to see what Rosina's looking at. The two girls look at her, not exactly smiling, but with a curiosity that is not unkind.

Is it true that this decision—where to sit at lunch—could define Grace for the rest of her high school career, quite possibly for the rest of her life? Is life that senseless and absurd? If her previous experiences are any indication, the answer is yes.

Grace had a plan, but maybe that plan was wrong. Maybe decisions should not be made out of fear. Maybe the goal isn't to blend in. Maybe Grace has been approaching this game all wrong, and the goal isn't to play it safe and try to stay in the middle. Maybe she doesn't have to play the game at all.

"Hi," Grace says when she reaches the lunch table, her heart pounding. "Can I sit with you?"

Erin tilts her head in a way that reminds Grace of either a cat or a robot. "Why?" she says.

"Erin," Rosina says. "Remember how you're not always supposed to say the first thing that comes to mind?"

"But I want to know why she wants to sit with us," Erin says, with no trace of cruelty. "No one ever wants to sit with us."

"Good point," Rosina says. "Why do you want to sit with us, New Girl?"

"I, um, I don't know? I guess I just met you both before, and you seemed nice, and I'm new and don't know anybody yet, and—"

"It's okay," Rosina says. "I was kidding. Of course you can sit with us."

"We're not nice," Erin says.

"Speak for yourself," says Rosina. "I'm nice."

"No, you're not."

"I'm nice to you."

"I'm the only person you're nice to."

"Well, maybe I'm going to want to be nice to New Girl, too. So far, she's being nice to me, so I'm definitely considering it."

Erin shrugs. "You're lucky," she says. "This is the best table in the cafeteria."

"Why's that?" Grace says as she sits down.

"It's the quietest," Erin says. "And it has the quickest escape route to the library."

Grace notices Erin's lunch in a small tin container with three compartments. It is not the lunch of an average teenager, not a sandwich or chips or anything resembling cooked food. Erin notices her looking. "This is called a bento box. It's from Japan. My mom got it for me because I don't like my food to touch."

"Are you on a diet?" Grace asks.

"Not on purpose."

"Erin's mom feeds her leaves and sticks so she won't hit herself anymore," Rosina says.

"Rosina's tone of voice implies sarcasm," Erin says flatly. "But the content of her statement is close to the truth. Except these aren't leaves and sticks."

"Okay, time to change the subject," Rosina says. "What's your name, New Girl?"

"Grace. We met yesterday, remember?"

"Yeah, I remember. You live in Lucy Moynihan's old house.

Shit!" Rosina fake slaps herself. "I promised I wouldn't utter her name again."

"Why not?" Grace asks.

"I do not want to contribute to this town's unhealthy obsession with that girl. It's been a whole summer and people are still talking about her. Get a life, Prescott."

"Was she your friend?"

"You're looking at my friend," Rosina says. "This bald girl eating rabbit food."

Erin looks up from her lunch of shredded vegetables. "People aren't going to stop talking about her until they stop feeling guilty," Erin says. "They can't let it go because it's still weighing on their consciences. Conscience. What's the plural of 'conscience'? I should know this."

"That was a very astute observation," Rosina says.

"Thank you."

"You're welcome."

"What exactly happened to Lucy?" Grace asks. "Did she say someone raped her? Who'd she say did it?"

Neither Rosina nor Erin says anything. They take a bite of their lunches in tandem.

"Did you believe her?" Grace says.

Rosina sighs. "Of course we believed her. Most everybody did, but they'll never admit it. Probably half the girls in this school have had some kind of run-in with one of those assholes." Rosina looks up from her barely-eaten sandwich. "But it doesn't fucking matter."

"Why doesn't it matter?" Grace says. "Of course it matters."

"On what planet?"

Grace has no idea how to answer.

"I would like to talk about nudibranchs now," Erin announces, kneading her hands together anxiously.

"Go for it," Rosina says. Grace looks to Rosina for a clue, but Rosina takes a bite of her sandwich as if this is a completely normal turn for the conversation to take.

"Nudibranchs are sea slugs," Erin says. "Which is a misleading name, because they are in fact some of the most beautiful and graceful creatures in the sea. *Nudibranch* is Latin for 'naked lung,' because their lungs are on the outside of their bodies, like feathers. They are gastropods, like mollusks and octopi. *Gastropod* means 'stomach foot.'"

"Gastropod," Rosina says, ripping the crust off her sandwich. "Great name for a band."

Then Grace hears a familiar kind of laugh nearby, the kind she got so used to at the end of her time in Adeline, the kind of laugh that has a target, a victim. Mean girls getting ready to be mean.

"Don't get too close to the freak table," a girl says in a fake whisper to her friend as they walk by.

Rosina's arm shoots into the air, her long middle finger outstretched. "Fuck off, pod people," she says calmly. "I don't want to catch what you got."

The girls roll their eyes and laugh as they walk away, and Grace feels something inside her collapse. A familiar pain surfaces, along with the fear that she picked exactly the wrong table.

"Fucking cheerleaders," Rosina says. "Can they be any more of a stereotype?"

"I'm leaving," Erin says, standing up abruptly with a pained look on her face and swaying slightly on her feet. She throws her things into her bag.

"See you," Rosina says as Erin turns and walks quickly down the hall.

"Wait," Grace says. "Where's she going?"

"Probably the library."

"Why?" Grace asks.

"Fucking cheerleaders," Rosina says, shaking her head, but Grace doesn't know if that's supposed to be an answer to her question or a comment on the state of the world. Either way, Grace is not feeling very optimistic.

US.

This girl joined the cheer squad because she loves dancing and the game of football. She didn't know that's not why most girls join the squad. She didn't think much about the uniforms, didn't think about the Fridays she'd be required to wear them to school, how the performance lasts way beyond the games, how it is part of her job to obsess about the cellulite on her upper thighs that no number of squats can get rid of, how the entire school has a right to judge her ass in close-up.

She holds her head high as she struts down the hall. It is her job to be confident and cheerful. So what if people are starting to talk about how she never seems to have a boyfriend? Someone so pretty should have a boyfriend.

The girl smiles so no one will suspect what she's thinking: *What if this wasn't my life? What if I didn't have to think about my body all the time, if I didn't have to be on display? What would it be like to be a different kind of girl?*

* * *

Prescott High's student body president wonders if maybe at Stanford girls are allowed to be more than one thing. Since everyone there has to be smart by default, maybe it's something you get to stop trying to prove all the time, so then you get to try being other things. Like maybe she can try wearing her skirts a little shorter, her shirts a little lower. Maybe she can wear some of that makeup her mom keeps buying her that she refuses to wear out of fear that people would stop taking her seriously. Maybe she can do something with her hair besides tying it up in this tight ponytail every day.

What would that be like, to be noticed? To be looked at? To be wanted as something besides a lab partner? To not have to choose between pretty and smart?

What guy wants a jock for a girlfriend? What guy dreams of hooking up with the school softball star, with her thick arms and legs, her drab orange ponytail, her see-through eyelashes and perpetually sunburned nose? They don't even see her in the locker room as she collects dirty towels from varsity football practice—a *girl*, in the locker room. She thought signing up to be team manager would help her meet guys, but the only time they ever talk to her is to ask her where Coach is or if she can get grape-flavored Gatorade for next practice.

So they certainly don't notice her in the corner disinfecting mouth guards as they towel off. They certainly don't know she's listening to their discussion comparing how many girls they slept with over the summer. Of course they're all probably lying. It's primal, their need to compete, this need to fight over territory.

"Let's make a bet on who can bag more this year," Eric Jordan

says. No surprise there. Even if he hadn't been one of the guys Lucy said raped her, everyone can agree he'd certainly be capable of something like that. "Virgins count double," he says. Most of the guys laugh. The ones who don't laugh look away or roll their eyes but say nothing. "Start with the freshmen. They're the easiest."

"Knock it off, man," one guy says. "My sister's a freshman."

"Is she hot?" says Eric Jordan.

The guy says a halfhearted "Fuck you," but it can barely be heard above the laughter. Maybe not all the guys are participating in the conversation, but certainly none of them is stopping it.

She knows the thought is wrong as she's thinking it, but she wishes, just once, a guy would try to take advantage of her.

If Erin DeLillo tolerated figures of speech, one might say she could do her homework with her eyes closed. Literally, of course, this is not true, but she does her homework quickly and with ease, even AP Calculus and AP Chemistry. Mom always reminds her how lucky she is to be so bright; few Aspies are so exceptional, so *special*. As if they need to be. As if that's the only way to be forgiven for the rest of what they are.

She sits on the couch with Spot and a snack of carrot sticks and homemade raw cashew "cheese" spread, having earned today's episode of *Star Trek: The Next Generation*. Episode 118, "Cause and Effect," starts with the senior crew playing poker. Data is particularly good at poker because his face shows no emotion. He has no tells. His poker face is permanent.

Erin has been working on her poker face. She doesn't cry as

much in public anymore. She's gotten better at hiding when she's hurt. The worst of the bullies have mostly gotten bored with her and moved on to other unfortunate victims. But there are still the looks when she says something weird, the snickers when she trips or does something clumsy, the ignoring, the exclusions, the talking to her like she's a child or hard of hearing—and that's from the nice people.

This is the episode of *TNG* where the *Enterprise* gets stuck in a time loop and keeps repeating the same day over and over and over again, and no one knows how to make it stop.

GRACE.

"Prescott, I am honored to meet you!" Grace's mother says from the pulpit with her arms open wide, as if she's embracing the entire congregation. She's got her magic smile on, the one that wrinkles her eyes and makes you feel hugged even if you're across the room. Grace looks around and sees people smiling, absorbing Mom's warmth. They feel it—her sincerity, her passion, her love. Just one sentence in, and Mom's a hit.

Grace remembers when their old church used to look at Mom this way, before she started talking about itchy stuff like social justice and the hypocrisy of conservative Christianity. Even the old curmudgeons who could never quite forgive her for being a woman couldn't help but be charmed by her infectious warmth. She was a feel-good kind of preacher, the kind that spent a lot of time on Proverbs, Song of Solomon, and the pretty parts of Psalms, talking about God's love and comfort and grace. The head pastor was the guy who did the fire-and-brimstone sermons; he was the guy who talked about sin. Mom warmed up the crowd with good news so they'd be ready for his bad.

Right now she's up there telling jokes. Their old church wasn't into funny. "A teacher asked her students to bring an item to class that represented their religious beliefs," she says in her thick Kentucky drawl. "A Catholic student brought a crucifix. A Jewish student brought a menorah. A Muslim student brought a prayer rug." She pauses for comedic effect before delivering the punch line. "The Southern Baptist brought a casserole dish." Everyone laughs.

"Yes, y'all, I come from a Southern Baptist tradition. My faith evolved, and I moved on. But I still love me a good, cheesy casserole." Laughter all around.

"We have to be able to laugh at ourselves," she says. "We must question ourselves, our most firmly held beliefs. We have to evolve and change and become better. The very *fact* of Jesus, His very existence, shows us that change is necessary, that change is God's work. Jesus came to change things. He came to make things better. We cannot insult Him by refusing to keep doing His work."

She never got to talk like this at her old church. "Change" was a dirty word, a sinful word. Their old, white, blue-eyed Jesus was a totally different guy from the one she's talking about today.

Grace has never heard her mother speak with this much passion, with this much joy. She can feel the electricity buzzing through the congregation. They are hearing her, feeling her. She is reaching inside and touching the parts of them where a little piece of God resides. Grace's father sits next to her, his phone lying next to him on the pew, recording the sermon. The church makes its own recordings to post on the website, but that won't go up until tomorrow at the earliest, and he will want to listen to this right away, to make

notes, to find pull quotes, to scour Mom's words for new angles to make her famous. They will sit at the dinner table tonight while Grace finishes the week's homework, talking late into the night about their two favorite subjects: God and business.

Grace is in the front row, but Mom seems miles away. Grace is just one of many, just a member of her audience, her flock. Grace's heart aches with yearning. *Just look at me*, she thinks. *Make me special.* But it doesn't happen. Mom is everybody's, not just Grace's.

Mom walks back and forth, abandoning the confines of the pulpit, taking up as much space as possible, reveling in this freedom she's never had before. This church isn't nearly as big as the megachurch they came from, but it's still big enough that she has to wear a mic on the collar of her robe. And the congregation is hers in a way she's never had before. All hers.

As they rise to sing, not out of the hymnal but from a photocopied handout of an old protest song from the sixties, Grace realizes her face is wet. She wipes her eyes and mouths the words of the song without making a sound. There is so much room inside her, so much space to fill. So much emptiness. Even here, she feels it. Even here, where God is supposed to make her whole.

After the service, Mom is like a rock star signing autographs for fans. She stands in front of the big, colorful mural decorated by Sunday school kids that says JESUS DIDN'T REJECT ANYONE—NEITHER DO WE. Half the congregation is lined up for a turn to talk with her, to shake hands and get a hug, to tell her how much they loved her sermon, to tell her how honored and grateful they are that she chose this church to be her new home. Grace still doesn't

quite understand how getting kicked out as an underling at a rural megachurch skyrocketed her mom to rock-star status, but here they are, and there she is, amassing her groupies. Dad's standing beside her, as always her devoted handler. Grace is standing in the corner between the wall and the foldout tables of snacks, shoving cookies in her face.

"Hey," says a very large teenage boy coming her way, the only young Black face in a field of white. "Aren't you the new preacher's kid?"

"Um, yes?" Grace mumbles, crumbs falling out of her mouth.

"You don't want to be part of the receiving line?"

She wipes her mouth with the back of her hand. Before she can think of an answer, the guy extends his big, meaty hand to shake. "I'm Jesse Camp," he says. Grace hasn't met a whole lot of people who make her feel petite, but he is definitely one of them.

"Grace Salter."

"You go to Prescott High?"

"Yeah."

"Me too. I'm a senior. Your mom's pretty cool."

"Thank you."

"This must be really different from where you're from, huh?"

"I don't know. We've only been here a week so far."

"I guess high schools are kinda the same everywhere, huh?" he says. "Same cliques. Same bullhonkey."

"Bullhonkey?" Grace says, with what may be her first smile of the day.

"I figured the word I really wanted to say wouldn't be appropriate in a house of God."

"Yeah," Grace says. "Same bullhonkey."

"Cool." Jesse grabs a cookie. So does Grace. They stand there in silence for a few moments, chewing. It is not an uncomfortable silence. He reminds Grace slightly of a teddy bear—endearing while not particularly attractive.

"My family used to go to a more traditional church when I was a kid," he says. "Prescott AME? Across town? You know, the one where all the black people go? All ten of them." He laughs at his joke. "My mom led prayer circles and everything. But then my brother came out as transgender two years ago and it made my mom kind of reevaluate where she felt welcome. Mom didn't like everyone calling her kid an abomination, you know?"

Grace nods. She does know. She knows all about a church rejecting someone. But why is this guy telling her all this over the cookie table?

"How many cookies have you had?" Jesse asks.

"Um, I don't know?"

"Me neither. They're not even that good, but I just keep eating them. It's like the one thing I look forward to about going to church."

Grace laughs. "Me too."

"But now maybe I have something else to look forward to," he says, smiling.

Grace chokes on her cookie.

"Are you okay?" Jesse says. He thumps her on the back with his pawlike hand. "Do you need some water? Here, have my lemonade." Grace takes a sip from his paper cup of watery lemonade.

"I'm okay," Grace says when the coughing subsides.

"Are you sure?"

"Yes," she says, but it's only half true. She may not be choking to death anymore, but she might die of embarrassment. "Tell me about your brother," she says. Changing the subject is always a good idea.

"I don't know. He's really smart. He's a vegetarian," Jesse says as he swallows another cookie. "The only thing I don't understand is the name he chose: Hector. I mean, if you get to choose whatever name you want, why the heck would you choose a crappy name like that?"

Grace thinks maybe she's supposed to laugh, but Jesse's face is serious, so she says, "Oh?" instead. She feels both a need to escape this conversation and also a desire for it to never end.

"Is it weird I'm telling you all this?" he says.

Grace looks at his big, soft face, into his warm brown eyes. "It's a little weird," she admits. "But I'm glad you did."

"It just sort of came out."

"It's okay."

"I'm kind of embarrassed."

"Don't be."

"Do people tell you a lot of stuff? Because you're the pastor's daughter? Do they, like, think you can give good advice or something?"

Grace can't help but laugh. No one in Adeline ever asked her advice about anything. She's not like her mom, not someone whose thoughts have ever mattered. "No," she says. "Not at all."

"Huh. Well, they should. You're really good to talk to. You have, like, this totally calm energy or something."

"Thanks."

A woman who must be Jesse's mother calls him from across the room, where she stands second in line to meet Grace's mom. "Looks like it's almost our turn," Jesse says. "It was nice meeting you. What was your name again?"

"Grace."

"Grace. I'll see you at school, I guess. Thanks for the advice."

He turns around and his wide back blocks Grace's view of her parents. How strange that he thanked her for her advice when all she did was listen.

Dad and Grace walk home while Mom stays behind to meet with some committee or other. One thing all churches, conservative or liberal, seem to have in common is they have a lot of committees.

"Wasn't she great?" Dad says. He hasn't stopped grinning.

"Yeah, Mom did really good."

"I have to start transcribing her sermon. There was definitely some stuff in there that deserves to go in her book."

"Uh-huh."

"You okay on your own for a while? Mom'll be home in a couple of hours and we'll all have supper together. I think I'm actually going to cook tonight instead of getting takeout. Can you believe it?"

"Sure," Grace says. "Yeah."

She climbs the stairs to her room and lies down. Over the past week since they arrived in Prescott, Grace has unpacked enough to put sheets and a blanket on her bed, but she is still living out of her suitcase. Unopened boxes are still piled throughout the room.

Grace turns on her side, toward the wall without the window. A mirror lays flat on her dresser packed in a misshapen bundle of towels and packing tape. She sees no reason to unwrap it. The wall is warped, bulging near the corner. And there, near the bottom where the wall meets chipped trim that used to be white, are little scribbles, minuscule, like graffiti made by a mouse.

Grace rolls off the bed and kneels in the corner for a closer look.

Hear me, the scribbles say.

Help me.

She stays on her knees, in a position of prayer, reading the words over and over.

ROSINA.

There are so many shitty things about a shift at La Cocina, it's hard to know where to begin. Maybe it's the coming home smelling like grease and smoked chiles, how the odor seeps so deep into Rosina's clothes, she can't wash it out, how the pores of her skin absorb it, how she leaves work feeling as if she herself has been deep fried and covered in stringy white cheese, mole sauce congealing in her nostrils, her ears, between her toes.

Maybe the worst thing about working at La Cocina is the boss (Tío José) yelling at Rosina all night for breaking a plate, even though it was an accident, even though she offered to pay for it. Sometimes he just has to yell, and sometimes Rosina just has to take it. It's not like she can go on strike or anything. It's not like there's a union for underage, under-the-table employees of a family business run like they're still in some village in Mexico where kids don't go to school past sixth grade. It's not like Mami's ever going to back Rosina up or take her daughter's side over the family's.

Maybe the worst thing is watching Mami slaving away in the

kitchen, seeing her hunched over in the corner with back pain but saying nothing. Maybe it's finding dead mice behind the forty-pound bags of cornmeal. Maybe it's refilling the hot sauce, how it makes Rosina cry even though she's trained herself to do it with her eyes closed. Maybe it's how Tío José is the boss even though Mami does all the real work. Maybe it's how he treats everyone like shit and gets away with it. Maybe it's how it's a scientific fact that people tip people of color less. Maybe it's everything.

Rosina rides her bike home fast and imagines the work grime flying off her, absorbed into the dark sponge of night. She is especially filthy after the final bag of garbage ripped just as she lifted it into the Dumpster, spilling raw chicken juice all over her leg. Maybe she should just lick the putrid mess, get salmonella, die of food poisoning, and end this joke of a life right now.

Snap out of it, Rosina tells herself. Suicide jokes are so cliché.

What she wants to know is if everyone else lives their lives in a constant state of humiliated fury, or if this is a particularly Rosina condition.

Whatever. One day this will be over. One day Rosina will graduate from high school and crawl out from under this layer of grease and run off to Portland to start her all-girl punk band, and she will never step foot in Prescott, or a Mexican restaurant, ever again.

There is at least some solace in arriving home. Abuelita is there, asleep on the couch in front of the television, her soft face illuminated by her constant stream of telenovelas. Rosina pulls the throw blanket up to Abuelita's chin, then heads to the shower, where she peels off her sticky work clothes, turns on the shower as hot as is

reasonable, and scrubs the evening off her skin, washes it out of her hair, watches the boredom and rude customers drain away in the soapy swirl. Her skin is hers again. She smells like herself.

She sits on her bed wrapped in a towel. She is at least grateful for her single bedroom, while all her cousins have to share. She can decorate it however she wants, paint the walls midnight blue and put up posters of her favorite bands, play her guitar and write her songs without anyone listening. But Rosina feels a twinge of shame at the thought that she benefits from the fact that her mother hasn't had the chance to have any more children, that, as far as Rosina knows, Mami hasn't even had sex since her father died seventeen years ago. Maybe that's why she's so grumpy all the time.

The house is silent. Mami is still at the restaurant, cleaning up the kitchen, prepping for tomorrow. The solitude is a welcome change from the whining crowd of her cousins or the demands of customers, but it is also lonely. Rosina suspects there is a place between these extremes, something besides loneliness and hating everyone around you. She pulls on a pair of leggings and an old T-shirt, shoves her phone in her waistband, not that anyone will call her, not that she'll call anyone. But there's always hope, isn't there?

Maybe that girl will actually call, the one she met at the all-ages show in Eugene she sneaked out of her house to go to last weekend. In a parallel universe, one that wasn't so small and backward, she probably wouldn't even care about that girl from the show. She wasn't really Rosina's type, and she wasn't really that nice or cute or interesting. But she was a girl. A queer girl. And Rosina hasn't hooked up with anyone since Gerte, her first and only real girlfriend, the

German exchange student who left in June. Before her, there were a few tipsy make-out sessions with curious straight girls freshman year, but they fizzled out as soon as the girls sobered up. Those girls could just shrug and giggle, collect a story to tell later, and be proud of themselves for being open-minded and adventurous, but what Rosina got was heartbreak. After the third time that happened, she swore off school parties—and straight girls—altogether.

Rosina pads downstairs and sits on the couch next to her grandmother. Even though Abuelita's asleep, the simple proximity of her body is a comfort. She is the only person in the world that Rosina doesn't have to fight.

"Alicia," Abuelita says in her sleep, calling Rosina by the name of her long-dead daughter.

Rosina squeezes her bony hand, breathes in the sour warmth of her breath. "Sí, Abuelita?" Rosina says. "Estoy aquí."

Abuelita mumbles something that Rosina doesn't understand but that she hopes means "I love you."

Rosina's phone rings. Erin rarely calls, but when she does it's to rant about something, to tell her about some fish she read about or an episode of *Star Trek* she just watched. With Rosina's luck, it's probably Mami calling to tell her to come back to the restaurant. Definitely not the girl from the show, who told Rosina she was too young and only reluctantly accepted the slip of paper with Rosina's phone number written on it in bloodred lipstick.

"Rosina?" the female voice says, from a number she does not recognize. Rosina's heart opens, just a crack. The world is suddenly a place that might include her.

"This is Grace? From school? You gave me your number at lunch the other day?"

It's just the plain girl who speaks in questions, Rosina and Erin's puzzling new lunch buddy. The rusty mechanism inside Rosina's chest closes back up again.

"Yeah?" Rosina says, running her fingers through her patchy wet hair. Maybe she should just chop it all off, shave her whole head like Erin, start over from scratch.

A pause, then: "I need you to tell me what happened to Lucy Moynihan."

The girl's voice—definitive, solid. The girl suddenly demanding, not asking permission.

Rosina sighs. If she could unknow the story of Lucy Moynihan, she would, in a heartbeat. Why this girl wants to know so badly, she has no idea.

Fine, she thinks. She'll tell Grace the story of the disappearing girl. She'll tell her the story no one says they believe.

LUCY.

She was not beautiful. She was small and mousy. Her hair was always frizzy and her clothes were always somehow wrong. She was a freshman at an upperclassman's party, accompanied by the default friends she'd had since kindergarten, Prescott natives like her. They were nothing special. They grasped on to their red plastic cups for dear life and huddled in the corner where they would not be seen.

But then. Her friends were gone and she could not find them. The room was dark and loud and tilted. He found her. Spencer Klimpt. He looked at her from across the room and she was suddenly someone: a girl, wanted.

He refilled her red cup. One time. Two times. More. He looked into her eyes and smiled while her wet mouth formed nervous words. The music was so loud, she could not hear her own voice, but she knew she was flirting. She was giddy with it.

She was a windup toy and he was waiting for her time to run out. He was patient, so patient. He was such a good listener, so chivalrous,

so good at getting her drinks, so good at watching her eyelids get heavy, at watching her power down, slowly, slowly, until she stopped speaking, until she was soft clay to be molded, perfectly malleable.

He took her hand and led her upstairs. He said things she could not hear to someone she could not see. Was there someone else in the room? She was laughing with her eyes closed. The world shook with her inside it. His strong arms kept her from falling. She thought: *This is it.*

When he laid her down on the bed, she was somewhere watching, narrating the shadowed events:

This is really happening. I'm fifteen and I'm about to make out with one of the most popular seniors in school. I should be so happy. I should be so proud. A little fear must be normal. I'm okay I'm okay everything is okay. Even though the bed is spinning even though I can't keep my eyes open even though I'm not even sure he knows my name even though even though even though his body is so heavy on top of mine and I can't move I can't breathe I don't want this I don't want this anymore I want to push but my wrists are pinned down and my pants are off and it's too late it's too late it's too late to say no.

Her last solid memory is pain.

Then black. Then nothing. Then her brain shuts off and scrambles the memories, rips them, tears them apart. There were so many red cups. So much darkness in the murky water, her head submerged. Her body torn apart by violent waters. She is nowhere. She is nothing. She disappears.

Then brief gasps for air, tiny moments, bright flashes in the darkness. Memories surface like tight bubbles.

Hands. Bed. Pain. Fear. A searing inevitability. A life taken and redefined.

A thought: *I did this to myself.*

A thought: *It will be over soon.*

Stillness. A heavy blanket of flesh, unmoving. She lets herself hope it is over.

Then movement. His voice: "Did you lock the door?"

Another voice: "Yeah. No one's coming."

His voice: "You ready, Ennis? Or are you going to be a pussy?"

Another voice. She knows this voice. Everybody knows Eric Jordan's voice. "Fuck Ennis. It's my turn."

A rhyme for children: *One, two, three: How many can there be?*

A thought: *I'm going to die.*

Rocking, thrashing, a violent sea. Then more. So much more. More than could possibly be imagined.

A voice: "Turn on the lights, man. I want to see her."

A hand on her mouth, shoving her voice back inside.

She sees nothing. She is dying. She is dead. She is a whale carcass being torn apart by eels at the bottom of the sea.

A voice: "Fuck, she's puking."

A voice: "Just turn her over."

Then a place even darker than black. Then time cut out of history. Then her mind is gone, her memories are gone. She is pulled underwater. They take her body, her breath. They bend and break and use her up until she is a memory no one can remember.

Sometimes the only thing worse than death is surviving.

It is morning and she is only mostly gone. Her hair is caked

with puke. She hurts all over. She hurts inside. The floor is littered with her crumpled clothes and half a dozen used condoms. How vile this tiny sliver of gratitude: they only destroyed; they did not plant anything live inside her.

The bottom-feeders have cleaned her skeleton of all its flesh. She is washed up onshore, tangled with seaweed, smelling of decay. She crawls across the storm-tossed beach, over the rocks and garbage, over the beer bottles and cigarette butts and lifeless bodies. Over so many red cups.

Bodies all over the place, bodies everywhere, people who didn't make it home last night. All these people down here while she was drowning.

Bodies stir. Eyes open and follow her ghostly walk to the door.

A laugh like glass breaking.

A voice in the darkness, giving her a new name:

Slut.

ERIN.

"You need to get a life," Erin tells Grace at
lunch because she won't stop talking about Lucy Moynihan.

"Manners," Rosina says.

"Being honest is more important than being nice," Erin says.
"I'm being honest."

Grace is being annoying. Erin doesn't understand why people
are so insistent on letting each other get away with being annoying.
If she's being annoying, she wants someone to tell her about it, like
Rosina does.

"Grace here hasn't had the time we've had to become hopelessly
apathetic," Rosina says. "She still gives a shit. We gave a shit at the
beginning, remember?"

"I never gave a shit," Erin says, because it's what she wants to
believe, but she's not quite sure she's telling the truth. A tinge of discomfort spreads through her, a vague suspicion that perhaps there
is a different truth beneath the surface that is staying murky and

hidden. Usually, she is a big fan of truth, but these sneaky kinds of truth are definitely not her favorite.

"Well, I cared," Rosina says. "I was fucking pissed."

Erin remembers Rosina going up to that football guy Eric Jordan and spitting in his face, how it dripped off his nose in slow motion, how the entire hallway was silent in those moments it took for the gob to reach the ground, how he just laughed in her face, called her a spic dyke, and walked away. Then, like everyone else, Rosina realized caring was a waste of time. Like Erin, she realized caring hurts.

Rosina never actually talked to Lucy, the girl she supposedly cared enough about to spit in someone's face to defend. But Erin knows there's a difference between an idea and a person, how it's so much simpler to care about something that does not breathe. Ideas do not have needs. They demand nothing but a few brief thoughts. They do not suffer or feel pain. As far as Erin knows, they are not contagious.

"Point the guys out to me," Grace says. "Are they here?"

"Eric has third lunch, I think," Rosina says. "But Ennis is here. Over there at the troll table." Rosina nods toward the center of the lunchroom, where the worst people sit. The girls who have been making fun of Erin since she moved here freshman year, the guys who don't even bother lowering their voices around her when they brainstorm about what it must be like to fuck "someone like her." Compared to the rest of them, Ennis is quiet, even soft spoken, the one you'd least suspect to be a monster.

"Ennis Calhoun is the one with the pubey goatee," Rosina says.

"And you've probably seen Eric around school. He always has a gang of trolls following him around. There was a third one, the ringleader, Spencer Klimpt, but he graduated. Works at the Quick Stop off the highway. Real winners, those guys."

"I don't think 'pubey' is a word," Erin says.

"Is Ennis that guy sitting by Jesse?" Grace says. Erin recognizes the look on Grace's face as disappointment, as if she expected that large, dopey boy named Jesse to be someone else, someone who does not sit by Ennis Calhoun at lunch.

"You know him?" Rosina says.

"He goes to my church."

"He's waving at you," Erin says. "He looks like a stuffed animal."

"You like that guy?" Rosina says.

"No," Grace says. "Never."

Everyone thinks Erin can't read people. That's what they've been telling her for her whole life. But Erin has no problem recognizing obvious emotions. She knows what crying means. She knows what angry shouting sounds like. She knows teasing. She knows the looks between people when she accidentally walks into the wall when rounding a corner, when she blurts out inappropriate things in class, when she rubs her hands together so hard they make a sound. It's the more subtle things that get confusing. Things like irony, attempts to hide feelings, lying. For these things, Erin's spent countless hours learning, getting tutored in reading facial expressions and interpreting body language. She has been trained to pay attention, to study human emotion and relationships with an intensity rivaled only by psychologists and novelists. Because it is

not intuitive, because she is an outsider, sometimes she sees things other people miss.

For instance, she suspects Grace may have been considering liking this Jesse guy. If she didn't like him, she'd have no reason to look so disappointed by the news that he may not be likable. Erin notices Jesse's happy stuffed-animal face turn sad as soon as he sees the way Grace's looking at him. Maybe he was considering liking her, too.

"They look so normal," Grace says. "Those guys. You can't even tell they—"

"Did you know that otters rape baby seals?" Erin says, knowing full well how shocking and inappropriate her words are, but she desperately wants to change the subject. Sometimes shocking people is the best way to get their attention. "People think they're so cute and cuddly, but they're still wild animals."

"Jesus, Erin," Rosina says.

"They can't help themselves," Erin says. "It's in their natures."

"Someone has to do something," Grace says.

"About sea otters?" Rosina says. "Like sensitivity training?"

"About Lucy. About those guys. They can't just get away with it. They can't just sit there eating lunch like nothing happened."

"You've seen the website, right?" Rosina says.

"What website?"

"Trust me," Rosina says. "You're better not knowing."

Grace looks at Erin for her opinion, but Erin just shrugs.

"What website?" Grace says again. "I want to know."

"It's more of a blog, really," Rosina says. "It's called *The Real Men of Prescott*. Hey, Erin. Give me your phone."

"You have a phone," Erin says.

"I have a crap phone," Rosina says. "I need yours."

"Who writes it?" Grace says.

"Nobody knows for sure," Rosina says, typing something on Erin's phone. "But most people think Spencer Klimpt is the main one behind it. It surfaced right around the time Lucy and her family left town. The blog had a couple hundred followers last time I checked." Rosina scrolls down the phone's screen. "Shit! It has more than three thousand now." She shoves the phone at Grace like she can no longer bear touching it. "Here," she says. "See for yourself."

They are silent as Grace scrolls through the blog. Erin hasn't looked at it since she first heard about it at the end of last school year, but she can only imagine what Grace is reading. Stuff about how to pick up girls. Rants about how feminism is ruining the world. Degrading descriptions of women the author has supposedly slept with.

"Oh my God," Grace says quietly. "This is horrible."

"There are a bunch of links on the sidebar to other sites just like it, even bigger ones," Rosina says with disgust. "It's called the 'manosphere.' All these guys online, a whole network of assholes who believe this shit. So-called 'pick-up artists' sharing advice on how to manipulate women. They call it a 'men's rights movement,' but basically they just hate women."

There is so much Erin has tried to forget. Not just this. Not just Lucy. The wrong is bigger than Lucy, bigger than their school and town, bigger than all of them. But it is also as small as her own private memories. It is a tiny box she locked them in and left back in Seattle.

"I don't want to talk about this anymore," Erin says, pulling her phone out of Grace's hand. She is thinking a trip to the library might be in order.

"I appreciate your passion, Grace," Rosina says. "But Lucy's gone. No one knows where she went. No one can help her."

"Maybe we could," Grace says. "We could help her."

Rosina laughs. Erin shudders. "Even if we wanted to—which we don't," Rosina says, "who would listen to us? Erin and I are like the freaks of the school and you're new, and no offense, but you're kind of sabotaging your social capital potential by hanging out with us."

Grace is different today, Erin thinks. Until now, she's mostly just sat quietly and a little hunched over, like she's not quite sure she has permission to speak. Now she won't stop talking. Erin thinks she liked the old Grace better. This new Grace is far too exhausting. This new Grace is bringing up things Erin doesn't want to think about, and certainly doesn't want to care about.

"Hey," Rosina says. "Think of the positive. At least we're not getting married off to old guys at nine years old and getting our clits cut off."

"Gross," Erin says. "Too much." She looks at the chopped nuts and veggies in her bento box, and for the moment she's glad Mom has made her a vegetarian.

"Why do you care so much?" Rosina says. "You never even met Lucy."

"I don't know," Grace says. "It's weird. I can't stop thinking about it."

"Maybe your house is haunted," Rosina says. "And you're possessed by her ghost. Except she's still alive." Rosina's face pales. "I hope."

Grace opens her mouth like she's going to say something, but then closes it and starts chewing on a fingernail. Maybe she does think her house is haunted.

"Get a hobby," Erin says. "You need a hobby."

"Or a job," Rosina says. "You can have mine. Do you want to get paid less than minimum wage and get yelled at all night by my uncle?"

"Yeah, maybe," Grace says, obviously not listening. She is looking over at the troll table like she's thinking the kind of thoughts that can get a person in trouble.

"You can't change nature," Erin says, but she knows Grace doesn't hear her, so she doesn't say the rest of what she was going to say, which is probably for the best because she knows Rosina would get mad at her. They've had this conversation before, and it ended in Rosina throwing a water bottle at her.

What Erin was going to say but didn't is that boys are animals, and they act like animals because it's in their natures, even the ones who seem cute and cuddly like sea otters. But like otters, they will turn ruthless in an instant if certain instincts are triggered. They will forget who you think they are supposed to be. They will even forget who they want to be. Trying to change them will never work. The only way to stay safe is to stay away from them completely.

Erin knows none of us are better than animals. We are no more than our biology, our genetic programming. Nature is harsh and

cruel and unsentimental. When you get down to it, boys are preda- tors and girls are prey, and what people call love or even simple attraction is just the drug of hormones, evolved to make the survival of our species slightly less painful.

Erin is lucky to have figured this out so young. While everyone else wastes their lives running around chasing "love," she can focus on what's really important and stay away from that mess completely.

US.

A girl sits in the corner of her classroom, looking at all the backs of heads, trying to take deep breaths and notice without judgment the feelings of rage bubbling up inside her. She tries to remember the mindfulness techniques she learned over the summer. *The only way out is through*, she repeats silently to herself. She waits for the feelings to drift away like clouds.

It's so strange how someone can be one person one day, then be transformed over the course of a few months, then come back to their previous life with completely different insides but all anyone still sees are the same old outsides. It's not like she thought she'd come back from rehab and suddenly be able to have a normal high school experience, but maybe a part of her hoped there'd be space for a tiny reinvention. She thinks maybe she should do something different with her hair, dye it some drastic new color. But all people would see is the same girl with different hair. Her place has been carved out for her already. There is nowhere else here for her to fit.

She watches a couple flirt next to her. She notices the rage

bubble up again, but focusing on her breath does nothing to distract her. She hates them with a fury that scares her. How dare they flaunt what this girl knows she'll never have—that innocence, that romance, that feeling of potential? Whatever possibility of that she ever had was burned out of her a long time ago, before she even had a chance to know it was something she wanted.

A few seats away, in the desk assigned to Adam Kowalski, sits another student, nameless. The student watches the flirting couple with yearning, with a thick, heavy sadness that makes it hard to breathe.

I just have to make it one more year, the student thinks. *One more year until I'm out of this school and out of this town, until I won't have to hide.*

But even then, they think. *Is there anyone who could ever want a freak like me? Is there anyone who can love someone whose outsides will never fully match their insides?*

On the other side of the school is a different set of students, kept mostly separate from the rest. Erin sits in the back of Mr. Trilling's AP American History class, trying not to look in the general direction of Otis Goldberg, in fear that he'll turn around the way he always seems to do at the precise moment she happens to be looking at him, his eyes making contact with hers like annoyingly precise lasers. Not that she looks at him often, or on purpose. She looks at all kinds of things. That's just what eyes do. Erin's eyes just happen to occasionally fall on him.

She can't help it. He's always raising his hand and saying sur-

prisingly smart things. He's always sitting there with his neck that's tan and just a little muscly from cross-country, with tiny blond hairs that catch the dim light streaming through the classroom window. Sometimes he even says hi to her, and she can never figure out what to say back in time. Everything about him is confusing. How can someone who has all the usual trappings of a nerd be so incongruously cute? How can someone so cute be so nice? No classification seems quite right for him, which is excruciating for Erin. It's almost like he *chose* to be a nerd instead of being forced into it like everyone else.

Otis Goldberg is very problematic.

This girl walks home after school, attempting to stay dry under her joke of a cheap umbrella. It's not even that windy, but the umbrella keeps getting blown inside out, like it actually wants to catch the air and carry her away, which wouldn't be that bad now that she thinks about it. Maybe then she could leave this world, this life, and she wouldn't have to hate herself yet again for sleeping with a guy last night who, she realized, as soon as he rolled off her, was never going to want her for anything more than that.

She doesn't want to go down the rabbit hole of counting how many times this has happened, how many times she's convinced herself maybe this time is going to be different, maybe those moments when their bodies are touching actually mean they're connecting, and those brief moments when he looks into her eyes actually mean he sees her.

She doesn't want to ask herself why this keeps happening, why

she seems doomed to repeat the same mistakes over and over again. It's like as soon as a guy touches her, she goes on autopilot. Her body moves to his, but it's like she's not even there anymore. It's like she's half awake. It's like she's half dead.

Another girl is on her way to Eugene, to the U of O campus, driving way too fast on the rainy highway. She can practically taste his lips already, and her lap is warm with anticipation. It's such torture that he lives so far away, that they must coordinate their love life with his college-dorm roommate. But it beats having to resort to the backseat of a car or worry about parents coming home early the way you do with high school boys.

She doesn't think she loves him, but it might be a possibility down the road. That's not important right now. All she cares about is ripping his clothes off and feeling his firm stomach rubbing against hers, his hands searching the warmest parts of her body until they find her breasts, her ass. She arches her back and presses her foot on the gas when she thinks about him inside her, the way it feels when everything fits so perfectly.

It's like as soon as he touches her, she goes on autopilot. Her body moves to his, and it is something so natural, so primal, so right. It is in these moments when she feels fully alive, fully in her body, fully herself, and she wishes there was a way she could stay forever.

The Real Men of Prescott

Quite a few readers have asked me for this, so here it is—a detailed inventory of all my lays, starting with the most recent. I would like to note that this list only includes the full conquests. If I included every blow job and hand job, I'd be here for days. So without further ado, here is:

AN ANALYSIS OF ALL MY HOOKUPS

1. Late-thirties MILF. Regular at my work, buys a bottle of cheap wine almost daily. Great body for her age, must do lots of yoga, definitely the oldest I've ever fucked. Did it doggie style in her basement while her kid played video games upstairs. She came into my business a few times afterward, but I made it clear I wasn't interested in her anymore. Must have started going somewhere else to buy her wine.

2. Early-twenties community college student. Picked her up at local bar where she was out with girlfriends. She was definitely hottest of the bunch. Negged her into submission by first hitting on her friend to make her jealous. A little too drunk, so she just sort of laid

there. Passed out in my bed, puked in my bathroom, and made me drive her home in the morning.

3. Midtwenties hippie chick with big tits. Didn't realize she had hairy armpits until it was too late. Her wildness in bed made up for it. Would consider adding her to my long-term harem if she agreed to shave and wash her hair more often.

4. Seventeen-year-old slut I knew from high school. Hot body, but too insecure to be high value. Being too easy makes it less fun. The conquest is part of the turn-on.

5. Trailer trash, indeterminate age, somewhere between twenty-five and thirty-five. Could have been number 4's mom for all I know. She was all over me at a bar, I didn't even have to throw any game. Okay sex, but a little too eager to please. She's still pretty hot now, but I can tell this one's on her way to becoming a fifty-year-old barfly.

6. Nineteen-year-old skinny, lazy stoner. Loved to fuck all night. Was part of my harem for a couple of months. Ended up in the hospital for a few days with some kind of infection, asked me to visit her. Fucked her in the bathroom when she was high on painkillers. Too doped up to say much, but whatever.

7. Eighteen-year-old blonde from out of town I met online. Dumb as a brick. Nothing special about this one. Did her in the back of my car, then never called her back.

8. Seventeen to eighteen years old. I made the mistake of actually agreeing to be this one's "boyfriend" for a year in high school, though of course I was still getting tail on the side. She started out hella hot, A+ grade, but got more and more pathetic the longer we were together. Finally got rid of her shortly after graduation. Good riddance to damaged goods.

9. Seventeen-year-old chubby girl from school. I had a girlfriend and she had a boyfriend, but she got drunk at a party when he was out of town and told me she'd had a crush on me since sixth grade. Fat girls are so easy. Mostly a pity fuck on my part. She was so grateful.

10. Sixteen-year-old redhead (whose carpet matched the curtains, by the way). Football groupie who talked too much and would do anything to party with the big boys. There's something so fun about virgins. It's so sweet how insecure they are, how they're so willing to do what they're told. You have so much power automatically, and they love it.

GRACE.

Grace is not in the mood for church today. For one, she hardly got any sleep last night. What started with reading *The Real Men of Prescott* blog turned into nearly three hours of torture as she started clicking on links until she found herself deep inside the manosphere, on forums where men exchanged date-rape tips, on websites that suggested men move to impoverished countries where women don't put up a fight and there are no laws to protect them.

The world is a sick place, Grace thinks. It is a place where people can post things like that, spreading hate and darkness, and no one holds them accountable. It is a place where hurting people is too easy, and where helping them is too hard. It is a place where the darkness is winning, where the darkness will always win.

And Mom's up there preaching, doing her job, trying to convince this church full of people that there is still light in the world, that it is within reach, that it is within us. Grace doesn't know if she believes this. She doesn't know what she believes anymore.

"John was a witness to the light," Mom says. "He came to testify.

He came to tell the truth of Jesus in a world that did not want to hear it."

She pauses and looks out at the silent, rapt congregation. She smiles like she's about to deliver the punch line of a joke. "And it was good news," she says, incredulous. "It was *great* news. It was news about God's grace and love and forgiveness!" She throws up her hands in mock exasperation. "But they didn't want to hear it. They said thanks, but no thanks. They said we're just going to keep doing things the way we've always done them, even if it's sort of stopped working for us. These guys were the definition of conservative." A statement like this would have gotten Mom beheaded at her old church. It gets a few laughs from the congregation, but Grace has no energy for humor.

"They had no interest in John's news," Mom continues, "because it was new and strange and because they knew it would change things. Because it was outside their understanding of tradition, and the way things had always been, and the way things ought to be. Change was scary. It was something to be avoided.

"Who was this guy leading people to the river and washing their sins away, saying everyone was worthy of redemption? Who was this guy preaching justice, telling soldiers not to kill, telling tax collectors not to steal? Who was this man preaching charity, who said in Luke 3:11, 'Let anyone who has two coats share with the person who has none; and anyone who has food do the same.' Who was this crazy guy claiming someone even greater than him, someone even *more* revolutionary, was on his way, some guy named Jesus, who had the power to wash them, not just in water, but in *fire*, in the very light of the Lord? The people said to John, 'Who the hell are you?'"

A few giggles at her creative paraphrasing of Scripture. She pauses to let her words settle, to give people time to get ready to adjust to a more serious vibe. Her face is earnest; her eyes are kind, imploring. She is electric. Her smile is fueled by a love big enough for everyone in the congregation, everyone in Prescott, everyone in the world. But Grace's heart aches a selfish ache, an ache that shames her, as she wishes the smile was meant for only her and not all these strangers.

"John 1:23," Grace's mom says. "And John said, 'I am the voice of one calling in the wilderness. Make straight the way for the Lord.'"

The congregation takes a deep breath.

"One calling in the wilderness." She pauses. "A lone voice in the wilderness." Her eyes are gleaming. "One solitary voice speaking truth in a loud, screaming world that does not want to hear it. But John speaks anyway. Because he has to. Because he knows the truth. Because his God makes him brave.

"My friends, the world needs us to be brave. We live in a world full of suffering and hate and fear and greed, full of injustice, just like John did. Just like Jesus did. It would be easy to throw up our hands and say, 'There's no use. This is just the way it is. There's nothing I—nothing one person—can do to change that.' And I say to you: Yes, the world is broken. Yes, our leaders are often corrupt and it is difficult to trust them. Yes, we struggle to make ends meet while a few of the world's richest men hoard enough wealth to house and feed all the starving people of the world. Bullies still seem to run things. The earth is getting sicker and sicker. This world is a hard, hard place to live. Yes to all these things." She pauses just long

enough for everyone to breathe. "But I want you to ask yourselves, is this broken world of ours worth saving?"

She gives them a moment to consider her question. Grace doesn't know if she can answer. She doesn't know if she wants to.

"Jesus thought so," Mom says. "John thought so. I think so. I think we are all worth saving."

Someone in the audience says, "Amen."

"The wilderness is large," she continues, gathering momentum, gaining speed. "It is loud and relentless. It is scary and vast. But our voices, they are louder than we even know. Even our whispers can send ripples that will spread farther than we could ever imagine reaching. One small kindness in a sea of cruelty, one word of truth among lies, these are the seeds that can change the world. Luke 3:8: 'Let your lives prove your repentance.'"

Someone says, "Hallelujah!"

"We must do the things that scare us," Mom says, her voice cracking with passion. "We must do the things we know are right even when everyone else seems to be doing wrong. We must listen to that tiny voice inside ourselves, God's clear voice in the wilderness of our souls, even when the world is noisy and doing all it can do to drown that voice out. Like John, we must be the voice of one calling in the wilderness. We must speak. John 1:5: 'The light shines in the darkness, and the darkness has not overcome it.' My friends, we must be the light."

Grace can feel the energy of the room surge, simultaneously crushing her and lifting her up. She can feel everyone eating up Mom's words, and she knows everything about her message is right and good,

but something about Mom's sermon is too hard to hear. It's making her skin itch under the fabric of her dress; it is making her sweat. While everyone else feels inspired, she feels judged. Reprimanded. Damned.

Grace whispers to her father that she's not feeling well. He smiles and nods but doesn't take his eyes off Mom. In the midst of everything she's feeling, Grace is struck with another sadness, a jealousy almost, a yearning. She knows her parents' love is unique, the way her father adores her mother, the way he admires her so deeply, completely, and without question. Grace has always suspected no high school romance could ever come close to this, so she's never bothered with boyfriends, never bothered letting anyone in. Has she been set up for a life of disappointment? Is she doomed to be alone? How could she ever dream of having her parents' fairy-tale kind of love? They live in a magic world where the queen is the one who rules the kingdom, one where the king follows her lead. It's a beautiful story. But a kingdom is so much bigger than a family. It is a place where a princess can get lost. It is a place where she can be forgotten.

Grace stands up and walks the full length of the church to the back exits. No disapproving, squinty eyes follow her, no muttered reprimands by thin-haired old ladies. After the heavy wood doors swing closed behind her, she expects the lump in her chest to dissolve, but it stays, heavy and stubborn. Why can't she just be happy for Mom? Why can't she believe in her the way Dad does? Why can't she be part of their dream?

The halls are empty and silent. Grace leans against the wall, hit with the realization that she has nowhere to go. She has no place for comfort, no place for refuge, no place that feels like home. Her house is still a

mess of half-emptied boxes. Her room is full of a lost girl's screams.

A bathroom door opens at the end of the hall. The large form of Jesse Camp steps out, wiping his wet hands on the legs of his pants.

"Oh, hi," he says. His face opens into a warm smile.

Grace wipes her eyes. Hardens.

"Are you okay?" he says. "Are you crying?"

"No, I am not crying," she sniffles.

"Hey, did I do something?" he says. "You gave me, like, dagger eyes at lunch the other day."

Grace glares at him, his face so misleading in its softness. "How can you be friends with those guys?"

"What guys?"

"You were sitting with Ennis Calhoun at lunch," Grace says. "Then I saw you in the hall later with Eric Jordan."

Jesse's eyes widen in surprise, but then he looks away and sighs with what Grace suspects is guilt. "Eric is on the football team with me," he says weakly. "Guys on the team are just sort of automatically friends, you know? And Ennis hangs out with him, so I guess we're kind of friends by default."

"You're just sort of friends with rapists by default? Like you don't have a choice in the matter?"

"There wasn't any proof," he says, his voice rising defensively. "That's what everyone said. They said that girl was lying."

"That girl has a name." Grace tries to kill him with her eyes. When nothing happens, she turns around and storms away.

"Wait, Grace," he says. She stops walking but keeps her back to him. "You don't understand. You weren't here. Everything was crazy

after Lucy said all that stuff. Everyone at school, the whole town was, like, falling apart."

"Yeah?" she says. "The *town* was falling apart?" She turns her head and looks him in the eyes. "How do you think *she* felt?"

Grace is suddenly, acutely, aware of a new feeling burning inside her. It is a shift away from the heavy stillness of sadness, toward something faster, hotter, something that until now had been out of her reach.

Anger. Fury. Rage. It takes strength just to feel it.

Jesse says nothing as Grace walks back into the chapel she escaped just moments ago. Nobody seems to notice as she walks down the aisle, as she sits back down next to her father just in time to catch the grand finale of Mom's sermon. The energy of the room envelops her and she is carried away with the rest of the congregation, her anger and sadness and feelings she cannot name swept up with the roomful of other lives, other passions and disappointments, other secrets, other loves, other lies. She closes her eyes and imagines she is one of many—nameless, faceless, not her mother's daughter. She listens to the powerful voice talk about how Jesus championed the weak and defenseless, how he embraced the misfits, how he loved the unlovable, how he spoke for those who could not speak for themselves. How he died for her sins. How he died fighting for all of us. How now it is our turn to fight.

The chapel rings with Grace's mother's words: "What are we going to do with our freedom, our power? What are we going to do with all this grace? What are we going to do with these blessed lives? What are we going to do to deserve them? How are we going to let our lives prove our repentance?"

Grace needs to leave, needs to be alone. She walks out again as everyone rises for the last hymn, their eyes clouded by inspiration. She can feel their hope as she escapes the chapel, all their fired-up good intentions to change some vague and abstract notion of the troubled world around them. Maybe they'll go home and get online and donate a hundred bucks to a worthwhile cause. The best of them will give a dollar and a smile to that homeless vet by the highway off-ramp with his cardboard sign asking for help. But what are they going to do for a girl who had been part of their community, who needed real help and was shunned instead?

Grace walks the few blocks home and goes straight to her room, the only place she can think of that is supposed to feel safe. But she imagines eyes watching her, like the room is alive, holding its breath, waiting for her to do something. Maybe the closet will be dark enough, small enough. Maybe in there she will not feel watched.

She crouches on the floor of the small closet, the hems of Sunday skirts and dresses brushing against her forehead. Light streams under the closet door as she pulls it closed from the inside. It is almost dark. She is almost hidden.

But there is still light. Still enough seeping in to let her know she's not alone. Enough to illuminate the words carved into the forgotten few inches of wall between the door and the corner, an unseen place, a place so dark, it could only be known by someone trying to be small—on the floor, with the door closed.

HELP ME, the scratches say. They are the texture of screaming, so rough they must have been carved by fingernails.

ERIN.

Sometimes dads leave and no one tells you why.
Then sometimes they come back, and no one tells you why then,
either. So you're left on your own to figure it out. This is when logic
comes in especially handy. Without logic and rational thinking, one
might be left to the much lesser device of emotion, which can create
all sorts of problems when left unchecked by reason.

Here's an example: 1) A dad leaves; 2) While he's gone, his
teenage daughter experiences something everyone says is traumatic;
3) The dad comes back; 4) The mom and dad still don't talk to each
other; 5) The mom and dad sleep in separate bedrooms; 6) The
mom and dad smile too much whenever the daughter's around and
pretend everything's fine.

Then the family ends up in Prescott, Oregon, landlocked,
exactly 81.7 miles from the ocean, in a town none of them particularly likes, and the girl has absolutely no say in the matter. Her
family is still intact, technically speaking, though her father is at
work far more than he's at home, the twenty-mile commute to his

office at the university a convenient excuse for his long hours and a convenient tool for avoiding the family he has little interest in being a part of, and the mother interacts with very few real, live people, preferring to manage her vast social-media empire of parent-support groups from her laptop perch on the kitchen island, right next to the fruit bowl, which is now devoid of bananas after she proclaimed them too sugary for her daughter's sensitive system.

Erin could be emotional about it. She could be anxious and stressed and confused. She might feel guilty, might blame herself for her father's unhappy return, might see herself as the toxic glue keeping her family intact. But she refuses to let emotions rule her. She knows she is better off without them, without pain, without thoughts and memories that serve no use but to hurt her. So she creates a world inside her head where these things will not bother her, a place where logic rules, a place she can control. She shoves the memories and feelings down so deep, they will not touch her.

There's no use in wishing her family were different. Wishing doesn't get anything done. Neither wishing nor thinking about the past is an efficient use of one's time.

So Erin will not think about the events that followed her father's leaving, not the handful of visits to the extended-stay hotel room that he absurdly called an apartment, prefurnished in durable beige fabrics, which takeout meals and late-night tears could not stain. She will not think about nights alone in the house with Mom's endless crying, how it made studying or reading nearly impossible, how the house was filled with it, so thick Erin had a hard time breathing. Of course she knew that wasn't possible—that her mother's emotions

could have an effect on the actual consistency of air—but regardless, Erin avoided the house as much as possible. She walked the whole length of Alki Beach as many times as it took to fill her pockets with shells whose species she practiced identifying by touch in the darkness, long enough to kill enough time so that Mom would probably be asleep when she got home. She checked the tidal charts each morning so she would know what to expect. The sea's rhythms were constants, predictable and comforting, while everything else was changing in the life of a girl who abhorred change.

Erin won't think about eighth grade. She certainly won't think about Casper Pennington. Not how he stared at her from the high school side of her private school's small auditorium every morning during announcements. How it made her body feel hot and good and a little bit scared. How it made her forget about the mess at home. How he walked by her one day in the hallway and told her she was beautiful. How she simultaneously didn't like his proximity to her but also wanted him closer. How his eyelashes were so long. How his blond hair was so blond. How his confidence and attention made her wonder if he could teach her how to be strong and not care about the world changing.

So what if she was only thirteen. So what if he was three years older than her. So what if she couldn't look people in the eye and didn't like to be touched most of the time and had an army full of specialists trying to teach her how to be normal. So what if her dad was gone and this Casper guy showed up telling her she was beautiful. You can always cram the wrong piece into the puzzle hole if you push hard enough and limit your definition of "fitting."

No, Erin will not think about these things. These are the kind of memories that serve no logical purpose; they do not contain useful knowledge or skills. Erin theorizes that sadness and regret are maladaptive features of the human brain, something the species will eventually evolve out of. We will ultimately merge with computers and never have to feel again.

Remembering is not on Erin's schedule. It has no place on her lists. If she let the memories in, they'd scramble all the order she's worked so tirelessly to create; they'd throw her back to the chaos. Better to keep things predictable, stable, simple. Peaceful.

That's all Erin wants: peace.

There is something soothing about doing homework at exactly the same time every day and having dinner at exactly 7:00 p.m. every night (the table almost always just set for two). But before dinner is the best time of day—time to watch Erin's one daily episode of *Star Trek: The Next Generation*, when she can travel light-years away and explore the unknown expanses of the universe with Captain Jean-Luc Picard, the whole crew's father figure (especially Data's, whose own father/inventor, Dr. Noonien Soong, was murdered by Data's brother, Lore, who turned defective and dangerous after being programmed with the emotion chip intended for Data).

Except today's episode is not one of Erin's favorites. Not only is the whole crew of the *Enterprise* inebriated and acting foolish because of the *Tsiolkovsky* virus, this is also the episode where Data has sex with Tasha Yar. Even though he's an android, he still caught the carbon-based virus (a plot inconsistency that, Erin notes with displeasure, has never been fully explained; she concedes that her

beloved show is not perfect). Even though Data had direct orders to take Yar to sick bay, he fell under the spell of her seduction.

Data made a mistake. Data is not supposed to make mistakes. His logical android brain failed him and he became too human, too animal.

When Tasha Yar asked him if he was "fully functional," he said yes. Even Erin knew what she meant by "fully functional."

Casper Pennington never asked Erin if she was fully functional. Maybe if he had asked, Erin would have had a chance to think about it. Maybe she would have realized her answer was no.

After Data's romantic interlude (which, thankfully, the viewer does not have to witness), after Dr. Crusher gives the crew of the *Enterprise* the antidote to the virus and everyone sobers up, Tasha Yar is embarrassed. She tells Data it never happened, then gets back to work. Is this the normal reaction after someone has sex with an android? To not want to speak to them ever again? To ignore them the next day? At least Tasha Yar didn't go bragging about it to her friends while simultaneously acting like Data didn't exist. At least Data couldn't feel the pain of rejection. He could process what happened as part of his ongoing anthropological research of the behavior of the human species. He could file it away in his android brain, and move on.

It is never clear if Data enjoyed it. He told Tasha Yar that he was programmed in many "techniques." He was born knowing how to give pleasure. But did he know how to feel it?

Was he programmed to feel fear? To feel the merging of these two opposite emotions until there was no more pleasure left, until

it was just a body on top of him, holding him down, grunting into his ear, pushing and pushing, again and again and again as he waited for it to end, as he prayed to a god he didn't even believe in to please make it stop, please make Casper stop, this is not what I wanted, I don't know what I wanted, but this isn't it, this is definitely not it.

Silence does not mean yes. No can be thought and felt but never said. It can be screamed silently on the inside. It can be in the wordless stone of a clenched fist, fingernails digging into palm. Her lips sealed. Her eyes closed. His body just taking, never asking, never taught to question silence.

Data's mind is a computer. He can wipe entire memories out if he wants to. Mistakes don't follow him, don't lodge themselves in his synapses and travel with him wherever he goes. His mistakes don't involve parents and school and courts. His mistakes don't make him stop talking for two weeks. They don't live in his body. Nobody has to call Data a victim. No one needs to place blame. That does not have to be a part of his story.

But it is part of Erin's story. Before she finally convinced her parents to drop the charges against Casper, the courts were ready to make the labels official, to proclaim her passive, a victim; to define her as powerless, unable to consent. Because of her age. Because of her Asperger's. Even though she is a sentient being. Even though she had wanted something, at some time, whatever it was. Even though she can't remember when she stopped wanting it. Even though she can't remember telling him one way or the other. It's true, he never asked. But is that job really his? Is it hers? And if the court says she was incapable of saying no, what does that mean for her capacity

to say *yes*? Who makes these decisions? Who writes these rules and defines words like "consent"? Who decides what makes something a "rape"?

She cannot say the word: *Rape*.

That word does not sound true. It wasn't rape, but it was something.

Unlike Data, Erin's emotion chip is not missing. Sometimes it feels like she was accidentally programmed with ten emotion chips, and they're all constantly malfunctioning.

There is no word for what happened with Casper Pennington. Erin has not been programmed with this knowledge. She does not know the word for what she is supposed to feel.

ROSINA.

"Erwin told me you have a new friend at school," Rosina's mother says as she scoops a cup of oil into a giant pan. "He says she's a white gordita." The oil sizzles with tiny bubbles.

"What, you have Erwin spying on me now?" Rosina says. Even at school, Mami has her in her clutches. It's like her family has invisible chains attached to Rosina; as soon as she figures out how to break one, another shows up.

"Is this new girl strange like your skinny friend?" Mami grabs a handful of gelatinous raw pink chicken out of a plastic bucket and throws it into the pan.

"You don't even know Erin," Rosina says.

"I know enough to know she's strange."

Rosina tries to think of a witty defense, but Mami interrupts her thought process: "Stack those glasses," she orders.

"Grace's mom's a priest. That should make you happy, right? She'll be a good influence on me and you can stop getting Erwin to spy on me at school."

"Women can't be priests."

"Pastor, minister. Whatever. Her family's a bunch of Christians."

"Christian is not the same as Catholic." Mami squints at Rosina, suspicion and grease smoke in her eyes. "What is her church?"

"That big brick one on Oak Street. Grace's mom is, like, the boss of it or something."

"The Congregationalist Church?" Mami's laugh hurts Rosina's ears almost as bad as the tinny music that pumps through her neighborhood out of cheap radios. "That place is not even a real church," Mami says. "Full of communists and homos."

"No one says 'homo,' Mom."

"Whatever," Mami says, her favorite Americanism. "Venga. You need to learn how to cook. A woman must know how to cook."

"You've made your opinion abundantly clear," Rosina says. "But like I've told you five million times already, I don't want to know how to cook."

"But one day you will have your own family. You will need to feed them. No one will marry you if you can't cook."

"Do you even realize how horrible that sounds? You are so oppressed," Rosina says, her voice rising above the sizzle of the frying chicken. "I don't even like Mexican food."

"Oh, you think you're so much better than me? You're so much better than your family?" Mami says, her eyes squinting the way they do right before she blows up. "If you're so sick of us, why don't you just leave? One less big mouth to feed."

"Then you might have to actually pay someone to do all the shit I do for free."

Mami takes a step forward but knocks her metal tongs on the floor in the process. As she leans over to pick them up, she shudders and lets out a tight squeal. Rosina rushes to her side.

"¡Chinga!" Mami curses between clenched teeth, holding her back as Rosina helps her slowly stand up.

"Your back again?" Rosina says, arm around Mami's shoulders.

"It's nothing," she says, cringing.

"You have to see a doctor," Rosina says.

"I did," Mami says, turning back to the stove, fishing a new pair of tongs out of a tray of clean cooking utensils. "All he did was give me a prescription for pain pills. He wants to make me a drug addict."

Rosina sighs. *How is it possible to love and hate someone so much at the same time?*

The restaurant's front door chimes. The frying chicken smokes. Mami flips the chicken, lips tight, blinking back tears of pain.

"You have a customer," Mami says without looking up from the stove.

"Are you okay?" Rosina says.

"Get out of here."

What if I just left? Rosina thinks. *What if I took my apron off and just walked out the door?*

But where could she go? With what money? With what skills?

All Rosina can think to do is go back to work.

"Surprise" is not the right word to describe Rosina's feeling when Eric Jordan and his family walk into the restaurant. Neither is

"shock." It's more like surreal disbelief. If she was anyone besides Rosina, perhaps even a little bit of fear. Is it possible for this night to get any worse?

"Hey, can we get some service over here?" the father says as the family crams itself into a booth without waiting to be seated. Eric hasn't noticed Rosina yet. He's busy, facedown in his phone, ignoring his mother's pleas to please-put-that-down-we're-having-a-nice-family-dinner. It's hard to hear her over the identical twin younger brothers' screams and yelps as they take turns punching each other in the shoulder. The men and boys wear crew cuts; the mother's hair is a mess of old perm and surrender.

Rosina takes a deep breath, grabs a stack of foggy plastic-coated menus from the front counter, and reminds herself she is the girl no one can shake.

"Hi there," she says as she approaches the table and hands out the menus. "Can I get you anything to drink while you look at the menu?"

"Aren't you supposed to say hola or something?" Eric says, leaning back that way young men do when they feel entitled to take up as much space as possible.

"Hola," Rosina says flatly.

"Nice to see you, too," Eric says. He looks at Rosina like she's already naked, like she's already caught.

"Oh, are you a friend from school?" his mom asks.

"Something like that," Rosina says.

"I'd love to be your friend," Eric says. "I can be a really good friend."

His mother is oblivious, haggard and worn. Father and son

have the same animal eyes, like everything is a potential meal. They both stare at Rosina, partners in the hunt. The longer Rosina stands there, the smaller she feels. The more like meat.

"What's all this stuff on here?" the dad says, looking at the menu.

"Traditional Oaxacan cuisine," Rosina says. How many times has she had to explain this? "It's our specialty. We have seven different type of moles."

"I thought this was a Mexican restaurant," he says. "I just want some tacos."

"The more familiar Mexican dishes are on the next page," Rosina says.

One of the young boys says, "I want pizza."

For once, Rosina wishes they served chapulines. Grasshoppers. She would recommend they order that. "Would you like something to drink?" she asks again.

"I'll have a beer," the father says. "Whatever's cheap and in a can."

"Boys, do you want Cokes?" the mother asks. They ignore her. "Boys? Do you want Sprite? Root beer?"

"Just order them something," the father says.

"Two Sprites," the woman squeaks.

"I'll have a Coke," Eric says. "One of those fancy Mexican ones in the glass bottle." Rosina doesn't look up as she writes down the drink orders, but she can feel his eyes like sharp teeth tearing into her breasts.

As she walks away, she can hear father say to son, "That one's pretty cute, huh?"

"Yeah," Eric says. "Too bad she's into chicks."

"Maybe she just hasn't met the right guy yet."

Rosina rushes into the walk-in fridge. She pauses after she grabs the family's drinks, looks out the fridge door's narrow window into the kitchen, where her mom is sweat-drenched and in pain, slaving away at the hot stove, cooking her sweat and anger and years of disappointment into the food she makes every night. Mami is the head cook, manages the kitchen, and even does the bookkeeping, in addition to housing and taking care of Abuelita, but still it is called José's restaurant. Still, he controls the money. Still, Rosina's mother is the daughter in a family with two sons.

"I fucking hate people," Rosina announces to a crateful of cabbage.

She returns to the table with the heavy tray of drinks and a basket of chips and salsa. The family ignores her as she places the items on the table. "Boys, let's go wash your hands, okay?" the mom says to the feral creatures, but they are too busy seeing how far they can bend each other's fingers back before they cry.

"You're such a girl," one of them says as the other withdraws his hand in pain.

"Boys?" Mom says. "Did you hear me? Time to wash your hands." But they act like she's not even there.

"Rob, can you help me here?" she implores her husband.

"Calm down," he says. "They're fine."

Rosina fights the urge to strangle the little shits. "Are you ready to order?" she says between clenched teeth.

"I want a number fourteen with beef," Dad says.

"Number eighteen," says Eric. "Pork." Rosina does not look up,

but the tone in his voice as he said "pork" suggested he was going for a double meaning.

"The boys will both have the kids' tacos, with beef, please," says the mother. "I'll have the taco salad with chicken. But just on a regular plate, not that fried tortilla bowl. And no cheese or sour cream or guacamole. And dressing on the side."

Rosina heads to the kitchen as fast as she can without running. She is relieved when two more parties enter the restaurant, even though they look like assholes too. Everyone around here looks like an asshole to Rosina. But there are gradations of assholes, and the new customers couldn't be anywhere near as bad as Eric's family.

As she seats the first new group, she can hear Eric and his father whispering. She can feel their eyes on her.

What can Rosina do? Storm over there and give them a piece of her mind? Make a scene? They'd just laugh at her. The other customers would freak out. Mami would freak out. It'd be bad for business. And if something's bad for business, the whole family suffers, the whole damn stupid family. The customer's always right, isn't he?

Rosina is immobilized, powerless. She is nobody, nothing. A waitress, a daughter, a body, a girl.

One of the twins knocks the basket of chips on the floor.

"Can we get some more chips over here?" the father says.

Just say yes. It's her job to always say yes.

She sweeps up the mess. She brings over a new basket of chips. She pretends not to notice the boys stabbing holes into the pleather booth with their forks. She pretends not to notice the fire in Eric's eyes as he looks at her, a mix of desire and violence, a sense of entitle-

ment that Rosina will never come close to knowing, an entitlement so effortless these men don't even know it's there. The privilege of always getting away with it. The privilege of getting to raise more sons just like them.

But worse, worse than anything, is the fact that Rosina, outspoken bitch extraordinaire, does nothing to stop them.

Rosina hears the bell ding in the kitchen announcing their order is ready. She sets the hot, glistening plates on a platter.

She spits a little bit of her rage into each one.

The Real Men of Prescott

All women are insecure and longing for male validation.
The fact that they hate themselves is our most powerful
weapon, and one of the most important tools of the game
is to learn how to use that self-hate to our advantage.
This works especially well for superhot girls, whose
whole sense of worth comes from their ability to control
men with their looks. Show them that you aren't being
controlled, by knocking them down a notch.

Ignore them. Tease them. Point out their little flaws.
Use their insecurities against them, then they'll do
anything and everything to get your approval. *You* will be
the one they want because they'll be so afraid *you* don't
want *them*.

—AlphaGuy541

GRACE.

Mom and Dad are still giddy from Mom's sermon yesterday. They hover over Dad's laptop at the breakfast table as he shows her the websites of different publishers and literary agents he's been researching. They don't even notice Grace enter the kitchen.

"I think it's finally time to finish my book," Mom says with a huge grin. Dad hugs her, holding her in his arms for a long time.

"It feels like the right time, doesn't it?" he says as he lets go. "God's calling us."

"He is," Mom says earnestly. "I just hope people want to hear my message. I hope they're ready."

Grace won't tell them how she spent all night on the computer, scouring the Web for any sign of Lucy Moynihan. Facebook, Twitter, Tumblr—everywhere, every sign of her, gone. Her old e-mail address bounced back. Her family seems to be unlisted, wherever they are. Lucy is invisible. She's been erased.

"God sure works in mysterious ways," Dad says with a laugh.

"I hate to say it, but people know who you are because of what happened in Adeline."

He didn't seem to hate to say it at all, Grace thinks as she pulls a carton of orange juice out of the fridge.

"As much as it hurt," Dad says, "it got us to where we are now."

What does he know about hurt? Grace thinks.

Mom sighs. "Who knew doing God's work would involve having to think about marketing angles?"

Dad hugs her again. "God will guide us in getting our message across, every step of the way." He chuckles. "Even Paul did 'marketing' in the early church. All of it matters. Every bit is holy."

They look at each other with a love that had always been a comfort to Grace growing up, when none of her friends' parents seemed to even like each other all that much. But now she's starting to find her parents' devotion annoying. The house is full of their positivity and faith—it's stuffed with it—leaving no room for what Grace is feeling. Their plans and dreams are so big and so complete, but Grace has no place in them. She does not matter.

She matters so little that her friends back in Adeline could just throw her away. She is no one. She is nothing. A girl no one sees. A girl no one remembers.

Grace grabs an apple and a granola bar for breakfast and walks out the door to head to school early.

She is so tired of being invisible.

Grace will have to make her own plans, then. She will have to find her own way to matter.

If you're already nothing, you have nothing to lose.

Grace prepares herself all morning for the speech she will give Rosina and Erin at lunch. She uses several pieces of notebook paper over the course of her first four classes, jotting down points she wants to make, retorts to potential objections. By the time she sits at their table, she is almost confident about her case. Almost.

Lord, give me strength.

Erin pulls out her bento box with its usual bird-food contents. Rosina plops down with a banana, a carton of chocolate milk, and some cheese crackers from the vending machine.

"That's all you're having?" Grace asks.

"Today's school lunch is tacos," Rosina says. "I hate tacos."

"Do you think an android could be programmed to enjoy sex?" Erin says while spooning a mysterious green substance out of one of her box's compartments. "And if it could, would there be a practical reason for it to have that ability?"

"Wow, Erin," Rosina says. "How about you start with something like 'how was your weekend?'"

"But that's small talk," Erin says. "You know I hate small talk."

"Now you're just being contrary."

"That's part of my charm."

"So, you guys?" Grace interrupts. "There's something I want to talk to you about." If she doesn't speak now, she knows she'll lose her nerve.

"Slow down, man," Rosina says. "Jeez, you both need to improve your social skills."

"Is this going to be about personal stuff?" Erin asks. "Because I don't like conversations about personal stuff."

"Not really. I mean, sort of?" Grace stutters. She freezes. What was she was going to say? Where are those notes?

"Hello?" Rosina says. "We're listening."

"Hold on," Grace says, pulling her notebook out of her backpack and flipping through the pages of her indecipherable handwriting.

Rosina shrugs, opens her bag of crackers, and throws a handful into her mouth. "So," she says with a mouthful of orange crumbs. "While you're trying to remember what you were going to say, I also have an announcement. I have decided that we do in fact have to do something to stop those assholes. Not just the assholes who raped Lucy, but all the assholes. We have to keep them from breeding more assholes." She peels open her banana and takes a big bite. "I think castration seems appropriate."

"Sounds messy," Erin says.

Rosina smiles. "That was funny, Erin."

"Thank you."

Grace puts her notebook back in her bag. Her body feels tingly, her surroundings surreal, like she's moving in slow motion while the rest of the world is speeding up.

"Are you serious?" Grace says. "What changed your mind?"

"It doesn't matter. Stop asking me questions or I might change it back."

Grace glances at Erin, who is chewing her food, watching them, listening. It is impossible to read her. She seems calm, but there is something else below the surface, something she is trying very hard to keep buried.

"What about you, Erin?" Grace asks her.

"Are you in?" Rosina says. "Do you want to be a part of our rebellion?"

Erin doesn't say anything for what seems like a long time. She is swaying slightly, her head down, like she is thinking hard, *feeling* hard, like there is a lot more going on inside her than what they're talking about. Finally she says, "That sounds like subversive activity."

"Yeah, so?" Rosina says.

"Subversive activity almost always involves breaking rules," Erin says, her voice growing agitated.

"That's kind of the point," Rosina says.

"We want to break the rules," Grace says, an energy building in her chest. The feeling of something happening. The feeling of something inevitable. The feeling of something that matters. "The rules are what keep us silent. The rules are what didn't get justice for Lucy. The rules are what's broken." Her words are full of fire, maybe not a full-on flame, but definitely at least a spark.

"Wow, New Girl." Rosina lifts an eyebrow. "You're just full of surprises."

Tell me about it, Grace thinks.

"But we need rules to keep order," Erin says, looking up for a moment with pleading eyes. "If everyone broke rules all the time, there'd be chaos. Then no one could get anything done."

"We're not talking about those kinds of rules," Rosina says. "We mean like the unwritten rules of our sexist culture. Like the way girls and boys are expected to act, like double standards, women only making seventy-eight percent what men make, that kind of thing."

"Guys getting away with rape even though everyone knows they did it," Grace says. "Girls living in fear for no reason except the fact that they're girls."

Grace sees something shift inside of Erin. Her face makes a pained expression and she stops rocking. She shakes her head. "But we're nobody," she says. "How are we going to fix any of those things?"

"That's what we're going to figure out," Grace says. "Are you with us?"

"With you for what? You don't exactly have a plan. And who's going to listen?"

Grace and Rosina look at each other. They deflate just a little.

Grace thinks about the messages Lucy left in her room. She thinks about telling Rosina and Erin about them. But something about that feels wrong, as if those words are secrets meant only for Grace, as if telling people about them would be betraying Lucy's trust.

"Erin's right," Rosina says. "It can't be just us. No one's going to listen to three weird girls."

"Let me state for the record that I still haven't agreed to anything," Erin says.

Grace bristles a little at the "weird" label, but then she reminds herself that she chose to sit with these girls at lunch. God led her here, He gave her a choice, and she made it.

"There has to be a way we can reach all the girls of the school and bring them together," Grace says. "Like have a meeting or something."

They sit in silence for a long time. No one is eating. The drama

of the lunchroom goes on around them, a wall of white noise. They cannot look at one another. They don't want to admit their idea is doomed just as it got started.

"You could e-mail them," Erin finally says, like it was obvious the whole time.

"How are we going to e-mail every girl in the school?" Rosina says.

"Easy," Erin says. "I can get their e-mail addresses from the office. I have access to everyone's information."

"So we'll send everyone an e-mail that says, 'Hi, it's us, three nobodies, and we're still pissed off about old news that everyone wants to forget about, and we're bringing it up because we want to make everyone's lives miserable. So who's with us?'" Rosina rolls her eyes. "Why don't we just toilet paper the guys' houses or something? That'd probably be equally as effective."

Grace feels something open inside her, a tiny whisper, a tiny light. "What if it wasn't us?" she says. "What if it was nobody?" She pauses for a second. "What if it was everybody?"

"What are you talking about?" Rosina says.

"The e-mail," Grace says. She is spinning. She is electric. "What if we sent it anonymously? It'd be coming from, like, *nowhere*. Then no one would know it was from us. And people would be intrigued by the mystery, right? They'd come to the meeting just to see what it's all about."

"'The Nowhere Girls,'" Erin says. "That's what we can call ourselves. On the e-mails."

"Yes!" Rosina says. "The Nowhere Girls! Erin, you are on such a roll today."

"I am not rolling anywhere," Erin says. "But thank you."

They sit in silence, all trying to imagine what a meeting called by nobody, from nowhere, would look like.

"But what's going to happen once everyone gets there?" Rosina finally says. "If we want to stay anonymous, who's going to lead the meeting?"

"Anyone could," Grace says.

"But what if nobody does? What if it's awkward and no one says anything? Or what if it's total chaos?"

"What if it turns into a riot?" Erin says.

The bell rings, signaling lunch is over. The movement and sound of hundreds of students intensify as everyone packs up to leave, and the girls feel their bubble quickly losing form. They will soon be swept back into the world of high school.

"It's not going to turn into a riot," Grace says, speaking fast. "We'll figure something out."

"It's time to go to class," Erin says.

"Can we meet after school?" Grace says. "To plan this?"

"My shift starts at five, but I can meet for a couple of hours," Rosina says. "Holy shit, we're really going to do this?"

They look at Erin. She's busy packing up her lunch.

"Erin?" Grace says. "What about you? Is after school today okay?"

She zips up her backpack. "After school is when I do my homework," she says. "Then I watch my episode of *TNG*. I'll have just enough time to do some extracurricular reading before dinner. If I meet after school, it will disrupt my schedule and throw everything into chaos."

"Really, Erin?" Rosina says. "Chaos? That's a little dramatic, don't you think?"

The lunchroom empties, and they are the last ones sitting in a sea of vacant tables, surrounded by dirty trays and soiled napkins.

"Erin," Grace says. "Look at me." Erin meets her eyes for almost a full second. "What's more important? Your schedule, or doing something to stop the rapist assholes holding this school hostage?"

"'Holding this school hostage'?" Rosina says. "That's good, New Girl."

Erin fidgets with the zipper of her backpack. "I'm going to miss my episode," she says, not looking up.

"So you're coming?" Grace says.

Erin takes a deep breath, squints her eyes closed, and nods slightly. "You're lucky I'm in a good mood today."

To: undisclosed recipients

From: TheNowhereGirls

Date: Tuesday, September 20

Subject: GIRLS! GIRLS! GIRLS!

Dear friends and classmates:

Are you tired? Are you scared? Are you tired of being scared?

Are you ANGRY???

We know what they did. Spencer Klimpt, Eric Jordan, and Ennis Calhoun. We know they raped Lucy. We know they have hurt others, probably many of us. We know they will hurt more.

But it is not just them, not just those three. It is everyone. It is the whole school, the students and administration, the whole community of Prescott, who let them get away with it. It is their friends and families and teammates who looked the other way. It is everyone who made excuses, everyone who thought "boys will be boys," everyone who thought it'd be easier to ignore Lucy than to give her justice.

When they raped Lucy, they raped all of us. Because it could have been us. It could have been any of us. Who will be next?

The rape continues as long as they remain unpunished for what they did.

Are you tired of enduring? Are you tired of letting things go? Are you tired of being silent?

We failed Lucy. We will not continue to fail ourselves. We will not continue to fail one another.

We will meet Thursday after school in the basement conference room of the Prescott Public Library. Enter through the emergency exit door in the alley off State Street. It will be propped open.

This meeting is intended to be a safe, anonymous, and confidential space. What is shared, and the names of who is present, will not leave the room.

Are you ready to do something? Are you ready to take matters into your own hands?

Join us. Together, we are stronger than they are.

We will not be silent any longer.

Love,
The Nowhere Girls

US.

"Nobody's coming," Rosina says.

"Yes, they are," Grace says.

"I had to *beg* my aunt to give me the afternoon off babysitting," Rosina whines. "Favors are really hard to get in my family, by the way. I used up a favor for nothing."

Rosina, Grace, and Erin are sitting on folding chairs in a long-forgotten room in the Prescott Public Library basement. Half the lightbulbs are out, and the walls are lined with dusty stacks of cardboard boxes. Erin pulls a book out of her backpack and starts reading.

Grace is on the edge of her seat, her knee bouncing away. "They're coming," she says. She looks at her watch. "It's only a little after three. People have to go to their lockers. Maybe stop somewhere to get a snack."

"I was sure at least a few people would show up," Rosina says. "Three people responded, 'This is awesome!' to the e-mail we sent out. With exclamation points. I thought those were definite RSVPs."

"The e-mail was sent to five hundred seven girls," Erin says. "It's probable that at least a few people will show up."

"Thank you, Erin," Grace says.

"Unless all the recipients are either lazy or don't care or think what we're doing is weird. That is also likely."

"I'm going to go check to make sure the back door is still open," Grace says. "Maybe people can't get in and they're too afraid to enter in the front?"

"Or no one's coming," Erin says. "That's the most logical answer."

"Maybe I can make it home in time to save my aunt's favor for later," Rosina says.

"So that's it?" Grace says with a quivering voice. "You want to give up?"

But then the doorknob rattles. Grace blinks back tears. The three girls turn their heads as the door opens to a blinking, freckled face.

"Um, hi," the girl says. Elise Powell: Senior, jock, undetermined sexual orientation. Not the top of the popularity totem pole, but definitely not the bottom. "Is this where the meeting is?"

She shuffles in, unsurely, and sits down on one of the chairs Grace set up in a circle. Following close behind are a pair of freshmen named Krista and Trista, both with badly dyed blue hair and thick black eyeliner. Then two more arrive—Connie Lancaster and Allison Norman, the gossips from Grace's homeroom. How many does that make? Eight? Not exactly enough to start a revolution.

"Oh, hey," Connie says to Grace. "You're in my homeroom, right?"

"Yes!" Grace says, too eagerly.

"Do you know who's in charge of this thing?" Connie says, running her fingers through her long dark hair. "Who sent the e-mail?"

"No one knows," Grace says, her face blazing red.

"This is weird," says Allison.

Then one more girl walks in. Rosina gasps. It is not just any girl.

"Hello!" the new arrival says in a cheerful voice that seems exceptionally loud coming from such a small body. Sam Robeson. Head of the drama club. Lead in last year's semiscandalous production of *Cabaret*, wearer of costume jewelry and endless expanses of scarves, and Rosina's hopeless crush all freshman year after she dressed up like a boy-band pop star for Halloween, proving definitively that there is nothing sexier than a femme girl in boy drag.

"So, what's up?" Sam says as she sits down. Rosina notices how her short pixie cut frames her perfect ears and jawline. "What are we going to talk about?"

"I think we're supposed to talk about Lucy Moynihan," one of the blue-haired girls says.

"I don't really care about Lucy Moynihan," Connie says, flipping her hair, reminding Grace that she's the meaner half of the homeroom pair. "I just want Eric Jordan to stop staring at my tits all the time." Krista and Trista giggle nervously. Rosina cringes.

"He totally groped me in the photography darkroom freshman year," Allison says. "I told Principal Slatterly, but she basically told me it was my fault and I shouldn't put myself in compromising positions."

"That's horrible," Grace says. "I can't believe she did that. Did you tell someone?"

Allison shrugs. "She's in charge. There was no one else to tell."

"You're new, right?" Connie says. "So you probably don't know yet that everyone in Prescott who's in charge of something—they're all friends. Principal Slatterly, the mayor, the police chief, city council, everyone. And they all go to Prescott Foursquare, the same church as Eric's, Spencer's, and Ennis's families. Chief Delaney's wife is cochair of the volunteer committee with Ennis's mom. This whole town is totally corrupt. There's a word for that, isn't there?"

"Nepotism," Erin says without looking up from her book.

"My parents go to that church, too," says Krista, or maybe it's Trista. "They force me to go. They're total fascists."

"Totally," says the other blue-haired girl.

Erin looks up from her book, blinks a couple of times as she looks around the room, then returns to her reading. Other eyes scan the circle, then stare back down at their laps or into some dim corner of the room. Sam pulls her phone out of her purse and reads a text message.

"So I have something I'd like to talk about," Elise Powell finally says. Eyes turn to her expectantly. "I'm the manager of the football team, and I overhear a lot of stuff in the locker room—"

"Oh my God," says Sam. "Do you *see* anything? Is there, like, hot guy-on-guy action?"

"Um, no," Elise says. "I'm not allowed in the actual showers."

"Bummer," says Sam.

"Anyway," Elise continues. "The other day all the guys were talking about making bets on how many girls they could sleep with this year. They're keeping track and everything. There's even money involved. Eric Jordan is the leader of the whole thing. He told everyone to start with freshmen girls because they're easiest. It was like

he thought he was the guys' teacher or something, like he was really helping them. Like he had this whole science about getting laid."

"Castration," Rosina says. "I'm telling you, that's the only solution."

"You'd think that after everything that happened last year," Sam says, "he'd try to fly under the radar a little, maybe try not to be such an obvious douche bag." She shakes her head and the beads of her dangling orange earrings clink together. "I can't believe I used to think he was hot."

"But maybe he feels even braver now that he got away with it," Elise says.

"It's kind of a tradition," says Connie. "The guys competing about sex. Poor freshmen don't see it coming. They actually think the guys like them. I almost fell for it once."

"I did fall for it," Allison says, lowering her eyes.

"We have to warn them," Elise says.

Krista's and Trista's eyes are big and round as they nod their heads in agreement. "How?" one of them squeaks.

"Maybe put up signs or something?" says the other.

"That's too dangerous," says Allison. "Couldn't they catch us with, like, forensic evidence or something?"

"CSI is not going to dust for fingerprints on a few construction-paper signs," Rosina says.

"I think we should make signs," Elise says. "And flyers maybe, too. We have to make sure everyone knows."

"At least you don't have anything to worry about," Connie says under her breath, but it is a small room with only nine people in it, so everyone hears.

"What's that supposed to mean?" Elise says, her freckles even darker against her skin's new crimson shade.

"I mean, like, you're gay, right?" Connie says. "So you don't have to worry about asshole guys like the rest of us."

"I'm not gay," Elise says, eyes on the floor, her enthusiasm snuffed out like a candle.

"Um, hello?" Rosina says. "Guys are still assholes to gay girls. Sometimes even worse."

"You know what I mean," says Connie.

"No, actually. I don't," Rosina says, leaning forward in her seat. "What exactly do you mean?"

"I mean, like, you're pretty so no one can really tell, but Elise *looks* like a—"

"I'm not gay!" Elise cries. Grace reaches over and tries to comfort her, but Elise pulls her hand away, shaking and sniffling as she grabs her backpack off the floor.

"Not cool, Connie," Rosina says. "What is your problem?"

"This is bullshit," Connie says. "I have better things to do than sit around complaining about boys." She stands up and Allison reluctantly follows, smiling apologetically as they walk out the door.

"Elise, wait," Grace pleads.

"I have to go," Elise says, fighting back tears as she leaves the room. The blue-haired freshmen duck out quietly behind her.

"Yeah, um," Sam says, wrapping her scarf around her neck. "I have to go run lines with my scene partner."

"Wait!" Grace says, but there's nobody left to hear her.

"I guess the meeting is over," Erin says as the door swings closed.

"Well, that was fun," Rosina says.

"I think I'm going to go back to my regular life now," Erin says.

"No," Grace says weakly. "You can't. We can't give up."

"Why?" Erin says.

"Because this is important," Grace says.

"But what's the point?" Rosina says. "We can't actually change anything."

"Maybe we can," Grace pleads. "If we keep trying."

"Lucy never asked us to do this," Erin says. "It's not our responsibility."

"Then whose responsibility is it?" Grace says.

Rosina hangs her head. Erin shrugs. Grace looks at them, back and forth, but they do not meet her eyes.

"I have to go home," Erin says. She looks at her phone. "I'm already six minutes behind schedule."

"I gotta go to work soon," Rosina says, picking up her backpack and standing up. "You coming, Grace?"

"I'm just going to sit here for a while," Grace says.

"Are you going to pray or something?" Erin says.

"I just want to think."

"Come on, Erin," Rosina says. "Time to return to our regularly scheduled programming." Erin follows Rosina out the door, leaving Grace to think or pray or whatever it is she does when no one's looking.

GRACE.

Lucy speaks to Grace from her gouges in the wall paint. *You failed me*, she says. *Nothing you did matters.*

Mom and Dad are already gone for the day, having left before Grace even woke up for school. They had to beat rush-hour traffic to get to the local NPR affiliate in downtown Eugene, where Mom is going to be interviewed on the morning talk show about progressive Christianity. She's out there changing the world while her inconsequential daughter makes inconsequential toast in the empty kitchen, boxes still piled in the corner with things that may never get unpacked: a crock pot, cookie cutters, a fondue set her parents got for their wedding twenty years ago that has never come out of its box.

Yesterday afternoon, in the dull, dusty light of the library basement, after shedding some good old-fashioned tears of self-pity, Grace prayed for guidance. "Lord," she said, "please show me my path. Show me what to do. Show me how to serve you and best help my fellow man. I mean, woman. I mean, girl. Girls." She couldn't even pray right.

Grace took a deep breath and squeezed her eyes tight. She pulled her hands against her chest, pressed the steeple of prayer against her heart. "Please," she said. "I know I have a purpose. I just want to know what it is. I just want to know what I'm good at. If there's anything I'm good at."

Then she opened her eyes with a startle, surprised at her own words. She felt her body, but not what was inside it. She was something empty, something that had not yet been filled, something waiting to know what it's made out of.

Overnight, the rain started. If Grace's research is correct, it will not stop until sometime in May. The stained ceiling in the corner of her room started leaking immediately, just as she suspected it would. She woke to the sloppy percussion of *drip, drip, drip* on her floor, and lay there for a long time considering her options: 1) Get out of bed, find a bucket and towels, and take care of it; 2) Get out of bed, get ready for school, and pretend like it's not happening; or, the most attractive option, 3) Go back to sleep.

Of course, she eventually went with the first option. At least she knows this one thing about herself: She is someone who does what she is supposed to do. She is someone who has been raised to always do the right thing.

Even with an umbrella and raincoat, Grace finds that by the time she gets to school, her shoes are full of water and her jeans are soaked from hem to knees, and they will stay that way for the rest of the day. The windows of the building are fogged with moisture; the halls are full of the sounds of wet clothes squishing and rubber soles squeaking on wet linoleum.

But there's something else. Voices are louder than usual. More urgent. Electric. It can't be the rain doing that. People are huddled in conversation, eyes wide and conspiratorial. They are looking at the walls, at lockers, at pieces of paper in their hands.

Grace walks fast to get a better look at a bright neon printout taped to a locker. WARNING! it reads. TO ALL THE GIRLS, ESPECIALLY FRESHMEN. BE CAREFUL WHO YOU TRUST! It goes on to describe the boys' sex competition in every disturbing detail. It is signed THE NOWHERE GIRLS.

"Oh my God," a girl says. She is young, probably a freshman. The girl turns to her friend. "Do you think that's why that senior asked for my number yesterday? I knew there was something weird about it."

A light burns in Grace's core. A small flame flickers in her dark expanses. God's wordless voice tells her this is the sign she was waiting for.

She turns around. She sees all these girls talking to one another, all these girls who normally wouldn't mix. Grace wants to celebrate. She wants to hug somebody. A twinge of pride surfaces: She wants to tell them *she* did this. Then shame takes pride's place. Does Mom's ego ever rear its ugly head like this? Does her chest fill with pride when she looks around at her rapt congregation? Does she forget to be humble? Does she forget we are only ever vessels of God, of His work? Does she ever, just a little bit, want to take His place?

A commotion in the halls. Coach Baxter and his football cronies march through, tearing down the signs. "This is unacceptable," Coach says, his face red, veins pulsing out of his neck. "Principal

Slatterly will not condone these rumors. This is *bullying*, ladies. That's what this is."

Somebody coughs, "Bullshit."

"Who said that?" one of the football boys barks. "Who the fuck said that?"

Then Elise Powell comes striding through the madness in the hall, a pure, beautiful smile on her freckled face. Grace catches her eye, and the warmth inside her grows and grows until she's full, until it can't be contained, until it bursts out of Grace's skin and through the hall and wraps Elise up inside it, and their smiles light the hall with their secret.

We did this, their eyes say. *We all did this.*

By the end of first period, most of the posters were defaced. By the end of second period, they had all been torn down. Someone wrote THE NOWHERE GIRLS SUCK!!! with lipstick across the first-floor girls' bathroom mirrors.

After the excitement of the morning, lunch is a letdown. Things haven't changed. People are sitting at their usual tables. The trolls are still central, still as cocky as ever, their voices and laughter even louder than normal as they joke about the morning's events.

How naïve to think one poster would change things. How stupid to think it would diminish their power.

"It's like everyone forgot already," Grace says.

"And you're surprised?" says Rosina.

"I have exciting news about sea urchins," Erin says, and begins a five-minute monologue.

Just as Erin starts to explain eversible stomachs, Elise Powell plops down next to her. Erin's eyes go wide in shock. Suddenly the three girls' tiny lunch table island is not so isolated. Suddenly they have achieved communication with the outside world.

"I just told Coach Baxter I'm quitting as manager of the football team," Elise tells them. "To protest the sexist culture they propagate in this school." She grins proudly.

"What'd he say?" says Grace.

"He was totally speechless at first," Elise says. "His mouth just hung open for a while. Then he got pissed. His face got so red, I thought smoke was going to start coming out of his ears. Then he was just like, 'Fine. Get out of my office,' like he was trying really hard to control himself. So I got out of his office."

"You go, girl," Rosina says, but Grace can't tell whether she's being sarcastic or sincere.

"Thanks." Elise smiles. "Well, I guess I'll see you guys later." Then she walks away to return to her usual table of girl jocks.

"That was weird," Erin says.

"See?" Grace says. "Things *are* changing."

"I hate to burst your bubble," Rosina says, "but I don't think Elise quitting as manager of the football team is a sign that we're destroying the patriarchy."

"Can you just let me have my moment, please?" Grace says.

But then something in the air shifts. Erin looks up in horror, as if she can smell danger. Grace can feel the presence behind her before the cruel voice speaks: "Oh, look, the two crazy bitches got a new fat friend."

Rosina spins around and glares at Eric Jordan, who is standing behind her. "This isn't your lunch, shitbird."

He holds up a hall pass. "Just passing through."

"Pass a little faster."

"You've got spunk, I'll give you that," Eric says with a grin. "And I like a challenge."

"Is that a threat?" Rosina says, standing up like she's ready to fight him.

Eric laughs. "It was supposed to be compliment."

"That was *not* a fucking compliment, you sexist piece of shit."

"Whatever," he says. He looks Rosina up and down one last time, like a wolf eyeing meat. "You're not worth the trouble." Then he walks away, laughing to himself as if the rest of the world is in on the joke.

Rosina is shaking with anger, her face red, her hands fists. "I feel homicidal right now," she says between clenched teeth. "This is why people shouldn't have guns."

"Oh my God," Grace says. She can't think of anything else to say, so she says "Oh my God" again.

"We have to get that fucking bastard," Rosina says. "We're getting together after school today, right? To figure out what to do next?"

"Absolutely," Grace says. "Erin, what about you?"

But Erin is hunched over, rocking back and forth. She is somewhere inside herself, trapped. She is not with them.

"Oh, shit," Rosina says.

"Erin, are you okay?" says Grace.

"I have to go," Erin says with a tight voice. She starts gathering her lunch from the table.

"Wait," Grace says. "Do you want to talk about it?"

"I want to be alone," Erin says, standing up. Her shoulders are so tense they're practically touching her ears.

"But we can go with you—" Grace protests, but Rosina touches her arm gently and shakes her head.

"No," Erin says, then turns around and shuffles away, her hip bumping hard into the edge of the table. They watch her make her way quickly through the hall, her shoulder against the wall, as if she doesn't trust herself to walk without the support.

Grace stands up. "Shouldn't we go with her?"

"Erin is one of those rare people who actually mean it when they say they want to be alone," Rosina says.

"But what if she's not okay?" Grace says. "What if something happens?"

"She can get to the library just fine on her own. The librarian, Mrs. Trumble, is good to her. I think she's a little on the spectrum herself."

Grace is not satisfied with that answer. Something about Eric scared Erin so badly she shut down. She had to run away. That's not something to ignore. That's not something going to the library and being alone will fix.

"She's not helpless, you know," Rosina says.

"I know," Grace says. *But just because she's not helpless doesn't mean she doesn't need help.*

* * *

"Erin went home after lunch," Rosina tells Grace as they walk to her aunt and uncle's house in the afternoon drizzle.

"And you think I shouldn't be worried about her?" Grace says.

Rosina sighs. "You can worry if you want, but I'm not sure it's going to do any good. This just happens with Erin sometimes. Things set her off and she gets overwhelmed, then she needs to recharge for a little while. She'll probably be back at school tomorrow. She just needs things to be quiet and go back to normal for a while."

But for Grace, going back to normal is unacceptable. Normal is where she gets lost. Normal is where she is nobody. Normal is where nothing happens. How can something be so different for two people?

"But I keep thinking about her being all alone," Grace says. "It seems like we should go check on her or something."

"Honestly," Rosina says, "I think that would stress her out even more. If you need to do something, why don't you text her? Let her know you're thinking about her. That'd make her feel good."

"You two have a fascinating relationship."

"Tell me about it."

"You really care about her, don't you?"

"Yeah, so?" Rosina says. "She's my friend."

Grace chuckles a little.

"What?" Rosina says.

"You act like you're such a badass."

"I am a badass."

They walk the rest of the way in silence, which allows Grace's

thoughts to wander back to herself. "Are you sure it's okay that I'm coming over?" she asks. She half hopes Rosina will change her mind. Grace is suddenly so nervous that even her leaking bedroom seems more comfortable than a first visit to a new friend's house.

Rosina is her *friend*. Going to her house (really her aunt and uncle's house) after school makes it official.

"I'm telling you," Rosina says. "I don't even need to be there. Those kids can totally survive without me."

Rosina wasn't kidding when she said she had a whole army of cousins. They are everywhere, underneath the tables, bouncing on the furniture, climbing up the walls. The open living/dining room is stuffed with mismatched furniture; toys, clothes, dishes, and papers cover every surface.

A tween girl sits close to the television, watching a reality show. "That's the one I'm trying to groom to take my position," Rosina says. "All she has to do is sit there like she always does. Lola!" The girl doesn't move. "Where's Abuelita?"

"At your house," Lola says without taking her eyes off the screen. It's the show about people who have strange addictions to eating weird things. On-screen, a woman is drinking dish soap out of a champagne glass.

"You know she's not supposed to be there by herself," Rosina says.

Lola shrugs. "She's sleeping." The woman on the TV burps and a bubble comes out of her mouth.

"Where's Erwin?" Rosina says.

"In the bathroom."

Rosina shakes her head. "These people," she mutters.

"Does Erin come over a lot?" Grace asks.

"She's not really into hanging out outside of school," Rosina says, throwing her backpack on the floor. "She's only come over a couple of times, and both times she had to leave after, like, ten minutes because she said the smells hurt her."

"What smells?" Grace says. "I don't smell anything."

"Food smells. She says she can smell the hot peppers my mom and aunt use in their cooking. Which is especially weird at my house because my mom hardly ever even cooks there. Erin was smelling, like, leftover smells from the restaurant. It's like she has superhuman senses or something."

A boy around two years old hands Grace a naked Barbie with no head. "Thank you?" Grace says as he toddles away.

"Over here," Rosina says as she opens a laptop sitting on the dining table. She moves a laundry basket off a chair and motions to Grace to sit down. They stare at the screen as Rosina signs into the e-mail account they created for the Nowhere Girls, with no real names or identifying information attached to it.

"Hey, look," Rosina says. "We got new e-mails!"

A fight breaks out on the other side of the room. "Mine!" says one of the kids.

"No, mine!" says another.

"Give me that," Lola says, grabs the toy from the dueling cousins, sits on top of it, and goes back to watching her show.

"See," Rosina says. "She's totally ready."

"What do the e-mails say?" Grace says. "Do you recognize any of the addresses?" All the school e-mail addresses are the same format:

lastname.firstname@PrescottHS.edu, but none of the names look familiar to Grace.

"If you haven't already noticed," Rosina says, "I'm not exactly a social butterfly. There are more than a thousand students at our school. It is highly unlikely that I know the first and last names of approximately five hundred of them."

"You sound like Erin," Grace says.

"I think this is from one of those little Emo girls at the meeting," Rosina says as she clicks on the first e-mail. "She says we should meet somewhere more secret than the library. Good point." Rosina clicks on the next one. "Here's one from Elise. She just wants to know when the next meeting is. Oh, man, I thought she was going to take credit for those signs. That girl has some cojones."

"You think she did it?" Grace asks.

"Of course she did it."

Rosina smiles at the computer screen. "Well, look at this. We got one from Margot Dillard."

"Who's Margot Dillard?"

"You don't know? Only your two-term Prescott High student body president," she says in a singsong voice. "Let's see. . . . 'Dear Nowhere Girls.' Isn't that polite? 'I am very interested in joining your group. It appears that you can do much in the way of promoting empowerment among the young women of Prescott High School. I am very devoted to fighting for women's equality and would like to be involved in your positive social action. Please let me know when and where your next meeting will be, and how I may be of service. Sincerely, Margot H. Dillard, Prescott High School Student Body

President.' Jesus!" Rosina says, leaning back in her chair. "It's like she's applying for a job at the fucking bank."

"What's that one?" Grace says, pointing to a "From" e-mail address not in the regular school format, just a bunch of randomly generated numbers and letters from a common e-mail provider.

"Huh," Rosina says, opening it. "Whoever it is must have really wanted to stay anonymous."

Grace leans over Rosina's shoulder as they read the e-mail in silence:

Hi, whoever you are.

When I got your first e-mail, I just ignored it. I thought it was bullshit. But after today and all the signs at school, I started thinking maybe it's not bullshit. I don't know if I'm ever going to come to your meetings, but I think you should keep having them.

The reason I'm writing is because the thing that the signs are talking about—that really happens. It happened to me last year. I was a freshman and he was a senior and I was so flattered he was into me. I thought he really liked me. It was at a party and he kept giving me drinks. Then he took me out to his car.

I told myself he must have not heard me say no. I blamed myself. I thought it was my fault for getting drunk.

I'm not going to tell you who this is, because if you go after him, he'll know it was me who told. But I just want you to know I'm grateful for what you're doing. I think a lot of girls are, even if they don't know it yet.

Thank you.

Rosina and Grace stand there for a long time, not talking, reading the e-mail over and over again.

A child in the living room starts wailing, breaking their trance. The cousin who must be Erwin pokes his head out of the hallway and says, "Rosina! Will you quiet that kid up?"

Rosina looks at Grace, her jaw set, her brown eyes sharp and glistening.

"When is our next meeting?" Grace says.

Rosina's hands shake as she starts typing.

To: undisclosed recipients

From: TheNowhereGirls

Date: Friday, September 23

Subject: ONLY YES MEANS YES (and info about our next meeting)

Dear friends:

There seems to be some confusion about this, so let us make something very clear:

Taking advantage of someone who is intoxicated is sleazy and wrong. IT IS RAPE.

Getting a girl drunk for the purpose of having sex with her is not "loosening her up." It is not a seduction technique. It is RAPE.

Having sex with someone who can't consent doesn't make a guy lucky. It makes him a RAPIST.

Got it?

Somehow we've all decided this is just the way things are. This is just what guys do. This is just what girls have to deal with. But we refuse to accept that anymore. We are done letting guys decide what they get to do with our bodies.

If this has happened to you, it is not your fault. We are here for you. We are here for all of us.

Together, we are so much stronger than this bullshit we've been putting up with for far too long. Together, we can change it.

Join us!

Our next meeting will be 4:00 p.m., Tuesday, September 27, at the old cement factory warehouse on Elm Road.

Love,
Your friends, The Nowhere Girls

The Real Men of Prescott

Hot girls are trained to make it hard for you to fuck
them. Being untouchable heightens their value. But all
girls want a strong man, not some sensitive beta pussy
who talks about his feelings. Girls want to be taken;
it's in their natures, so sometimes they put up a fight
hoping you'll get a little rough. The truth is, sometimes
no doesn't mean no. Of course, the feminazis will never
admit this, but I'll bet you a hundred bucks most of
those chicks like it rough.

Women want a man who takes charge. They want a master.
But remember, only when you gain complete control of
yourself will you be able to gain complete control
of her.

—AlphaGuy541

US.

"I think this is considered breaking and entering," Erin says as they walk into the empty warehouse. "This is most definitely illegal. I am not comfortable with this."

"We're not breaking anything," Rosina says. "The door was wide open."

"I'm not convinced," Erin says, but she doesn't seem as upset as she should be.

The space is huge and empty, just a concrete floor surrounded by walls of multipaned, dirty windows, with no furniture anywhere. There are already over a dozen girls here, including every one of the girls from the first meeting, even Connie Lancaster, the girl who essentially ended it. Everyone is slightly damp from the day's relentless drizzle, standing around looking suspicious, huddled tight in their usual cliques, eyeing each other with disdain. It seems more likely that they're about to go to war than join forces.

"I don't think they like your location selection either," Erin tells Rosina.

"How did you even know about this place?" says Grace.

"Let's just say I have made it somewhat of an art form to discover places where my family can't find me," Rosina says.

Gray light filters into the empty space through clouded windows, muting all color. Everything is a gradation of shadow. Someone whispers, "What is *she* doing here?" and everyone assumes the "she" means herself.

"I don't like this," Erin says. "Everyone looks mean. What if they're mean? What if this ends as badly as the last meeting?"

"It hasn't even started yet and you're already panicking about how it's going to end?" Rosina says.

"There are so many more people," Grace says nervously.

"Dude," Rosina says. "That's a good thing."

"I thought Grace was supposed to be the positive one," Erin says, wringing her hands. "Why isn't Grace being positive?"

"Oh, thank God!" Rosina says, looking over Erin's and Grace's head. "Margot Dillard's here. Finally, someone's here who will know what to do. Or at least pretend she does."

"Oh, this is so exciting!" Margot Dillard, Prescott High School student body president, exclaims, clapping her hands together. She goes around the room greeting everyone, as if this is her party and she invited everybody, as if she doesn't even notice the dismal surroundings.

"Holy crap," Erin whispers. "*Cheerleaders*. I can't handle this."

Four girls walk into the room, statuesque, impeccably groomed, and somehow impervious to rain.

"Big deal," Rosina says.

"It is actually kind of a big deal," Grace says.

"I don't understand why everybody gets so excited about cheerleaders," Rosina says. "None of them is particularly accomplished at anything except jumping up and down and occasionally spelling 'Spartans' out loud. I can spell a whole lot of words way more complicated than 'Spartans' and no one ever cheers for me."

"You like that one cheerleader," Erin says. "The nice one."

"No, I don't," Rosina says.

"Yes, you do. You said she's the most beautiful girl in school."

"No, I didn't."

"Oh my gosh," Grace says. "There are like twenty people here already."

"*Oh my gosh*," Rosina teases.

"Twenty-three," Erin says. "I counted."

"Does this group have a designated facilitator?" Margot Dillard says with her big, presidential voice.

"It's like she has a microphone built into her throat," Rosina mutters.

"The last meeting was pretty unfacilitated," Sam Robeson, drama club girl, says.

"Well, every meeting needs a facilitator," Margot says. "Would anyone like to nominate a facilitator?"

"I nominate Margot to be the facilitator," says Elise Powell.

"Thanks, Elise," Margot says with fake surprise. "Does anyone want to second Elise's nomination?"

"I second it," says either Trista or Krista.

"All in favor, raise your hand," says Margot, and all the hands in the room go up.

"Thank God," Grace says.

"Thank gosh," says Rosina.

"How about we all sit down in a circle," Margot says.

"On the floor?" says one of the cheerleaders as everybody shuffles into position.

"You won't die if you get a little dirty," says another cheerleader—Melissa Sanderson, the one with the sweet smile and kind eyes who has brought Rosina's wandering grandmother back home more than once, and who has always stood out as a little different from her pack of popular girls.

"Before we get started," Margot says after everyone gets settled, "I just want to say thank you to whomever started this. I know you want to stay anonymous, which I understand completely. But if you're in this room, and I think you are, I want you to know that this is the kind of grassroots organizing that leads to real and lasting change." There are some halfhearted nods around the room, a few shrugs, a few muted sneers and snickers.

"It's like she's practicing for a real run for office," Rosina whispers. The cheerleader named Melissa laughs as she sits down right beside her, and Rosina looks down at her lap. Erin glares at both of them.

"Why did you blush?" Erin asks Rosina. "You never blush."

"Shhh," says Grace.

"I'd also like to suggest that the group stop using our school e-mail for communication, because it's too easily traceable," Margot continues. "I'd recommend disabling it entirely. We can spread news by good old-fashioned word of mouth."

"She's really taking over, isn't she?" Melissa whispers to Rosina. "Do you think she's the one who started it?"

"Are you blushing *again*?" Erin says.

"Now," Margot says, "I think we should go around in a circle and introduce ourselves and say a little about why we're here. I'll go first. My name's Margot Dillard. I'm a senior and your student body president, and I'm here because I want to change the misogynist culture at our school. Okay, your turn."

"Um," the next girl says. "My name's Julie Simpson. I'm a sophomore. I don't know. I guess I just wanted to see what this is all about?"

"My name's Taylor Wiggins," says another girl. "I'm here because I'm sick of the way guys treat girls. Like how they always tell their buddies whenever they hook up with someone, without even thinking about her privacy or anything."

"Yeah," says another girl. A few more nod their heads in agreement.

"I'm Lisa Sutter. Senior. Captain of the cheer squad. But you all know who I am, right? Anyways, I'm here because my boyfriend, Blake, cheated on me and I want to punish him."

"I'm Melissa Sanderson," Melissa says. "I guess I'm just tired of everyone expecting me to be a certain way because I'm a cheerleader or whatever. Like maybe I'm not really who everyone thinks I should be, but I feel like I have to hide it. I don't know, maybe that doesn't have anything to do with what this group is about. But it feels like it does, or at least it should. Because, I don't know, there has to be more than one way to be a girl, right?"

"Totally," Rosina says.

"Why are they looking at each other like that?" Erin whispers to Grace.

"Shhh," Grace says.

"Hey, weren't you guys friends with Lucy Moynihan?" someone says, and everyone's attention immediately focuses on two nondescript girls on the other side of the circle.

"Can I pass?" the first girl says meekly.

"Isn't the Mexican girl next?" says the other.

"Mexican girl?" says Rosina.

"You were at the party with her that night," someone else says. "I remember you. Both of you."

"Come on, Jenny," says the first girl. "We knew we were going to have to talk about her. That's why we came here."

"You were friends with Lucy?" Grace says, then immediately shrinks back, as if startled by the sound of her own voice, so loud, in front of this many people.

"No," says Jenny, at the same time her friend says, "Yes."

"Which is it?" says Margot.

"We weren't, like, close or anything," Jenny says, not looking anyone in the eye. "We just knew each other."

Her friend looks at her in disbelief. "Jenny, we were friends with her since kindergarten."

"Were you with her at the party that night?" Margot asks.

"Yes," says the girl who is not Jenny.

"We weren't with her when it happened," says Jenny. "She was totally flirting with Spencer Klimpt all night, and then she, like,

ditched us to go do whatever with him. You remember that, don't you, Lily?"

"She drank a lot that night," says Lily, looking down. "He kept giving her drinks. She'd never really gotten drunk before that night."

"Yeah," says Jenny, but her voice is different from her friend's, as if they are remembering two completely different girls. "She was drunk."

"So you blame her?" Rosina says with an edge to her voice. "Because she was drunk?"

"She could barely keep her eyes open," Lily says, her voice cracking. Tears well up in her eyes as she stares at Jenny, who refuses to look up at her. "He was practically dragging her up the stairs."

"Jesus," someone says.

"We should have done something," Lily says. Her lips are wet with tears. "Jenny, why didn't we do anything?"

Jenny just shakes her head. She looks folded, like she's trying to squeeze herself into two dimensions, like maybe if she is small enough, she can slip away from all these girls staring at her and demanding answers.

"She called me the next morning," Lily says through her tears. "She was crying so hard I could barely understand her. She said something bad happened, something really bad, but she wouldn't say what. And I kept asking her, 'What happened, what happened,' and she kept saying, 'I don't know.'" Lily pauses and looks over at Jenny, who still won't look up. "I was still so mad at her for ditching us at the party. We both were. Lucy was the one who made us go in the first place. Jenny and I didn't want to."

"She always wanted to be popular," Jenny says, but now she doesn't seem so angry. Now she just seems sad.

"I said, 'Did you hook up with Spencer Klimpt?'" Lily says. "And she didn't say anything, she just kept crying. So I hung up on her."

"She would do anything to be popular," says Jenny, but now she's crying too.

"She kept trying to call back, but I wouldn't answer," Lily continues. "Then she just stopped trying."

Lily takes a deep breath. "I didn't hear anything until Monday, when she wasn't at school, and neither were the guys, and everyone was talking about how she and her parents talked to the cops, and there were so many different stories and no one knew what to believe. But it didn't matter because everyone knew it was three guys who mattered against one girl who didn't. I mean, no one even knew her name. They were calling her 'some freshman girl.' They didn't even know her name and they already decided she was lying."

"What did you think?" Grace says softly. "Did you think she was lying?"

After a long pause, Lily says, "No. I believed her." She looks at Jenny. "But I pretended I didn't, just like everyone else. I was still so mad at her."

"I didn't believe her," Connie Lancaster says. "I'm sorry, but I didn't. I believed what everyone was saying, that she made it all up to get attention."

"I don't get it," Rosina says. "Why didn't you want to believe her?"

"I don't know," Connie says, looking down, ashamed. "I hated her for talking about it. It was like she screwed up *my* life somehow."

Connie looks up briefly, then looks back down with a shudder. "I know how bad that sounds."

"I remember she only lasted half a day when she came back to school," Elise Powell says. "People were tripping her in the hall and calling her a slut everywhere she went."

"And we just watched it happen," says Sam Robeson, wiping her eyes with a purple scarf.

"Didn't the ambulance come to get her?" says Trista or Krista. "I heard the school nurse called them because she was having a nervous breakdown in the office."

"An ambulance showed up, but she didn't go with them," Connie says.

"I think her parents picked her up," says Allison.

"And now she's gone," sniffles Sam.

"That is so fucked," Rosina spits. "This is so incredibly fucked up."

"I should have done something," says Lily, quietly. "That night. I shouldn't have let her go upstairs with him. I knew how drunk she was. I knew something bad was going to happen." She starts sobbing. "But I thought it was her fault. I blamed her. She didn't deserve that. I should have done something."

"We all should have done something," Sam says softly. "It wasn't just you. We all ignored her when she came back to school. Nobody helped her. No one stood up for her."

"A lot of people were at the party that night," says Melissa Sanderson. "I was there. I saw her talking to Spencer. I knew what he wanted. I had no idea it was going to be anywhere near as bad as it was, that Eric and Ennis were going to be involved, but I knew

enough. I knew Spencer was an asshole. I knew he had a habit of taking advantage of drunk girls. I knew she was a freshman. I knew it was wrong." She closes her eyes, shakes her head.

"But it doesn't have to be like that," Rosina says. "It can't be like that."

"It's only like that because we let it be," Melissa says, locking eyes with Rosina. "We can help each other, but we don't."

"It's time for things to change," Margot Dillard says, with energy in her voice, like she's getting ready to make a speech.

"But what exactly are we going to *do*?" Rosina says.

No one says anything for a very long time.

And then, in the silence, a small voice calls out: "What about a manifesto?"

"A what?" someone says.

"A manifesto," Grace says a little louder. "Let's write our manifesto. Let's tell them exactly what we think."

"We have to do more than that," Rosina says. "We have to punish them. We have to do something to make them hurt too."

"I have an idea," Grace says.

ATTENTION:

Boys and Young Men of Prescott High School

We are sick of your shit. We have been putting up with it for too long.
That ends now.

Our bodies are not toys for you to play with. They are not pieces in a game
for you to manipulate and trick. We are not notches on your bedposts.

We believe Lucy Moynihan. She was telling the truth. In your hearts,
you know it too. You know who hurt her. You see her rapists at school
and in the community every day. You sit by them in your classes. You
party with them on the weekends.

But you do nothing. You look the other way and let your friends hurt,
use, and rape more girls. Or worse, you encourage them. You cheer
them on. Or worse, you do it too.

Guys, we know you can do better. Call out sexism when you see
it. Tell your bros their rape jokes aren't funny. When you hear guys
talking shit about girls behind their backs or bragging about their lays,
call them on it. Help girls when you see them being harassed or taken
advantage of. Be the bigger man.

Don't keep silent when you know something wrong is happening.
Don't look the other way.

We won't. Not anymore.

So until you face these facts and take action to change your behavior, and to hold your friends accountable for theirs, you do not deserve us.

Our demands are simple. We require:

1. Justice for Lucy Moynihan

2. That the male students of Prescott High School treat us with the respect we deserve

We do not want war. We want you on our side.

But until that happens, and until our demands are met, we will not engage in any sexual activity with the male students of Prescott High School. This includes but is not limited to: sexual intercourse, oral sex (aka blow jobs), manual sex (aka hand jobs), kissing, frenching, necking, making out, heavy petting, dry humping, wet humping, porking, screwing, banging, boning, boinking, and any other ridiculous word for hooking up that you can think of.

Do we have your attention yet?

Let us be clear: Rape is not about sex. It is about power and violence and control.

We know a sex strike cannot stop rape. Our strike is meant to get the attention of those of you who think you are off the hook, those who do not rape but who allow it through your silence about those who do, through the tiny things you do every day that make girls feel like they are less than you, that make girls feel afraid. Even if you do not rape, you still hurt women. Even if you do not rape, you feed rape culture by not actively trying to stop it. It is time for you to know this. It is time for this to end.

We hereto declare that the young women of Prescott High School are officially on a sex strike.

Make friends with your hands, boys.

Sincerely,
The Nowhere Girls

US.

The notes are everywhere—on walls, on ceilings, on floors, inside lockers and backpacks and purses—bright fluorescent late-night printouts from some unsuspecting parent's printer. The school is littered with them. They will be cleaned up, but they cannot be unseen.

"What the fuck is this shit?"

"Is this serious?"

"Have Eric and Ennis seen this?"

"Fucking bitches!"

These are the words said out loud, with laughter, with rage, with ridicule. But there are also slight smiles, imperceptible nods of the head, invisible support that is so far hidden.

Girls walk through the hallway a little taller. They meet one another's eyes, share smiles with girls they never would have thought to acknowledge before. They keep their secret, and it burns like sunlight in their chests.

* * *

Erin sits at a desk in the back corner of the school's front office entering data into a computer spreadsheet. Her desk is not quite hidden, but it is pretty close. She is almost comfortable.

One thing Erin has learned during her time in the office is that Principal Slatterly likes to keep her office door open, and she always has a fan going. "She's going through *the change*," Erin overheard Mrs. Poole say while gossiping with one of the guidance counselors.

Erin overhears a lot in her corner. Sometimes people forget she's there. Or even if they know she's there, they somehow think she's not capable of hearing them.

Like right now, Erin can hear every word of a phone conversation Principal Slatterly is having in her office. She heard Slatterly say, "This is Regina Slatterly returning Chief Delaney's call." She heard her silent waiting. Then she heard a series of almost meek "Yes, sirs," as if Slatterly were a child being scolded.

"We're working on getting all the flyers down," Slatterly says. "The situation will be contained."

Erin stops typing.

"I don't think we have anything to worry about," Slatterly says. "The girls aren't doing any harm. It'll fizzle out in time. . . . Yes, sir. . . . No, sir. . . . It's just, I'm not so sure they're actually doing anything illegal. . . . No, of course not. . . . I understand. . . . Yes, I'll take care of it. . . . Okay, I'll talk to you later. Tell Marjorie and the kids I say hello."

Erin hears the phone rattle back into the console. Then she hears quite possibly the loudest sigh in the history of sighs.

She turns her head very slowly until she is looking over her

shoulder, straight into the principal's office, straight at Slatterly seated behind her big desk with her head buried in her hands, her fan ruffling the thinning hair on the top of her head like soft feathers.

Amber Sullivan has Beginning Art for second period. It's already a throwaway class, even without today's substitute teacher. They're supposed to be working on self-portraits, making a collage of the things they most care about, things that define them. Some students are texting or playing games on their phones; a few are asleep, heads cushioned by arms and jackets. But, mostly, people are talking.

Amber sits at her table in the corner and silently flips through old, wrinkled magazines, looking for pictures to add to her collage. She cuts out a picture of a tree. A mailbox. A cat. She glues them on her piece of red construction paper in no particular order. She cuts out no pictures of people, nothing resembling skin or body parts. The only intention she has for this project is that it should be impossible to read any meaning into it, that it should reflect nothing real of herself, that it should not give her away the way art always claims to do.

The only other person in class who appears to be working on their project is Grace, who is sitting on the other side of the room. School has been in session for three weeks already, but Amber only just started noticing the plain, chubby girl who always seems to be staring at her whenever she looks her way. It's like she suddenly appeared out of nowhere, and now it's impossible to ignore her. She doesn't look at her the way other girls look at her, with a mix of ridicule and hostility in their eyes, the words "slut" and "white

trash" on the tips of their tongues. Maybe this girl just doesn't know any better.

"Fucking chicks, man," says the asshole named Blake at the table next to Amber's. It is impossible to ignore him, too. "I bought Lisa a quadruple grande caramel some kind of bullshit that cost like six dollars, and she wouldn't even give me a fucking hand job."

"Lisa?" says another guy. "She's in on that Nowhere Girls bullshit now too?"

"Yeah, can you believe it? She was all, 'I don't have to hook up with you if I don't feel like it,' so I was like, 'Then why are you wearing that skirt that's so short I can practically see your ass?' and she was all, 'I can wear whatever I want,' and I said, 'Yeah, but if you wear something like that, you can't expect me to behave myself,' which is like totally reasonable, right?"

"Totally."

"But then she started bitching about how blaming women for sexual assault because of what they're wearing is, like, bad or something, and I was like, 'Who said anything about sexual assault? I just wanted a hand job,' and then she threw the fucking drink in my face!"

"She has a point, though," says a third guy at the table. "It is kind of a dick move to just expect her to want to hook up with you whenever you feel like it."

Blake and the other guy look at him, like they're waiting for him to say, "Just kidding."

"What the fuck, dude?" Blake finally says. "She, like, totally ruined my car seats."

The guy just shrugs.

"But at least there's still one girl left who won't say no," Blake's friend says, not even bothering to lower his voice. "You should have called Amber."

Amber tenses as soon as the words pierce her skin; she arms herself against their laughter. They know she heard them, but they don't care, or maybe they even wanted her to. Like she's not even a person, not someone with feelings, not someone who can get hurt. Just an object. Just something they can use. And she does not try to prove them otherwise, does not speak or otherwise engage, neither denies nor confirms their statements. What she does is harden, her own special defense mechanism—fight or flight or turn to stone.

The bell rings. Students put away the art supplies none of them was using. The boys leave without acknowledging Amber's existence, laughing all the way out the door. Even the guy who defended Lisa is in on it, because Amber and Lisa are very different kinds of girls.

Amber takes her time cleaning up. She is giving the guys a head start. The worst thing is to get stuck in the hall with a pack of them.

The classroom finally empties. Even the sub has disappeared. Amber zips up her bag and throws it over her shoulder. Only five more periods until the end of school, when she can sneak away to the computer lab and hide at her favorite desk in the corner while the tech club nerds congregate on the other side of the classroom pretending she's not there. It's her secret—this small joy, that tiny space behind the computer where she feels capable and creative, where she can leave her body and enter a world that makes sense,

a world made of ones and zeros that she can manipulate, a world where she is in control.

"Hey," a voice says behind her, making her jump. She turns around to find Grace, who somehow sneaked up on her without her noticing. "You're Amber, right?"

Amber doesn't say anything, just looks at Grace with an angry squint in her eyes, ready to deflect the inevitable abuse that's coming, that always comes. She is ready to snarl back, ready to prove the other side of her reputation true: cruel, mean, nasty. There are reasons she doesn't have any friends.

Grace lowers her voice even though there's no one around to hear her besides Amber. "You've heard of the Nowhere Girls, right?"

Amber nods, and for a brief moment the squint in her eyes softens.

"Do you want to come to the next meeting?" Grace says. "I think you'd like it. The meetings are actually pretty fun."

"What do you guys do exactly?" Amber says sharply, but the real question in her head is, *When was the last time a girl invited me to anything?*

"We talk mostly. You can talk about anything. We talk a lot about guys, I guess."

"So you just sit around complaining about guys?"

"That's part of it," Grace says. "But other things, too."

"Like what?" Amber's body is angled toward the door, instinctively ready for a getaway.

"Like how to not let them bother us anymore."

Amber's bag is packed and over her shoulder, but she's not

walking away. She won't look at Grace, but she wonders if Grace can feel her wanting to, can feel her full of questions, can sense Amber wanting to feel something besides anger and suspicion.

"You don't have to decide right now," Grace says. "If you give me your phone number, I can text you info about the next meeting."

Just then Amber's phone beeps with a new text message. She pulls it out of her bag. From a number she doesn't recognize: **Hey, want to hook up tonight?** Amber sighs. She is too tired for her seventeen years. She opens her bag and rips out a piece of notebook paper, scribbles something on it, folds it, and hands it to Grace. "Okay," Amber says, without looking Grace in the eye, then turns and walks out the door.

"Hey, boys!" calls a girl across the lunchroom. "Miss us yet?"

"There's more where you came from," calls a boy from the other side.

People laugh. It's all they can do. Some laughs are giddy, triumphant. Some are the peculiar mix of cruelty and embarrassment—the laughter of bullies. Still, some burn with a rage and hate that was already there but hidden, before any of this began.

"Miss this?" says another boy, standing up and fake unbuttoning his pants.

"Miss *what*?" says a girl. "There's nothing there."

Clear lines are drawn. The lunchroom is tense. Allegiances are shifting; tables are emptying as members defect to the other side. A vague no-man's-land exists between them, a neutral zone of people with their heads down, just trying to eat their lunches. The taunts

fly over their heads like war fire, back and forth, a hit here, a ricochet there. Shrapnel flying and seasoning everyone's food.

"Look at Ennis over there," Rosina says. "He looks like he's going to throw up. I almost feel sorry for him." His head is down, his face covered by the bill of his baseball hat. His friends are silent, hunkered down and steely eyed. All except Jesse Camp, Grace's almost-friend from church, whose doughy, bewildered face rises above the hunched figures of his lunch mates, looking around the lunchroom as if he's been misplaced. "God, I wish we had the same lunch as Eric," Rosina says. "I want to see the look on his face."

"Sam said he hasn't been at lunch the past few days," Grace says. "He's been going off campus."

"Can I have your French fries?" Erin says.

"What happened to your raw, organic, vegan, gluten-free diet?" says Rosina.

"All this social upheaval is making me hungry."

"It's important," a girl says to her boyfriend in her bedroom after school, removing his hands from her waist. "I have to do this."

She's having a hard enough time believing her own words without him touching her. Her body wants her to forget her promise. His mouth is on her neck and his breath is warming her skin, and he's not the enemy, is he? He's not a rapist. He's a nice guy. She loves him. Why should he suffer?

She melts. She turns warm. She closes her eyes. She lets his hands sculpt her.

Then she thinks of Lucy, alone and scared, with nobody to

help her. She remembers seeing her in the hall the day she came back, how the boys threw things at her—pencils, wadded-up paper, chewed gum—how the girls looked the other way. She thinks of her own body, her boyfriend's. She thinks of this privilege of pleasure.

"No," the girl says, and pushes her boyfriend away. "I need you to support me on this."

He sighs. He squints his eyes tight. He breathes in and out. "I do support you," he finally says. "But this is kind of painful." He looks down at his lap, at the expectation bulging in his jeans. "Like physically painful."

"So go to the bathroom and take care of it if you have to," the girl says, her resolve back. She has lost all sympathy for decisions made by body parts.

He looks her in the eye. "I'll survive," he says, trying to smile. He puts a pillow on his lap.

"You will," she says. She can see that he is trying. She softens. "Thank you."

He looks out the window, at the relentless, pounding Oregon rain. God, what a perfect day to have sex. What a perfect day to be warm and close and under the blankets. "So what do we do now?" he says.

"I don't know," the girl says, sitting up on her bed, making sure none of her body parts touches any of his. "I guess we talk."

The Real Men of Prescott

We have to stop letting the bitches manipulate us. They
think their passive-aggressive games are going to force
us to behave how they want, but we're stronger than that.
We call the shots, not them. We will not bow to a mob of
feminazis. We don't need them. They're too much trouble.

Don't worry, men. In the great scheme of things, these
girls are nothing. Real women want a strong man to take
control. They want to please. They want to be wanted.
They'll do anything to get you to say you love them.

So let's move on. These bitches aren't worth our time.
There's plenty of other pussy out there, and we know how
to grab it.

—AlphaGuy541

ROSINA.

Fuck this school. Fuck Principal Slatterly.

"Come on, Miss Suarez," says the dopey security guard. "I don't have all day."

Fuck you.

A handful of girls sit on the plastic seats in the school office, the best selection of burnouts and antisocial weirdos the school has to offer.

"What is this?" Rosina says to the black-haired girl with white streaks sitting next to her—Serina Barlow, the girl who notoriously just got back from a summer in rehab.

"I have no idea," Serina says.

Mrs. Poole steps out from the back, fanning herself with her short chubby fingers. Her forehead shines with beads of sweat.

"You all right, Denise?" the security guard asks her.

"Yeah, *Denise*," one of the burnouts says, and a couple of others cackle with her.

"Yes, yes," Mrs. Poole chirps. "Busy day, that's all."

"What are we here for?" Serina asks. "I haven't done anything."

"*I haven't done anything,*" one of the burnouts mocks. "You think you're some kind of princess just because you have three months sober? All of a sudden you're better than us?"

Serina ignores the girls' hateful stares. Rosina likes her immediately.

"Hey," Rosina says. "Did you know our names are almost the same if you rearrange the letters?" Serina just looks at her and blinks. "If we get out of here alive," Rosina whispers, "I have something I want to talk to you about."

"Rosina Suarez." Mrs. Poole sighs. "Why don't you go next?" She waves her in the direction of Principal Slatterly's office.

This isn't the first time Rosina's been in the principal's office. There was that time she spit in Eric Jordan's face, of course. There was also the time she defaced the library book about Intelligent Design as a birthday present to Erin (which Erin did not appreciate nearly as much as she should have). There was the time she called her PE teacher an asshole when he shouted "Hurry up, hot tamale!" at her during a running test.

"Why am I here?" Rosina says as she sinks into the way-too-soft armchair across the desk from Principal Slatterly. Everything in the room is floral patterned and wicker. An oil painting of baby rabbits in a gaudy gold frame hangs above a filing cabinet. If a person didn't know any better, they might think this was the office of a sweet old grandma. But they would be oh so wrong.

"I was hoping you could tell me that," Slatterly says, leaning forward in her chair and folding her hands on top of her desk.

"I'm here because you told the security guard to come get me out of class."

"And why do you suppose I did that?"

There are a lot of things Rosina could say, most of which would probably get her suspended. So Rosina says nothing. She leans back, shoulders relaxed, and looks out the window at the dreary wet parking lot as if she couldn't care less. This is a look she has perfected, which comes in especially handy in moments like this, when she cares way too much.

"You were quite vocal last spring about how you felt about those allegations against three of our male students," Principal Slatterly says. "You created quite a few disturbances."

"I created one disturbance," Rosina says. "And it wasn't much of a disturbance."

"There have been quite a few disturbances lately," Slatterly says. "Would you agree that I am justified in suspecting you might be behind those?"

"Really?" Rosina laughs. "You think I'm a part of this protest or whatever?"

Slatterly doesn't blink.

"Dude, I'm not a part of *anything*," Rosina says. "It's like a group, right? Like a bunch of dumb girls got together and decided to play pretend freedom fighters and change the world? Do you really think I'd be a part of that? Nobody likes me. I like nobody. I don't do groups, and I definitely don't do optimism or whatever it is you need to believe anything you do can actually make a difference."

Slatterly's lips go tight and thin. Rosina can't help but smile a

little—no doubt she won that round. But then the principal hoists her chin in the air and raises her eyebrows. Round two.

Slatterly takes a deep breath. If Rosina didn't know any better, she might think the gesture seemed sad.

"You may not believe this," Slatterly says, "but I was young once too."

It takes all Rosina's strength to not laugh in the principal's face.

"You might even say I was a little like you," Slatterly says. "I tried fighting. I tried yelling to make myself heard."

Rosina wonders what kind of manipulation strategy this is. Some kind of reverse psychology?

"But you know what?" Slatterly continues. "I didn't get anywhere that way. I used up all my energy trying to prove something to the world, but no one was listening." She shifts some papers around on her desk. "I know you girls think you're doing the right thing, picking these fights. And trust me, I'm with you—I don't want anyone to get raped. I don't want girls getting pressured into having sex. Hell, I don't want girls your age having sex at all. But the truth is, you can't expect the boys to take you seriously like this. You can't expect them to respect you when you're yelling at them." Slatterly pauses, attempts a smile, maybe even a real one. "Thankfully I learned before it was too late, and that's why I'm here talking to you, as your principal, in a position of leadership. In a position of *power*. It was not easy to get where I am, Miss Suarez, and there's no way I could have done it if I hadn't been willing to make some compromises."

Rosina doesn't know if she's supposed to say something now.

She doesn't know what she's supposed to think, what she's supposed to feel. A part of her is angry, but most of her is just confused.

"It's a man's world," Slatterly says, and for a moment Rosina thinks she sees something human break through Slatterly's usual hard-ass demeanor. Something vulnerable. Something maybe even a little scared. "They make the rules, Miss Suarez. And if you want to get anywhere in this world, you have to play like a man. Being a strong woman doesn't mean fighting men; it means acting like one."

"Why are you telling me all this?" Rosina says.

"I want you to succeed, Rosina. I don't want you to get mixed up in any pointless activity that gets you in trouble."

"I'm not," Rosina says. "So you have nothing to worry about."

Slatterly sighs. She closes her eyes for a moment, then adjusts the small fan on her desk so it is pointed straight at her face. Rosina fidgets in her seat. Is Slatterly *sweating*?

"How many people in your family have graduated high school?" Slatterly finally says.

"What?" Rosina says. "How is that relevant?"

"I imagine your success in school is important to them. They would be very disappointed if you didn't graduate, for instance."

"My grades are fine."

"Surprisingly, yes," Slatterly says. "But your attendance is abysmal. That can be grounds for suspension. Even expulsion in extreme cases."

"I doubt I'm an extreme case."

"Well, that's the thing, Miss Suarez. You are not the judge of that. I am."

Rosina says nothing. Here's the principal she knows. Here's the royal bitch.

"You don't want to disappoint your family by not graduating, do you?" Slatterly says. "There aren't a whole lot of opportunities for uneducated women out there. I suppose you could spend the rest of your life waiting tables at your uncle's restaurant."

Slatterly's face is blank as she lets that sink in, as she lets it fester and poison Rosina from the inside. "So," she says, "what do you think, Miss Suarez? Do you want to take those risks? Do you want to keep making trouble for yourself, for your family?"

"No," Rosina whispers.

"Then I think we are in agreement. No funny business, right?"

"Right," Rosina says between clenched teeth.

Slatterly smiles. "I'm glad to hear that."

"Can I go now?" Rosina says.

"Yes," Slatterly says. "Please send in the next student, will you, dear?"

Rosina stands up, her muscles a tangle of knots and snarls. She walks out without saying anything, out of the front office, down the hall, and out the school's front doors. She unlocks her bike and rides through the rain as fast as she can. She doesn't care about getting wet. She doesn't care about mud puddles. All she needs is to get to her destination, one of her favorite hiding places on the edge of town, a place where no one but her ever goes, a place where she can sing and scream as loud as she can and no one will tell her what to do, and no one will tell her to be quiet.

ERIN.

Tonight's big event is a rare dinner at home with *both* of Erin's parents. Mom has gone all out with a baked lentil loaf and mashed cauliflower. It's a special occasion when Erin gets to eat cooked legumes. Dad drove straight home after his Friday afternoon class. He does try once in a while, but usually only after serious badgering by Erin's mom.

"I can't believe you still have Erin on this crazy diet," Dad says, picking at his food.

"If you were ever around," Mom says, "you'd have noticed that it's actually made a huge difference in her mood and behavior."

"Did you know there's a group of sea slugs that feed on algae and can retain the chloroplasts for their own photosynthetic use?" Erin says. "It's called 'kleptoplasty.' Get it? *Klepto?*"

"That's nice, honey," Mom says.

"How's school, kiddo?" says Dad. "Still acing all your classes, of course?"

"Erin has a new friend," Mom says.

"Oh, yeah?" Dad says. "That's great."

"She's the daughter of that new pastor at—what is it, honey? The Unitarian church?"

"Congregationalist," Erin says. Spot follows the conversation from his place next to her on the floor.

"Well, at least it's not one of those backward churches they have around here," Dad says, sipping his wine. "You can't go a block without running into some idiot who actually thinks the world was created seven thousand years ago."

"Jim," Mom says. "That's not nice."

"What? It's true. There's nothing wrong with me not wanting my daughter to hang out with ignorant and willfully anti-intellectual people. Those people are destroying this country. I think it's perfectly reasonable to not want them to brainwash my daughter."

"I don't think this has anything to do with your daughter," Mom says.

Neither does this dinner, Erin thinks.

"Honey," Mom says. "Quiet hands at the dinner table."

Erin stops rubbing her hands for approximately five seconds before her anxiety feels like it's going to kill her. She stands up, even though she's still hungry, but she's used to being hungry. "I'm going to my room."

"No, sweetie," Mom pleads. "We're having a nice dinner."

"I started my period," Erin says, and walks away, Spot following close at her heels. That always works.

"Look what you did," Erin hears Mom say as she heads upstairs.

"You're the one who turned this into a fight," says Dad.

"Why can't we just have a nice dinner as a family? Just once. That's all I ask."

"*That's* all you ask? You can't be serious."

Erin closes her door, finally safe in the familiar order of her room, where everything is precisely placed, all her books organized by subject and then alphabetized by author. Spot goes to his usual place on the foot of the bed. Erin turns on her white-noise machine to the preset station of waves and whales singing, lies down on her side on her perfectly made bed, and presses the soles of her feet against Spot's warm, sturdy body. She closes her eyes as she rocks back and forth, as she imagines herself deep underwater, in a ship of her own design, so far down that sunlight can no longer reach her.

But thoughts still creep in. Even this far underwater. Even inside her submersible with steel walls nearly three inches thick. There are the usual things. There is this Nowhere Girls business, how it makes her think about things she's worked so hard to push away, how some strange urge makes her keep showing up for meetings even though they terrify her. But fresh in her mind is a newly troubling issue: the boy named Otis Goldberg in her AP American History class.

While Erin will reluctantly admit it is pleasing that Otis Goldberg slightly resembles Wesley Crusher from *Star Trek: The Next Generation*, he also has a man-bun, which is unacceptable. But because he is only a teenager, he is technically not a man, so the term is not completely accurate. He is closer to a boy. Otis Goldberg has a boy-bun.

What Erin is specifically not comfortable with about Otis Goldberg is the fact that he keeps talking to her in class when it is

obviously not academically required. She purposely sat in the back of the class to avoid situations like this. Also so no one would notice her stimming, which would make her self-conscious, which would make her anxious, which would make it impossible to pay attention. Sometimes she just has to flex her fingers or rub her hands together or rock slightly. Sometimes moving her body is the only thing that can still her mind. The "quiet hands" Mom always wants her to have are a meltdown waiting to happen.

Otis Goldberg is always doing strange things like asking how Erin is or saying he liked her presentation on the Iroquois Confederacy. Today was by far the worst, because he kept asking about the Nowhere Girls, if Erin is in the Nowhere Girls, if she's been to the meetings, if she knows who started it; and Erin had no idea if he was talking to her because he was trying to get information, or if he actually wanted to talk to her, and she didn't know which one was worse, or which one was better, and she certainly didn't know which one she wanted, or if she's allowed to want anything, if it's safe to want anything. So she just forced herself to keep her mouth closed, which just made him talk more, so he started talking about himself, and how he thinks the Nowhere Girls are great, how he totally considers himself a feminist, how he has two moms who would kill him if he didn't consider himself a feminist, and by then Erin couldn't keep her mouth closed any longer, so she blurted out "Can you please be quiet?!" so loud the whole class turned around to stare at her, and Mr. Trilling said, "Erin, are you *all right?*" in that way all the teachers do, even nice ones like Mr. Trilling, which really means, "Erin, are you about to get all Aspergery on me?"

Then Otis was quiet. And Erin was confused because she thought she was supposed to be happy because silence was what she wanted the whole time he was talking, but then when it finally happened, something about it didn't feel good, something hurt inside and Erin had no idea why, so she told Mr. Trilling she had to go cool off, which means go to the library to read about fish, which is what she says when everyone is acting so stupid she has to leave, except this time she had to leave because *she's* the one who acted stupid, and all she wanted was to take back what she said to Otis Goldberg because she realized he did nothing but be nice to her.

Erin should be watching the real Wesley Crusher on her daily episode of *TNG* instead of thinking about the fake boy-bun Wesley Crusher named Otis Goldberg, but instead she's trapped in her room while her parents monopolize the whole downstairs with their fighting, which is where the TV is, which is where she watches *TNG*. Erin is forbidden from watching shows in her room, because Mom does not want her to isolate any more than she already does, which is a lot, but not nearly as much since this whole Nowhere Girls business started, which has completely thrown her off schedule, which has quite frankly changed everything, and Erin is still not quite sure how she feels about it, except that she misses her room, she misses Data and Captain Jean-Luc Picard and all her friends on the USS *Enterprise*, she misses her old house in Seattle, she misses her old beach, she misses her old school and her old life and everything she had and everything she was before she did the thing with Casper Pennington that made her have to leave.

The world is moving too fast and she cannot adapt fast enough.

It is getting harder to push bad thoughts away. They are a poison, spreading. Everything is a reminder, threatening to pull the memories from deep inside where she has them buried. Every day Erin is getting less like Data and more like the raw nerve she's worked so hard to hide. She is falling apart. She is falling. She is lost in space and she has nothing to hold on to and she has no control over anything.

Erin wonders why Spot is getting up, why he's climbing over her to move to this end of the bed. She only realizes she's crying when he starts licking the tears off her cheeks. "I love you," she says to Spot, and he's the only one she ever says it to.

US.

Mom and Dad are both busy tonight with church stuff, so Grace is eating her microwaved dinner in front of the computer while she Facebook stalks her old friends in Adeline. Judging from recent pictures and vague, heavily exclamation-pointed status updates, nothing much has changed. One of her friends is "really excited!" about her new kitten. One of them is "really bummed!" that she got a B on her chemistry quiz. One of them is asking her thirty-seven Facebook friends for prayers as she sends in her application to Boyce College. One reposted some meme with a picture of a defiant toddler making a fist and "Back off devil, I belong to Jesus!" written in Comic Sans font.

And that's it. Four friends. Grace can't really think of anyone else to Facebook stalk. She grew up with these girls, spent almost every weekend with at least one of them, yet she feels no trace of missing them. She wonders what they would think of her new friends, about what she's doing, what she's becoming. They might pray for her, but only after they talked behind her back and vowed to never speak to her again.

Grace always yearned to feel a part of something, and for a long time she felt secure with her place in youth group, in her church, in her tiny clique of friends. It was a small, sturdy box she shoved herself inside because there didn't seem to be any other reasonable choices. But this, now, whatever *this* is, feels different. It's not even a box. It's something she's building to fit *her*, a place in the world that is adapting and growing and changing as she changes. She's a part of something she's helping to create, not something premade that someone else decided was good for her.

It was Grace who decided this was good for her.

Grace decided.

Two friends kiss.

"Are we allowed to do this?" one of them says.

"There's no rule against kissing girls," says the other.

"I wonder if all the Nowhere Girls are kissing each other now," says the first.

"They should," giggles the other.

This girl cringes as she points her phone toward her naked body and presses the button to make the image permanent. She only glances at it as she types out the words: Remember you promised to not show this to ANYONE!

She didn't want to do it, but he begged and begged until she said yes. He said if she wasn't going to have sex with him during the strike, she had to give him *something*. Better a picture of her than porn. Better her than someone else.

But as soon as she presses send, her stomach lurches. *What have I done?* she thinks. Now the photo is out there, uncontrollable. He owns this image of her body. He owns her.

A girl lies on her bed facing her boyfriend.

"Come on, tell me," he teases, stroking his fingers lightly across her arm the way he knows always gets her excited.

She picks up his hand and places it back on the bed. "You know I can't tell you who comes to the meetings," she says. "That'd be breaking so much trust."

"At least tell me some of the stuff you talk about. You don't have to name anyone."

"It's confidential."

"Fine," he says, rolling over onto his back. "Whatever."

"What do you mean, *whatever*?" The girl sits up.

"I mean, whatever." He does not look at her.

"I feel like you're not supporting me," she says.

He takes a deep breath. He closes his eyes. He opens them. He looks at her for a moment, then stares back up at the ceiling. "It's getting hard to support you," he finally says. "It feels like the whole thing is about hating men or something. And I'm, like, a man, so I kind of take it personally."

"I don't hate men," she says, her voice shaking with hurt, or anger, or both. "I just hate what some men do. I hate that they get away with it."

"I get it," he says, sitting up to face her. "I hate that stuff too. But you're all talking about the bad stuff all the time, so it seems like

that's all you think there is. But there are good guys too. And most guys are probably somewhere in the middle. What about them?" He pauses. He waits for her to meet his eyes. "What about me?"

She thinks she hears his voice crack. He looks away, but not before she notices the new wetness in his eyes. She opens her mouth to speak but nothing comes out.

"I know I'm not perfect," he says. "But I try to be a good boyfriend. I love you."

"I love you, too," she says.

His eyes bore into hers, begging. "Do you think I'm like them?" he says softly. "Do you think I'm a bad guy?"

"No," she says immediately, because she knows it's the answer he needs to hear. She wraps her arms around him because she knows he needs to be comforted. They hold each other for a long time, and she can feel the relief in his body just as she notices the rising tension in hers. She knows it's true that she loves him, but she wonders if maybe there is a little part of herself, deep down, that doesn't trust him, that believes there is some latent animal part of him, part of all men, that's like those guys, that's bad, and there's nothing he, or she, or anyone, can do to fix it.

Krista's and Trista's families sit beside each other at a wedding that is like almost every other wedding they've attended. Same music, same suits, same floral arrangements. Same words coming out of Pastor Skinner's mouth. Same tired old reading from Ephesians:

"Wives, submit yourselves to your own husbands as you do to the Lord. For the husband is the head of the wife as Christ is the

head of the church, his body, of which he is the Savior. Now as the church submits to Christ, so also wives should submit to their husbands in everything."

Krista and Trista look at each other and roll their darkly penciled eyes.

A girl takes her dog out for his afternoon walk. She feels her phone buzz in her pocket with a new text message: U like? The attached photo glares at her from the screen and hijacks the good day she was having until now, replacing it with a sick feeling that spreads through her entire body.

When did she ever give that douche bag in her economics class the impression that she wanted him to send her a picture of his pink, crooked dick? How can it be so easy for him to force his body into her vision like this, without her permission?

She looks away from the dick pic and sees her dog crouched over the ground, concentrating. She bends down, holds out her phone and clicks, then presses send to reply with a picture of her dog's fresh warm turd and the text message: U like?

A girl searches on the Internet: *How do girls masturbate?*

ROSINA.

In a miracle of scheduling, Rosina has a whole glorious Saturday off work and babysitting until the Nowhere Girls meeting tonight. Is this what it feels like to be a normal teenager? To have hours on end to sit around and do whatever you want, to do *nothing*, to listen to music and stare at the ceiling and dream about the life you're going to have, someday, as soon as you make it out of this one?

Mom's at work, of course. Tía Blanca is watching all the kids next door. Rosina already finished her homework, so now all she has to do is go downstairs to check on Abuelita once in a while. Otherwise, she's free to turn her music on as loud as she wants (Abuelita's hard of hearing) and let the voices of her idols carry her away to a place where she is strong and fearless, where she can imagine herself onstage with them—harmonizing vocals with Corin Tucker, playing guitar next to Kathleen Hanna.

Bang bang bang, says the door.

"Rosina, open up," says her mother on the other side.

No, Rosina thinks, closing her eyes. Something seizes in her chest. Mami has an uncanny sense of the exact right time to crush Rosina, always right at the moment she is starting to feel free.

"Rosina!" *Bang bang bang.*

"It's not locked," Rosina mumbles. Of course it's not locked. Mom had Uncle Ephraim remove the lock as soon as Rosina started puberty.

Mami has a way of opening the door that always seems somewhat violent to Rosina. Like she's a ball of anger and everything she touches explodes.

"Turn that noise off!" Mami shouts over the music.

Rosina rolls over on her bed and shuts off her stereo, saying a silent good-bye to the Butchies. "What?" she says in her best bitchy teen snarl.

"Elena called in sick," Mom says, scowling at a poster of a sweaty, tattooed, and scantily clad female musician onstage. "You have to come in to work."

Rosina bolts upright. "No," she says firmly. "Absolutely not."

"Don't give me that," Mami says. "You're not going to skip work just to lie around doing nothing."

"I have plans," Rosina says. "I have to leave soon."

"What plans? Watching TV with that crazy girl?"

"I told you not to call her that."

"Whatever it is can wait until another time," Mami says, rifling through the pile of clean laundry on the floor that Rosina still hasn't managed to fold and put away. She picks up a black shirt, smells it, then throws it at Rosina. "Here."

Rosina throws it back. "I'm not going."

Their eyes lock. Mami stands completely still. A rock. A mountain.

"You are going to work," Mami says slowly. "Get dressed."

"It's my day off," Rosina says.

"Your family needs you."

Fuck my family, Rosina thinks. But it's like Mami heard her, like she read Rosina's mind, because her eyes narrow as if in response. Rosina can read her mother's mind too. She hears her when she thinks, *This means war.*

"How did I end up with such a lazy and ungrateful daughter?" Mami says.

"Lazy?" Rosina says. "Are you insane? I work my fucking ass off for you people."

"Watch your mouth," Mami hisses.

Rosina stands up. "I'm in high school, Mami. In case you didn't know, I'm supposed to be learning shit, maybe even—God forbid!—having fun once in a while. I'm not supposed to be working almost every school night. I'm not supposed to be taking care of everybody else's fucking kids."

"How dare you talk to me like that," Mami says, stepping closer. "You need to treat your mother with respect. I do everything for you."

"This isn't about you!" Rosina shouts. "All I'm saying is I don't want to go to work on my day off. I have plans. That's my right."

Mami takes another step forward until they are only inches apart. She has to lift her head to meet her daughter's eyes. "Your *right?*" she says. "You want to talk about your rights?" She stabs her pointer finger into Rosina's chest. "Your family and the restaurant

are what keeps a roof over your head and gives you food to eat. If you don't appreciate it, maybe you don't need it. Maybe you don't deserve to live in the house I work so hard for. Maybe you need to be out on your own, see what the real world is like with all your *rights* you care so much about."

"Mami, that's not what I—"

"All you care about is yourself," Mami says. "You don't care about me. You don't care about your family."

Something inside Rosina breaks. How dare she say that? All Rosina has ever done is take care of her goddamned family and try to make Mami happy.

"Maybe you should try it sometime," Rosina says, staring daggers into her mother's eyes. "Maybe *you* need to think about yourself more and less about this family. That's why you're so mad. Because you're jealous of me. Because I'm at least trying to have my own life, when all you do is what other people tell you."

"You'd have nothing without your family," Mami says. Low. Snarling. "You wouldn't even be here. You'd be nothing."

I'm already nothing, Rosina thinks.

"But what if this isn't what I even want?" Rosina says.

And then the something inside Mami breaks too. "Fine!" she shouts, pushing Rosina in the chest so hard she falls back on her bed. "If this isn't what you want, get out! Get out of my face! Get out of my house! You ungrateful puta."

Rosina jumps up and storms past her mother, knocking her as hard as she can with her shoulder. *This is it*, she thinks. This is the time she doesn't come back. This is the time Mami throws all of

Rosina's shit on the front lawn and changes the locks and she never sees her family again.

She storms downstairs in nothing but a ratty pair of leggings and an old T-shirt. She is burning, on fire. Her blood is made of lava. But even in her rage, she does not forget Abuelita. Good, sweet Abuelita. How did such a kind and gentle woman create such a monster? Rosina must at least kiss her good-bye. Even if Abuelita won't remember. Even if she doesn't even know who Rosina is.

But where is she? She's not on the couch watching TV. She's not in her bedroom taking a nap. She's not in the bathroom. Not in the kitchen.

"Abuelita!" Rosina calls. "¿Dónde estás?" Nothing. "Abuelita!" she screams.

"What happened?" Mom yells as she runs down the stairs.

"She's not here," Rosina cries. "I looked everywhere."

For a moment they forget to be mad at each other. At the same time, their heads turn toward the front door. The weak early evening light shines through the open crack.

They burst out the door. They call for Abuelita. Nothing. The day is overcast, a thick blanket of gray clouds hanging low in the sky, so misleading in their softness. Rosina's eyes scan the neighborhood for any sign of a shuffling old lady, but everything is still. There are usually kids playing in front yards, people washing cars or pruning bushes, but it is eerily quiet today, as if everyone's hiding.

"Get in the car," Mami commands.

"But wouldn't it make more sense if—"

"Get. In. The. Car."

Rosina hops in the passenger seat while Mami starts the car. She starts driving before Rosina has a chance to fasten her seat belt.

They roll down the street, calling for Abuelita out the window. There are more signs of life as they get closer to the highway—other cars, people walking.

"Shouldn't we talk to someone?" Rosina says. "Shouldn't we ask people if they've seen her?"

But Mami's eyes stay glued to the road, her hands fists on the steering wheel, her thin lips so tight they're nonexistent. This family does not ask outsiders for help. This family takes care of itself.

They turn onto the busy street that leads to the highway on-ramp, all six lanes and a median, the fast cars and stoplights, the turn lanes and crosswalks, the big-box stores and fast-food restaurants, the bright lights and blinking signs. Abuelita must be so scared, Rosina thinks. Does she remember that things like this exist? Or does she think she still lives in the little Oaxacan mountain village she left years ago? Is she wandering around here, lost, thinking she stumbled onto another planet?

"There!" Mami shouts, pointing at an intersection a block away. The car speeds up and they swerve just in time to avoid rear-ending a car turning right.

Abuelita is standing calmly at the corner, pressing the button for the crosswalk. The car screeches to a halt in front of her, and Mami jumps out. Rosina pushes the hazard lights on and pulls up the emergency brake lever. For a brief moment she wishes Mami could have witnessed her quick thinking, could have seen her taking care of things.

"Mami," Mami says gently to Abuelita. She puts her arm around her and says, "Vámonos."

Abuelita blinks, confused but trusting. Mami speaks to her cheerfully in Spanish, all of her previous rage suddenly gone. Rosina has to turn her head. Something about witnessing her mother's softness hurts. Because Rosina never feels it. Because it is never directed at her.

Rosina gets out and opens the door to the backseat as Mami guides Abuelita back to the car. She looks across the lanes of traffic, at the Quick Stop gas station and mini-mart. She wonders if Spencer is working right now. She wonders who he's hurt lately.

Then *thwack!* Rosina stands, stunned, as she realizes the side of her face is burning. She turns her head to see Abuelita right next to her, her open hand raised in the aftermath of a slap, eyes wild with a combination of anger and terror.

"¿Qué has hecho con mi hija?" Abuelita demands. *What have you done with my daughter?* "¿Qué has hecho con Alicia?"

"Soy yo," Rosina says. "Soy Rosina."

"Tienes su cara, pero no eres ella." *You have her face, but you are not her.* Abuelita thwacks Rosina again. "¡Demonio!" she screams. *Demon!*

"Mami!" Rosina's mother calls, reaching for Abuelita's arm, but the old woman wrestles herself free. Rosina covers her face with her hands while her grandmother hits her with everything she's got. Rosina doesn't fight back. She doesn't try to stop her. Each impact seems somehow earned. She deserves this.

"¡Basta!" Mami shouts. *Enough!* "Rosina es su nieta. Ella te ama." *Rosina is your granddaughter. She loves you.* "Ella es buena." *She is good.*

No, Rosina thinks. *Mami's lying. She doesn't believe that.*

Rosina and her mother manage to wrestle Abuelita into the back of the car. She stops fighting as soon as her bony butt hits the seat, as if, just like that, something switched in her head and she forgot her torment. How nice it would be to turn off feelings like that, Rosina thinks as she leans in and buckles Abuelita's seat belt. Something wet from her face makes a tiny splash on her grandmother's knee.

They drive home in silence. Abuelita falls asleep as soon as the car starts. "Like a baby," Mami says softly. "You used to do that. When you wouldn't stop crying, I'd put you in your car seat and drive around the block. Worked every time."

But it's not working now. Rosina is turned as far away from her mother as possible, her forehead pressed against the cold window. It has started to rain, and the thick drops outside match the ones falling down Rosina's cheeks.

Rosina gets out of the car as soon as it comes to a stop in front of the house. She lifts Abuelita out of her seat, and her bony arms hold tight around Rosina's neck as she carries her into the house. Rosina lays her down in her bed, pulls the blankets up her to chin, and tucks in the sides slightly. Rosina knows Abuelita likes her blankets tight, just like Rosina.

Mami is standing in the doorway of Abuelita's bedroom. The room is dark and Rosina cannot see her face. She steps quietly away from the bed and says, "Excuse me." Mom gets out of her way.

"I'm going out now," Rosina says. In the darkness, she can see her mother nod.

US.

"At least this place is a lot cleaner than where we had the last meeting," Grace says.

"But it's probably even more illegal," Erin says.

The big stone sign at the entrance to the road says OASIS VILLAS, but there is neither an oasis nor villas in sight, only acres of muddy, bulldozed land dissected by a tangle of roads that circle around and go nowhere. The only signs of life are abandoned tractors sitting on piles of dirt and, way off in the distance, far from the main road, this one empty, perfect house on top of a hill, which the girls are sitting in right now. The sign stuck out front says MODEL HOME! in cheerful green letters, but there is nothing cheerful about it.

"Oh, look," Rosina says. "I'm not the only brown person here anymore. There's Esther Ngyuen and Shara Porter. We have our token Latina, Asian, and Black girls now. Aren't we just the model of intersectional feminism?"

Rosina plops down in the corner and leans against the wall, glaring at the rest of the room.

"What's your problem?" Erin says as she sits down beside her.

"I don't have a problem," Rosina says.

"You're even bitchier than usual," Erin says.

"You do seem kind of down," Grace says. "Are you still upset about your meeting with Principal Slatterly on Thursday?"

"Fuck Principal Slatterly," Rosina says, but without her usual enthusiasm. She touches her red and slightly swollen left cheek. "My mom told me I had to come into the restaurant today," she says. "Even though it's my day off. Seriously, it's like third world conditions. Being in my family is like living in a sweatshop."

"Is that racist?" says Erin. "Are you being racist against yourself?"

"But you're not at the restaurant," Grace says, still standing in front of her two seated friends.

"Yeah, well, that's because I said no."

"That's good, right?" Grace says.

"Not when it sets off a fight that's so bad we don't notice my grandmother leaving the house until she's already made it five blocks away and is about to get herself killed trying to cross the six-lane street by the highway. And then when we try to get her in the car, she thinks I'm a demon impersonating her dead daughter and punches me in the face."

"Oh no," Grace says. "I'm so sorry."

Rosina shrugs her best I-don't-care shrug, but it is not convincing. She looks around at the growing crowd of girls cramming themselves into the pristine, empty living room, trying to maneuver

for prime spots near their friends. Even here, where everyone's supposed to be on the same side, social cliques and hierarchy still reign.

"Why don't you just quit?" Erin asks.

"What, quit my family?" Rosina says. "I wish."

"Quit your job."

"I need the money."

"Could you at least quit babysitting like you were talking about?" Grace says. "Get your cousin to start doing it?"

"My family doesn't exactly understand the word 'no.'"

"Margot's talking," Erin says.

"When is she not?" Rosina says.

"It's time to be quiet," Erin says.

Someone has turned on the gas flames of the model home's fake fireplace, and Margot Dillard, student body president, is standing in front of it trying to get everyone's attention.

"Grace, are you going to sit down?" Rosina says. "You're making me nervous."

Grace looks at her feet, then at Margot, then back at her friends sitting in the corner. "I think I'm going to sit closer to the middle?" she says. "So I can hear better?"

"Whatever," Rosina says. "Knock yourself out."

"There are thirty-one people here," Erin says, her hands in knots. "That's too many for this room. It's too crowded. It's just a matter of time before the meeting descends into total chaos."

"*Descends into total chaos,*" Rosina sings in a growly heavy-metal voice. "*Duh duh duh.*" But Rosina's teasing of Erin is interrupted as Melissa the cheerleader sits in the empty spot right next to her.

"Is it okay if I sit here?" Melissa says, smiling.

"Um, okay?" Rosina says, immediately hating herself for the question in her voice.

"I am not comfortable with this at all," says Erin, to no one in particular.

"Does anyone have topics they would like to propose for today's discussion?" Margot says from the fake fireplace.

"Can we talk about how all the boys are being big babies?" someone says, which makes people laugh.

"I'm curious how things feel different for people," Melissa says. "Like if anyone feels like things are changing with how guys are treating them, or how we're treating one another. Or even how we feel about ourselves."

"Yes," Margot says. "Does anyone want to speak on what Melissa brought up? How things are changing?"

"I feel more confident," says Elise Powell. "Like, less insecure around other girls. Not as worried about everyone judging me all the time. Because it feels like we're all on the same side for once."

"I feel braver," says another girl.

"Yeah," says Elise. "I feel like *we're* different. The girls are. But the guys seem exactly the same."

"If not worse," someone says.

"We're forcing them to show who they really are," says Sam Robeson. "Nothing like a little obstacle to bring out someone's true character. It's basic dramatic theory."

"What are we supposed to do now?" says another girl. "Just sit around and wait for the guys to get their shit together?"

"Basically, yes," says Elise. "They know what we want. It's up to them to figure out how to change."

"They can always ask us for pointers," Rosina says. "Like here are the top ten ways to not be a douche bag. Number one: Don't rape girls."

"Number two," says Melissa. "Don't let your friends rape girls."

"Number three," someone says. "Have girls as friends, not just girlfriends."

"Number four," says Margot. "Don't call us 'fucksocks.'" The room erupts in laughter.

"Who calls women 'fucksocks'?" Sam says.

"I read it on *The Real Men of Prescott* blog," Margot says.

"Oh, God," says Rosina.

"Number five," says Melissa. "Don't read *The Real Men of Prescott* blog."

Then the laughter suddenly fizzles out. One by one, everyone turns her head, on high alert, like prairie dogs sniffing for danger.

"Holy shit," says Connie Lancaster. She does not bother whispering.

Amber Sullivan is standing in the doorway, a defensive scowl already on her face. The room is silent as everyone stares in her direction. Tense. On guard. Amber doesn't move, as if she's being held in place by their suspicious glares. For a moment it seems like the girls have decided to block Amber's entrance with nothing but their eyes.

"Why's she here?" someone whispers.

"I don't trust her," whispers someone else. "She's totally going to tell on us."

"Amber!" Grace finally says. "I'm so glad you came." Grace seems to be the only person who's happy Amber showed up, including Amber.

People half relax as Grace ushers Amber into the room. A few people even say hi, as if Grace's small act of inclusion was all it took to think of Amber as someone suddenly worth knowing.

"Wow," Melissa whispers to Rosina. "It's brave of her to come. Girls *hate* her."

"Do you?"

"No, of course not," she says. "I feel sorry for her."

"That's worse," Rosina says. "If someone hates you, at least they think you have some kind of power."

Melissa looks at Rosina in a way she can't read, forcing her to look away. For a moment Rosina wonders if maybe she's a little autistic herself, like Erin. It was almost painful, that eye contact. She feels the ache somewhere in her chest, in the place Erin's panic attacks start.

"Okay, ladies," Margot Dillard says. "Everyone comfortable? Do we want to check in about how the sex strike is going for everyone? Has anyone experienced any pushback from their boyfriends?"

"You mean ex-boyfriend?" says head cheerleader Lisa Sutter. "I always knew he was an asshole, but this whole thing has brought it to a new level." She looks at Amber with a homicidal gleam in her eye.

"Yeah, I had to dump mine, too," says another girl. "He laughed at me when I told him I was doing the strike."

"They're like little kids," Lisa says. "They don't understand the word 'no.' It just, like, doesn't compute in their tiny brains."

"Not all guys," another girl says. "My boyfriend's being really supportive."

"Yeah," says Sam Robeson. "I still don't understand why the nice guys have to suffer. I don't understand why *we* have to suffer. Girls are being punished by this sex strike too, you know."

"If it makes you feel any better, Sam," Lisa says, "I don't think Amber's doing the sex strike."

A few surprised gasps. A few nervous giggles.

"Amber still has sex with lots of guys, right?" Lisa says.

"Lisa," Melissa says gently. "I think you need to drop it."

"Drop it?" Lisa says. "Why should I drop it? You think I should be nice to her? She slept with my boyfriend."

"Ladies," Margot says in a high-pitched, nervous voice. "Let's not forget that we're here to connect and create a safe space for all girls. So let's try to come together instead of driving one another away. Okay?"

Girls murmur. Some nod in agreement. Some roll their eyes. "Whatever," Lisa says. "Majority rule, right? I'll just keep my mouth shut for the rest of the meeting since no one wants to hear what I have to say."

"That's not true," Margot says. "We still—"

Lisa puts her hand up like a stop sign. "It's fine. Seriously. I don't want to talk about it."

"I'm so sorry, Amber," Grace whispers, but the room is so quiet everyone can hear her.

"It's not like I don't know what people say," Amber says. "I know what you think of me. I know you all think I'm a slut."

"No, we don't," someone says weakly.

"That's sweet," Amber says with a voice that is anything but sweet. "But you're full of shit."

"It's not fair," Sam Robeson says. "Guys can have as much sex as they want, but as soon as a girl does, she's labeled a slut."

"But they still want you to be sexy," says another girl. "Or else they don't even see you."

"But not too sexy," says Margot. "Especially if you want people to take you seriously."

"So do you even like sex, Amber?" Connie Lancaster asks.

"Connie!" her friend Allison whispers.

"I'm curious," Connie says. "Really. I'm not being mean."

The room turns silent, waiting for an answer.

Amber doesn't say anything for a long time, just looks around the room at everybody looking at her. Their eyes are more inquisitive than hostile, like they actually want to know what she thinks and feels, like they actually want to know *her*. "I don't know," Amber finally says. The eyes have softened her. The surprise of this strange place and these strange girls, looking at her in this strange new way.

"But you hook up with a lot of guys, right?" Connie says, her voice almost kind.

"Yeah, I guess so."

"But you don't like it?"

"Sometimes," Amber says. "But not always."

"Why would you do it if you don't like it?"

Amber takes a long time to answer, as if the question was in a foreign language and she is taking time to translate each word.

"I don't know," she finally says. " I guess it just seems like . . . why wouldn't I?"

A few almost imperceptible nods around the room. Hate turning into pity turning into something else entirely.

Amber straightens up, turns hard again. "Yeah, so maybe I don't like it every time. So what? I just don't think sex is all that special. I don't see what the big deal is."

"The youth pastor at our church says virginity is like a flower," says Krista. "Losing your virginity before marriage is like plucking the petals off a flower. No one wants a flower without petals."

"No offense," Sam says. "But that's crap."

"Amber," Grace says. "We don't have to talk about this anymore if you don't want to."

"I think we should stop talking about this entirely," someone says.

"No," Sam says. "This is exactly the kind of thing we need to talk about."

"Well, I think we can all agree," Lisa says, "if anyone needs to go on a sex strike, it's Amber."

"Lisa, stop," says Melissa.

Lisa motions a zipper closing across her mouth.

"You really think a sex strike is going to make them respect you?" Amber laughs. "You think they could ever respect you? You think they respect any of us? It's a waste of time trying to get guys to respect you. So I'm using them just like they're using me. It's totally equal."

Somewhere in the shadows, someone whispers, "Poor Amber,"

but it is loud enough to make Amber flinch, to remind her why she should never have come here, why she doesn't belong with these people.

"You know what's weird?" Connie says. "No one at school talks about Sam being a slut, but she totally sleeps around, right? Why is Amber a slut but Sam is not?"

"I've heard people call Sam a slut," says one of Sam's drama club friends.

"Thanks," says Sam.

"But still not as much as Amber, right?" says Connie. "Like, not with as much hatred. Like if you had to choose who was considered a bigger slut by the majority of students at Prescott High School, Amber would win, even though they both have sex with lots of guys."

"Can we stop using that word? Like right now?" Sam says. "Can we all agree to just stop using that horrible word? I mean, it's bad enough what guys do, what they say about us. Do we really have to do this shit to each other?"

No one realizes that Amber is gone. They see her still sitting with them, but they do not know about her talent of leaving her body when it gets too painful to stay inside it. She doesn't want to think about what makes her different from Sam. She doesn't want to think about the hole inside her that nothing will fill.

"There's judgment on the other side, too," Grace says. She clears her throat and looks around the room. She takes a deep breath. "For virgins. For girls who choose to stay virgins. The way we talk about sex sometimes, it's like we assume everyone's having it. But we're not. I'm not."

"Me neither," Krista and Trista say in tandem.

"Me neither," Elise grumbles. "But not willingly."

"I'm not either," says someone else. "All the high school boys I know are losers. I'm waiting until I get to college to find someone worthy."

"I'm still a virgin," says another girl. "But I am *sooo* ready not to be. It's my boyfriend who says he's not ready."

"I can't believe we're actually talking about this," says another.

"I'm curious," Grace says, her voice a little louder. "Who here is still a virgin?" Slowly, hands pop up, one by one, until about half the girls have their hand in the air. "See," Grace says. "We're not some weird minority."

Erin did not raise her hand. She is looking down, into her lap, wringing her hands. Rosina tries to make eye contact, but Erin is trapped inside herself, trying to stay safe.

She didn't raise her hand.

Rosina feels the floor crumble and fall away, and her heart goes with it. Erin has a secret Rosina never even considered.

"Erin," Rosina whispers. "What's going on?" But Erin does not respond.

"Our church tells us to save ourselves until marriage," Trista says. "But you know what's weird? It's really just the girls who are considered damaged if they have sex, not the guys."

"We're supposed to be so scared of sex," Krista says. She looks around the room, takes a deep breath. "And I am. I'm terrified."

Erin's eyes are down and she is rocking slightly, her back softly padding the wall behind her. Rosina knows she would have left by

now if she wanted to leave. There must be a reason Erin is staying, something safe here despite all these scary words, something contagious in the bravery it takes to say them.

"That's how my old church was for sure," Grace says. "Girls wore purity rings and everything. But I'm not like that. My mom's definitely not like that. She's not telling me I'm going to hell if I have sex before marriage. It's just my choice, you know?"

"Amen," someone says.

"All the purity-ring girls are just letting other people make decision for their bodies," Trista says. "They're letting the church make decisions for their bodies. Their *dads* buy them the ring and give it to them like he's, like, her *boyfriend*. Or like Jesus is her boyfriend. It is so gross."

"There's some truth in that, for sure," Grace says. "But maybe try to look at it from their side for a minute. Most of them really think they're doing the right thing, and for some of the same reasons we're doing what we're doing. They believe choosing virginity is a way to respect themselves and their bodies. It makes them feel strong, just like we're trying to feel strong, because they're not giving in to peer pressure, not doing something just because everyone else is. And I don't know, I don't think there's one correct faith for everyone in the world, and I don't judge anyone in here for their choices." Grace looks around the room, sitting tall, meeting people's eyes. Her voice is strong as she says, "But, personally, yeah, I kind of agree with them. My old church was backward in a lot of ways, but some of the things stuck with me. Like how sex should be sacred, between two people who are committed and love each other. How our bodies

are temples. When I have sex, I want it to be with the person I want to spend my life with. I don't want to share that with anyone else."

Barely anyone notices Amber Sullivan get up and slip out of the room. Some girls are so good at being invisible.

"But why not?" Sam says. "No offense, but who decided sex was this precious, holy thing that has to be so deep and special all the time? Why can't it just be fun? I mean, if you take away all the religion and repressive sexist bullshit, sex is this super fun thing that bodies are, like, *made* to do. What would happen if we just ignored all the people who make it seem like something evil and did what feels good and didn't feel bad about it?"

"Yeah!" someone says.

"People would have sex all the time," Krista says with wide eyes. "With *everyone*. And then everyone would get pregnant and have gonorrhea!"

"Jesus Christ," Rosina says, hanging her head in her hands.

"Honey, that's why you get yourself on the pill or an IUD pronto," Sam says. "And use a condom *every single time*. No matter what."

Krista looks horrified at this prospect.

"I totally respect your point," Grace says carefully. "But for me personally, I think there's more involved in the decision than just my body. Like my head, and my heart and soul."

Sam lets out a big sigh. "I like thinking our bodies are less like temples and more like amusement parks," she says. "Less sacred, more fun."

"I don't think it has to be either/or," Melissa says.

"It can be both," someone says.

"So you're going to wait until marriage?" someone asks Grace.

"I don't know," Grace says. "Maybe not. Maybe I'll fall in love and it'll feel like forever and I'll want to do it then. And maybe that's not the guy I'll end up marrying. All I know is I'm not in a hurry. Life is complicated enough already."

"I wish I'd waited," says an unfamiliar voice—Allison Norman. "But I thought that's what I had to do if I wanted to be popular. I was so afraid of saying no." Her eyes fill with tears. "Fourteen is so young." Connie puts her arm around her friend.

"So what's the right age?" someone says.

"There's no one answer," Sam Robeson says. "We have to decide for ourselves. And adults can't handle that. They won't trust us to make decisions for our own bodies."

"But do you blame them?" Grace says. "They must be terrified. Look what can happen—we can get pregnant, we can get diseases, we can make decisions that screw up our lives forever. We can get hurt in all kinds of ways guys can't. It's not fair, but it's the truth. Parents' instincts are to protect us, and that's what they think they're doing."

"Maybe your parents," someone says.

Erin raises her head for a moment and looks at Grace. She blinks, as if surprised to find herself suddenly here, in this room with all these people, not alone inside the small space of her body.

"Hey, I have a question," says a voice in the back. All heads turn toward the pale girl with black and white hair: Serina Barlow, rehab girl. "Do any of you actually *like* sex?" The tone in her voice makes it clear that she thinks the answer should be no.

"Yes!" Sam says enthusiastically, immediately, without thinking.

A few nervous giggles. A few pink, blushing faces.

"Me too," says another girl. "Is that, like, okay?"

"Me three," says another. "But I feel like I'm supposed to hide it. Like I'm a slut if I like it too much."

"But you're also a prude if you don't," Margot says. "There's no way to win."

"I kind of like sex," says another girl, confusion written across her face. "I don't know. I mean—sorry if this is TMI—but I can get so horny sometimes when we're making out, and I totally want to do it. But then it happens so fast, and I'm just like, 'Is that it?'"

"Yes, totally!" says another girl.

"Oh my God, yaaaaas," says another.

"It's so frustrating," says the first girl.

"Well, do you say that?" says Sam.

"Say what?"

"Say 'Is that it?' To your guy?"

The girls laugh, then all suddenly stop when they realize she's serious.

"How do you expect him to know you want more if you don't tell him?" Sam says.

"But he's, like, *done*," the first girl says.

"So what? Make him wait his turn until *you're* done. Or, he can come, then you tell him what you want, and he can do a little mouth and hand action for you, then he can go again. Everybody wins! It's not like it takes these guys very long to recharge. They're ready to go again in like three minutes."

"Oh my God," someone giggles.

"I like sex, and I'm not ashamed of it," Sam says with a flip of her scarf. "No one should be."

"You're kind of my hero right now," Trista says.

"I'm still kind of freaked out by this whole conversation," says Krista.

"Wait," Allison Norman says. "How do you do that? How do you *tell* him?"

"You just tell him what you want," Sam says. "Or if you don't feel like talking, then you show him."

"You make it sound so easy," Allison says. "But I don't think I could do that. And even if I could, I don't even know what I'd say."

"So what do you do?" Sam asks Allison. "During sex?"

"I guess I just sort of lie there," Allison says, then emits a small, sad laugh. "To be honest, I was pretty relieved when we decided to go on a sex strike."

"Me too," another girl says.

A few heads nod around the circle. Sam looks from face to face, her own face twisting into recognition of something new, something horrible she had not before considered—that sex could be about something very different than pleasure, that it could be a burden, a job, something to be endured.

"Sometimes I offer to give a blow job when I really don't want to have sex with a guy," another girl says. "So he won't be mad at me."

"No," Sam whispers.

"You're lucky, Sam," Serina Barlow says. "I'm happy for you.

Really, I mean it. And I think most girls probably have a chance of figuring this sex thing out, how to make it something good, like it is for you." She pauses. "But some people are probably never going to be okay. You think Lucy Moynihan's ever going to have a great sex life? Not likely."

"You don't know that," Sam says.

Serina shakes her head. "What happens to you when you're young, it, like, brands you for the rest of your life. Nothing as bad as that ever happened to me, not really. But I lost my virginity when I was barely thirteen. The guy was seventeen, and I was high. I wasn't thinking clearly. It wasn't rape, but it wasn't good. And it feels like that programmed me, like that's the way sex is always going to feel, no matter who it's with. It's like I'm cursed."

"But it was rape," Margot says. "If he was seventeen, it counts as statutory rape. And if you were so high you didn't know what was going on, you couldn't consent."

"Whatever you want to call it," Serina says, "it's done. It happened. There's nothing I can do about it now."

"Maybe you can go to therapy or something?" Elise offers.

"Girl, I've *been* in therapy." Serina laughs bitterly. "But I'm damaged goods. Part of me is broken and it's never going to get put back together."

"But what if—"

"It's like my instincts have been rewired," Serina says. "Even if I like a guy, if I genuinely like him and think he's cute, as soon as he shows any interest in me, I fucking hate him. It's like a physical thing, like disgust, like I'm physically sick with how angry I am, like

I want to kill him. Just because he looked at me a certain way. Just because he might want me."

"Rosina," Melissa whispers. "I think something's wrong with Erin."

Rosina looks beside her and sees Erin's eyes are wide and darting. Her rocking is more frantic. Her breaths are shallow and fast.

Where are Erin's walls? Where are her defenses? Serina's words are cutting into her, slicing her open, and she can feel everything.

"Erin," Rosina whispers. "Are you okay?"

Erin shakes her head.

"And I think," Serina continues, "maybe if my parents had talked to me about sex, maybe if someone had told me it was something I got to *choose* to do, something I was supposed to want, maybe it would have turned out different, you know? Because I didn't even really know that 'no' was an option. I thought if a guy wanted me, that meant the decision had already been made."

"Breathe," Rosina whispers to Erin. "Count backward from one hundred."

"I'm sorry, guys." Serina sighs. "I didn't mean to bring everyone down. I've been in rehab for the past three months where I was in group therapy for like ten hours a day and all anyone does is talk about their feelings. All. The. Fucking. Time."

Rosina whispers, "One hundred, ninety-nine, ninety-eight, ninety-seven . . ."

"How can we all be so screwed up already?" Margot says with a strained voice, emotion betraying her usual flawless confidence.

"I just know that if I ever have a daughter, I'm going to teach

her that sex is supposed to make her feel good," Serina says. "It should be obvious, right? But it's so not."

"Breathe," Rosina whispers to Erin. "Eighty-eight, eighty-seven, eighty-six, eighty-five . . ."

"I think I know how you feel," says another girl. "At least a little bit. Even though I'm really lucky. My first time was actually really romantic, and my boyfriend is awesome and totally support-ive of what we're doing. I've never been abused or raped. I get along with both my parents. My mom's a strong woman. My dad isn't an asshole. But just being a girl, I get nervous sometimes, like I don't know what could happen."

"Look around the room," Rosina whispers to Erin. "Look at the corners. Feel the floor under you."

"We can't keep living like this," someone says.

"We're not," Grace says, and her clear voice reverberates around the room. "What we're doing here, right now. Just being here with each other and talking about what we're talking about. We're chang-ing *everything*."

"I need to go," Erin says.

"You're okay," Rosina says. "The meeting will be over soon. Can you wait till then?"

"No," Erin says, on the verge of tears. "I need to get out of here."

"Do you want me to come with you?"

"No," Erin says, standing up.

"Are you sure?"

"Rosina, leave me alone!" Erin shouts, and she stumbles over the mass of people sitting on the floor, out of the room, and out

the front door. The room is silent for a moment in her wake.

"Well," Lisa Sutter says, standing up. "I guess the meeting's over."

"Oh," Margot says as people start moving. "Unless anyone else has anything they'd like to say—"

"I need ice cream," someone says.

"I need beer," says someone else.

"I guess the meeting is adjourned?" says Margot, but no one is listening.

The house empties, so many things still unsaid.

The rain has stopped. The night brightens in increments as a couple of dozen cars turn on their headlights. Rosina finds Erin standing next to Grace's mom's car in the muddy makeshift parking lot on the side of the hill not visible from the road.

"I just want Grace to give me a ride home," Erin says before Rosina has a chance to open her mouth.

"She's on her way," Rosina says. "But can we talk about what happened?"

"There were too many people in too small a space," Erin says. "I made a mistake not sitting by the door. I feel much better now that I'm outside."

"Okay, but—"

"It's better than in there with all those people and their perfume and scented deodorants."

"You didn't raise your hand when Grace asked about being a virgin," Rosina says. "And you got really upset about what Serina was saying. And—" Rosina has to stop talking. There is something in

her throat, something not made out of words. Her eyes are stinging. She is fighting the urge to do something Erin would never forgive her for—throw her arms around her and hold on tight and never let go.

"I'm done talking," Erin says.

"But—"

"Rosina, I said no."

"Okay, but—"

"And I don't want to talk about this later. I don't want to talk about this at school. I don't want to talk about it ever."

"Okay." Rosina sighs.

"Why would Grace lock her car?" Erin says, pounding on the door with her fist.

"I don't know."

"I want to go home," Erin says.

"I know," Rosina says, even though she has little clue what that feels like.

US.

Grace tunes out during most of Mom's sermon about the renunciation of worldly goods. That doesn't seem too relevant to her life right now since she doesn't own much of anything.

She notices Jesse looking at her a couple of times during the service, but quickly looks away before having to admit to herself how nice his smile is. As soon as the service is over, she runs home without stopping at the bathroom even though she has to pee like crazy. That's how desperate she is to avoid talking to Jesse Camp.

As she sits on her bed, ready to lose herself in the current book she's reading, it suddenly hits her that, outside of what was required in classes or church activities, Grace has hardly ever talked to boys. Something in her softens. Maybe, deep down, she's not so much angry at Jesse as she is scared—he's a boy and she has no idea how to talk to him. What makes it worse is she suspects she probably wants to.

But what would that mean, if Grace let herself talk to Jesse? Would that mean she likes him? Would that make them friends? Would that mean she wants to be *more* than friends?

Grace cringes. She looks around her room, as if embarrassed that someone might have heard her thought, shamed that she even briefly considered something as ridiculous as that. She knows this line of thinking is off-limits to someone like her. She knows fat girls don't get boyfriends in high school, especially semipopular ones like Jesse. No one has to tell her that her body makes her irrelevant to that entire conversation.

Grace has never questioned her body's place in the world. She's always believed the laws of movies and TV shows: Chubby girls are sidekicks, not romantic leads; sometimes they get to be funny, but more often they're the butt of jokes; if they're powerful, they're evil—they're Ursula the sea witch from *The Little Mermaid*; they are not heroines and they are certainly not sexy. These are the rules. This is the script.

But life now looks so much different. Maybe those rules don't apply anymore. Maybe they never really did. Maybe real life is not like movies at all. Maybe in this one, in this life, fat girls get to be heroines.

How r u doin? the text from Rosina says.

Erin hates how Rosina doesn't spell out words properly.

Fine. She texts back, period and all.

Want to talk bout what happened at mtg? U ok?

Let it go. She texts back. It's so much easier to be rude in writing than in person.

I'm worried about u.

Busy now. See you tomorrow. Erin shoves her phone in

her pocket. She hears it ding with another text as she walks downstairs, but she doesn't check it. Spot rubs up against her leg like he's trying to tell her something. Is he on Rosina's side now?

Mom is at her station in the kitchen. "Oh, good, you're here," she says as soon as she sees Erin. "I want to talk to you."

Erin opens the fridge and searches inside for something that will fill her stomach for the rest of the afternoon. It's not looking good.

"I made you a snack," Mom says. "It's in the green bowl."

Erin pulls out the unappetizing green-specked gray mush. She sniffs it. It smells like nothing. "I want something crunchy," Erin says.

"Honey," Mom says. "I've been working on figuring out a night for our next family dinner, but Dad's schedule is pretty hectic with midterms and everything, and I know you must be terribly disappointed, but—"

"Why would I be disappointed?" Erin says, dipping a baby carrot into her mush. "Nobody likes family dinner."

Mom looks at her blankly. "Carrots aren't a part of this snack," she says.

"Why do you keep trying to force these family dinners to happen?" Erin says.

"Because we're a family, honey," Mom says, trying to smile, but the corner of her mouth is twitching.

"That's a stupid reason," Erin says. Why can't Mom just leave it alone? Why can't Rosina leave it alone? Why is everyone always trying to tell Erin what's good for her?

"Erin, I don't think you should be eating carrots right now."

"Trying to force people to be a family does not make them a family," Erin says. She can feel her chest heating up, her shoulders tensing. Spot paws at her leg. "Pretending we are isn't good for anybody. All we're doing is lying. You're lying. Dad's lying."

"Honey, don't yell," Mom says.

"You know he doesn't want to be with us."

"Honey, take a deep breath."

Spot steps on Erin's feet and leans into her shins, but his comfort can't stop her.

"You should have gotten a divorce the first time," Erin says, and she feels a brief flushing of relief, an emptying. And then panic. Then a locking, a sealing shut.

Mom's face is red. "Erin, I think you need to go upstairs and cool down." She sounds like she's choking.

Erin couldn't agree more. What she needs right now are her heavy blanket and her whale songs. What she needs is to be at the bottom of the ocean. Fish don't have families. The babies hatch out of their eggs and are on their own. Sure, most of them are eaten up by predators, but that's nature for you.

There's a pack of those Nowhere Girls, probably on their way to one of their secret meetings. For a brief moment this girl considers following them, finding out their meeting place and who's in charge, and turning them in. Maybe then her school could have some peace back. Maybe then it wouldn't feel like going to a war zone every day. Maybe the students wouldn't be so divided.

But it wouldn't work, she thinks. The girls would see her and know she wasn't one of them. They'd know she was a spy. Everyone knows she's the president of Prescott High School's Students for Conservative Values Club. They will judge and condemn her immediately. They're so prejudiced, the girl thinks. They're such hypocrites.

They keep talking about "rape culture," but it doesn't even exist. Rape is illegal in this country, isn't it? Women aren't all victims. Men aren't all evil predators waiting to get them drunk and take advantage of them. How does that attitude empower women? What about girls' own responsibility? All these Nowhere Girls are doing is jumping on the feminist bandwagon of blaming men for all their problems. They don't believe in equality, they believe in crushing and humiliating men.

They talk about women's solidarity, but it's only for certain kinds of women. There's no place in their feminism for girls like her—for conservatives, for Christians, for people who are pro-life, for women who value family. They call girls like her an idiot. They say all girls who disagree with them are wrong. As if you have to call yourself a feminist, as if conforming to everything they believe in, is the only way to be a strong woman. But this girl knows she's a strong woman. She doesn't need their dogma or their labels to validate that.

Sam keeps telling herself the sex strike is just about the guys at Prescott High. It doesn't include guys outside the school. So this is fine. She has nothing to feel guilty about. Plus she never wanted to do the sex strike in the first place.

But she can't help feeling a little bad. Even if she doesn't agree with everything in the Nowhere Girls' manifesto, does she have the responsibility to do it anyway, out of solidarity? Is there room for dissent? Is she a traitor for listening to her body?

As soon as her boyfriend puts his mouth on her nipple, she's suddenly confident the answer is no.

She knows it is not just his body she is responding to. There is something inside him that seeps into the air and wraps itself around the something inside her. It is not just their skin touching. They are something more than flesh. Sam suspects that maybe she is starting to love him.

She had always planned to go to UCLA or USC for college, but the University of Oregon has a theater department, doesn't it?

No, she thinks. She is not going to change her plans just because of some boy. But then he touches her in a brand-new way that gives her wings, and maybe, just maybe, she might consider it.

A girl searches on the Internet: *Where is the clitoris?*

GRACE.

The morning bell rings, but nobody's quieting down. The class is way too animated for a Monday morning.

"Oh my God," Allison Norman says, and it takes Grace a second to realize she's talking to her. She's still not used to having friends. "Did you hear what happened over the weekend?"

Besides Grace going to church on Sunday and avoiding Jesse Camp, reading two entire books, emptying the bucket under her leaky ceiling, and eating frozen pizza two meals in a row? "No," Grace says. "What happened?"

"The rumor is that Eric Jordan and Ennis Calhoun showed up at Bridget Lawson's party over the weekend and, like, half the people there wouldn't even talk to them," Allison says.

"Then Fiona and Rob had a huge fight because she was mad at him for still being friends with them," Connie Lancaster adds. "And then she totally dumped him. In front of *everyone*."

"Pipe down!" Coach Baxter yells, but the room quiets only slightly.

"And did you hear about Friday's football game?" a boy sitting

near them says, a member of the marching band. "The team was practically laughed off the field. The other school made signs making fun of them. One of them said something like, 'Prescott can't score *any* kind of touchdowns.'"

"Hey," Connie whispers, leaning forward. Grace and Allison follow, until they are almost touching foreheads. "Do you know when the next meeting is?"

A loud bang silences the room. A metal filing cabinet is dented from where Coach Baxter just kicked it.

"Do I have your attention now?" he growls.

"Yes, sir," say a couple of jocks in the front row. The rest of the class is silent.

"Everybody open your books," Coach Baxter says. "Silent reading for the rest of the class."

"He's really going for teacher of the year, isn't he?" Connie says, and Grace doesn't even try to mute her giggle.

"You!" Coach roars at Connie. "To the principal's office. Right now."

"Are you serious?" Connie says.

"Take your bag and get out of my face."

"This is crazy," Connie says as she stands up. She looks out at the class, as if they might have some answers for her, some explanation of what she did wrong. All Grace can think to do is say a little silent prayer, *God, please help her to not get in trouble.* And then Connie is gone, the door whispering shut behind her.

When Grace gets to lunch, her usual table is almost full. Rosina's practically glowing, but Erin's face is buried deep in a book. Sitting

with them are a handful of people Grace recognizes from the Nowhere Girls meetings, including Elise Powell and Melissa the cheerleader. A popular girl. At her lunch table.

"Hi, Grace," Melissa says as Grace sits down.

"Um, hi?" Somehow it feels different to be talking to her at school, outside the meetings. Here, Grace is just her normal, boring self. But at the meetings, she's becoming someone different. Someone who can talk to people without everything being a question. Someone with ideas. Someone with an identity.

"Melissa was just telling us how she quit the cheer squad," Rosina says.

"Yeah," she says. "Some of the girls are kind of mad at me right now."

"I'm sorry," Grace says.

"They'll get over it."

"Why'd you quit?"

Melissa crunches thoughtfully on a chip. "I think I finally got honest with myself and realized I didn't really like it. I thought I was supposed to like it, and I kept waiting to like it. But it wasn't anything like what I thought it would be. Most of the girls don't even know anything about football. Like they literally have no idea what is going on at the games. That's crazy to me."

"Football's crazy to me," Rosina says.

Melissa nudges Rosina with her shoulder. "You're crazy," she says with a grin. Are they *flirting*? Grace notices Erin bury her face even deeper into her book.

"Cheer squad isn't really about the games, at least not at this

school," Melissa continues. "It's about this role you have in the school, and it's something you have to do all the time, even when you don't feel like it. And, I don't know. I guess I realized that I don't ever really feel like it."

"Good for you," Rosina says. "Now you can hang out with us peasants."

"Does that mean you're going to sit at our table all the time now?" Erin mumbles from behind her book.

"Don't be rude," Rosina says.

"It's just a question."

Melissa laughs. "I haven't really made any plans beyond today."

"Well, you're welcome to sit here whenever you want," Rosina says, giving Erin the stink eye. "Regardless of what that one says."

"Thanks."

"Looks like the troll table has had some defections too," Elise says.

Grace turns around to see that the usually full table has a handful of guys at it now, and only two girls.

"Kayla Cunningham and Shannon Spears," Elise says, shaking her head. "They'll never come over to our side. They'd probably deflate if you separated them from their boyfriends."

Ennis is nowhere to be seen. Grace's eyes search the lunchroom and find Jesse Camp, sitting with a new group several tables away. Their eyes meet just as she realizes she was in fact looking for him.

"Dammit," she says, turning around as fast as possible.

"What?" Melissa says.

"Nothing."

"Your friend Jesse switched tables too, huh?" Rosina says.

"Jesse Camp?" Melissa says. "You guys are friends? He's a great guy."

"No," Grace says. "We're not friends."

Melissa shrugs. Rosina lifts her eyebrows like, *Yeah, right.*

Erin says, "Do you want to know the longest fish name?"

"No," says Rosina, at the same time Melissa says, "Sure."

"It's humuhumunukunukuapua'a," Erin says. "It's the Hawaiian state fish."

"That's interesting," says Melissa.

"Don't encourage her," says Rosina.

"Hey!" Jesse says, catching Grace in the hall just as she's about to step inside her fifth-period class.

Her stomach does something strange, like she's on an elevator that dropped down too fast. Is it indigestion? Did she eat something bad?

Grace's head is suddenly crowded with questions. How can someone's face be this friendly? How can his eyes be so warm? Is it normal to simultaneously feel both dread and a sense of relief around the same person?

"I tried to find you after church yesterday," Jesse says, "but I guess you had already left."

Grace doesn't tell him it's because she ran straight home afterward for the sole purpose of avoiding him. "I'm going to be late for class," she says.

"There's still like four minutes until the second bell rings."

Grace tries not to feel bad as Jesse's face goes from cheery to

perplexed to disappointed. "Oh," he says. "You're still mad at me."

"I don't really have time to talk right now," Grace lies.

"I'm not friends with them anymore," he says.

Grace says nothing. She's afraid if she looks him in the eye, she'll accidentally forgive him.

"I don't understand why you're so mad at me," he says. "You know I'm on your side, right?"

Grace has no response. The truth is, she doesn't know why she's so mad at him either. Or why she wants to be. But she's not about to tell him that.

Jesse sighs. "I was trying to be friends with everyone. It's one of my faults, I guess—wanting people to like me. But I should have let some of those guys go a long time ago. You wouldn't believe some of the racist shit that comes out of their mouths. I just pretend I don't hear it. I pretend it doesn't hurt. And some of the stuff they said about my brother when he was transitioning?" Jesse looks away. He swallows. "I didn't stick up for him. I didn't stick up for my own brother."

"Why are you telling me this?" Grace says, and she hates herself for sounding so mean.

"I thought I could remain a neutral party. I thought if I didn't say or do anything, then everyone would like me. But I realized that wasn't going to be possible. Now I know there's more important things than trying to be liked by everyone. So I picked a side. I picked the right side." He tilts his body so that his face is at the same level as hers, so she has no choice but to look at him. "I picked yours."

Grace doesn't understand what she's feeling. Part of her wants to forgive him, to be his friend, to get to know him. But then part of her is terrified by that entire train of thought and where it might lead, so terrified that staying mad at him for questionable reasons, and pushing him away even though all he's doing is trying to be nice to her, seem like completely logical things to do.

"I don't know if I believe people can just change like that," Grace says.

She can't read the look on his face. It's something like pain, something like confusion, but also something almost like pity.

"If you don't think people can change," he says slowly, as if he's trying to make sense of the words as he says them, "then what's the point of any of this?"

The bell rings. "I have to go," Grace says. But she doesn't really care about getting to class on time. All she knows is, she doesn't know the answer to his question.

The Real Men of Prescott

Guys, we have to stop putting bitches on a pedestal.
The more you get to know them, you realize there's no
such thing as sweet and innocent. They're all selfish,
lying manipulators who want stuff for free. They're the
original players, but they get mad about us having game?
They're just begging to be put back in their place.

I'm going to be totally honest with you—girls are good
for fucking and making sandwiches. That's it. This may
sound shocking, but in your hearts you know it's true.
The feminists have been ruling things for so long they've
made us ashamed of speaking the truth.

I, for one, will not be silenced any longer.

—AlphaGuy541

ERIN.

"Miss DeLillo," Principal Slatterly says, with a smile on her face that Erin knows does not mean what most smiles mean. "How are you doing?"

"Fine," Erin says. She knows Slatterly does not want to know how she's doing. All morning, Erin has watched everybody file in to talk to the principal, one by one—Mrs. Poole, the vice principal, guidance counselors, everyone who works in the office. Now it's Erin's turn. For the past thirty minutes, she's been doing her best to prepare, scribbling an if/then flowchart of possible scenarios and complications. She lost track of the number of times she's counted backward from one hundred. She's even had to do the alphabet backward, which she reserves for truly serious situations. And this is serious.

"Are you getting all the support you need this year?" Principal Slatterly says with a tone that Erin would normally associate with kindness, but right now she's not so sure. Slatterly is the enemy, right? And enemies are usually not known for being kind. "How is your IEP working out?"

"Fine," Erin says, but she is uncomfortable with the fact that Slatterly technically asked two different questions. "Yes," she says, to answer the first question. But now the two answers are out of order.

Z, Y, X, W, V—

Erin doesn't try to stop her rocking. It's the only thing keeping her from running out of the room.

"That's wonderful, dear."

This is where logic has led Erin: she did the actual stealing of e-mail addresses. While everyone else in the Nowhere Girls is guilty of minor things, few of them probably even illegal, Erin is the only one so far who has done an actual serious crime. Rosina and Grace have tried to convince her that it doesn't matter, that the school can't actually prove the e-mail addresses were stolen. Because all student e-mail addresses follow the same format, the Nowhere Girls technically could have figured out every single one and typed it in by hand—no stealing necessary.

While Erin will admit this is a reasonable explanation, it is also a lie. Lies get caught and liars get punished. The e-mails are school property and Erin stole them. Erin broke a rule, a *law*.

Erin reminds herself that lying isn't always bad. Even Lieutenant Commander Data lied in Season 4, Episode 14, of *Star Trek: The Next Generation* (episode title: "Clues"). In order to protect his ship and everybody on it, Data had no choice but to allow the Paxans to wipe the memories of the entire crew of the *Enterprise* and feed them with a false story of what happened, leaving Data with the responsibility of carrying the truth, alone. His lie saved

everyone he cared about. (That is, if he had the capacity to care.)

"I'd like to ask you a few questions, Erin," Principal Slatterly says. "Would that be all right with you?" She's speaking slowly, enunciating each word. Slatterly thinks Erin's an idiot. If she actually took the time to look at her IEP files, she'd know the opposite is true.

"Okay," Erin says, realizing she can use Slatterly's ignorance and sterotypes to her own benefit.

"You're friends with Rosina Suarez, aren't you?"

Erin shrugs. What would an idiot do? "Rosina lets me sit by her at lunch," Erin says as she sticks her finger in her ear.

"And she's your friend," Slatterly says. If this were *Law & Order*, Erin would say, *Objection, your honor. Leading the witness.*

Erin twirls her finger in her ear a little. "I don't know. We don't really talk to each other or anything. Do you have to talk to someone to be their friend? Maybe we're not friends. I wish we were friends." Erin stares into space and lets herself rock as much as she wants to.

Principal Slatterly sighs the sigh that means frustrated. Erin is not giving her the answers she wants. The anxiety in her chest is turning into something else, something not quite painful. She is a better liar than she thought. Maybe she will add acting as one of her interests. Maybe that is something she can talk to Sam Robeson about, since that is Sam's main interest, in addition to sex.

"It must be hard for someone like you to make friends," Slatterly says. "Maybe you'd be willing to do things you normally wouldn't do, in order to make a friend. You might be persuaded by someone like Miss Suarez to do something bad. Something only you could

do because of your work in the office, maybe? Because you have access to certain information other students don't have?" Slatterly stares at Erin for a moment, to make sure she understands. Erin must still look like an idiot because Slatterly keeps talking. "I know Miss Suarez can be very convincing, Erin. Very charming. There's no shame in being taken advantage of by someone like that. You're vulnerable, Erin. You have . . . limitations. It's not your fault."

Slatterly pauses to let that sink in. Erin knows she is supposed to feel safe now, supposed to trust the principal because she gave her permission to be vulnerable. She's good; Erin will give her that.

"We failed to protect you," Slatterly continues. "That's our job. That's on us. It's reprehensible for someone to take advantage of you like that, to make you do their dirty work. To make you steal for them. But you can make this right. You have the power to do that. This could all be over in a second if you turn the troublemakers in. You'd be a hero. You know that? Everyone in the school would love you for ending this crazy disruption, and everything could get back to normal. Wouldn't you like that? Wouldn't you just love to be a hero?"

"Like Superman?" Erin says. "Would I get to wear a cape? I would really like to wear a cape."

"Sure, honey," Slatterly says with a smile that seems close to genuine. She thinks she's getting somewhere. "You can wear a cape."

"A red cape?" Erin says. "A shiny one?" She never knew lying could be so fun. She never knew she'd be so good at it. How is it possible she is so in control right now? The old Erin would be in full meltdown mode by now. Since when is there even a new Erin? When did that happen?

"Whatever you want, dear. You're the hero."

Erin stares at Principal Slatterly, her jaw slack. She tilts her head to the side the way Spot does when he's confused, the way actors do when they're playing stereotypes of people like her. "What are we talking about again?"

Slatterly's breath comes out in a big huff. "What is it you do in the office exactly?" Her voice is sharp. She is done playing nice.

"I type the letters and numbers in boxes on the computer screen. I move the papers from one pile to another pile. I refill Mrs. Poole's coffee cup sometimes."

"Do you do anything with student e-mail addresses?" Erin can't tell if Slatterly's on the verge of screaming or the verge of crying.

"Are those the words with the *A* in the middle with the circle around it?" Erin says.

Slatterly's face is red and bulging. Erin suspects her anger is contributing to a serious medical condition. Hypertension. Heart disease. Ulcers. Erin wonders what Slatterly eats, if her diet consists of foods low in sodium and refined sugars and high in fiber and antioxidants, as it should. Mom could probably help her with an appropriate nutrition plan to reduce inflammation.

Erin's smile is not part of her act. She is not scared. She feels too much of something else, something close to triumphant. Playing dumb has made her feel pretty damn smart.

"What do you want to talk about now?" Erin says, looking Principal Slatterly in the eye for almost a whole second. "I have a special interest in fish. Would you like to talk about fish? I can tell

you all about hagfish. They are spineless and jawless and covered in slime."

"No, I would not like to talk about fish." Erin can almost hear the word "retard" at the end of Slatterly's sentence. She can feel her want to say it. "You can go now, Erin."

So Erin goes back to her desk in the back of the office, where she could do so much damage if she wanted to.

"We're partners!" Otis Goldberg says as he pushes his desk toward Erin's in AP American History.

"I hate group projects," she tells him.

Today the hair tie around his boy-bun is purple. The classroom is noisy with moving desks, which would normally make Erin agitated, but she still hasn't come down from the high of her meeting with Principal Slatterly. She is less annoyed with Otis than usual.

"This is going to be great," he says. "What luck, huh? The two smartest kids in the class get to be partners."

"I don't believe in luck."

He scoots his desk closer. His desk is practically on top of Erin's now.

"Do you believe in fate? Like, destiny?" he says.

Erin scoots her desk three inches away from his.

"So what have the Nowhere Girls been up to lately? Anything cool planned, like some kind of subversive action? Can I come?"

"You talk too much," Erin says.

"All right, class," Mr. Trilling says. "Let's stay focused on the task at hand."

Otis pushes his desk against Erin's again. He doesn't even seem aware that he's doing it. It's like he has some deep, subconscious need to always be touching someone. He is the exact opposite of Erin.

"Do you have any ideas for our project?" he says. Erin shrugs. "Because I was thinking we could do something about Manifest Destiny and westward expansion, how if you analyze the ideology in psychological terms, it's like certifiable narcissism, probably border-line personality disorder, maybe even sociopathic."

"I don't think that's the kind of project Mr. Trilling wants us to do," Erin says.

Despite today's events, Erin feels surprisingly unagitated. Lying to Principal Slatterly wasn't nearly as hard as she thought it should be. The noisy classroom. The group project. And now this, whatever it is. This talking to Otis Goldberg that is not completely unpleasant. She does not have to look him in the eye to notice the pleasing symmetry of his face. And even though he talks far more than is necessary, his voice is not as grating as most people's.

Today is a strange day. Erin feels strange. But maybe strange is not necessarily the same as bad.

Erin feels so many things, but she doesn't know how to classify them. When she asks herself what Data would do, all she hears is silence.

US.

A yellow construction-paper poster reads WE BELIEVE LUCY MOYNIHAN! Someone has written SLUT across it in thick red marker.

Another sign reads FIGHT RAPE CULTURE AT PHS! Someone has added WHORE to that one.

"That is so fucked up," a guy says next to Elise Powell as he stares at one of the defaced posters. Benjamin Chu. He's in Elise's calculus class, perpetually late, but possessing a smile that consistently convinces the teacher to not punish him. Elise waits for him to arrive every day and fills with relief when he falls panting into his seat across the aisle from her.

"What's fucked up?" Elise says, ready to either get defensive or fall madly in love.

"What some assholes wrote on these signs," he says. "What is wrong with people?"

"You like the signs?" Elise says. She has pitched tied games in the fourteenth inning. She has pitched the state semifinals. She has

pitched games that were regionally televised. But she has never been so scared as right now.

"Hell, yeah," Benjamin says, smiling his detention-evading smile. "Don't you?"

"Yeah," Elise says. "I do."

Elise feels her face burn and she knows it's red, she knows her freckles are popping out like they always do when she's embarrassed. But this is a different kind of embarrassed, a different kind of being seen, and it is not entirely horrible. And the not-horribleness of it turns her desire into a brief, giddy moment of courage.

"Hey, um, Ben?" Elise says. "Do you maybe want to hang out sometime? With me?"

He says yes way too quickly. Elise waits a moment to give him time to realize he made a mistake. But instead he smiles, his face almost as red as hers.

The bell rings in Grace's homeroom. Connie Lancaster rushes in, breathless. "Holy shit!" she says, falling into her seat. "You guys totally just missed a major fight."

"What happened?" Allison says.

"I don't know all the details," Connie says. "I got there just as the security guards were breaking it up. But Elise was there and said she saw the whole thing. She said Corwin Jackson was talking to this girl in the hall and she kept trying to walk away but he wouldn't let her, then these two freshmen guys totally stuck up for her and started telling him to stop bothering her, and Corwin got up in their faces and shoved one of them, and then the girl hit Corwin with her

purse, and then shit got crazy and they all ganged up on Corwin, and that's when I heard everyone in the hall yelling and ran over to see what was happening, but by then everything was pretty much over, but Corwin had his hand over his eye and his lip was bleeding and he was totally *crying*." Connie fans herself with her hand. "It's like a war zone out there."

"I wish things didn't have to get violent," Grace says.

"They already were violent," Allison says.

Coach Baxter enters, shoulders hunched, face clouded with anger. He doesn't bother trying to quiet the class down. The football team everyone had such high hopes for has lost every one of its games so far this season. They are the laughingstock of the greater Eugene metropolitan area and the entire Willamette Valley.

"Poor Coach," Connie says in a fake whisper, which elicits more than a few giggles. Yes, Coach Baxter is a sexist jerk with a whole team of guys who look up to him that he's doing nothing to lead in the right direction, but Grace can't help but feel a little sorry for him. She can't help but feel a little sorry for whoever this Corwin guy is, even if he is an asshole, even if he started it. It's hard for her to see anyone suffer, even if maybe they deserve it a little. She wonders if all growth has to hurt. She wonders if change always requires some kind of pain from someone.

She wonders about Jesse, if what he said about his own change is true. She wonders why she's so afraid of believing him.

"Attention, Prescott High School," booms Principal Slatterly's voice from the ceiling speakers. No "Good morning," no "Hello." She sounds as grumpy as Coach Baxter looks.

"I want to make something very clear," Slatterly says, her voice serious and gruff. "I am implementing a zero-tolerance policy for the kind of disruptive activity that has been going on recently. This is an institution of learning, and I will not tolerate any behavior that makes Prescott High School an unsafe environment for learning. This escalating hostility between students is unacceptable. Anyone caught posting things on school property without administrative approval will be immediately suspended. Computer techs have been hired to investigate the theft and illegal use of school e-mail addresses. We will discover who is behind all the recent upheaval, and they will be brought to justice."

"Yeah, right," a girl says in front of Grace.

"Justice, my ass," says the marching-band guy.

"That is all," Slatterly says. "Oh, and the chess club is meeting in Room 302 this afternoon, not Room 203. Go Spartans."

"Well, that was depressing," a guy says a few seats away, one of Sam Robeson's friends from drama club.

"Shut up, faggot!" says one of the football players.

"You shut up!" the guy says right back.

"Don't call him that!" usually quiet Allison yells at the football player.

"Everyone shut up!" yells Coach Baxter. "You're all giving me a headache." He sits down at his desk. "Independent reading time," he says. "Get out your books."

"Do you think it's for real?" Melissa Sanderson says. "Do you think Slatterly really has people checking the Nowhere Girls' e-mails?"

"She's totally bluffing," Rosina says. "Even if she could access the e-mails, we don't have anything to worry about. I'm sure whoever started this thing was smart enough to keep any personal info off their e-mail account."

"Yeah," Elise Powell says. "Plus the e-mails stopped days ago. And I'm pretty sure they always went out to everyone, so no one was singled out or anything. They can't punish all the girls of the school for just receiving e-mails."

"I don't know," says Krista, whose hair is now purple instead of blue, while Trista has changed hers to orange. It is getting easier to tell them apart. "Can't they trace the e-mails back to the sender, even if it's an anonymous account? Like triangulate where the message was coming from, and send like a SWAT team there or something? I think I saw that on a show one time."

"That's cell phones," says Trista.

"Shhhh," Elise says. "Security guard, one o'clock."

All heads turn toward the large man in blue who has inched closer to their table over the course of the conversation. Rosina flashes him a big smile and waves. He takes one step away, pretending to not have seen her.

"We're being watched," Erin says severely. Rosina tries to stifle a laugh, but that just makes the whole table crack up. Even Erin smiles. The security guard looks away.

"I saw Sam in the hall this morning," Elise says. "She has second period with Eric. She said he was barely conscious and totally reeked of booze."

"I guess that's one way to deal with it," Rosina says.

"Has anyone read *The Real Men of Prescott* blog lately?" Melissa says.

"Why would we?" Rosina groans.

"We have to see what we're up against," Melissa says.

"Whoever's behind it sure is pissed at us," says orange-haired Trista.

"You know it's Spencer Klimpt, right?" Melissa says.

"No!" Trista says. "Really?"

"Yeah," Melissa says. "I thought everyone knew that."

"No one knows for sure," Elise says. "It's not like he's admitted it or anything."

"But it's pretty obvious," Melissa says.

"But didn't he graduate last year?" Krista says. "Why would he care what's happening here?"

"Because he hasn't gone anywhere," Melissa says. "He's still working at the Quick Stop, still hanging out with his old friends. High school is the best life he's ever going to have."

"What a loser," Rosina says.

"A loser with four thousand one hundred seventy-two followers," Erin says, looking at her phone.

"Jesus," Rosina says.

"The stuff he says really resonates with some guys," Melissa says. "It's scary."

"The same kind of guys who think immigrants are ruining the country and stealing their jobs," Rosina says. "They have to blame someone for their lives sucking. So why not pick someone whose life sucks more than yours?"

"Exactly," Melissa says. "These guys can't get laid, so they hate women. Couldn't possibly be something wrong with *them*."

"Wait," Trista says. "That means those girls on the list he posted, the girls he slept with? Some of them must go to this school still. They're, like, people we *know*."

"Yeah, but no one's going to come out and admit it," Rosina says. "Can you imagine? 'Oh, yeah, number whatever is me. I'm the ugly one who was bad in bed.' A couple of them are pretty obvious though."

"Which ones?" Krista says, wide-eyed.

"It's none of our business," Melissa says with an uncharacteristic sharpness in her voice. "Come on, you guys. Those girls don't deserve that."

The table is silent.

"Do you think one of the girls on there is Lucy?" Trista says softly.

The bell rings but the girls don't move. They stay seated, silent, while the lunchroom erupts into its usual chaos. Slowly, they begin to pack up. They grab their things and head to class, weighted down by the unfinished conversation.

Melissa and Rosina both stay behind, Melissa looking at her phone, Rosina poking around in her bag. "Um, bye?" Melissa says. Rosina thinks she hears something in her voice, a hint of not wanting to leave, too. But she doesn't know if she can trust her ears, if hope and want are making her hallucinate.

"Bye," Rosina says, and then the inches between them turn into feet, into yards, and magnets pull at Rosina's heart and pound it against her rib cage as it tries to follow Melissa out of the lunchroom.

A girl sits in her classroom, her body pulsing with a formless, pressured yearning. She looks around at the boys, some of them hot, some of them mildly disgusting, and she thinks to herself, *I'd probably hook up with any of these guys if they asked me.*

She wonders if this makes her pathetic, if the desire to be wanted is some sign of weakness.

She wants to make someone hungry. She wants to be devoured.

Rosina, Grace, and Erin are standing next to the third-floor girls' bathrooms, which have been out of order since the beginning of the year. It is a place nobody goes, which makes it an excellent location for a clandestine meeting.

"Let's make this fast," Erin says. "We only have three minutes and twenty-eight seconds to get to our next class."

"Okay." Grace scans the hall and sees no one within earshot. "The group never decided on a time for our next meeting."

"Large groups are not capable of making decisions," Erin says. "I liked it better when we made all the decisions."

"But that's not how democracy works," Grace says.

"But aren't we the leaders?" Erin says. "I thought we were the leaders."

"We're not the leaders," Grace says. "We just started it."

"Doesn't that make us the leaders?"

"It makes us the founders, that's all," Rosina says. "I think we should have a meeting on Saturday night. We can make it like a party. I know the perfect spot."

"But the meetings aren't supposed to be parties," Erin says. "We're supposed to talk about serious things."

"I think the last meeting was serious enough to last at least a couple of weeks," Rosina says.

"Maybe we don't have to be serious all the time," Grace says. "Isn't being happy part of empowering ourselves?"

"But parties don't make me happy," Erin says.

"Erin, honey," Rosina says, holding Erin's shoulders for just a moment before Erin wiggles away. "This is a good time to practice being flexible and compromising."

Erin sighs an epic sigh so Rosina will understand how hard this is for her. No matter how many times Erin explains it, Rosina will never truly understand the sensory overload of the crowd and the unfamiliar surroundings, the exhaustion of processing how to act in front of so many people who already think she's weird. But maybe the last meeting wasn't so bad, at least until her meltdown. Maybe it's actually kind of nice to have something to do on a Saturday night besides read and take a bath and watch *TNG*. "Fine," she says. "I'll compromise. But I won't like it."

But they are not the only people in this forgotten corner of the hallway.

Grace notices Amber Sullivan hovering nearby, within hearing range. How long has she been there? What has she heard?

Grace smiles, and Amber smiles too. There is something like trust in her eyes, something like light. Grace decides they have nothing to worry about. Grace has faith that their secret is safe.

GRACE.

"Hey, Grace," someone yells. "Wait up."

Grace's instinct is to freeze. Most of her semirecent experiences with people yelling her name in a school hallway resulted in either tripping or name-calling, or the occasional cruel-eyed promise to pray for Grace's soul that sounded a whole lot more like a threat than Christian compassion. But that was a different school, a different school year, a different state, and what Grace is starting to think of as an entirely different Grace.

She turns around and finds none other than Margot Dillard, two-term Prescott High School student body president, striding in her direction. Grace didn't know Margot even knew her name.

"How are you?" Margot says. "Got any exciting plans after school?"

"Not really," Grace lies. For some reason, she has decided to keep her real plan a secret. It's embarrassing how excited she is, and how terrified. It's confusing how the combination of these feelings is making her feel something strangely similar to happy.

"I have a favor to ask you," Margot says.

"Okay," Grace says. People ask favors of their friends. That means Margot considers Grace her friend.

Margot leans in closer. She smells like watermelon candy. "I can't make it to the meeting tomorrow night," she whispers. "The debate team is traveling to Salem for a really important meet, and I can't get out of it. I'm so bummed. Can you lead the meeting for me?"

Grace's first instinct is this must be a joke. A cruel trick. Like that movie *Carrie*. A bucket of blood will be waiting for her at the meeting, ready to dump on her head for thinking she could possibly lead anything.

"Grace?" Margot says. "Can you do it?"

The only thing Grace can think to say is "Why me?"

Margot smiles. "Your comments are always thoughtful and smart. You seem really steady and calm, and not swayed by people's disagreements and emotions and everything."

"But I'm too quiet," Grace says.

"You don't have to be loud to be a leader," Margot says. "People respect you. That's what's important."

Grace is light-headed. Her body, which usually feels so heavy and cumbersome, is suddenly made out of feathers.

There are so many things running through her mind, so many ways to respond. In her brain, new synapses are firing, working frantically to make connections where none had been before. They are trying to rewire her, trying to make sense of the disparity of how others see her versus how she's always seen herself. They are trying

to let Margot's words in, trying to make them stick, trying to make Grace believe them.

A tiny spark ignites inside her, a soft voice finds its way through her depths, through the previously empty expanses that are slowly filling, through the place in her throat where so many thousands, maybe millions, of words have gotten stuck over time. The spark finds Grace's tongue, her teeth, her lips, finds Grace's voice, and opens her mouth: "Yes," Grace says. "Yes, I'll do it."

"Great!" Margot says, and hugs her quickly before bouncing away. "You're going to do great!" she calls when she's halfway down the hall. Grace knows Margot is rarely wrong about anything.

But still, the question remains: Why her? Why Grace? Of all people? Margot could have asked Melissa or Elise, born leaders. Even Rosina would have been a stronger, though possibly volatile, choice. Was it because Margot was in a hurry and Grace was simply the first person she saw? Or was it something deeper, one of God's mysterious workings, one of His miracles? Was Margot right? Is Grace a leader? Is there something of her mother in her after all?

Is there any use in asking these questions? If it's God's will, it's God's will, plain and simple. If it's not, Grace will certainly find out when the meeting turns out to be a disaster and she lets everyone down.

Grace is shocked to realize this thought does not fill her with the usual terror. Somehow all the potential catastrophes of failure and humiliation she can imagine do not actually feel like the end of the world. Perhaps she will be embarrassed in front of a few dozen girls from her school. Maybe they will never want her to lead the

meeting again. And so what? When she asks herself what's the worst that could happen, the answers are not that scary. Because even if she fails, it is a small failure. Even if she's embarrassed, it will not last forever. The girls will still be her friends. The Nowhere Girls will still meet, still plan, still make each other stronger. No matter what happens, she will still be part of them.

Grace stands alone in the empty hallway. It seems like just seconds ago that she was surrounded by hordes of students slamming lockers and running to catch their buses. She does not know how long she's been standing here, feeling the ripples of Margot's wake. Echoes of noise and movement fill the space around her, carry her down the stairs and out the door as she remembers what she was on her way to do before Margot intercepted her.

Grace goes the long way home. It is not her usual route through the carefully manicured front yards and white fences of the neighborhood around the school, into the more modest houses and smaller lots of her own neighborhood. This route takes her onto the busy street lined with chain stores and fast-food restaurants that leads to the highway. She inhales five blocks' worth of exhaust fumes until she reaches her destination just before the street empties into the on-ramp.

Grace is nervous as she approaches the Quick Stop. It's weird to have spent so much time thinking and talking about someone she's never met. The distance has kept Spencer Klimpt somewhat hypothetical until now. She needs a face to attach to the stories. She needs to see him in the flesh, needs to remind herself that *The Real Men of Prescott* blog is more than words. It is the weapon of a man

who hurts girls, of a man who teaches other men how to hurt girls. She needs to make him real. On her own. Alone.

When she finally sees him for the first time, the experience is anticlimactic. She expected a sadistic rapist to look a little more like a cartoon version of a bad guy than what she finds when she enters the Quick Stop. She imagined his face in a mug shot, his eyes dead and cruel, the lighting around him dramatic and sinister instead of these too-bright fluorescents. He just looks like a guy, the boy next door, someone who could even be handsome if his eyes weren't so sunken, if his skin wasn't so greasy, if he were wearing something besides a gas station uniform and a scowl on his face. Nothing about him says "rapist." Nothing about him is particularly intimidating. There's no clue to stay away from him besides his crappy job and unfortunate haircut. There's nothing about him that screams evil. Someone like him could be anyone.

But still, Grace's skin prickles with the knowledge of him. He is not just some guy behind a counter writing notes on a clipboard, taking inventory of the cigarettes. Grace knows what he did. She's reminded of it every second she spends in her bedroom, Lucy's pain scratched into the walls of a place she is supposed to feel safe.

"Do you need something?" Spencer says, and Grace jumps. She feels his eyes bore into her, and it makes her skin crawl. Just his gaze is a violation.

"No," she mumbles. "I mean, yeah." She starts to panic. She reaches for something, anything, to make her look like a normal shopper, not some weird girl who came just to stare. She grabs a pack of gum, a candy bar. She walks up to the counter, puts the

items in front of him. His hands are dirty, scabbed at the knuckles, his chewed-up nails black with grime. Grace imagines those hands touching Lucy's body, her friends' bodies, her own. So unclean. So marked by violence.

He says something. She cannot look at him. She did not hear it.

"Hello?" he says again. "That'll be two sixty-five."

Grace fumbles for her wallet, pulls out a five, hands it over. His fingers brush hers, and a surge of rage pulses through her. How can he be in the world so easy like this, selling girls candy, touching their hands?

Grace runs out as soon as he hands over her change. She tries to do what Erin does when she feels anxious. She counts backward as she walks away from the store, focuses on the feeling of her feet hitting the ground, the smell of gasoline in the air, the wet breeze of a coming rainstorm. Then without thinking, before she turns the corner toward her house, she turns around for one last look at Spencer Klimpt.

She is still close enough to see that he is typing something onto the smart phone in his hand, an amused smile on his face. Then he looks up, his face turned in her direction, and for just a moment their eyes meet. A shiver runs down Grace's spine; she feels caught, trapped, like a deer in headlights who sees danger coming but is incapable of moving. He could walk out of the store right now and grab her. But he just laughs and looks back at his phone, releasing her. Grace speed walks the rest of the way home.

Grace is sweaty and out of breath when she gets home. She knows Mom and Dad are at a meeting at church all afternoon, so

she opens the candy bar and sits down in front of the computer in Mom's office. There's a picture of Grace on the desk from early last year. In the picture, Grace still has braces and is even chubbier than she is now. Her outfit is atrocious—pink leggings, a yellow T-shirt with a kitten on it, a frizzy ponytail on the top of her head. She looks like a little girl, so naïve, so ignorant. That girl looks happy. She hasn't yet lost her friends and moved across the country. She hasn't lost her mother to more important things. That girl doesn't even know what rape is.

Grace takes a bite of her candy bar, but it doesn't taste as good as she wants it to. She turns on Mom's computer, types a web address in the browser window. *The Real Men of Prescott* blog opens.

A new entry was posted five minutes ago.

The Real Men of Prescott

Homely and kinda fat girl just walked into my work,
was totally checking me out. Obvious she wanted me.
If I wasn't so hungover, I would have played that. She
probably wouldn't have been too bad with the lights out.
Nice lips, lots of nice pieces to hold on to. A lot of
the time, plain girls can be way better fucks than 9s and
10s because they know they have to work harder. Sometimes
the hottest girls don't even try. They think they just
have to lie there.

This one would have been an easy score. Am now regretting
not picking her up. Unless she's one of those ugly girls
with a feminist mommy who raised her to have more self-
esteem than she deserves. But if she makes you work for
it and then pulls some shit later saying she didn't want
it, she's the kind of girl everyone will know is lying
through her fat face.

—AlphaGuy541

US.

"You guys are crazy," Rosina says. "This is a great place to have a meeting."

"It's not structurally stable," Erin says. "And it's a fire hazard. It is highly likely that it's going to catch fire and we're all going to be burned alive."

"Maybe it wasn't a great idea to tell people to bring candles," Grace says.

"But we need light, right?" Rosina says. "And who knows when this place last had electricity?"

"Flashlights," Erin says. "Battery-operated lanterns. We should have specified no open flames."

The old Dixon Mansion has been sitting uninhabited on the edge of town for as long as anyone can remember. The three girls stand on the porch of the crumbling three-story building as it towers in front of them, the ornate columns framing the entrance tilting at an unnerving angle. Pale light flickers from inside, through cracked and scum-coated windows. The wind is

hard tonight. A strong gust might tip the whole place over.

"You ready?" Rosina says to Grace.

"No," Grace says.

"You're going to be great," Rosina says. "Right, Erin?"

"Do you want my honest answer?" Erin says. "Or do you want me to be supportive?"

"What do you think?" Rosina says.

"Grace, you're going to do great," Erin says flatly.

Grace sighs. "I can't screw it up too much, right? Because the meetings usually pretty much lead themselves?"

"Or they end up like the first meeting at the library," Erin says.

"Erin," Rosina says softly.

Erin blinks. "I'm sorry, Grace," she says, looking away. "I want to encourage you because you are my friend and I care about you."

"That was really sweet," Rosina says.

Erin shrugs. "Even if Grace totally bombs, it's okay. Because we'll still like her and so will everyone else."

Grace looks at Erin with the beginning of tears in her eyes. "Erin, that is the nicest thing you've ever said to me."

"Yeah, well," Erin says. "Don't get used to it."

"I kind of want to hug you right now," Rosina says.

"Don't you dare."

"I love you guys," Grace says with a quiver in her voice.

"Ugh," Erin says. "You are both unbearable." And she pulls open the creaking front door.

The inside of the mansion looks like the set of a horror movie, complete with a rotted, half-collapsed grand staircase leading to a

second-floor landing, the rusted metal carcass of a car-size chandelier in the middle of the floor, the crystal ornaments stolen long ago. The girls follow light and voices into the adjoining ballroom, where a few dozen girls cast ghostlike shadows.

"This place is so creepy!" someone squeals.

"Whoever had the idea to meet here is crazy," says someone else as she guzzles a can of beer.

"This house is definitely haunted," says another.

"See, Grace," Erin says. "You're not the only one who's scared."

"I think it's great," says a possibly tipsy Samantha Robeson, leaning against a stone fireplace that is at least a foot taller than she is and could fit at least five of her inside it. "It's a perfect metaphor, if you think about it. The house symbolizes our fears, and we're joining here to face them."

Standing next to Sam is a laughing Melissa Sanderson. "Oh." Melissa stops laughing. "You were serious."

"Melissa!" Rosina calls, then hurries over to greet her.

"Was Rosina skipping?" says Grace.

Erin rolls her eyes in answer.

The huge ballroom is drafty, and the candlelight flickers, casting weird moving shadows over the stained walls and ceiling. Peeling wallpaper gives the impression that the house is disintegrating while they are in it. The sound of pounding wind is somehow amplified, made hostile. The room is dusty and dry, but there is a sense of being underwater, of being fish in a human-size aquarium.

Something creaks. Girls scream. Melissa grabs Rosina's arm and pulls her into her. Then she looks up, giggles, blushes, and lets go.

But she is still close. Their hips are touching. They can feel each other's warmth through their jeans.

Music is playing out of someone's phone. Girls are passing bottles around. Erin has taken it upon herself to go around the room asking everyone if they have a designated driver. Preppy girls are talking to nerds, jocks are talking to artsy girls, loners are talking to popular girls. Sam Robeson spins in place, whipping her red feather boa around her head like a gleeful tornado. Girls are dancing, freed of their usual inhibitions, liberated from the need to be sexy for an audience of boys.

"Come on," Melissa says, taking Rosina's hand and pulling her into the small circle where people are dancing.

"I don't dance," Rosina says.

"Everybody dances," Melissa says. "You don't fool me. I know you're not as cool as you act." She leans in, her soft hair brushing against Rosina's cheek. "Hey," she says, her lips, her breath, warm in Rosina's ear. "Do you want to hang out sometime?"

"Are you drunk?" are the words that come out of Rosina's mouth.

Melissa pulls away, hardens slightly. "No," she says. "I'm not drunk."

"I'm sorry," Rosina says. "I don't know why I said that."

A heavy silence passes between the girls. "I'm sorry," Rosina says again. "I'm just not used to girls like you talking to me."

"Girls like me?" The corners of Melissa's eyes squint in a smile. "What exactly is a girl like me?"

"I don't know," Rosina says, looking at her feet. "Popular. Seemingly well adjusted. Not weird." Melissa laughs. Rosina looks up,

into Melissa's light-blue eyes sparkling with candlelight. "Kind of beautiful."

"You're beautiful too," Melissa says. "Really beautiful."

"Shouldn't we start the meeting?" Erin says sharply, appearing out of nowhere, pulling Rosina away from Melissa. "It's already seventeen minutes past the meeting start time."

"Hi, Erin," Melissa says warmly. Rosina is still in shock, unable to form words in her mouth that was just so close to Melissa's skin.

"This dancing," Erin says sternly, "or whatever it is you two are doing, is not a constructive use of our time. Grace!" she shouts, even though Grace is only a few feet away. "Shouldn't you start the meeting?"

"In a few minutes," Grace says. "People are having fun."

"But this is not supposed to be about fun," Erin says, with a frantic edge in her voice. "We should be sitting in a circle and taking turns talking. We need to be organized. We need to be planning our subversive action. We need—"

Melissa circles Erin in her arms and gives her a big squeeze, then lets go before Erin has a chance to freak out. She waves her arm toward the rickety dance floor, at all the girls dancing like no one's watching. "This *is* subversive action."

"You two are useless," Erin says, then stomps away.

The music abruptly stops. Erin holds the offending phone in her hand.

"Hey, that's mine," says Connie Lancaster.

"It's time to start the meeting," Erin says.

"At least give me my phone back," Connie says.

"You have to promise not to play any music," Erin says. "The dance party is over."

"Okay, y'all," Grace says in an almost-loud voice. "Um, let's get in a circle, everyone. I'm Grace. Margot asked me to lead the meeting while she's gone."

People slowly find seats on the dusty wood floor. Erin sits by Grace, Rosina sits by Erin, and Melissa sits by Rosina. Melissa does not notice Erin's eyes shooting daggers in her direction.

"I wonder where Amber is," Grace says to no one in particular.

Across the circle, Lisa Sutter says, "Who cares?"

"That's not nice," says one of her cheerleader friends.

"She's not nice," says Lisa.

"Hey, y'all?" Grace says. She clears her throat. "Can we try to focus on what can bring us together rather than what divides us? We're not going to get anywhere if we keep fighting each other."

"Or sleeping with each other's boyfriends," Lisa mutters under her breath.

New beers are opened as empty cans are crushed and thrown into dark corners of the room. How many of these six-packs were purchased from Spencer Klimpt at the Quick Stop? How many girls recognize the irony of this?

"Where's Elise?" Rosina says.

"She has a date," says one of her softball friends.

"She's skipping the meeting for a *date*?" Connie Lancaster says. "Doesn't that go against everything she believes in?"

"Dude, just be happy for her," Rosina says. "If anyone deserves a little romance, it's Elise."

Melissa leans against Rosina with her whole body, and Rosina forgets how to breathe.

Everyone is seated. The room is dark around them, faces illuminated by the unstable light of candles and flashlights as the girls sit in a circle facing each other. There are almost forty girls here. They're practically piled on top of each other.

"Oooh, are we going to have a séance?" someone says.

"Let's play Truth or Dare!" says someone else.

"I need to say something," Sam announces before Grace even has a chance to decide what she is going to say next. "I think we need to call off the sex strike," she says.

"You're just horny," her friend says.

"I'm not joking," Sam says. "I never wanted to do the strike. From the beginning, I thought it was a bad idea."

"Oh, poor you," a girl says, obviously drunk. "So you're not getting laid? Big deal. At least you *can* get laid. Some of us here will probably die virgins." Her friend is trying to shush her, but it's not working. "I've never even kissed anyone. How pathetic, huh? Some of us might never get boyfriends."

"Or girlfriends," mutters someone else.

"But you all have hands," Rosina says. "I hope you know how to use them." Melissa giggles next to her.

"It's not just about that," Sam says. "I think the strike sends the wrong message. We're protesting rape, right? But rape isn't about sex. It's about power and violence."

"We're protesting a lot of things besides rape," Melissa says. "And like you said, rape is about power. It's about their physical power over

us, about them using their bodies to overpower ours. So we're asserting our power, right? By not letting them have our bodies?"

"But we're not just withholding sex from guys," Sam says. "We're withholding it from ourselves. It's like going on a hunger strike because they're pelting us with tomatoes. It doesn't make sense. We're still suffering because of them. They're still controlling our bodies."

"Personally, I don't feel like it's that much of a sacrifice," Connie says. "But I don't have a boyfriend, so I guess I don't have a whole lot to give up."

"Sam," Grace says, sitting up a little straighter as she speaks. "What do you propose we do?"

"I don't know. I don't know how to fix it. All I know is it doesn't feel right to me."

"But we can't just take it back," Rosina says. "That would be like surrender. That would be like them winning."

"No, it wouldn't," Sam says. "It'd be us making a decision for ourselves. They have nothing to do with it. I mean, look at what we've done so far. Look at how things have changed. It had nothing to do with the sex strike. It was about us supporting each other. It was about standing up for ourselves and not taking any more shit. Sex is ours, too, you know? Empowerment isn't just about saying no. Isn't our pleasure empowering too?"

"I don't think it's time yet," Melissa says.

"I agree with everything you said, Sam," Grace says. "I think most of us probably do. But, honestly, I don't know if people will listen to us otherwise." She sighs and looks around the room

apologetically. "It seems like sex is still our best tool for making sure we're heard."

"Well, that is supremely fucked up," Sam says.

"Everything's fucked up," says Rosina.

"Don't you see it?" Sam pleads. "We're using sex to get what we want. We're still playing by their rules. How is that okay?"

The room is silent. No one has an answer. No one has a solution.

Grace clears her throat. "I think what Margot would do right now is take a vote."

"That's her solution to everything." Sam sighs. "But deciding something doesn't necessarily make it right."

"It's the only thing I can think of," Grace says. "I'm sorry if it's not perfect. But unless someone comes up with a better idea, I think it's all we have right now." She clears her throat and looks around the room. "Does anyone have anything they want to add before we vote?"

The room is quiet.

"Okay," Grace says. "All in favor of keeping the sex strike, raise your hand."

The room is full of hands, but the faces attached to them are resigned, unenthusiastic.

"All opposed," Grace says.

Far fewer hands fill the air now.

Sam shrugs. "It was worth a try."

"Are you still with us, Sam?" Grace says.

Sam smiles a tired smile. "Of course I am."

Then something in the air shifts, some kind of invisible move-

ment. Eyes follow eyes until they are all focused on the same thing. Lisa Sutter gets up and walks across the room to meet the figure that has appeared in the doorway.

"Abby?" Melissa Sanderson says, wide-eyed, like she's seen a ghost.

Lisa stands almost protectively next to the girl who has materialized out of the shadows.

"Who is that?" Grace whispers to Rosina.

"Abby Steward," Rosina says with disdain. "Graduated last year. One of the queens of the troll table. Total mean girl."

"Hey, Melissa," says the girl named Abby. "Hey, Lisa." She is something close to beautiful, but there is something too sharp in her features, something strained and hard.

"She could be a spy," Erin says. "What if she's a spy? What if she's going to turn us all in?"

"Oh my God, Abby!" says one of the cheerleaders. "How have you been since graduation?"

"I'm all right," Abby says. "Taking some classes at PCC and working at Applebee's."

"That's great," the cheerleader says. "So nice to see you."

"Yeah," Abby says. "Whatever."

"If someone could be murdered by uncomfortable small talk," Rosina says, "I would definitely be dead right now."

"Why's everyone being weird?" Grace whispers.

"Abby is Spencer's Klimpt's ex-girlfriend," says Rosina.

"I can't stay long," Abby says, backing up half a step toward the door. "Lisa told me about your meetings and everything. And I just—I wanted to come by and tell you something."

A ballroom full of girls are sitting at Abby's feet, staring at her, waiting.

Abby picks at something on her fingernail. "So, like, you guys know I dated Spencer Klimpt almost all last year?" She leans against the wall, trying to look relaxed, like she couldn't care less about what she's doing. But she doesn't know what to do with her hands. She puts one in her coat pocket, tucks an imaginary strand of hair behind her ear with the other, then folds both arms across her chest. She covers her mouth with thin, trembling fingers, as if they could hide her words, as if they could protect her from what she came here to say.

"So, he was, like, bad," Abby finally says. "Like really bad. Like I think he's crazy. I think he likes hurting girls." She looks up briefly with a startling softness, suddenly not the bitchy mean girl of her reputation. "He was really controlling, you know? Like he always had to know where I was and who I was with. And he'd get rough, like violent, sometimes." She twists a ring on her right hand. Her eyes dart around the floor, the walls, the ceiling. She looks anywhere but into another person's eyes. "It wasn't really rape, right? Because I was his girlfriend?"

"It was rape," Lisa says.

"It was absolutely rape," says Melissa.

"The first time he did it, I cried afterward," Abby says. "He told me to shut up and just left me lying there because he said I was annoying him. When he did it again, I knew not to cry. After that, I just knew to never say no."

Lisa leans against Abby and puts her arm around her. Abby stiffens but lets her.

"I never told anyone before, besides Lisa," Abby says. "I kept it a secret. I got really good at covering up bruises with makeup." Lisa hugs her closer. "But now I know I have to talk about it," she says, looking up. "You all have inspired me, I guess. I knew I had to tell you. Someone has to do something."

"You have to tell the police," Connie says.

Abby shrinks into herself. "No," she says. "I have no proof. They didn't believe Lucy Moynihan, they won't believe me. I was his *girlfriend*." She looks out at the circle of girls, her eyes pleading. "You have to do something."

"We're trying," Lisa says.

"Eric Jordan's a pig with no respect for women," Abby says. "He'll do anything to get laid. And Ennis, I don't know. I think he's just following Spencer and Eric. But Spencer, he's a bad guy. A really bad guy."

The room could not be more silent. It could not be more still. Everyone is holding their breath, frozen with the weight of what they must do.

"I don't think she's a spy anymore," Erin says.

Then with a flip of her hair, Abby's eyes go blank. She turns back into the girl people remember, a girl who would never come here asking for help. She shakes off Lisa's arm around her shoulder. "I gotta run," she says.

"Wait," Lisa says. "Stay with us."

"No," Abby says, pulling away from her. "No offense, but I'm done hanging out with high school girls." Her laugh is bitter, biting. "I just want that sick bastard to hurt. So good luck, I guess. Hurting

him." And before anyone can figure out what to say, Abby slides out the door and is gone.

A circle of eyes blinks at one another, like lights going on and off.

"Wow," someone finally says.

"That was intense," says Sam.

"Total buzz kill," says the drunk girl.

Lisa Sutter sits down and puts her head in her hands. The room seems suddenly darker, more full of shadows.

"She has to tell the cops," Serina Barlow says.

"She doesn't have to do anything," Melissa says.

Trista and Krista are huddled over a phone, their faces illuminated by the unnatural glow. "She's number eight, isn't she?" Trista says.

"You guys, stop," Melissa says. "She's humiliated enough already."

"I'm not making fun of her, I swear," Trista says. "I was just thinking. There are a couple of girls on the list that sound really bad. Like number six: 'too doped up to say much.' And number eleven: 'got her so drunk she couldn't say no.' I mean, he basically admits to raping them, right? We don't know who they are, but maybe if Abby came forward and, like, verified that Spencer is definitely who's behind the posts, maybe the police would investigate what he did to those girls. Abby wouldn't even have to say all that stuff he did to her. She'd just have to admit to being on the list."

The only movement in the room is a sea of darting eyes. The only sounds are the walls shuddering around them and the muted howls of the wind outside, as if it's trying to get in.

"That's actually a really good idea," Grace finally says.

"And there are so many other girls, too," Krista says. "If it was like a whole group that came forward with Abby, the police couldn't ignore them."

Trista looks up from her phone. "Like maybe some of the girls are even in this room." She can't help herself. She looks at Lisa Sutter. *Number Twelve: Boring and needy. Apparently she's head cheerleader now.*

All eyes are on Lisa. The room is waiting for her to speak. Waiting for her to come forward and risk humiliation. Waiting for her to be brave.

But what she does is grab her purse, stand up, and walk out of the room.

"What's her problem?" Serina Barlow says.

"Really?" Melissa says. "You all try to bully her into admitting she's on that list, and you're surprised that she's upset?"

"Who was bullying?" Serina says. "No one even said her name."

"You didn't have to."

"You know what?" Serina says. "Lisa *should* feel bad. She has the power to possibly get Spencer for some really bad shit he did, and she's more worried about being embarrassed? Everyone already knows she's number twelve anyway. The longer he's out there and not in jail, the more girls he's going to hurt. And what about those other girls? Number six and eleven? He needs to go to jail for what he did to them."

"But who even knows what they want?" Melissa says.

"They want justice, obviously," Serina says.

"We can't assume that. We can't assume they want people to

know. We can't assume they want to talk to the police or testify in court or any of that."

"That's bullshit," Serina says. "They have to."

"We can't force anyone to talk about their rape," Melissa says. She looks around the room, her eyes stopping at Erin, silent and hunched over, trapped inside her mysterious pain. "They've already been forced to do something they didn't want to."

Rosina follows Melissa's eyes to Erin in a ball beside her. "Erin?" she whispers.

"So we're fucked," Serina says. "We can't do anything."

Morose faces around the room.

Erin is unreachable.

"That's not true," Grace says. "Look at us. Look at what we're doing. We're changing things already."

"What's changing?" Serina says. "Lucy still got raped. Those assholes are still free. We're not doing anything."

"These meetings are something," Grace says. "We're changing ourselves."

"We're changing the culture at Prescott," Melissa agrees.

"Erin," Rosina whispers. "Do you need to go?"

"But we don't even talk about Lucy anymore," Serina says. "We hardly ever talk about Spencer, Eric, and Ennis, either. And aren't they the whole reason this thing started?"

Without thinking, Rosina places her hand lightly on Erin's back. In a split second, Erin bursts out of her quiet huddle, arms flailing, knocking Rosina over in the process.

"Jesus, Erin!" Rosina says, rubbing her arm. But by the time

Rosina gets herself upright, Erin is already on her way out the door.

"And we can't forget about the girls who aren't here," Sam Robeson says. "The ones who aren't fighting yet. We need to fight for them."

"So what do we do?" Melissa says. "How do we help them?"

"We could host a self-defense class," Connie Lancaster says. "We could pool our money and hire someone to teach us."

"That's good," Sam says. "We should definitely do that."

Rosina runs out of the room after Erin. The last thing she hears is Serina Barlow say: "Yeah, but it's still not enough."

It takes a few moments for Rosina's eyes to adjust to the darkness outside. The wind has been replaced by a downpour. The world outside the leaking shelter of the porch is a wall of solid water.

"Erin?" Rosina says softly. "Where are you?"

She hears wood creaking. She searches with her flashlight until the beam finds Erin, sitting on an old crate in the shadows at the far end of the porch, rocking to a rhythm only she can hear.

Erin holds her hand over her eyes. "Will you please not shine that in my face?"

"Sorry," Rosina says, shutting the flashlight off. "Are you okay?"

"I'm fine."

"You don't seem fine."

"You're entitled to your opinion."

"Can we talk?"

"Why don't you go talk to your cheerleader instead?"

"Erin, what's going on with you?"

"Nothing."

As Rosina moves closer, she notices Erin flinch.

"Come on," Rosina says. "You had near meltdowns in the past two meetings."

"You know I don't like large groups of people," Erin says, looking out at the rain. "I need to be alone sometimes."

"I don't think that's it, though. This is about more than that." Rosina pauses, waits. But Erin says nothing. "They were talking about things. About sex. About rape. Things that triggered you." Rosina takes one tentative step closer. "You can tell me. I'm your best friend."

Erin stands up and starts pacing the length of the porch. "What about what your cheerleader said? What about not forcing people to talk about it?"

"I want to help you. I—"

Erin stops abruptly in front of Rosina. Her entire body is shaking. "It's none of your business!" Erin shouts. "Why do you think everything about me is your business?" She starts pacing again, this time faster, this time with her hands flying. "You're as bad as my mom. You think I can't handle my own feelings. You think I'm completely helpless."

"I'm sorry," Rosina says. "That's not what I—"

"I don't need your help," Erin says with a strained voice. "I can take care of myself."

"I know you can."

"Don't patronize me!"

"Erin—"

"Just go away," Erin says, returning to the shadows in the corner

of the porch. "Just leave me alone. I don't need you. I don't want you here."

There are no words for what Rosina's feeling, no response to what Erin has said. She could tell herself it's Erin's stress talking right now, that she's lashing out because she's scared, that she doesn't really mean what she's saying. But Rosina knows there is something real in Erin's anger, something damning, and a heavy pressure seizes her from inside her chest and grabs her throat like a hand, strangling her.

"Fine," Rosina manages to choke out. "I'm walking home. You can get a ride with Grace."

Rosina steps off the porch and is instantly drenched. She does not turn around, does not check for Erin's response. Erin's right— she doesn't need Rosina. Nobody does.

Rosina is grateful for the rain, grateful that she can focus on the sound and the feel of it on her body, the new heaviness of her clothes, the cold wet of her skin. She does not turn on her flashlight as she walks away, even though the moon is covered by thick rain clouds and there are no streetlights nearby, even though the road is overgrown and rocky, even though the trees are tall and thick and slightly terrifying. Rosina does not try to fight the darkness. If she can't see, then she has to be even more aware of her surroundings. She has to use all her inner resources just to manage walking. She has to focus on moving forward, focus on surviving. And when you're focused on surviving, there's nothing left for pain.

You're alone, the darkness tells her. *Nobody wants you.*

The rain is so loud, even if Rosina was crying, no one would hear her. The night is so dark and she is so drenched, even if there

were tears on Rosina's cheeks, no one would be able to see them.

Two miles later there is not a single part of Rosina that is dry. She's careful to clean up the puddle she makes when she strips off her clothes in the living room. Best to be invisible. Best to leave no trace. Best to not create any new reasons to make Mami mad again.

The house is silent. Mami and Abuelita are both asleep in their rooms. Rosina and Mami have barely spoken to each other since their fight last weekend, except for what is absolutely necessary. Take the garbage out. Order ready for table four. Help Abuelita with her bath.

Rosina doesn't know which is worse—this Cold War silent treatment or the sporadic high-octane screaming fights. At least actual fights are over quickly. They usually have some closure. They burn themselves out. But this, whatever it is, is like a smoldering fire, a constant ache. There's a voice in Rosina's head, so soft it's more like a subliminal message, on repeat, a low dirge: *You are not even important enough to scream at anymore.*

GRACE.

"Oh my God, you guys," Connie Lancaster says. "You'll never guess what I heard." It's Monday morning, the bell for homeroom hasn't even rung yet, and Connie is already primed for gossip. "A bunch of girls just started a feminist club at East Eugene High and, like, *guys* are joining."

"That's awesome," Grace says.

"But this is the best part," Connie says, leaning in. "They're calling themselves the Nowhere Girls."

Something catches in Grace's throat, a mix of gratitude and pride. A great gasp of love.

The homeroom bell rings. "Attention, please," Slatterly's voice booms over the loudspeaker before the class even has a chance to get seated.

"This is gonna be good," says Connie.

"I am pleased to announce that the administration has made significant progress in our mission to uncover the perpetrators responsible for the Nowhere Girls activity."

"'*Perpetrators*'?" Allison says. "Is this a joke? Did she really use that word?"

Grace's momentary high crashes. Hard.

"Our technical advisers have successfully traced e-mail correspondence and have identified several people of interest."

"Oh, shit," says Connie.

"Would the following people please come to the office immediately?"

Grace closes her eyes. She cannot remember how to breathe.

"Trista Polanski," Slatterly says.

"Oh no," Allison says.

"Elise Powell," Slatterly says.

The jocks in the front row bust up laughing. "No surprise there," one of them mutters. "Fucking dyke."

"Fuck you!" Connie yells across the room.

"Language," Baxter scolds half-heartedly. But he is leaning back in his chair, almost smiling; this is his first win of the season.

"And Margot Dillard," Slatterly says, and even over the loudspeakers, Grace thinks she can hear something like pain in the principal's voice.

"Holy shit," laughs one of the trolls. "Queen Margot's going down!" The boys are beside themselves. They haven't been this happy in weeks.

"Oh my God," Allison whispers, tears welling up in her eyes. "Not Margot."

Grace's tears are already falling.

"What are we going to do?" Connie says.

What have we done? Grace thinks.

Rumors fly like crazy. Some say the girls have been suspended for a week. Others say they've been expelled, even arrested. Rumor is Elise has been kicked off the softball team and will lose her U of O scholarship; Margot is disqualified from Stanford. Trista is being sent to some kind of boarding school where they do things like "convert" gay kids. The truth is impossible to decipher from all the gossip.

"I tried calling Margot and Elise," Melissa says at lunch. "It keeps going to voice mail. Have you talked to Trista?"

Krista can barely even shake her head. She's inconsolable. She's been crying since homeroom.

"Margot wasn't even at the first meeting," Grace says. "It doesn't make any sense. Why her?"

"They wrote *to* the Nowhere Girls e-mail address," Erin says. "That's how the computer techs must have identified them." Everyone looks at her. Everyone but Rosina. "Maybe," she adds. "I don't know. It's a theory."

"So that's it?" Melissa says. "They sent an e-mail and now they're taking the fall for everyone? That's ridiculous. That can't be legal."

Rosina and Erin are sitting in their usual spots across from each other, but they haven't spoken; they haven't even looked at each other. Grace knows almost nothing about what happened between them on Saturday night, only that she came outside after the meeting was over to find Erin alone, pacing the porch and crying. All Erin told Grace was they got in a fight and Rosina decided to walk home in the rain. She was silent on the ride home as she stared out the window and, Grace suspected, searched for signs of Rosina.

"This is so fucked up," Melissa says. "Look at Ennis sitting over there. He thinks it's safe to show his face again."

"What are we going to do?" Krista cries. "We have to help them."

"Hey, bitches!" one of the guys from the troll table yells across the cafeteria. "How's your revolution going?"

"Catch any rapists lately?" says another, and the table explodes in laughter.

The girls say nothing. Not even Rosina has the energy for a response.

Grace stares at Rosina until she meets her eyes, but nothing passes between them but fear.

In the three hours between lunch and the end of school, Grace experiences a kind of regression. She goes back in time to a pre-Rosina, pre-Erin, pre–Nowhere Girls version of herself. Fear can do that to a person. Fear can do all kinds of things.

There is nothing lonelier than fear. In Grace's language, it is the opposite of faith. It is when you need God the most.

But Grace cannot think of God right now. She is stuck inside herself with her shame, her secrets. Grace did this. Grace made this mess. Good people are being punished, and it's her own damn fault. Three lives are being ruined because a nobody wanted to be somebody, because pride got in the way of a good sheep staying a sheep.

What made Grace think she could change anything? What made her think she could even change herself? People can't change. That's just a lie to keep therapists and preachers in business. She never should have bothered. She should have just kept her head down, just kept to the invisible middle of the herd where she belongs, where she's always belonged, along with the other sheep, with the other invisible girls.

She should have painted over those words on her bedroom wall as soon as she saw them. She should have never learned the name Lucy Moynihan.

Grace wants to go back to being empty. Being empty did not hurt like this. There is no risk when you are no one. There is nothing to lose when you have nothing.

Emptiness. What Grace wants is emptiness.

But where can she find it? The house is not empty. Is that Mom Grace sees through the kitchen window? Is she boiling water for tea? Or is it another ghost, another figment of Grace's yearning?

Grace considers turning around. She could go to one of the places the girls have claimed—the model home, the old Dixon Mansion, the vacant warehouse, the library basement. But as usual, she's too slow. Mom looks up and sees Grace through the window, and a smile spreads across her face, the kind of smile Grace has been aching for, a look of acknowledgment, the look of being seen, and suddenly all Grace wants is to fill up that not-empty house with her. All she wants is to be her mother's daughter and nothing else.

"Hey, sweetie," Mom says when Grace enters the kitchen. "Want a cup of tea?"

What Grace means to say is yes, but instead she starts crying. Mom's arms are instantly around her, and they are not the pastor's arms. Grace is a girl again, before everything changed, before all this caring and worrying and growing up, and for a few brief moments she is no longer afraid.

"Oh, Gracie," Mom says, and leads her to the couch. For a moment love makes Grace brave, and she thinks maybe if you miss

someone, you should tell them. Maybe if you want something, you should do something about it instead of feeling sorry for yourself.

"I miss you, Mom," Grace says.

"Oh, honey, I miss you, too." And now Mom is crying too. "I'm so sorry I've been so busy. I haven't been here for you."

"Everything's changing," Grace says. "Every single thing in my world is changing."

"I know," Mom says. "I know. But I'm here. I'm still here. I promise." And she rocks Grace in her arms, and she is something Grace can hold on to, something solid and familiar and hers.

"Can we do something?" Grace says. "Just you and me."

"Let's have a dinner date," Mom says.

"When?" Grace sniffles.

"Tonight. I'll cancel my meeting at the church. Anywhere you want to go."

Was it always this easy? All that time missing her mom, all she had to do was say something? All that time wanting, all she had to do was ask? Grace wonders how much of her life she has wasted waiting for things to come to her, too afraid to take chances, too afraid to make herself and her desires known. As if it is everyone else who knows things, as if they are the ones who hold the secret to God's will for her. As if God doesn't speak through her, too.

Grace decides she is sick and tired of waiting. Her fear is not gone, but it is wavering. It is love that did that, love that gave her the need, and then the faith, to open her mouth and risk speaking. Maybe that was her prayer. She spoke to her mother, she asked for help, and God answered through her.

ROSINA.

Rosina sits in the front passenger seat of Melissa Sanderson's car. Right next to her. In her car. Their legs are inches apart.

"It feels weird, like, just hanging out while Margot, Elise, and Trista are in such big trouble," Melissa says as she pulls out of the school parking lot.

And while my best friend and my mother both hate me, Rosina thinks.

"I wish there was something we could do for them," Melissa says.

"Do you want to cancel?" Rosina says. "We could do this another time." For a moment she hates those three girls for potentially ruining her first maybe date with the girl of her dreams. She hates Mami and Erin for infiltrating her thoughts.

Melissa looks at Rosina and smiles her intoxicating smile. "Of course not."

"Keep your eyes on the road, lady," Rosina says, mostly so Melissa will not see the goofy grin she cannot keep from forming

on her face, despite the toxic sludge of gloom swirling around in her chest.

"What should we do?" Melissa says. "Where should we go?"

"We could go to my house," Rosina says. "No one's there."

"Great," Melissa says. "I happen to know exactly where that is."

The few seconds of silence that follow are too much for Rosina. She must fill them. "So, um, you like football, huh?"

Melissa laughs. "I love it. You probably think that's really stupid."

"I think it's surprising," Rosina says. "I like surprising."

"Can I tell you something and you promise you won't laugh?"

"I will try not to laugh. I will promise to try."

"What I want to be someday, more than anything in the world, is a professional sportscaster. I want to do *Monday Night Football*."

"Wow," Rosina says. "That's so . . . surprising."

"What do you want to do?"

"I have no idea," Rosina says. No way she's going to admit to her dream of being a rock star.

"I think I'm so into football because my dad is," Melissa says. "I'm an only child so I'm the one Dad watches games with and takes to Ducks games. Football's our thing. Always has been. There's a series of photos of me in the stairwell at different ages since I was born, and I'm next to a football in all of them. Newborn me. Three-month-old me. Six-month-old me. It goes all the way up to ten years old."

"That is both adorable," Rosina says, "and a little insane."

"I know," Melissa says. "I kind of love it."

"I think cooking was supposed to be my thing with my mom,"

Rosina says. "It's the thing she loves to do, what she's really good at, and she's always trying to teach me. But I hate it. I hate Mexican food. I hate Oaxacan food. I hate beans and corn. I hate tortillas. I refuse to go to church, and I like girls, so basically I'm like the worst Mexican daughter ever." Why does she feel like crying all of a sudden?

"Probably not the worst," Melissa says.

"No?"

"Maybe the second worst."

Rosina smiles. As nervous and full of self-pity as she is, talking with Melissa is so strangely easy.

"What do your parents do?" Rosina asks. "Like as a job?"

"My mom's a kindergarten teacher," Melissa says.

"That must be why you're so nice."

"My dad does something with pencils."

"Pencils?"

"Yeah, like the distribution of pencils."

"Wow."

"He manages a pencil distribution office."

"No!"

"Yes!"

"That's fascinating."

"Tell me about it."

They ride the rest of the way to Rosina's house with grins on their faces.

It's been a whole week since cousin Lola took over babysitting duty, but it's still a shock to Rosina every time she enters her empty, quiet house after school instead of the chaos of her aunt and uncle's

place next door. Despite having not a single shred of faith, she can't help but say a silent "Thank you, Jesus" as she closes the door behind them.

There was significantly less bloodshed involved in Rosina getting out of babysitting than she expected. Her aunts didn't care who did it as long as they were dependable and—most important—free. At least there is one perk of her mother's silent treatment—Mami didn't get involved. All it took was Rosina promising to pay Lola fifteen dollars per afternoon to take her place, which is almost all her tips from a night of work, but that is a small price for freedom.

And right now, what Rosina's new freedom looks like is Melissa Sanderson standing in her house, unsupervised, the whole afternoon in front of them until Rosina's shift at the restaurant, when she must pretend like she did not just spend the past couple of hours with the most beautiful girl in the world.

"Where's your grandma?" Melissa says. "She's such a sweetie."

"Next door, at my aunt and uncle's house. My cousin is watching her. Used to be my job, but I quit."

"You have a lot of jobs."

"That's the understatement of the year."

They stand in the entryway of the house that is identical to the one next door, the living room open on the left, the dining area and kitchen on the right. Their coats are still on, their bags still on their shoulders. Rosina realizes she has no idea what to do. "Um," Rosina says. "Are you hungry? Do you want something to drink?"

"I'm okay," Melissa says, looking at the brightly colored print of la Virgen de Guadalupe hanging above the dining table.

"Don't judge me," Rosina says.

"About what?"

"That."

"Why would I judge you?" Melissa says. "She's beautiful."

"It's so . . . Catholic," Rosina says.

"What's wrong with that?"

Rosina searches Melissa's face for a hint of sarcasm. Is she really like this all the time? This open? This positive?

"They don't exactly have the highest opinion of people like me," Rosina says. *Or like you?* Rosina wants to say. There is so much she wants to say.

"I'm sure not all Catholics are so closed minded."

Rosina shrugs. They are still standing in the same spot with their coats and bags on. "Do you want to watch TV or something?"

"Can I see your room?" Melissa says.

Rosina almost chokes. "Sure," she says. "Yeah."

She is leading the most beautiful girl in the world to her room. Rosina should be giddy, excited, all those cliché teenage romantic feelings, but as they climb the narrow stairway to the second floor, her nervous joy is interrupted by thoughts of Erin, how she didn't raise her hand at the meeting where Grace asked who the virgins were, how she looked so scared, how she shut down, how she keeps shutting down, how she's full of a pain she refuses to share, how Rosina can't fix it, how Erin won't even let her try. And Erin made Rosina ashamed of that, as if wanting to help her was somehow wrong. Rosina would do anything for Erin. Why is that bad?

Is this what Mami wants Rosina to feel about the family? The

kind of selflessness that would make her do anything for them? Can love be the same as duty and obligation, words that make Rosina bristle and want to fight?

Can love be forced? Can someone be shamed into it? Is it still love if it suffocates you? Is this what Rosina's doing to Erin? Is she suffocating Erin with her love the way Mami and Rosina's family suffocate her with theirs? Is that why Erin pushed her away?

"Wow," Melissa says. "Your room is so cool."

"Thanks," Rosina says, using every bit of strength to pull herself back into the moment.

I don't deserve her, she thinks. *I don't deserve this perfect girl.*

"What are all these bands?" Melissa says. "I don't recognize any of them."

"These are all vintage posters I found at this record store in Eugene," Rosina says. "Most of these bands don't exist anymore. They were around in the nineties. This is Bikini Kill. Heavens to Betsy. L7. The Gits. Sleater-Kinney is the best one. I have all their albums. They're still around too. They didn't just have the attitude, they're also really talented musicians."

"They all look so . . . fierce," Melissa says.

"They are."

"Like you."

Rosina opens her mouth but no words come out. Melissa smiles.

"You play guitar?" Melissa's fingers brush the strings of Rosina's acoustic leaning against her bed.

"Yeah," Rosina says, hoping Melissa didn't notice her shiver. "I sing, too. I write songs."

"I had no idea!"

"I don't exactly talk about it all the time."

"Why not? It's so cool."

"It's kind of personal, I guess," Rosina says.

Melissa takes off her coat and shoes and sits cross-legged on Rosina's bed. Rosina says a second silent *Thank you, Jesus* that she made her bed this morning.

"Will you play one for me?" Melissa says. "One of your songs?"

"No," Rosina says immediately.

"Why not?"

"I've never played them for anyone."

"There's a first for everything," Melissa says. "You want to play them for people eventually, right?"

"I don't know."

"Really? You write songs just to play for yourself?"

Rosina smiles. Of course not. She writes them to sing at the top of her lungs on a stage in front of an audience of people who adore her.

"Okay," Rosina says. "But you have to be nice."

"I'm always nice," Melissa says. Which is true.

Rosina takes a deep breath, picks up her guitar, and sits on the bed next to Melissa. She starts the quiet fingerpicking of her most recent song. Her whispery vocals come in, with a melody like a lullaby crossed with a funeral dirge, pretty yet heavy, with lyrics alluding to a bird trapped, caged. The single guitar notes slowly build to strumming, Rosina's voice breaking into a full-bodied wail. Her dark thoughts are released—Mami and Erin, gone. She sings of

escape, of flight. The music vibrates inside her. It shakes the room. Her voice, her words, are her wings.

When she is done, she puts her guitar down and slowly lifts her eyes to Melissa. There is the look she's imagined while writing her songs in secret. There is the audience she's dreamed of every night singing to herself. There is the love, the adoration. In front of her is someone moved to tears.

"Say something," Rosina says.

"I can't."

"It was that bad?"

"Oh my God, no." Melissa takes Rosina's hands in hers. "That was quite possibly the most amazing thing I've ever heard in my life."

Rosina looks away. Her smile takes up the whole room.

"Why don't you perform?" Melissa asks. "Why don't you have a band?"

Rosina shrugs.

"That's crazy. You have to let people hear you. They need to hear you."

"Maybe someday," Rosina says.

"Someday soon," Melissa says. "Please."

"Okay."

Their smiles cannot get any bigger. Melissa's eyes cannot get any deeper. The space between them shrinks as the rest of the room falls away, until all that exists is this twin bed and these two girls and their strong hearts pounding beautiful in their chests, willing their bodies closer so they can catch each other's rhythm, so they can beat together, so they can make music.

Rosina suddenly realizes they've been holding hands this whole time, and looks down to see the entwined lattice of their fingers. She thinks this is where she'd normally say something sarcastic, something to diffuse the intensity of the moment, to make Melissa think she doesn't care, to make her think she's not quickly turning to jelly, starting where her fingertips rest soft in the palm of Melissa's hand, up her arm, her chest, her heart, aching a beautiful ache that could turn ugly at any moment. The yearning is so close to pain. It could turn into a monster, a great clawed thing, and jump out of Rosina's chest, so desperate to hold every piece of this beautiful girl only inches away.

But Rosina stays silent. She lets the moment last. But she does not look up, cannot look Melissa in the eyes, cannot let her see the blinking neon in her own eyes that will tell her everything Rosina's too scared to let her know.

But then a soft touch on Rosina's chin, a gentle lifting. And then two eyes bright with the same yearning, two lips soft and open, and suddenly the world is too beautiful for Rosina to feel scared.

GRACE.

Grace wonders if this is kind of what it feels like
to be on a date—nervous and excited, hopeful but slightly wary of
the night not living up to her expectations. As she and her mom
drive to dinner, thoughts of Jesse Camp creep into her head, how
easy and pleasant it was to talk to him that first time at church, then
the strangely overblown feeling when she saw him sitting with Ennis
Calhoun at lunch, as if he had personally betrayed her, how both
feelings tug inside her every time she sees him. Grace wonders how
it would feel to go on a date with him, if it was Jesse in the passenger's seat instead of her mom.

"So your friend's family owns this restaurant we're going to?"
Mom says.

"Rosina's mom is the head chef," Grace says. "And Rosina's
working tonight, so you get to meet her."

"Oh, good!" Mom says, and she seems genuinely excited. "I
can't wait to meet one of your new friends. And I've heard great
things about this place."

She makes it sound so normal, Grace thinks. *One of your new friends.* As if it isn't a miracle.

Rosina spots them as soon as they set foot in the restaurant. "Gracie!" she calls as she runs over to give her a hug.

"Gracie?" Grace says. A *hug*? Something's wrong with Rosina.

"Is this your mom?"

"Hi, Rosina," Mom says. "It's so nice to meet you."

"So nice to meet you, too, Mrs. Salter," Rosina says, shaking her hand. "Or should I call you Pastor Salter?"

"You can call me Robin," she laughs.

"Where do you guys want to sit?" Rosina asks. "The booths are comfy."

"A booth would be perfect," Mom says.

As Rosina leads them to their table, she whispers to Grace, "Guess who just came over to my house after school?"

"Melissa?"

"Yes!"

"You're like seriously swooning."

"I know!"

"It's kind of disturbing how happy you are."

"My mom's been yelling at me all night and I totally don't care!"

Rosina seats them and takes their drink orders, then dances away.

"She's sweet," Mom says.

Grace can't help but laugh at that description. "She's usually a lot grumpier. But I think she's in love."

"How nice," Mom says. "What about you, Gracie? Anyone catch your eye?"

"Ugh," Grace says. "No." But maybe she's lying just a little.

"It's okay to date, you know," Mom says. "I know the culture back in Adeline was a little backward about stuff like that. But I want you to know it's okay with your dad and me. As long as he treats you right."

"Noted," Grace says, racking her brain to find something to say to change the subject.

"Or . . . she?" Mom says.

"He, Mom," Grace says. "But thanks."

"Honey," Mom says. "Is there anything you want to know? About dating? About . . . being intimate? We can talk about these things, you know."

"No," Grace says. "Thanks. I'm okay." What she really wants to say is how do you expect me to talk about that stuff when we haven't really talked about anything lately?

Rosina returns with a tray of chips and waters in one hand, her other hand tugging the sleeve of a woman behind her who must be her mother. Rosina's mom is half a foot shorter than Rosina and much plumper around the middle, her black hair up in a tight hairnet-covered bun, her face a mix of hesitance and surprise as Rosina drags her across the restaurant floor.

"This is my mom," Rosina announces. "Maria Suarez."

Rosina's mother wipes her hands on her apron and smiles shyly. "I'm happy to meet you," she says with a girlish voice. This is the evil tyrant Rosina is always complaining about?

"Hi, Mrs. Suarez," Grace says. "I'm Grace. It's nice to meet you."

"Hello, Grace." She smiles. "It's nice to meet you, too." She seems to genuinely mean it.

"I'm Grace's mom, Robin," Mom says, extending her hand for a shake.

"Thank you for coming to the restaurant," Mrs. Suarez says.

"See, Mami," Rosina says. "Grace is totally normal and totally a good influence on me." Both sets of moms and daughters laugh.

"Rosina is a good influence on me, too," Grace says.

"I doubt that," Mrs. Suarez says, but with a hint of her daughter's signature sass.

"Maria!" a man calls from the back of the restaurant.

"Tío José beckons," Rosina says, rolling her eyes.

"I have to return to the kitchen," Mrs. Suarez says. "It was very nice to meet you, Grace. And Mrs.—?"

"You can call me Robin."

"Very nice to meet you, Robin. I hope you enjoy your meal."

Rosina bounces away after her mom, and Grace can't help but smile, imagining her as a little girl with pigtails, full of the same fire but in a much smaller and less coordinated body.

"Seems like you've settled in pretty well here," Mom says.

"Yeah," Grace says. "I guess I have."

"I'm proud of you, honey," Mom says. "I know things ended kind of badly in Adeline with your friends."

Grace feels the sting of sudden tears in her eyes, but she shrugs in feigned indifference.

"People can be very cruel and closed minded when faced with things they don't understand." She pauses and looks down. She smoothes the napkin on her lap. "I want you to know I'm sorry. You

suffered because of things I did. That wasn't fair to you. I wish it could have been different."

"You were called," Grace says. "You had to answer."

"That's true." Mom smiles. "But I'm taking you with me, aren't I? I never asked you if you wanted to come."

"I was mad at you for a long time," Grace says. Something in her body is different. Her bones are harder; her blood is thicker. "But now, I think maybe it happened for a reason. For you, obviously. But for me, too. Those girls weren't ever really my friends if they could drop me that easily. What happened brought us here. And I think I like it here. I think I'm happy."

Grace realizes the truth of these words as they come out of her mouth. As much struggle as she's had here, as much heartache, she has found something she never had in Adeline, something she never even knew she wanted.

"Oh, honey," Mom says. "That makes me so glad."

"So thank you, I guess," Grace says. "For totally destroying my life and making me move across the country to this weird town."

"You're very welcome," Mom says. She raises her glass. "To us."

"To us," Grace says, raising hers.

Grace and Mom sit on the living room couch, eating mint chip ice cream out of the container.

"I can't believe I even have room for this after that dinner," Mom groans. "It was so good."

"Remember, all Salters have a separate dessert stomach," Grace says. "That stomach is still empty."

"Ah, yes," Mom says. "Right you are."

"What should we watch?" Grace says, clicking through the channels.

"I don't know. I haven't had time to watch TV in so long. I don't even know what shows are on anymore."

Grace stops clicking. She blinks. She wonders if she's hallucinating.

The title on the screen reads: TROUBLE AT PRESCOTT HIGH SCHOOL.

"My school's on the news," Grace says, turning up the volume.

"Oh, yeah," Mom says. "I can't believe I forgot to tell you. They interviewed me this morning about all the vandalism that's been happening and the secret girls' club—what's it called?"

"The Nowhere Girls," Grace says.

"That's right. Do you know anything about it?"

Grace hesitates. "No," she lies, and something twists inside her as she does. Why can't she tell her?

"I wonder if they're going to show my interview," Mom says, licking her ice-cream spoon.

A male reporter stands in front of the school with a microphone in his hand. It is long after school hours; the shot is empty and dark, almost sinister, as if a violent crime has been committed. The reporter says with journalistic gravitas: "A local high school is mired in conflict resulting from the activities of an underground feminist group calling themselves the 'Nowhere Girls.'"

Cut to a close-up of crumpled posters in a garbage can. "In recent weeks Prescott High School has been plagued by vandalism

and increasingly volatile altercations between students. The group is also suspected of stealing sensitive computer data from the school. It is unclear how many members the group has, but the school administration believes it consists entirely of female students."

Cut to a shot of the empty football field. "Targets of the group have included the Prescott High football team, who were last year's regional champions but have a total losing streak so far this season, which Coach Dwayne Baxter believes is a direct result of bullying and slander by propaganda spread by the Nowhere Girls."

The screen cuts to Coach Baxter, sitting at the desk Grace recognizes all too well. "You wouldn't believe the team's loss of morale," he says. "They're just devastated. These girls are accusing them of awful things, stuff I know my guys wouldn't do. These are good guys. They've trained hard for this season. And now all their talent is being wasted because a group of troublemakers is going around spreading lies. These are hate crimes is what they are. Pure and simple. My guys are being singled out because they're boys, because of their gender."

The reporter returns. "Some are calling it an adolescent war of the sexes. Some say it's a result of hormones gone awry. And some are saying the Nowhere Girls have legitimate concerns stemming from the events of last year that threw Prescott High School, indeed the whole town of Prescott, into chaos, after one girl accused three male students of a brutal sexual assault. The charges were quickly dropped, but the unfortunate event sent ripples through the community that seem to have inspired the recent disruptions at Prescott High."

"We asked Prescott residents what they think of the so-called 'feminist uprising' at the high school, and here are some of their responses."

The screen cuts to an old woman standing outside the grocery store. "I think it's disgusting," she says between thin lips. "What these girls are up to. Our boys don't do things like that."

A middle-aged man in front of his truck: "They're just a bunch of girls who want attention. Just like that girl last year."

A dreadlocked, scruffy-bearded man of indeterminate age and questionable sobriety: "Yeah, girls. Fight the power." He pumps his fist in the air.

"*That's* who they chose to speak for the other side?" Grace says. "Objective reporting, my ass."

Mom raises her eyebrow. "Sorry," Grace says.

Cut back to the reporter, chuckling. "One thing's for sure, Prescott is full of opinions. We also spoke with Dr. Regina Slatterly, principal of Prescott High School, who is at the epicenter of the current difficulties and is struggling to keep her students safe and focused on their education."

Principal Slatterly sits behind her desk, hands folded in front of her. She is wearing more makeup than usual. "You know," she says, "we live in such a culture of entitlement and blame and playing the victim card when we feel we don't get the kind of treatment we deserve. I think the girls involved in this need to stop for a moment and ask themselves what their part is in their dissatisfaction. Maybe then they will stop blaming boys for all their problems and stop using them as a scapegoat. Don't get me wrong; I do believe most of

the girls involved are probably good girls at heart. But they're young and full of emotions they don't understand, and they've found the wrong outlet for it. Girls this age are naïve and impressionable, and I have reason to believe that there is a mastermind at the center of this who is responsible for leading them astray and putting all these ideas in their heads. But I want to make one thing clear: This is not your usual run-of-the-mill case of peer pressure. This is serious. The escalating disruption at Prescott High has created a hostile environment that is not conducive to learning and is, quite frankly, not safe for the students. And I am determined, with full support from the Prescott police force, to find the person or persons behind this and bring them to justice. I *will* get my school back."

There is so much Grace wants to say, none of which would be appropriate in front of her mother. More than anything, she wants to throw the remote control at the TV screen, straight at Principal Slatterly's smug face.

"Many of the people we spoke to echoed Principal Slatterly's sentiments, but there is one response that stands out, from a relatively new member of the Prescott community—Dr. Robin Salter, new head pastor at Prescott Congregational."

"Mom, you're on TV!" Grace says.

"Oh, my forehead looks so shiny," Mom says.

"Shhh!" Grace says. "I want to hear you."

"I wasn't here last spring," Mom says in front of the church's big rainbow mural. "So I don't know firsthand what this community went through. And I don't think anyone knows what really happened between the young woman and the three young men except those

involved. Whatever the truth is about that night, it sounds like the young women of this community have thoughts and feelings that need to be heard, and whether or not we agree with their tactics, I think we can all agree that we care about these girls and we want to hear them."

Grace's Mom is replaced by a fat white man standing at the front of a large modern church, the stained glass of a suffering Jesus on the cross towering behind him. The camera shoots from below so he looks more powerful, kinglike. The reporter's voice is dubbed over: "But Pastor Robert Skinner of Prescott Foursquare, Fir County's largest congregation, has a different take on the matter."

"They cut out all the good parts of my interview," Mom says.

"Of course they did," Grace grumbles.

The pastor speaks: "I have to tell you, something like this would never have happened ten years ago, when the people of Prescott really cared about family values. But people from outside the community, with different values and priorities, are moving here and changing the culture, changing the way we do things, creating conflict and problems where there have never been any. You know, I sympathize with these girls, I do. I know how hard it is being a teenager, what with all their hormones and pressures from school, and disappointments from dating, and the mixed messages they get from the media. I can see how that would lead to some destructive feelings, and then you add the mob mentality of this thing, and it's just getting out of control. I think what these girls need to do is take a deep breath, go home to their families, and pray."

"That guy is such a blowhard," Mom says.

"And there you have it," the reporter says. "It'll be interesting

to see where this goes. Principal Regina Slatterly was able to tell us that three members of the group have recently been identified and are receiving disciplinary action, but the leader of the group is still unknown. Of course, we'll keep you posted with any new developments. I'm sure I speak for all of Prescott when I say I hope this gets resolved soon and things can go back to normal for the students at Prescott High. Back to you, Jill."

Grace turns the TV off. She grabs the pint of ice cream from her mom and sticks a big spoonful in her mouth to keep herself from saying something she'll regret.

Mom shakes her head. "Interesting they didn't ask any of the students what they think."

Grace sucks on her ice-cream spoon.

"Do you know anything about this group?" Mom says. "These Nowhere Girls?"

"I've seen their posters around school," Grace says, digging in for another scoop.

"So you're not involved or anything?" Mom says.

Grace shakes her head. She thinks the spoon sticking out of her mouth is the only thing keeping her from spilling everything.

"It's intriguing," Mom says.

Grace pulls the spoon out of her mouth, fights the smile that wants to form on her lips, fights the urge to throw her arms around her mother.

Instead of any of these things, Grace stands up and says, "Did Dad tell you my ceiling has a leak?"

"He must have forgotten to mention it," Mom says.

"Well, it does."

"Then I guess we need to take care of it."

"Yeah," Grace says. She hands her mother the ice cream. "I'm going to head up to bed now. Thanks for dinner and everything."

"Okay, honey."

"You did really good on your interview."

Mom smiles and opens her arms. "Come here."

Grace lets herself be held. She closes her eyes and for a moment imagines telling her mother everything. Maybe Mom wouldn't be proud exactly, but at least she'd know what Grace is capable of. She might get mad, she might be disappointed, but she'd certainly be impressed.

But Mom can't know. It's bad enough what happened to Trista, Elise, and Margot; there's no way Grace is going to take that chance with Mom. She can't burden her with that knowledge. She can't ask her to keep that secret. Mom has way too much at stake.

"We're doing good," Mom says, squeezing Grace's shoulders.

"We are," Grace says. But what she's thinking is, *You have no idea.*

The Real Men of Prescott

Bad news, men. The feminist apocalypse may be upon us. If you live in Prescott, you already know what I'm talking about. If not, here's the short of it—the girls of Prescott High School have been possessed by evil feminist cunt forces and have decided to declare a sex strike. Something about wanting "respect" from guys and "justice" for some girl who got fucked last year and cried rape because she thought being a victim would be cooler than being a slut.

And it's not just the ugly girls who have their granny panties in a bunch. Even some of the dumb hot princesses who have nothing to complain about have gotten the idea in their head that the best way to get respect is to turn frigid. Really, girls? You think guys will respect you more if you take away the only thing we actually like about you?

Have they ever stopped to think that maybe if they say no all the time, guys will stop taking no for an answer?

—AlphaGuy541

US.

Today's homeroom announcement from Principal Slatterly: School employees, at their discretion, have authority to separate girls who are congregating for nonschoolwork-related reasons.

"She's not even pretending to not be a fascist anymore," Connie says.

Coach Baxter is late. He storms in, throws some papers on his desk. "The cheerleaders?" Coach Baxter rants at the front of the classroom. "I'm sick of this. The marching band was one thing, but now the *cheerleaders* are boycotting games?"

"They should have done it a long time ago," says the boy who plays trumpet in the marching band.

"Get out!" Coach Baxter growls. "Get out of my classroom right now."

"Gladly," says the boy as he picks up his bag and walks out the door.

"I'm coming with you," says the girl who sits next to him, one of the marching-band drummers.

"This is ridiculous," Coach says as the door closes behind them.

"All of this. What happened to respecting authority? What happened to tradition?"

No one has an answer for him.

"Hey!" Melissa says as she practically leaps into her seat at the lunch table. "You guys will never believe this!" She leans in, bouncing with excitement. It is almost impossible for her to keep her voice down. "I convinced Lisa to talk to the cops about being on Spencer's list."

"Really?" Grace says. "Oh my God."

"Melissa!" Rosina beams. "You're amazing."

"Get a room," Erin mumbles.

"She says she thinks she can convince Abby to do it too," Melissa says.

"It just takes one person to be brave," Grace says. "Then others will follow her lead."

"Yeah, well," Melissa says, "I think Lisa's thinking more like blackmail. But whatever, that's between the two of them."

"You guys?" Erin says.

"Grace, you're friends with Amber, right?" Melissa says.

"I'm not sure you would call it that, but yes, I guess so."

"Do you think you could talk to her?" Melissa says. "Maybe she'll come forward too."

"She's on the list?" Rosina says.

Melissa nods. "Number four. I'm like ninety-nine point nine percent positive."

"Hey, you guys," Erin says again.

"She wasn't in class today," Grace says. "But I can call her."

"You guys!" Erin yells.

But it is too late. The security guard is towering over them. "That's it," he barks. "Party's over. Break it up."

"What do you mean?" Melissa says.

"I mean move."

"Where are we supposed to go?" Rosina asks.

"I don't care," the guard says. "You just can't sit together."

"This is bullshit," Rosina says.

"What was that?" he growls.

"I said 'Yes, sir.'"

"If you girls aren't separated in ten seconds, I'm sending you all to Principal Slatterly's office."

So they move. One by one, they join other tables. Rosina sits with Serina Barlow. Melissa sits with a handful of cheerleaders, who are apparently still allowed to congregate. Erin heads to the library. Grace picks up her tray and looks around the lunchroom, is stunned to realize she could join half these tables and feel something close to comfortable. But there is one in particular that catches her eye, mostly a mix of athletes from the school's less-fashionable sports like golf and fencing. At the end of the table, with a cheeseburger in his hands, is Jesse Camp.

Grace thinks about her mom. She thinks about how sometimes doing a scary thing makes it less scary.

"Hi," Grace says as she sits down next to Jesse, just as he takes a big bite of burger.

"Mrumph," he mumbles with a full mouth, his eyes wide with surprise.

"You have a little ketchup." She points to a spot on her chin.

Still chewing, Jesse tries to wipe it off but misses. Grace picks up a napkin from the table and wipes it off.

Jesse swallows. "Um, thanks."

"I just got booted from my table by the rent-a-cop."

"You're such a rebel," he says, smiling.

"I know," Grace says, smiling back.

"So you're not mad at me anymore?"

Grace takes a bite of French fry and shakes her head.

"So we can be friends now?"

Grace chews and nods.

"So," he says, setting his burger down. "Things are pretty crazy around here these days."

"You could definitely say that."

"Are you friends with the girls who got suspended?"

"Yeah," Grace says. "Pretty good friends, actually."

"Have you heard anything from them?"

"It sounds like Elise's parents are pretty cool and she didn't even get grounded. Margot's freaked out this'll ruin her chances at Stanford, but I'm sure she'll be fine. Her parents are threatening to sue the school or something. Elise's too, I think. They're filing a formal complaint with the school board. The other girl, Trista, she got it the worst. She's like grounded forever. Her parents are going to make her do some kind of spiritual counseling with the youth pastor at their church."

"Wow," Jesse says. "That sucks."

"Yeah," Grace says. "Especially since none of them is guilty."

"How do you know?"

"I just know."

"Because you're in the Nowhere Girls," Jesse says. "I already figured that out."

"The first rule about the Nowhere Girls"—Grace smiles—"is you do not talk about the Nowhere Girls."

A girl looks around the lunchroom and can't help but laugh a little at all the groups of girls being forced to separate by security guards. Since when are groups of white girls considered a threat? Must be that Nowhere Girls stuff. Some girls from her softball team invited her to a meeting a couple of weeks ago and she thought about checking it out, but she knew she never would.

Because this feminism or whatever it is they're doing—it's a white-girl thing. When they go around making demands and yelling, people call them fired up and passionate.

But black girls don't have that privilege. When black girls stand up for themselves, people call them hostile. They call them dangerous. They call them other things.

Amber decides she needs a day off of school. She needs a break from being herself.

The problem is there's nothing good on TV. There's nothing good in the fridge. Mom's at work and her boyfriend-of-the-week is who knows where (thank God), and the trailer is feeling damp and toxic. Some kind of dark-colored mold is growing around the edges of all the windows. Condensation drips down the glass and forms tiny puddles on the windowsills.

There's that guy she met at that PCC party last weekend. Chad

something. He texted her yesterday and she never texted back. Maybe this one's different. Maybe he's more mature because he's older and in college.

Chad picks her up two blocks away. Amber thinks maybe if he doesn't see where she lives, he won't jump to certain conclusions. And maybe because he's not part of her high school world, he won't have any preconceived ideas about who she is. She can start with a clean slate. She could be anyone.

She tells him she's hungry. She hopes maybe he'll take her out for a real date at a real restaurant. Her heart drops when the car slows and turns into the McDonald's drive-through. But at least he pays for it.

"Let's go to my place," Chad says. In the few minutes it takes to drive to his apartment complex, Amber eats her burger and fries and swallows whatever pride foolishly dared to surface this morning.

Amber has seen apartments like this before. Dishes piled in the sink for who knows how long. Cheap and mismatched secondhand furniture. Stained, drooping couch. Large bong on the coffee table amidst empty bags of chips and beer cans. A rank smell of dirty socks, rancid food, and ball sweat. Walls bare except for one crooked poster of a car Chad will never in his life be able to afford, with a bikini-clad woman on top he will never sleep with.

Amber's phone rings. The caller ID says it's that girl Grace from school. What is her problem? Why does she keep bothering Amber? Is it a weird Christian thing? Is Grace trying to save her? Well, too bad. It's way too late for that.

"Here," Chad says, handing Amber a plastic cup. She takes a sip of what she guesses is about five shots of cheap vodka with a splash

of SunnyD. They talk for approximately four minutes before Chad unceremoniously leans over and puts his mouth on hers, his hand on her breast. He tastes like the room smells.

Amber wishes she'd gone to school today after all. Grace invited her to sit with her weird friends at lunch, but Amber hasn't taken her up on it yet. Even though Amber doesn't trust her, even though she has no clue what her angle is, sitting next to her at lunch and wondering what Grace wants from her sure sounds a lot better than this.

She pushes Chad away. "What's wrong, baby?" he mumbles as he pulls her back. She tries to wiggle out of his arms, but he holds her closer. She hears her phone ring again, and she moves to reach for her purse on the floor, but Chad doesn't let go.

"Stop," she whispers, the word so foreign and strange in her mouth. She thinks maybe he didn't hear her. She says it a little louder.

Chad laughs and pushes her down on the couch. "Yeah, right," he says, both hands under her shirt, pressing against her ribs, holding her in place.

"No, really," Amber says, the taste of fear in her mouth. "I'm not joking."

He pretends not to hear her. He pushes her shirt up until it is gathered around her neck like a noose.

Amber knows she must make a decision. To fight or not to fight.

She is so tired. She thinks today was not a good day to try to not be herself.

She thinks, *It doesn't count as rape if I give up.*

She thinks, *Different rules apply to different girls. Someone like me doesn't get to say no.*

"You guys!" Melissa yells, running up to Rosina and Grace in the hall after school. Sam Robeson follows, silky multicolored scarves trailing after her. "Stop everything you're doing and come with us," Melissa says.

"What's going on?" asks Grace.

Rosina doesn't need to know. She'll go wherever Melissa asks her to.

"We're going to the police station," Melissa says. "Like, right now. Lisa and Abby are already on their way."

"Numbers nine and ten have come forward, too," Sam says.

"Holy shit," Rosina says. "This is really happening."

"Did you ever get ahold of Amber?" Melissa asks.

Grace shakes her head. "I tried. She never answered."

"It's okay," Sam says. "Four girls is totally enough."

"We have to find Erin," Grace says.

"I already talked to her," Sam says. "She's not coming. She said she had something really important to do after school."

"What's more important than this?" Grace says.

"Probably just taking a shower and watching *Star Trek*," Rosina grumbles.

"I'm ready for you two to stop being mad at each other," Grace says.

"Let's go," Melissa says. "You can both ride with me."

ERIN.

Otis Goldberg's car is clean and tidy inside. Erin finds this acceptable, maybe even pleasing. She might be comfortable if she wasn't so anxious.

"Take a right here," she manages to say, though what she wants to do is open the door and jump out of the moving car.

"Okeydokey," he says.

"What is this music?" Erin says. "And who buys CDs anymore?" She realizes the words may have sounded rude. She reminds herself to work on this. This may have been something she would have asked Rosina to help her with, but not anymore.

"In answer to your first question," Otis says. "This is Muddy Waters, the greatest blues musician in history. In answer to your second question, I buy CDs because I can get them used cheap. All kinds of cool old music like this."

Erin likes the straightforward and logical way he structured the answer to her questions.

"It's the blue house on the left," Erin says. "Also, you are an excellent driver."

"Is that a compliment?" Otis says. "Did you just give me a compliment, Erin DeLillo?"

"I am capable of giving compliments," Erin says. "But I do it selectively."

"I am honored to have been selected."

Spot is the first one to greet them when they enter the house. He licks Erin's hand like he usually does, then he circles around Otis, sniffing. When he's made it all the way around, he licks Otis's hand too.

"Spot approves of you," Erin says. "He's a good judge of character."

"I'm honored again," Otis says, rubbing Spot behind the ears.

Then Mom bursts through the kitchen door and attacks. "Otis, it is so nice to meet you! May I take your coat? What is your project about? Oh, isn't that interesting! What do you think of Mr. Trilling? Erin thinks quite highly of him, and you know how demanding she can be, ha ha ha! I made snacks!"

Mom runs to the kitchen, leaving Otis and Erin and Spot in the living room.

"Let's get to work," Erin says. "I sit here. You can sit there."

Otis doesn't question her instructions. "Your mom is nice," he says as he sits down.

"She doesn't get out much."

"Here you go!" Mom sings as she enters the room with two plates. She sets one in front of Erin that has celery and carrot sticks and a small bowl of raw almond butter. The plate in front of Otis

has cheese and crackers. "All right then," she says. "Otis, do you need anything else?"

"No," he says. "Thank you."

"Mother," Erin says, "we are unlikely to get much work done with you hovering."

"Yes, of course. I'll be in the kitchen if you need anything."

"So what's up with the different snacks?" Otis says as soon as she's gone.

"I'm not supposed to eat dairy or wheat," Erin says, opening her laptop.

"What happens if you do?"

"Probably not too much if I just have a little right now."

"Oh. Do you want some?"

"Yes." She reaches over and counts out exactly half his crackers and slices of cheese, and puts them on her plate. She counts out half her carrot and celery sticks for him. "We can share this almond butter," she says. "But do not, under any circumstances, double dip."

"It's a good thing nothing had an odd number of pieces," Otis says.

"Mom knows better."

Otis is smiling in a way that Erin knows is not mean, but it still feels like he's laughing at her. Is it possible to laugh at someone in a friendly way? Erin wishes Rosina was here to ask, but she's probably out on a date with that cheerleader. This is how it starts, the loss of people. They start drifting away and they never stop.

Erin feels the little reminder she's been trained to feel, the internal voice telling her to try to act normal, to not say weird

things, to not get emotional. Along with this reminder is the realization that she cares whether or not Otis likes her. These are the kinds of feelings she's tried to eradicate, the insecurities and yearnings that only ever lead to pain.

This is too hard, this talking about snacks. Spot seems to agree, and licks Erin's hand.

"I already put together an agenda for this afternoon," Erin says, pulling up the document on her laptop. "To make sure we use our time most effectively and get the most done."

"Do I get to have any input?" Otis says.

Erin looks at him and blinks. "I'd rather you not."

"I'm pretty smart, you know."

"Usually teachers don't make me do group projects."

"I asked Mr. Trilling to make us partners."

"What?" Erin says, panic rising in her voice. "That's not fair. You can't go behind my back and make decisions for me like that. You can't just sneak around manipulating things. Why'd you do that?" Spot paws at her. He rubs his face against her leg.

"I'm sorry," Otis says. "I didn't know it would upset you so much. I just thought it'd be fun to do a project together."

"Why?"

"Because I like you."

"Why?"

"I don't know. Because you're smart and speak your mind. Because you're real. You're also not bad to look at."

Erin's anxiety is not gone, but it has changed shape. It is a nervousness she and Spot can live with, at least temporarily.

"Not bad to look at?" Erin says. "Is that supposed to be a compliment?"

"I thought you'd hate it less than if I said you're pretty."

Erin shoves a stack of cheese and crackers in her mouth. The salty crunch and creamy softness calm her. Mom's food theory is so wrong.

"Let's get to work," Erin says through the mass of crumbs in her mouth.

Erin is pleasantly surprised that Otis manages to stay on track for the next hour and a half. He is, indeed, smart. She might even say they work well together. There is no more talk of liking or prettiness. Confident that he will not be needed, Spot takes a little nap on the floor next to Erin's feet.

"We made really good progress," Otis says.

"I agree," Erin says, closing her laptop.

"So now what?" Otis says.

"Now what, what?"

"What are you doing right now?"

"After homework and before dinner, I watch an episode of *Star Trek: The Next Generation*."

"Can I join you?" Otis says. "I don't have to be home until dinner."

Erin narrows her eyes as she tries to think of a good reason why not. *Because that's how I've always done it* does not seem like an adequate reason. And maybe it wouldn't be so bad to sit next to someone besides Spot while she's watching it. It'll be like an experiment, she thinks. Another way to challenge herself.

"Fine," she says.

"Great!" says Otis.

Erin pulls out her phone and taps a few times.

"What are you doing?"

"I have an app on my phone that randomly generates numbers. That's how I choose which episode to watch."

"That's quite a system."

"It's so I can practice being comfortable with surprise."

Otis does that weird smile again, the one like he's laughing at her but in a nice way. "How's that working out for you?"

"Fine, thank you."

The number is one hundred seventeen. The episode is "The Outcast."

"What's wrong?" says Otis.

"Nothing," says Erin. "What makes you ask that?"

"Your face," he says. "You looked sad for a second."

Erin is not sad. She feels something, and maybe it was strong enough to do something to her face, even though she's not quite sure what it is. The thing is, this is one of her all-time favorite episodes. She is not sure she wants to share it with Otis Goldberg. She is not sure she is ready to let him see something she loves.

"Have you ever watched this show before?" she says.

"I think so," he says. "Maybe a couple of times on the Syfy channel or something."

"It is the greatest show ever on television."

"Okay."

"So don't talk during it."

"Okay."

"Try not to move too much either. It's distracting."

"Okay."

Erin finds the episode and presses play. She folds her legs and puts a pillow on her lap. She tunes Otis out as she enters deep space, as she joins the crew of the *Enterprise* as they encounter a genderless alien species called the J'naii, for whom sex and gender specificity are considered an abomination. To be male or female, to *want* someone who is male or female, is primitive, unevolved. The only right way to be is androgynous. Sexless.

But Soren, one of the J'naii crew members, is different. She considers herself female. She falls in love with Riker, the epitome of the human male. She is an abomination. She must be fixed. Riker can do nothing to save her. Their love is not strong enough. She is not strong enough.

Soren allows herself to be reprogrammed, to be turned back to "normal." She lets her people convince her that loving Riker was a sickness, that her gender was shameful, that sex was shameful. It is a mistake she vows to never make again. Better to be safe. Better to blend in. Better to keep her distance from the destructive influence of desire.

"Well, that was intense," Otis says as the credits start to roll.

"If you don't have anything nice to say," Erin says, "don't say anything at all."

"I liked it," he says. "I really liked it. You kind of look like that Soren character."

"Is that a compliment?"

"Yes." That infuriating smile again.

Erin forgets to look away. By the time she does, it's too late. They made what could be described as meaningful eye contact. For a moment Erin's chest simultaneously burns and feels caved in. For a moment she wishes Rosina were here. She wishes she could ask her what it is she's feeling.

"It's almost time for dinner," she says. "You should leave now."

As if on cue, Erin's mom bursts through the kitchen door. Was she listening this whole time?

"How are you doing, kids? How was the episode? Oh, looks like you enjoyed the snacks, ha ha ha. Otis, would you like to stay for dinner? No? Well, you're welcome any time. Really, I mean it. I really hope to see you again soon. Right, Erin? Honey?"

Mom is quiet just long enough for Otis to leave, then the verbal firing squad starts right up again. "He seems like such a nice boy. So glad you invited him over, sweetheart. I wish you would invite friends over more often. You know, I haven't seen Rosina lately. How's she doing? Do you think Otis is going to come over again soon? Oh, I really hope so. Honey, I'm so proud of you. You've been showing so much growth lately. You're taking a lot more chances socially and—"

"I ate cheese," Erin says.

"What?"

"I ate cheese and my stomach hurts so I'm going to skip dinner."

"Oh. Okay."

"I'm going upstairs now."

Strange feelings follow her, and they have nothing to do with

cheese. Missing Rosina. Memories of Otis's smile. The way his body threw off the balance of the couch, how Erin listed slightly toward him over the course of the episode, how when it was over they were only inches apart. How he said she looked like Soren.

Erin is due for her biweekly head shaving. Also a good time for a bath. She strips naked and stands in front of the bathroom mirror, watches the reflection of her long, thin fingers as she pulls the electric razor in careful tracks over her head, leaving a clean quarter inch of hair. When she is done, she looks at herself in the mirror. Maybe she does not hate what she sees. Maybe she does not blame the image reflected back at her for everything bad that has happened.

US.

"Ladies!" the cop at the front desk yells. "I need you to calm down!"

There are at least twenty girls crammed into the tiny waiting room of the Prescott police station. Without Margot there to take control of the situation, everyone is talking at once, trying to explain to the cop why they are there. No one's getting very far, especially Sam Robeson, whose theatrical bent has reached epic proportions; she seems to have slipped into a Shakespearean accent accompanied by dizzying hand motions as she attempts to lecture the clueless cop.

"It's a good thing Erin's not here," Rosina says to Melissa. "All this noise would kill her."

"Someone's got to do something," Grace says, to no one in particular.

"Um, hello?" Rosina says. "Maybe that someone is you."

Without giving herself time to talk herself out of it, Grace pushes her way to the front desk. She turns around and faces the crowd, raises her arms in the air until eyes start moving in her direc-

tion. "Hey, y'all," she says. "Can we quiet down a little?" To Grace's amazement, the room actually hushes and listens. "Unless anyone has any objections, I'm going to talk to the officer and explain what we're doing here. If I miss anything, please feel free to chime in, but I think we'll be more effective if one person handles most of the communication right now. Does that sound okay?"

There is a consensus of "Yes" around the room. Someone shouts "Go, Grace!"

Grace turns around. "How can I help you, young lady?" the officer says. He's already exhausted.

"We are here to report a rape," she says. "Several rapes, actually. We have proof. It's online. I can give you the website address to Spencer Klimpt's blog, where he basically confesses to—"

"Stop right there, honey," the cop says. "I'm going to have to call in the chief on this. You girls sit tight."

"Can't we talk to you?"

"No, I think this is really something for Chief Delaney." He hands a clipboard to Grace. "Will you have everyone sign this?"

"What is it?"

"We need a record of who's here if you want to file a formal complaint."

"Oh, okay." Grace takes the clipboard and starts working on getting everyone signed in. Rosina texts her mother that she can't come to work tonight. The room throbs with energy. The girls are electric.

"Yeah, hey, Chief," the cop says into the phone. "O'Malley here. Sorry to bug you. I have a couple of dozen girls here in the station who say they want to report a rape or something. . . . Something about a

website and that Klimpt boy, and I remember you said you wanted to handle anything concerning . . . Yeah, I know. . . . Sorry. . . . Yep. See you soon." He hangs up the phone, looks around the room, and sighs. "Chief Delaney is on his way. But it may be a while, so you probably want to make yourselves comfortable. I'm sure not all of you gals need to be here."

There are only two benches in the waiting area, so most of the girls sit on the floor. Grace confers with Lisa Sutter, Abby Steward, and the two other girls mentioned on the blog, to go over what they're going to say to the police chief. Some girls do homework. Others mess around on their phones. Rosina avoids repeated phone calls from her mother.

A buzzer rings as the door opens.

"Hey, everyone," says Elise Powell, who is soon tackled with a barrage of hugs by half the room.

"I can't believe your parents let you come," someone says.

"They don't exactly know I'm here," Elise says. "I'm supposed to be at the library studying."

"I can't believe parents still fall for that one," Sam says.

But Elise is not the only new arrival. A large, sheepish figure emerges behind her in the doorway. "Look who I found in the parking lot," Elise says.

Jesse Camp smiles and waves awkwardly. "Hi," he says. "I heard about what you guys were doing and I wanted to help. I thought I could come and give a statement about Spencer's character or something, since I've heard him brag about this stuff for years." He looks down. "I don't know," he says. "Do you think that could help?"

"Yes," Grace says, stepping over her friends on the floor to get to him. She puts her hand on his arm. "Of course that will help. Thank you for being here."

"They make a cute couple, don't you think?" Rosina whispers to Melissa.

"Does she like him?" says Melissa.

"She won't admit it, but yeah. She totally likes him."

Rosina's phone buzzes. "Dammit," she says. "This is like the tenth time my mom has called in the past twenty minutes."

"Maybe you should answer," Melissa says.

"Stop being so reasonable."

Rosina grimaces as she looks at her phone. "Here goes," she says, and she answers.

Melissa can hear Rosina's mom screaming. The words are unintelligible, but the anger behind them is clear. Rosina holds the phone away from her ear and winces. "She's threatening to throw me out if I skip work anymore," Rosina says.

"I'm sure she doesn't mean it," Melissa says.

"Oh yes she does," Rosina says. "She's been trying to get rid of me for years."

"Don't say that."

Rosina's eyes are suddenly shinier than usual. It's almost like they're wet. It's almost like there are tears forming.

"Mami," she says into the phone, her voice breaking slightly. "I'm sorry. It's an emergency. Please trust me." Then she hangs up.

Melissa reaches for Rosina's hand. They don't speak, but their fingers stay entwined, their shoulders pressed together, for the

next five long minutes, until Police Chief Delaney comes bursting through the door.

"Jesus," he grumbles at the mass of girls blocking his way to the front desk. "Is it a full moon or something?"

"Chief Delaney," Grace calls. "We're ready to make a statement, sir."

"Are you the leader of this?"

"No," Grace says. "We don't have a leader. I'm just helping to organize things a little."

"Well, isn't that noble of you," he mutters. "So you want to talk to me? Who else? I'm not taking all of you back into my office."

"It'll be me, Lisa, Abby, Juna, Lizzy, and Jesse."

"Jesse?" the police chief says. "Jesse Camp? Aren't you one of Prescott High's linebackers?"

"Not anymore, sir," Jesse says. "I quit the team."

"Might as well," he says. "This year's gone to shit anyway." He looks at his watch. "I'm missing the kickoff for this, you know? Seahawks versus the Patriots. You'd better make it quick."

Grace and the five others follow Chief Delaney to his office. Everyone else waits.

It is only twelve minutes before they come back out.

Chief Delaney makes it out the door before the waiting room full of girls has a chance to register that he's leaving. Grace, Jesse, and the handful of Spencer's victims emerge from behind the front desk. Tears are falling down Lisa Sutter's cheeks. Abby Steward's face is red with fury.

"What happened?" Elise asks.

"Nothing," Abby spits. "I knew this was a waste of time. I can't believe I let you talk me into this, Lisa. I fucking sat there telling him what Spencer did to me, and he wasn't even listening. He was reading Spencer's blog. He was fucking laughing."

"He said there isn't sufficient proof that the website belongs to Spencer," Grace says flatly. "And even if there was, there's nothing on there that's prosecutable."

"That's bullshit," Elise says.

"I told him I've heard Spencer talking about some of these girls," Jesse says. "But Delaney said it's just gossip. He said he couldn't arrest people based on rumors and the word of a bunch of disgruntled ex-girlfriends."

"'Disgruntled ex-girlfriends,'" Lisa sobs. "Like that's all we are. Like that makes everything we say useless."

The room is silent, seething. The air is made of teeth.

"He didn't even take a statement," Grace says in disbelief. "He said it wasn't worth it. He said it wasn't worth his time."

"So what now?" Rosina says. "He's just going to wait to do something until those bastards rape again? Or maybe someone has to die before he gives a shit."

"He's just trying to save his own ass," Melissa says. "If the police start looking back into what happened last year, they'll find proof that Delaney totally screwed up the case, maybe even on purpose. He'd be ruined."

"Fuck, you're right," Rosina says. "He's never going to be on our side."

The cop behind the front desk has mysteriously disappeared.

There is no one with any authority anywhere to be seen. Just a roomful of outraged girls and one boy. They are teenagers. They're just kids. They are not worthy of being listened to.

"Fuck it," Abby says. "No one cares. I don't care." And she walks out the door.

"I have to get home before my parents suspect anything," Elise says. She hugs Grace. "This isn't over. I'm not giving up."

Within minutes, the station is empty. Everyone is on their way home, where they will have to pretend today was any other day, where they will have to decide if it's worth it to keep fighting, where they will sit through dinner wondering what you're supposed to do when the person you ask for help says no.

Melissa drives Grace and Rosina home. "You did a really great job today," Melissa says as she pulls up in front of Grace's house.

"Not good enough, though," Grace says.

"That wasn't your fault," Rosina says. "That asshole made a decision to not help us before he ever set foot in the station."

"Yeah," Grace mumbles. "Maybe." But all the fight in her is gone. She's exhausted. She wants nothing more than to sit on the couch watching TV and eating ice cream out of the carton with her mom. She wants a world where that is enough.

ROSINA.

Rosina doesn't get out of the car when Melissa pulls up to her house. The sky has exploded into a full-on thunderstorm, and the car reverberates with the pounding rain. "I'm not going in there," Rosina says. "I'm running away."

"Don't you need more than your school backpack if you're going to run away from home?" Melissa says.

"Good point." Rosina leans her head back and closes her eyes. "I am so fucked."

"Maybe it won't be as bad as you think. Maybe you're not giving your mom enough credit." Melissa reaches over and takes Rosina's hand in hers. "It's going to be okay."

"You don't know that."

The car is full of the thick echoes of raindrops and the warmth of their bodies. Thunder shakes them, pulls them closer together.

"So, are you, like, gay?" Rosina says. "Or are you going to realize next week, 'Oh I was just experimenting, let's just be friends'? Because that would be really lame. Because the more I know you,

the more I don't want to be your friend. I mean . . . You know what I mean."

Melissa takes off her seat belt, leans over, and kisses Rosina. Not a peck. A long, slow, soft kiss. Not a friend kind of kiss at all.

"Rosina," Melissa whispers. "You are not an experiment."

It takes Rosina a few moments to open her eyes.

"Okay?" Melissa says.

"Okay."

"Call me and tell me what happens with your mom."

"Okay."

Rosina enters her house, floating. The usually irritating sight of Lola watching TV on her couch doesn't even bother her.

"Is Abuelita sleeping?" Rosina asks her.

"You owe me twenty bucks," Lola says.

"Hello to you, too."

"I had to watch her because you skipped work so my mom had to go in."

"Yeah, looks like really hard work."

Lola sticks out her hand. Rosina sighs and fishes in her wallet for a twenty. Normally, Rosina would fight, but she's saving her energy for Mami. Just one minute with a member of her family, and it's like Rosina's kiss with Melissa never even happened.

Rosina goes up to her room and waits. She doesn't bother trying to go to sleep because she knows Mami will wake her up as soon as she gets home from work. She picks the strings of her guitar softly for a few minutes, mindlessly experimenting with various chords and rhythms and patterns, until that mysterious force she cannot

name and never talks about seems to speak through her fingers, directing Rosina, making decisions for her. Thirty minutes later she is somehow playing the loose structure of a new song—three arpeggiated chords of a verse and another three of a chorus. She is humming the beginnings of a melody as she thinks about Melissa, about her lips, how Melissa seems to glow whenever she enters a room, how the light of her makes Rosina's shadows bearable.

But then *knock, knock, knock, knock.* Rosina's room shakes with Mami's fist on her door. Before Rosina has a chance to say "Come in," the door swings open and Mami barges in.

"What the hell were you doing that was so important?" she growls.

"I can't tell you," Rosina says. "I'm sorry."

"No," Mami says, shaking her head so violently Rosina thinks it might fly off. "That's not acceptable. You do not get to do that."

"I'm sorry" is all Rosina can think to say.

"Who do you think you are?" Mami says, marching closer. She grabs Rosina's guitar out of her hands and throws it on the floor. The wooden frame knocks and the strings chime dully as it hits the floor. Rosina's eyes go wide. Not her guitar. Anything but that.

But Rosina suddenly feels a strange calm. She stares at her mother's red, furious face, and she almost feels sorry for her, sorry for her angry, lonely life. What's the point of meeting her rage with more rage? What's the point of fighting someone who's always angry no matter what happens? Rosina could have dropped a plate on the floor. She could have been two minutes late. She could have killed someone. And Mami would still be the same kind of mad.

Rosina skipped work tonight and won't tell her mother why. She knows Mami has a right to be angry. But Rosina also has a right to own her decision. She accepts her mother's anger, but she does not have to fight it.

Rosina says nothing. She looks into her mother's eyes, her face blank, free of defiance, free of shame.

Mami is the one to look away first. "You make me sick," she spits. She spins around and walks out of Rosina's room. The door simply closes behind her because it is too light to slam.

Rosina's room is silent in Mami's wake. She picks up her guitar to inspect it for damage, and finds that it just needs a slight tuning adjustment.

Her instinct is to be alone. But there is something new, something stronger than instinct.

Rosina picks up her phone and calls Melissa. It's nearly midnight, but somehow she knows Melissa is still awake.

"Hey," Melissa says after two rings.

"I just had a fight with my mom. I don't want to talk about it."

"Oh, Rosina. I'm so sorry."

"It's actually kind of okay," Rosina says, confused by her own words. "I think."

"Yeah?" Melissa says. "That's great."

"Let's talk about something else," Rosina says. "Let's pretend nothing sad happened today."

"What do you want to talk about?"

"I just want to hear your voice."

"Oh, okay."

Silence.

When Melissa giggles, it feels like butterfly wings fluttering everywhere in Rosina's body, blowing the pain away.

"Say something," Rosina says.

"Do you want to come over to my house for dinner sometime?"

The butterfly wings stop fluttering. The butterflies are stunned stupid. "Like, with your parents?" Rosina says.

"Yeah."

"I'm supposed to say yes, aren't I?"

"I hope you say yes."

"Okay, yes," Rosina says. "But I'm a little terrified."

"It's okay to be terrified."

"I'm peeing my pants a little."

"You should probably get that checked out."

"What'd you tell your parents about me?"

"I told them you're awesome."

"Oh."

"I also may have told them that I kind of want you to be my girlfriend," Melissa says.

And that's it—there are now officially too many feelings to fit inside the confines of Rosina's ribs. Her heart explodes. She's a goner.

US.

Amber Sullivan is in Graphic Design, her best hour of the day. It's her chance to fool around on a decent computer and feel halfway good at something. Who knows what she'd be capable of if she actually had one at home to practice on.

Not only is this her best class, it is also her best seating arrangement. She is assigned to a computer right next to Otis Goldberg, who is usually on the other side of the school in the smart-kid classes, and who, at this point in her life, is the only person whose company Amber actually enjoys.

"What are you working on?" Otis asks her, as if she's an actual person.

"Oh," she says. "Um." He is the only boy she doesn't know how to talk to.

"That looks cool," he says, leaning sideways to better see her screen, his shoulder touching hers. "Is it animated?"

"Yeah," she says. She presses the button to start the animation. It's nothing, really. It took her fifteen minutes to create.

"Wow," Otis says, and he seems genuinely impressed. "How'd you do that?"

"It's really easy programming," Amber says. She switches to the screen where she wrote it.

"You wrote all that code? How'd you learn how to do that?"

Amber shrugs. "I guess I just taught myself."

"You're really talented," Otis says. "You could do this professionally if you wanted to."

Amber has to look away from his searing eyes. He's the only one who's ever told her she can do anything.

"Slut," Olivia Han fake coughs as she walks by, knocking Amber's computer with her hip.

"Shut up, Olivia," Otis says. "Not cool."

Olivia looks at Otis for a moment, dumbfounded. When has anyone ever stood up for Amber Sullivan? "Whatever," Olivia finally says, and walks away.

"You didn't have to do that," Amber says. "I'm used to it."

"That doesn't give her the right to do it," Otis says. "You don't deserve that."

The strange thing is, he actually seems to believe it.

The strangest thing is, for a brief moment, looking into Otis's eyes, so does Amber.

Someone sits in the desk designated for Adam Kowalski, but that is just the name on her birth certificate. Her real name is Adele now, but nobody knows it yet. *Just one more year*, she thinks, the mantra on a constant loop in her head.

She watches a group of girls in a huddle, whispering. Something yanks inside her chest, wanting to join them. She knows they're talking about the Nowhere Girls; that's all anyone talks about these days. She yearns to be a part of it, but would they even let her in? Is someone like her allowed? If she showed up to a meeting, would they scream at her to leave? What is her claim to womanhood if it isn't in her body?

Of course Margot Dillard has already finished the homework Mom picked up for her at school. She has already had an encouraging conversation with the dean of admissions at Stanford, who waxed nostalgic about her own trouble with the law protesting apartheid in the eighties. Certain that their daughter can do no wrong, Margot's parents are preparing to sue the school district over her suspension, and they have a very good lawyer.

Margot does not think about her great luck, about this privilege of being trusted. She is sitting in front of the mirror applying makeup. She replays the YouTube video about how to create a smoky eye, which she's already watched six times because of course it has to be perfect. She looks in the mirror and pouts out her plump red lips.

Sexy, she thinks. *Holy shit, I'm sexy.*

Trista's father installed a new doorknob on her door that locks from the outside. She can't come out except for once every two hours to use the bathroom. Mom brings her food and prays with her. After dinner the family has the incredible honor of being visited by Pastor Skinner. Trista is let out of her room to sit with him in the living room to talk about honoring her parents and the church.

As he drones on about respecting authority, Trista thinks about how she's been raised to always ask herself "What would Jesus do?" She says nothing to Pastor Skinner about how Jesus fought for what he believed in, how he stood up against corrupt people in power, how he showed women kindness and respect at a time in history when they received little of either. But that is not the Jesus who Pastor Skinner is talking about. In fact, the pastor isn't talking much about Jesus at all.

Trista is being held hostage, and that's not even teenage hyperbole. This is really, truly a hostage situation. But there's nothing she can do. She's a kid. She has no rights. Her parents get to decide what's right and wrong for her, even if they're wrong.

Elise Powell knows this suspension is supposed to be a punishment, but she's lying in bed with a grin on her face, looking at the ceiling and not feeling particularly guilty about anything. She already made it through the initial terror of her future being destroyed like Principal Slatterly promised—her parents' disappointment, getting kicked off the softball team, losing her scholarship to U of O. After their visit to the principal's office, as Elise explained her side of the story to her parents, she swears she saw her mom fighting a smile. Most important, they believed her. And when Elise called her coach in tears begging not to be kicked off the team, after a short pause and what sounded like a door closing, Coach Andrews whispered, "Don't tell anyone, but, girl, I am so proud of you. And I'm pretty sure my friends over at U of O will feel the same way."

But there is something even bigger than all that, something more unexpected and magical and earth shattering, something she

is happy to spend her weeklong suspension replaying in her head over and over and over again: She had a date. With a boy. A cute, awesome, wonderful boy.

Elise should maybe feel guilty that she skipped a Nowhere Girls meeting to hang out with Benjamin Chu, that she kept it secret. She should feel guilty about her priorities being skewed, about caring more about a boy than solidarity with her friends and the cause, how instead of joining everyone at that creepy old house on Saturday, she played video games with Benjamin in his den, how it was kind of hot and he kept apologizing for the thermostat being busted, how their glasses of lemonade were sweaty, how his upper lip was sweaty, how Elise was so distracted by wanting to taste the sweat on his lip that she kept dying in the video game in embarrassingly lame ways, how he teased her for it in a way that made her feel magnificent, how he looked in her eyes for so long he died too, how she barely registered the tiny voice in her head crying, "What about the strike?" as she leaned over and pressed her lips to his, how when they finally separated, he could barely open his eyes, how he mumbled through his dopey grin, "The strike is over?" and she said, "Don't tell anyone," and he said, "I can wait," and she said, "No way," and he said, "Are you sure?" and as she kissed him again, her body said *I'm sure I'm sure I'm sure I'm sure.*

Elise lies on her bed, remembering the salty-sweet lemonade taste of Benjamin Chu's lips. She thinks maybe she should be a little sorry, but mostly she thinks not. Because maybe the Nowhere Girls would be happy for her. Because maybe sometimes saying yes is just as important as saying no.

ERIN.

Erin doesn't know exactly what happened last night at the police station while she was at home with Otis, but clearly it was bad, and clearly the news spread to people who had no business knowing it. The three girls who came forward as being on Spencer's list all had their lockers vandalized by the time they got to school. Someone stuck a bumper sticker on Lisa Sutter's locker that said DUCT TAPE: TURNING "NO NO NO" INTO "MMM MMM MMM" SINCE 1942.

Principal Slatterly is on a rampage. Four new rent-a-cops have been hired to patrol the halls and lunchroom. Rumor is at least eight girls have received detentions or gotten suspended today so far, and it's only fourth period. Because of some list Slattery got from Delaney of who showed up at the station last night, she knows just who to target, and she certainly knows how to come up with bogus reasons.

Erin knows she should feel bad for them. She should regret not being there last night. Those would be the right things to feel. But she is too busy feeling something completely different.

And now, on her way to class, she has reason to feel that different feeling even more. There, at the other end of the hall, is Otis Goldberg getting something out of his locker. Something inside her jumps. It feels reptilian—a darting snake, a lizard flicking its tail. Before she even has a chance to think, Erin has what feels strangely like the beginning of a panic attack but also the opposite of a panic attack, which leads to the thought that maybe she would like to say "Hi, Otis" out loud, which would catch his attention, which would make him smile, which would cause him to walk toward Erin and talk to her, which would make Erin feel even happier because, Erin now suddenly realizes, as clear and unclouded as a perfect geometric proof, she likes him. She likes Otis Goldberg. She likes Otis Goldberg in a way that is different from and bigger than how she likes Rosina and Grace. She likes Otis Goldberg as something more than a friend.

But then she sees Amber Sullivan next to him, standing very close. Erin has spent years studying body language and personal space, and she knows Amber is standing closer than a friend is supposed to stand. Erin knows friends do not tuck stray hairs behind each other's ears. They do not rub their boobs on each other's arms.

Girls like Amber are the ones boys like. Girls with curves and smiles, with compliments and eye contact. Not weird androgynous freaks like Erin. Not girls who only know how to feel too much or too little.

So, just like that, as quickly as Erin discovers her feelings for Otis Goldberg, she vows to shove them away, to make them not exist. She can will herself to stop feeling. Her mind is stronger and more stable than the volatile and unpredictable chaos of her heart. Not the actual organ, of course, but the mysterious muck around it, the oddly placed

neural cells in the middle of her chest that connect to her brain and mysterious other things that cannot be observed or measured, the place in her body that feels panic and love and cannot tell the two apart.

Erin should have known better. She was not thinking like an android. She let feelings infect her. She was not doing what Data would do.

It is true that an android can get its wires crossed. It can perceive something without complete information and come to an incorrect conclusion, but these occasional inaccuracies should not lead to emotions, which may or may not lead to further conclusions that could lead to other, even stronger, emotions, and thoughts, and even actions, but then maybe another observation interferes with the first and throws the whole series of previous neural firings into question, and the wires get stretched and tangled and extremely uncomfortable, which may or may not lead to other, completely different, emotions, and everything turns into a big fat mess.

Erin wonders if this is a metaphor. Erin hates metaphors.

She just needs a little time, a little space. She will hide here behind this stairwell until the halls empty, until everyone is in class. She will use the silence to recharge herself. All she needs is a few minutes. She will be a little late for class, but she has weighed the pros and cons of that transgression and has come to the conclusion that it is more important that she be sturdy and in one piece than be on time for class.

There. Better. Otis and Amber are gone. Everyone is gone, even the ubiquitous security guards. It is now safe for Erin to emerge from her hiding place and make her way to class.

But then footsteps. A throaty laugh. Erin looks around to find

Eric Jordan at the other end of the hall, more tired and bedraggled than she's ever seen him. His sunken eyes are focused intently on her. His signature smirk has lost all charm.

"Stop looking at me," Erin says.

Eric laughs. "I know you don't mean that." He keeps walking. He gets closer and closer. "You like me looking at you, don't you?"

"No," Erin says.

"Even someone like you must have needs," he says, nearly upon her. She can smell the stale liquor on his breath, his unwashed body.

Erin knows she should run. She should get away. But she can't let him know she's afraid. She can't give him that satisfaction. She wants to hurt him back.

"Why are you even talking to me?" Erin says. "Now that you can't get any of the girls here to talk to you, you're talking to me, the school freak? You must be really desperate. How pathetic."

Then something crosses his face, something terrifying, a look of such rage and hatred, and for the moment Erin sees herself reflected in his pale eyes, she forgets she's even human. He is not looking at something human.

Erin feels the pressure in her chest and her feet leaving the ground as he shoves her across the hall and into the lockers. She feels a locker handle dig into the small of her back.

"Don't you dare talk to me like that." He spits the words in her face. She feels them stick to her skin.

"I can talk to you however I want," Erin says. She doesn't know where the words come from. Somewhere down deep, somewhere with the pain and memories and dark corners, but also with light that slices

through the shadows, somewhere where fear turns into courage.

"You think I need the bitches at this school to talk to me? You think I want to talk to them?" He is half laughing, half choking. He is verging on hysterical. "I don't want to *talk*. I don't want to talk to you. I can get what I want without talking."

He pushes her against the lockers with his left hand and grabs her crotch with his right. Through the thick denim of her jeans, Erin can feel his muscular fingers grabbing, tugging, trying to tear through her. It is not sexual. There is nothing sexual about it. He wants to hurt her. He wants to turn her into nothing.

She is back in Seattle. Casper Pennington's distant eyes look through her. She disappears under the weight of his body. She stops fighting. "No" may have never left her mouth, but her body said it. It is Casper who chose not to hear.

Erin cannot move even though all she wants to do is move. She cannot make him stop. She cannot scream. She cannot cry for help. This is what it is to be caught, to be powerless and frozen, to be turned into nothing. This is when your own body, your own voice, becomes your enemy, when it won't even listen to you because it's his now, because he's stolen it, because he controls it with your own fear.

First, you are an object. Then you are taken. Then you are destroyed and pounded into dust.

Then a sound down the hall, a walkie-talkie the security guards carry around. Eric lets go, but only part of Erin is free.

She doesn't look at him, doesn't look toward where the sound was coming from, doesn't look anywhere. She just runs. She moves so fast she can't think, she can't feel. She runs out the door and down the street,

and even though she isn't breathing, even though she forgot how, and her bones feel like breaking, and her veins feel like knives, and everything in the world wants to hurt her, everything in her body is a threat, her mind violent static, razor blades, glass, even though her entire existence is a war zone, she runs and runs and runs until she falls through the door of her house, until she lands on her knees, a pile of bruises and broken skin, until she finds the corner where there is at least one thing in the world that is sturdy, and she backs up against it, and Spot arrives, ears erect, just in time to hear the moan escape from Erin's broken-glass lungs, the sound like a whole soul deflating, a whole life imploding under the pressure of too much gravity, too much weight, elephant bones in a bird-girl's body, breaking, breaking, breaking.

This is what happens when feelings are stronger than will, when everything that was stuffed away explodes out of the shadows. This is what happens when the feelings win and Erin loses.

She is rocking with the pulse of a bigger heart, her body a metronome, the back of her head banging against the wall as it keeps time, one two one two one two, and Spot to the rescue, nudging Erin with his nose, trying to put himself between her body and the wall, trying to make himself a pillow. She needs impact, something touching, something pounding, something marking the violence of her body existing in this world.

Spot softens the blow with his body. He is a living, breathing cushion. But Erin is not done hurting, not done breaking. She hits her face with her own hand. She hits and hits and hits. She hurts herself because she has to, because everything hurts so much already, because it is the only way to change the hurt, to move it somewhere

else, so it will not swallow her up entirely. She has to fight, she has to fight something, and she is the only thing here to fight.

But Spot is there, his sharp teeth so gentle as he takes Erin's hand in his mouth and pulls it away, like a mother with a wandering puppy and the loose, trusting flesh at the scruff of its neck, and it is this tenderness that ultimately wins, not Erin's fighting herself, it is Spot wedging his eighty-plus pounds of dog into Erin's lap, on top of her arms so she can do no more damage, so her only choice is to hold him, to feel the comfort of his weight on top of her, to be silenced and stilled by a creature who is programmed to do nothing but love her.

And that's when Erin's mother walks through the front door with her arms full of groceries. In this moment Erin cannot reach the world outside herself, cannot hear the grocery bags fall to the floor, cannot hear the cracks and splats of the eggshells, cannot hear her mother cry, "What happened? What happened?" In this moment Erin is only vaguely aware of her mother's presence, and she knows nothing of the world inside her, the locked-up place where her mother is screaming too—helpless, powerless, tortured by love, as she kneels beside her unreachable daughter and knows there is nothing she can do to help. She knows she cannot touch her, cannot wrap her in her arms and rock her the way her instincts demand. And Erin cannot even consider that comfort in this moment, cannot see outside her body's dense world of pain, cannot comprehend that there is anyone in the world who wants to help her, that there is anyone in the world who can.

Spot starts to whimper. He cannot escape Erin's tight embrace. She won't let go. She can't. Her arms are vises that her mother has to carefully pry away.

ROSINA.

"Get over here right now," Mami growls as soon as Rosina enters the restaurant kitchen.

"I'm not even late!" Rosina answers. In fact, she's early. She didn't even put up a fight when Mami told her to come in an hour early to help deep clean the walk-in fridge.

"Your principal called me today," Mami says.

"What'd she want?" Rosina says coolly, despite the sudden panic in her chest.

"I don't know yet," Mami says, her eyes narrow, suspicious. "She left a message that she wanted to talk to me about something important. She said I could call her on her cell phone any time."

"So why didn't you call her?"

"I wanted to wait for you to be here."

"How nice of you," Rosina says, trying to act like the floor is not crumbling beneath her feet, like there is still ground for her to stand on. As Mami takes her phone out of her pocket to call Slatterly back, Rosina tries to look relaxed as she sits on a crate in

the corner of the kitchen, but she can barely feel her legs.

"Hello? Mrs. Slatterly?" Mami says. "This is Maria Suarez, Rosina Suarez's mother?"

As she watches Mami listen to whatever Slatterly's saying, Rosina thinks she may know, just a little, what crucifixion must feel like—being tortured, unable to move, victim to the whims of whoever's in power. With every uh-huh and yes Mami answers, her eyes fill with fire, they explode with rage and disgust, and Rosina shrinks, hardens, turns into ice.

"She wants to talk to you," Mami says, the words barely able to make it out of her clenched jaw as she shoves the phone in her daughter's face. Rosina stands up and lifts the phone to her ear, turns around and looks at a discolored patch on the wall, and wishes it could absorb her like so many years' worth of grease stains.

"Hello?" Rosina says.

"Hello, Miss Suarez," says Principal Slatterly with her fake sweetness. "How are you this afternoon?"

"Fine," says Rosina. She can feel Mami's eyes burning a hole into her back.

"That's good to hear," Slatterly says. "I'm going to be direct with you, honey. I'm worried about you. And I wouldn't be doing my job right if I didn't share my concerns about students with their parents."

"What'd you tell her?"

"I'm sure she'll tell you after we're done talking. But I wanted to talk to you directly about certain things I chose not to tell your mother."

Rosina waits. The silence nearly kills her. She knows Slatterly is purposely prolonging the torture, that she gets some kind of sick pleasure out of it.

"You know, Miss Suarez, I have nothing against you personally," Slatterly says. "I appreciate your independent spirit. In some ways, I even admire it. But the truth is, I'm under a lot of pressure to bring you and your friends' little club to an end." She pauses. "You have no idea what kind of pressure I'm under," she says with a strained, high-pitched voice. "No idea." For a moment Rosina fears that Slatterly's going to start crying. This is the voice of someone on the edge.

"I'll admit it," Slatterly continues. "I'm actually a little proud of you girls for how far you've taken this thing. But you've had your fun, and now I think it's time to put it to rest. Some things are better left alone. Am I clear?"

"I don't know what you're talking about."

Slatterly's heavy sigh blasts through the phone. "Miss Suarez," she says. "I didn't want it to come to this, but you've left me no choice." She pauses, and Rosina wishes she could see Slatterly's face right now so she could figure out what the pause is made of, if the tinge of remorse Rosina thinks she hears is real. "I'm aware that the immigration status of your grandmother is not—how should we say it—up to snuff?"

Everything in Rosina's body stops—her heart, her lungs, the blood flowing through her veins. Every cell inside her simultaneously surrenders.

"I know you wouldn't want to do anything that might get your

family in trouble. Maybe send the health department to your uncle's restaurant? All it would take is a call from a concerned citizen." Her voice is suddenly robotic, soulless. It is no longer a human saying these words.

Without thinking, Rosina turns around to see her mother, still standing there, staring at Rosina with that same fire in her eyes. Two women, poised to hurt her more than any man could. Rosina turns back around to face the wall. She is trapped.

"What do you think, Miss Suarez?" Slatterly finally says. "Do you want to make trouble?"

"No," Rosina whispers.

"You know, I could forget about all of this if you'd help me a little. If you'd tell me what you know about this Nowhere Girls group. Perhaps when and where the next meeting will be, who the leader is, what kind of plans they have in store. That information would be very helpful to me."

"I don't know anything," Rosina says. "I already told you that."

"Of course you did," Slatterly says.

Again, the agonizing silence.

"Well, I'm sure your mother is eager to speak with you," Slatterly finally says, way too cheerfully and way too fast, as if she is trying to end this conversation as quickly as possible, as if she is trying to convince herself it wasn't as bad as it really was. "The good news is, if you stay out of trouble, you have nothing to worry about. But you're on probation, Miss Suarez. One wrong step, and you're gone. Understood?"

"Yes."

"And of course, if you happen to remember something about your friends' little organization, I'm all ears. If the information is useful, I'll have no reason to pay such close attention to you anymore. All right? Wonderful. I'm glad we had this talk. Please tell your mother I say good-bye, and I hope you have a great weekend." Then Slatterly is gone.

"Drugs?!" Mami screams as soon as Rosina faces her.

"What?"

"The principal told me you're on drugs," she says, grabbing the phone out of Rosina's hand. "So that's where you've been sneaking off all the time. That's why you can't babysit. Because you're getting high? You're choosing drugs over your own family? I knew you were up to something, but not *that*. Even I didn't think you could sink that low."

"I haven't done a drug in my life!" Rosina says. "Slatterly doesn't know what she's talking about."

"She said you've been skipping classes. She said you've been hanging out with bad kids at school."

"Mami, you've met my friends," Rosina says. "You know they're not bad."

"What I know is that girls lie," Mami says. She steps forward, forcing Rosina up against the wall. "What I know is that you lie. You have been lying to me since the moment you could speak."

"Mami," Rosina cries. "I'm telling the truth. I'm not doing anything bad. I swear to God."

Mami grabs the front of Rosina's shirt and pulls it tight, catching Rosina's breath in her grip. "Don't you dare," she growls. "Don't

you dare talk about God. Don't you even utter His name."

Rosina can't speak. She can't breathe.

"One more call from the principal and you're gone," Mami says, almost calmly, which is so much worse than her rage. "I've had enough. This family has had enough. I am done being your mother."

When Mami lets go, Rosina stumbles against the crate and falls to the ground. Now that the noose around her neck has loosened, everything is bubbling up, all the tears she hasn't cried, and Rosina is sobbing, she is a heap on the floor, she is reaching for her mother's feet, crying "I'm sorry, I'm sorry," but all Mami does is look at her like she's a mangy street dog, too sick and dirty to love.

"Clean yourself up and get ready for work," Mami says.

Rosina looks up at her, face red and blotchy and drenched with tears. "Mami," Rosina says, forcing herself to meet her mother's eyes. "Please. I'm sorry. I love you."

For a split second, Rosina thinks she sees her mother soften, but just as quickly, it is gone.

"You make me sick," Mami spits, and walks away, and Rosina couldn't agree more.

ERIN.

The blanket on Erin is heavy, like those X-ray bibs dentists use. It is a special kind of blanket for people on the spectrum, like a hug for people who don't like to be hugged. She has spent most of the weekend under it, either reading in bed or dragging it downstairs to watch randomly generated episodes of *TNG*. She skips the ones with Wesley Crusher.

Erin has been nonverbal for two days. Mom has been trying to reach her all weekend. She's asked her repeatedly if something happened at school. She called Slatterly's office, but the principal never called back. She's made calls to Erin's doctor and therapist and specialists, even her old OT in Seattle. They have all told her to wait, to let Erin decide when she's ready to talk. But patience is not Mom's strong suit. Giving Erin space is not Mom's idea of fixing a problem.

Erin sat through dinner tonight, listening to Mom's desperate, tear-filled attempts to fill the silence. "Was it the bullies, honey? Did they say something? I thought they were leaving you alone this year. You haven't done this in so long. You've been doing so well. Is this a regression?"

Erin did not say answers to these questions out loud, but that doesn't mean she didn't have them. She was having a full dialogue with her mom in her head. *This is not about regression,* she thought. *I am not linear. I just hurt. I just want the world to be quiet.*

Erin thinks maybe she will start talking again tomorrow. Monday is always a good day to start over. But tonight she just wants to be in her room. She wants stillness. She wants silence. She wants to make herself solid again.

Her phone has been buzzing with calls and texts from Otis for the past half hour, so she turns it off, not reading or listening to any of his messages. She is employing her oldest and best defense—she is choosing not to care. The whales and waves of her noise machine sing to her. She is underwater, so deep the pressure would crush a normal human, but she is safe, boneless.

But just as she is drifting off to sleep, Erin hears something new, something close. Something real and here, not a recording, not an electronic buzz. A series of small taps at her second-floor window. A freak hailstorm? Kamikaze birds?

She opens the window and looks outside, hears rustling below, sees a shadowed figure in the shape of Otis Goldberg, arm raised in midthrow.

"Ow!" Erin says, rubbing her suddenly stinging forehead. "What was that?" These are the first words she's spoken since Friday. Since Eric.

"Oh, crap," Otis says. "Sorry. It was a rock."

"Why?"

"I need to talk to you."

"Why? How'd you know where my bedroom is?"

"Lucky guess. Can you let me in?"

"No," Erin says. "It's the middle of the night."

"Please."

"Good-bye."

"Erin, stop being difficult."

"You're the one throwing rocks at my head."

"Dammit, Erin!" Otis shouts. "I just got my freaking ass kicked." He fiddles with his phone, turns the flashlight on, and shines it on his face. He is bloody. His lip is cut. His right eye is swollen half closed.

Erin forgets everything she's thought or felt or decided about Otis since Friday afternoon. She forgets about Amber. She forgets about silence. She even forgets about Eric. She's not thinking about her parents, if they're still awake, if they will hear. The only thing on her mind is how fast she can get downstairs to let Otis in, how fast she can get him safe in her room, how fast she can help him stop hurting.

Spot follows Erin downstairs and stands beside her as she opens the front door. Otis is leaning against the wall of the front porch, holding on to his side. Erin stands there, frozen, looking at him.

"What do I do?" she says.

"Help me."

Erin takes one tentative step forward. One more. Spot nudges the back of her calf with his nose. She reaches out her hand and Otis takes it. She feels his warmth, his weight, as he puts his arm around her waist and leans on her. He flinches with each step as she guides him into the house and up the stairs. She wonders why this weight is scary but that of a heavy blanket is not.

"Don't get blood on anything," Erin says as she closes her bedroom door behind them.

Otis's laugh quickly turns into a grimace. "Ouch," he says. He unzips his jacket and pulls up the side of his T-shirt to inspect a bruise the size of his hand forming on his ribs. "Well, that doesn't look good." He collapses into Erin's desk chair.

"Don't move," Erin says, and runs out of the room.

She returns with a pile of wet washcloths and enough first-aid supplies for a small hospital. Without saying anything, Erin sits on her bed facing Otis. With slow and gentle hands, she commences to wash his blood away. Spot follows her lead, licking Otis's hand as it rests on his knee.

"Spot is a very empathetic dog," Erin says.

"I can see that," Otis says.

"Stop smiling," Erin says. "It's making your lip bleed more."

"Are your parents going to hear us and freak out? Because I don't think I can handle getting my ass kicked twice in one night."

"Their bedroom is downstairs on the other side of the house," Erin says. "So, we're fine unless you start screaming at the top of your lungs."

"Be gentle then."

Erin notices that she feels strangely comfortable with Otis in her room. She likes being so close to his face. She likes dabbing it with hydrogen-peroxide-drenched cotton balls, likes soothing his little twitches with antibiotic gel and pressing Band-Aids on his warm skin. She likes the silence and the stillness of this touching, how it feels like they are talking even though no one except the noise-machine whales are saying anything.

"This is trippy music," Otis says.

"It helps me relax," Erin says.

"You're pretty good at this. Have you thought about being a doctor?"

"Doctors have to talk to people."

Erin leans back and admires her work. All cleaned up, Otis's face is starting to resemble its usual symmetrical self again, at least as much as it can with a quarter of it swollen.

"Are you going to tell me what happened?" Erin says.

"I was wondering when you'd ask me that."

"I was busy taking care of you."

"Does that mean you care about me?" Otis says with a smile so big it makes both of them flinch.

"Stop smiling," Erin says.

"Since you're dying to know, I'll tell you."

But Erin doesn't know if she wants him to. She's enjoying this too much. This being with him in the silence. This bubble of stillness before the bad news.

"I went to the Quick Stop," Otis begins. "I wasn't thinking. It was like ten o'clock and I just finished writing that big paper for Ms. Eldridge's class, and I was fiending for a bowl of Honey Nut Cheerios, which is like my favorite late-night snack. Do you like Honey Nut Cheerios?"

"I don't know," Erin says. She can't remember the last time she had them. "Do Honey Nut Cheerios have anything to do with why your face got smashed?"

"We were out," Otis says. "So I decided to walk to the Quick Stop to get a box."

"At ten o'clock at night."

"Yes. Like I said, I needed them. Desperately. You don't understand my relationship with Honey Nut Cheerios."

"That's weird."

"So I walk through the door, but I guess the doorbell dinger thing was broken, because no one noticed I was there. The place was empty except for Spencer Klimpt behind the counter. And guess who else was there? Eric Jordan. And they were talking all serious, so my detective instincts took over and I knew I had to listen to what they were saying."

"Why do you have detective instincts?" Erin says.

"I'm going to be a journalist when I grow up. I like asking questions and making people uncomfortable."

"Oh."

"They were talking about a girl named Cheyenne who lives over in Fir City, and it sounds like—" Otis pauses. He looks Erin in the eye. She does not look away. "It sounds like they did the exact same thing to her that they did to Lucy." Otis looks away before Erin does. "I don't know if I can say it out loud."

"You have to," Erin says.

Otis takes a deep breath, looks up. Spot licks his wrist. "I remember Spencer's exact words," he says. "He said she should feel lucky they even wanted her. Then Eric said she just laid there." Otis looks like he's going to be sick. "Eric said he likes it better when they fight a little."

Erin realizes she's holding Otis's hand.

"Then Eric started complaining about how Spencer always gets

to go first, how he wants to go first next time. Like they're planning a next time. And then Eric started talking about Ennis and asking Spencer if he thought Ennis was going to tell, how he never should have been a part of it, how he's a pussy and they can't trust him. But that's when I fell over where I was sort of crouching in the cereal aisle, and I knocked some boxes off the shelves."

"Oh no," Erin says.

"Oh yes."

"Then what happened?"

"Spencer said something like, 'What do you want?' and Eric said, 'Oh, shit, do you think he heard us?' and then I just sort of ran away."

"You sort of ran away?"

"I ran away."

"But they caught you."

"Eric did. I was running, but I'm not a very fast runner, and he's, like, a football player. I heard him coming and then I just felt myself getting pulled back by my jacket. And then I was on the ground and he was punching me. He kicked me in the stomach. I didn't even fight back."

Erin dabs Otis's tears with a cotton ball.

"I begged him to stop and he just laughed at me. And in that moment I think I knew, just a little, what it felt like to be Lucy. To be Cheyenne."

And me, Erin thinks. And then she's crying too. And Spot is frantic, his face snapping back and forth as he tries to lick them both.

"Then Eric stood up, like totally calm," Otis says, wiping his

nose with his sleeve. "He said I'd get worse if I told anyone what I heard. And then he spit on me and walked away."

"You need to tell the police," Erin says.

"Yeah, right," Otis says. "Like they'll believe me. We both know they're not going to do anything. Eric's dad plays poker with the police chief. And weren't they, like, in Desert Storm together or something?"

"Why'd you come here?"

"I don't know. I feel safe here. With you."

"That's ridiculous."

"I'm okay with that."

"Why are you looking at me?" Erin says. "Do I have snot coming out of my nose? I'm not good at crying."

"I just like looking at you."

"You're ridiculous."

"I know."

"I can't breathe," Erin says. "I think I'm having a heart attack."

"You're too young to have a heart attack."

"But it hurts," Erin says. "Here." She puts her hand over her heart.

Otis puts his hand on top of hers.

"It's my fault you got hurt," Erin cries. "Because of the Nowhere Girls. Because I'm one of the people who started it. If we hadn't started it, you wouldn't have gotten hurt."

Otis smiles. "Just when I thought I couldn't like you any more."

"What?"

"I do."

Erin's trickle of tears turns into real sobs. She covers her face with her hands. "But you're so ugly!" she cries. "I'm sorry. That's not what I meant. You're not ugly. Your face is. No, wait—"

"I think you're beautiful," says Otis.

Erin stands up and starts pacing the room, Spot following close behind. She needs an anchor, something familiar and soothing to counter all this weirdness. "Have you ever thought about how deep-space travel like on *Star Trek* is similar to deep-ocean exploration?" she says. "It's all about going where no one's gone before, finding new life-forms, and expanding our knowledge. Did you know that less than five percent of the ocean floor has been explored? Did you know that we know more about the surface of the moon than we do about the seafloor? Did you know that there are whole ecosystems down there that don't rely on the sun, like all the energy comes from chemicals that come through hydrothermal vents, and there are six-foot-tall tube worms that live around them, where the water's like eighty degrees Celsius, and there are copepods that eat chemo-synthetic bacteria, and eels and crabs that eat *them*, and what this all means is there could be life on other planets, maybe even intelligent life, that isn't based on photosynthesis." Erin stops pacing. Otis and the weirdness are still here. "Wait, what are you going to tell your parents?"

"I'll say I fell off my bike riding to the store."

"They'll believe that?"

"Sure."

"Your parents must not be very smart people."

"Erin?"

"What?"

"Did you hear me say you're beautiful?"

She starts pacing again. "You only have one eye right now," she says. It is a shiny brown rock sprinkled with light.

"What do you think about that?" Otis says.

Erin's hands flap wildly. "This is who I am. You think this is beautiful?"

"Don't you?"

Erin stops. She looks Otis straight in the eye. "You're delusional."

"That's entirely possible." Otis stands up, facing her.

"Why are you standing up? You're hurt. You're supposed to be sitting."

He doesn't say anything. He just looks at her that way he does, his face so open, so not afraid of any of the things Erin finds so terrifying.

"I'm not a project," Erin says. "You're never going to change me. I'm never going to be normal. I'm autistic. I want to stay autistic."

"I don't want to change you."

"Then what do you want?" she shouts. Spot presses his body against her legs.

Erin doesn't understand what's going on. Why is Otis looking at her like this? Why is he being so nice to her? Why are they standing face-to-face like this? She doesn't know what she's supposed to say now, what she's supposed to do with her body, if she's supposed to look him in the eyes, and if so, for how long? Most of all, she doesn't understand why Otis likes her, why she likes him, why all this is happening when she promised herself she'd never let it.

"Do you want me to leave?" Otis says gently.

"No. Yes. I don't know," Erin says. She takes a deep breath. She sits down on her bed. "I need space. Sometimes I just need space."

"Whatever you want is okay."

"If I ask you to leave, it doesn't mean I don't like you."

"Okay."

"Because I do," Erin says. "Like you."

"I like you, too."

"Okay."

"Okay."

"Now will you leave?"

It is after midnight when Otis sneaks back out of the house. Erin knows she will not sleep tonight. She knows there is no hope of guessing what Data would do in a situation like this.

She texts Rosina and Grace: EMERGENCY! Cancel all after-school plans. We need Grace's parents' car.

Erin turns off her whale songs and gets on the computer. She has work to do. This is no time for being underwater. This is no time for being mad at her best friend. Some things are just too big to be afraid of.

ROSINA.

It's Monday, and Margot, Elise, and Trista are back from suspension, and everybody's treating them like war heroes, even though all that happened was they basically got a vacation from school. Margot's prancing through the halls like she's an even bigger deal than she thought she was before, Elise can't stop smiling and giving high fives, and even little Trista (hair stripped of purple and back to its natural brown) looks like she's walking taller.

Rosina knows she should be happy for them. She should be happy for all the Nowhere Girls, including herself. Slatterly was trying to send a warning with the girls' suspensions, but it totally backfired. They're martyrs now, proof of the cause's righteousness. The Nowhere Girls are more popular than ever. It's like no one's even scared of Slatterly anymore.

No one but Rosina. Fearless, fierce Rosina. She wants to punch the irony of this in its face.

Rosina has no more chances. Apart from school and her shifts at

the restaurant, she is on house arrest. If she gets in any more trouble at school, she will be expelled. If she gets in any more trouble, period, she is no longer her mother's daughter. That's what Mami said: *No serás mi hija.* Rosina's fought the world so hard, she fought her way out of her family.

She fell asleep in Abuelita's bed last night, unsure whether her grandmother heard the latest screaming match with Mom, if she had any idea what it was about, if she knows what Rosina's been accused of, or if she slept through the whole thing. All Rosina knows is Abuelita's skinny arms held her close as she cried, her frail body surprising with its warmth. She shushed Rosina to sleep like a baby, calling her Alicia, her dead daughter's name.

There is no fucking way Rosina is letting anyone at this stupid school see her cry right now. She punches a locker with her fist. Her eyes dry up as her knuckles burn.

"What'd that locker do to you?" she hears Erin say behind her.

Rosina sucks up the pain and spins around. Erin immediately shoves a stapled stack of papers in her face.

"I need you to review this packet by the end of the day," Erin says.

"I thought you weren't talking to me," Rosina says.

"I am calling a temporary cease-fire."

"Wait a minute," Rosina says. "First tell me what's going on. What the hell was that text about last night?"

"No time," Erin says. "I'll explain on the car ride there."

"On the car ride where?"

"Fir City."

"Why do you want to go to Fir City?"

"Read the packet."

"I have to be at work at five," Rosina says. "I can't get in trouble anymore."

"This is more important than work," Erin says. "We have to help Cheyenne."

"Who's Cheyenne?"

"A girl that Eric Jordan and Spencer Klimpt raped two nights ago."

"Shit," Rosina says. "No. You're lying. This can't be happening." But Rosina knows Erin does not lie.

"Otis Goldberg overheard them talking about it at the Quick Stop. Then Eric Jordan beat up Otis Goldberg. Then Otis Goldberg told me about it. Then I texted you and Grace. Then I stayed up all night making this packet."

Erin keeps talking as Rosina lets this sink in. She is numb because there is too much to feel.

"Cheyenne Lockett. Sophomore at Fir City High School, Fir City, Fir County, Oregon. Address is Eleven Temple Street. Here is a map and driving directions." She flips a page. "Here is a synopsis of an article on how to best talk to a victim of sexual assault." She flips to another page. "Here is a bulleted list of information we need in order to build a rape case that is so solid even the most apathetic and corrupt cop can't ignore it."

"I can't," Rosina says. "I can't go after school."

Erin looks at her. Blinks. "You are not Rosina," she says. "Rosina would never say that. If you see the real Rosina, tell her to meet Grace

and me in the parking lot immediately after school." Then she turns and walks away.

Erin is right, Rosina thinks. She is not the real Rosina. She is someone who needs a home more than she wants to help people. She is not brave. She is not a hero.

She is scared. She is so fucking scared.

AMBER.

Mom's new boyfriend spent the night again.
Amber wakes up to the sound of him pissing in the toilet, which
is about a foot away from her head, with only the thin trailer-wall
partition between them. The length of time and the heaviness of
the stream makes Amber think last night was at least an eight-drink
night for each of them. She has this shit down to a science.

She doesn't take a shower because she doesn't want to chance
seeing him in the hall again wearing only a towel. So far, all he's
done is look, but she knows where those looks lead. He's no different from the others. A couple of weeks of looks, then a couple
of weeks of comments when Mom's not in earshot, then luckily by
then they're usually gone. But if they last much longer, their comments turn into touches, into grabs. And that's when Amber starts
looking for other places to sleep. It's hard to say if those other places
are much better. But at least they're her choice.

The suspended girls are back and the school is practically throwing them a parade. But it's not like anyone in that weird club has

done anything besides sit around and talk about how much they're changing the world, even though nothing's really changed. They're all patting themselves on the back for nothing. The only reason they think things are different is because they haven't been hanging out with the boys. They're going to be real disappointed when they end their stupid sex strike and find out guys are still assholes.

Except for one. But he's not at school today. The seat next to Amber in Graphic Design is empty.

She's supposed to be working on her midterm project, but she's online looking up Web design classes at Prescott Community College. She always figured she'd start waitressing full-time at Buster's like Mom as soon as she graduated, but maybe there are other options. Like maybe she could work part-time and get student loans to pay for college. Maybe she could find a roommate and a cheap apartment. Maybe there are possibilities she hasn't even thought of yet.

Otis Goldberg told her she was good at computers. She's better than *him* even, and he's one of the smartest kids in school. No one's ever told Amber she is good at anything, except for the things she's not exactly proud of being good at.

Amber's started thinking about other things, too. Like maybe that Chad guy can be the last guy she ever sleeps with on the first date. She thinks maybe she can decide if she likes a guy *before* she has sex with him, not after.

Sometimes she walks by Otis's house, just hoping he'll happen to be in the front yard and she can talk to him outside of school, outside of everybody looking at her the way they do. She wants to know what it feels like to have only him looking at her, as if his look

could change her, as if it could tell her who she really is. There must be something like Cinderella's glass slipper for Amber, something that could transform her in an instant and sweep her away from this life she inherited in a cruel twist of fate—if only she could make it fit. Otis's desire could save her. His desire could turn her into a princess. All she has to do is be wanted by the prince.

People think Amber's dumb, but she knows some things about people. Like how they get used to the way people look at them, how someone starts it and then everybody follows, and then before you know it, everybody looks at you that way, including yourself, and no one can remember where it started, and no one cares, and there's nothing you can do about it.

But then maybe someone looks at you a little different. And maybe you start thinking you can be someone beside who you've always been, ever since Uncle Seth started looking at you when you were ten, when his eyes traced your body and told you who you are—not a princess anymore, not someone allowed to dream—when he started to do more than look, and then that's all anyone ever did, all they ever wanted, and you were branded, like your body was made out of red flashing lights that told everybody the one thing it was good for, and their eyes told you who you are, and their eyes told your story.

But then one day, you stopped to think, *What do I want?* You stopped to think, *Maybe I can tell my own story.*

The only reason Otis Goldberg would ever miss school is because he's sick. He's that kind of person. So here Amber is now, ringing the doorbell of his house. She's supposed to be in third period, but who is she kidding? Amber is not the kind of person

whose life is going to be changed one way or another by how well she does in Math Fundamentals.

Otis will never know how much he's done for her, but she can thank him. If he's sick, she knows she can make him feel better. She knows she can't do many things, but she can do that.

The door opens and Amber almost screams.

"Oh," Otis says through cracked, bruised lips. "Hi, Amber."

One of his eyes is swollen completely shut. He's holding an ice pack on his side.

"I fell off my bike," he says. "I'm not very coordinated."

"I thought you were sick," Amber manages to say. "I came to see how you were doing."

It's hard to tell if he smiles, because his mouth can't move much. But Amber thinks she sees it in his one good eye, the way it crinkles at the side.

"Do you want to come in?" he says. "I'm watching a documentary about squid."

His house is nice. It's like TV-show nice. It's obvious a real family lives here. Amber sits by Otis on the couch, and he doesn't even seem to notice that she chose the spot in the middle, right next to him.

"Where are your parents?" she says.

"Both at work," he says. "It was nice of you to come check on me."

"I was worried about you." Amber scoots closer so their legs are touching. She stares at him, waiting for him to meet her eyes so she can give him *the look*, but his eyes are on the TV.

"I never realized the ocean was so cool," he says. "My interests have always been with history and current events and figuring out why

people do things, but I guess science can be pretty fascinating too."

"Oh, really?" Amber says. Guys love it when you act interested in what they're saying.

"Yeah, like this Humboldt squid is supposed to be as smart as a dog. And it doesn't even have a spine!"

Otis is different, yes. But he is still a boy, and as far as Amber knows, he is a boy who likes girls. He speaks the language of boys. It is a language Amber knows. It is the thing she does well. People act like this is something to be ashamed of. But when you get right down to it, everybody's playing the same games.

Amber leans over Otis and grabs the remote control from the side table. She presses her breasts against his chest, just briefly, just long enough to make him gasp. She turns the TV off. She places her hand softly on his unbruised cheek. "Does it hurt?" she whispers.

He opens his mouth but no sound comes out. His eyes are wide. He is still trying to figure out what she is doing. Amber thinks he must not be used to girls like her, girls who speak his body's language, girls who know what he wants.

She leans in closer. She can feel his chest breathing against hers. Amber's lips are close to his ear, her hand on his knee, his thigh, inside, higher. She knows exactly what boys want. What men want. They have taught her.

"Stop," he says, springing up so quickly Amber falls backward on the couch. "What are you doing?"

"I like you, Otis," she says. "Don't you like me?" She reaches for him but he backs away.

"As a friend," he says. "I like you as a friend. That's it."

"I can be more than a friend."

"I'm not interested in you that way, Amber."

"It's okay, Otis," Amber says. "It's not like I need you to call me your girlfriend or anything. We can have fun, that's all. We can have a good time."

Otis tries to back away, but his legs knock against the coffee table. He is trapped.

"I'm in love with someone else," he says. "I don't want to be with you."

Amber sees something dark in his eyes. He is looking at her like she never thought he could—with pity.

"Who's the lucky girl?" she says. She can feel herself harden. She can feel herself turn. She is becoming the other Amber—the bitch, the one everyone hates.

"Erin DeLillo," he says, with a completely straight face.

"You can't be serious," Amber laughs.

"I am very serious."

"So that's your thing, then?" she says. "Some guys like big tits, some guys like black girls. I guess your thing is retards."

"Don't you dare call her that," he snaps. "She's smarter than both of us combined."

"No, it's cool. I get it. I'm not your type. You can only get it up for retards."

"What is wrong with you?" The look on his face reminds Amber who she is, who she's always been, who she always will be. Amber was wrong about Otis. He's nothing special. He's just like the rest of them.

"Leave," he says. "You need to leave right now."

She feels a sick satisfaction as she walks away, a comfortable inevitability settling in her stomach. The universe is in order. She knocked him off his pedestal. He's no prince. He's no different from the others, the innumerable, uncountable others. He is one more who says "What is wrong with you?" and looks at her with disgust and tells her to leave.

Amber doesn't bother closing the front door behind her. She keeps walking even though she doesn't know where she's going.

Amber can't believe how stupid she was. How stupid to think things could change, that someone like Otis could like her, that she could ever be friends with those girls, that there was a place for her in their stupid secret club. Fuck Erin for getting the only good guy in the school, and fuck her little weirdo friends. Fuck that Mexican dyke and that fat bitch Grace, who thinks she's so smart. Fuck Grace for tricking Amber into coming to that meeting. Fuck those girls for starting this whole thing in the first place.

If things had just stayed the way they were, Amber never would have made a fool of herself with Otis. She wouldn't have even considered it. She would have just kept doing what she was doing. Maybe it wasn't perfect, maybe it wasn't a great life, but at least she didn't think about it, at least no one told her the lie that she deserved better. Amber never should have been so stupid to believe it.

That's the worst part. Being tricked into hope, and then having it stolen away.

It's those girls' faults. Amber wants them to hurt. She wants them to hurt as much as she does. And she knows just what to do to make them hurt.

GRACE.

Grace barely got any information out of Erin at lunch before the security guard broke them apart. Something about Otis overhearing Spencer and Eric at the Quick Stop. Something about a girl in Fir City who needs their help.

Before Grace knew even that much, when all she had was Erin's middle-of-the-night text message to go on, she told Mom she needed the car after school because she had to help a friend. It would have been so easy to tell her then, to tell her everything, but that would make Mom complicit. It could ruin her. So Grace looked Mom in the eye and said she couldn't tell her why she needed the car. She said, "I need you to trust me."

Mom looked in her eyes for a few moments and then nodded. She didn't ask any questions. Who knows what was going through her mind, what she thought Grace could be doing. Helping someone move? Driving a friend to a clinic for an abortion? What could possibly be so serious to warrant a secret, but also her permission?

God, Grace prays. *Please don't let me abuse her trust. Please let this be worth it.*

It's the middle of sixth period and Grace can't sit still. She's wandering the halls carrying her Spanish class hall pass—a nearly two-foot-long rubber chicken with "El Pase de Pasillo de Señor Barry!" written on it in blue Sharpie.

When she turns the corner into the main hall, she sees two policemen walking through the front door in full cop regalia—bulletproof vests, walkie-talkies, billy clubs, Tasers, guns. Grace watches, frozen, as they enter the main office, then walks quickly to catch up as soon as they're inside. She leans against the wall next to the open door so she can see the front desk, just barely, without them seeing her.

"Oh my," says Mrs. Poole. "How may I help you, officers?"

"We're looking for three students, ma'am," one of them says. "Rosina Suarez, Erin DeLillo, and Grace Salter. Is there a way you can get them all down to the office quickly?"

Grace thinks she's going to throw up.

"Of course," Mrs. Poole says. "Let me just call in Principal Slatterly. I'm sure I can guess what this is concerning."

"I'm sure you can."

Grace has never run so fast in her life. She is suddenly fifty pounds lighter; she is pure speed as she makes her way to Rosina's sixth-period chemistry class. She takes a moment to collect herself and catch her breath, to put on her best invisible-girl face, then she tosses the rubber-chicken hall pass aside, knocks, and open the door.

"Hello, sir?" Grace says, with the question in her voice Erin

hates. "Um, Principal Slatterly wants to see Rosina Suarez in the office?"

"Why doesn't that surprise me?" the teacher says. "Miss Suarez, you heard her. You're wanted in the office."

Rosina stands up displaying her usual confidence, but with a questioning look on her face meant only for Grace.

"You might want to bring your bag," Grace says.

"What's up?" Rosina says as soon as the door closes behind them.

"We have to get Erin," Grace says. "Do you know where her class is?"

"Yeah," Rosina says. "But are you going to tell me why?"

"No time," Grace says as she scuttles down the hall.

"Wait," Rosina says. "Are we skipping class? I can't skip class anymore. There's just one period left. Can't this wait an hour?"

"No. We have to go now. Trust me."

Rosina stops. "I can't get in trouble anymore."

Grace turns around. "Rosina, the police are here. They're looking for us. Skipping class is not your biggest problem right now."

Rosina's eyes go wide. "Oh, fucking shit fuck," she says.

They run.

Rosina goes to get Erin out of class while Grace hurries back to Spanish. "I have to go, Señor," she pants as she grabs her backpack. "It's an emergency."

"En Español!" he shouts.

"Adios!" Grace says as she hurries out the door. She hears him yell, "Dónde está mi pase de pasillo?" as the door swings closed behind her.

"I'm dead," Rosina says when Grace finds her and Erin in the parking lot. "This is the end of me. As of now, I am most likely homeless."

"Did you read your packets?" Erin says as they climb into Grace's mom's car.

"Wait," Grace says. "First you need to tell us exactly what happened."

As they drive out of Prescott, Erin tells them, in excruciating detail, all about Otis coming to her house, what he said he heard, what Eric did to him. When she is done, Rosina and Grace are both speechless for a long time. It sinks in what they are about to do: They are going to try to help a girl Spencer and Eric raped, a real girl, a girl who is here right now, hurting right now. Not Lucy. Not someone already gone. Not someone hypothetical. This is someone they're going to have to look in the eyes, someone they're taking a kind of responsibility for. If they don't do this right, they could hurt her, too.

"This is too much," Rosina finally says. "I can't do this."

"What are you talking about?" Grace says. "This is our chance to finally get those bastards. We finally have proof."

"This girl isn't *proof*," Rosina says. "She's a person. A person who just got fucking raped. What if she doesn't want anything to do with us? We can't force her to talk to the cops. We don't even know her. What if she doesn't even want our help?"

"But what if she does?" Erin says softly from the backseat. "Maybe she's all alone right now. Maybe she's scared and thinks there's no one to help her. Maybe she's waiting for us."

The car is quiet. After a moment Rosina turns around to face Erin in the backseat. Grace can't see what is happening between them, but she can feel it.

Finally Erin speaks again: "We have to at least let her know we're here, that we believe her. We have to let her know someone's on her side. Then she can decide what she wants to do."

ERIN.

It takes exactly forty-two minutes to drive from Prescott High School to Cheyenne's town of Fir City, which is approximately half the size of Prescott. "We're in the country now, boy," Rosina says with her fake redneck accent. Erin hates it when she does that.

The sky is gray and low with clouds. Erin remembers something she read about how the Willamette Valley is one of the worst places in the world for people with chronic migraines because of something to do with its unique barometric-pressure system. Erin wishes she knew more about barometric pressure. She wonders if, had she grown up here instead of by the beach, meteorology would have been her interest instead of marine biology.

Rosina tells them they're entering white supremacist country. "This is where all the survivalist crazies live," she warns. "And they have machine guns."

"I'm sure not everyone out here's like that," Grace says. "That's like saying everyone from the south is racist."

During the drive, Erin quizzes Rosina and Grace on the instructions she prepared about how best to talk to a rape victim. She's moderately confident that they have the most important things down—don't push her to share anything she's not comfortable with, don't criticize or judge her, don't get too emotional, don't touch her, don't try to fix her, don't make it about you and your experiences, don't tell her what to do, don't pressure her to report it if she doesn't want to.

"What if we forget one?" Rosina says. "Is that going to screw her up forever? Is the fact that we have no idea what the hell we're doing going to add to her trauma? What if we make things worse?" She shakes her head. "You guys, I don't think I can do this."

"Of course you can," Grace says.

"Aren't you supposed to be the brave one?" Erin says. Rosina is always the brave one. She's always the one who knows exactly what to do.

"But I'm not," Rosina says. "It's just an act. It's always been an act."

Erin wonders what's gotten into Rosina, why she's acting so un-Rosina-like. All this Nowhere Girls business has turned everything upside down, has turned each of them into their opposites— Rosina's scared, Grace is brave, and Erin is skipping class to do something spontaneous and possibly dangerous, and she's not even all that anxious. She hasn't had to count backward at all today.

"But that's exactly what being brave means," Grace says. "Doing something even when you're scared."

"You make it sound so easy," Rosina says. "You do know that

people out here are just waiting to shoot people like me, right? Hello? I'm brown *and* gay."

"We're almost there." Grace turns into a cul-de-sac of small ranch-style homes. "It should be on the left," she says. "There. The white one." She pulls up in front and turns off the engine. No one moves.

"What the fuck do we do now?" Rosina finally says.

"She's probably not even home from school yet," Grace says. "Should we just wait out here until we see her?"

"That feels creepy," Rosina says. "Like we're stalking her or something."

"I think we've already crossed that line," Erin says.

Rosina turns around and glares at Erin in the backseat. "Why the hell are you so calm?"

Erin shrugs. "We should go up there now," she says. "In case Cheyenne's already home."

"What are we going to say?" Rosina says.

"My old OT said you should usually start with 'Hello,'" says Erin.

"Are you trying to be funny, Erin? Now is really not the time."

"I think Grace should speak first," Erin says. "Since she's the nicest and most normal-looking."

"Okay," says Grace, and she opens her door. "Let's go."

"What?" Rosina says. "Now? We don't have a plan. Grace, what are you going to say?"

"We've prepared as much as we can," Grace says. "Now we just have to trust that the right words will come."

"Is that one of your God things?" Rosina says. "Because I really don't think I can handle that right now."

Without answering, Grace steps out of the car and shuts the door behind her. Definitive. Decisive. Erin decides she likes this new Grace better than the old one.

The three girls converge on the front porch and, without speaking, stand facing one another.

"Did you know the triangle is the strongest geometric shape in nature?" Erin says.

They meet one another's eyes, one by one by one. They breathe. They swallow. They turn toward the door. Grace presses the button of the doorbell. They hold their breath and wait.

The sound of footsteps. Locks unlocking. The door creaking open to a tiny crack, just enough to reveal a girl's face.

"Can I help you?" the girl says. Her voice quivers. She is already afraid.

"Cheyenne?" Grace says gently.

"Yeah?"

"Hi, I'm Grace. I'm here with my friends Erin and Rosina. We go to Prescott High."

The door opens a little more. Cheyenne sticks her head out—pale skin with freckles; long strawberry-blond, curly hair. Her blue eyes are red rimmed. Haunted. She takes a long look at each of the girls.

"I don't really know how to say this," Grace says. "We're here because . . . Well . . ."

"We thought you might need our help," Rosina says, stepping forward.

A wave of recognition passes through Cheyenne's eyes, then a tremor of surprise. She opens the door a little more.

"A friend of ours overheard a couple of guys talking," Grace says. "Guys we already know have done bad things to girls. They mentioned your name. They were talking about something they did. Something horrible."

Erin is trying to hide behind Rosina. She is no longer calm. All of a sudden she wants to run back to the car. She wants to curl up in the backseat, where she felt safe just moments ago, lock the door, and wait for this all to be over.

Cheyenne's eyes dart between the girls. Erin knows that look. Erin knows that panic.

"We're so sorry about what happened," Grace says. "We want to help. We want to support you in any way you need."

"Does everyone in Prescott know?" Cheyenne says. She sounds mad. "How many people know?"

"Just us," Grace says. "The guys don't know we know."

Cheyenne takes a deep breath. "This is crazy," she says. She closes her eyes for a moment. "What the hell? I guess I should invite you in."

"Only if you want to," Grace says.

Cheyenne looks Grace in the eyes. "I want to," she says softly, almost too quietly to hear. She turns around and they follow her inside.

Erin thinks the living room looks like the kind of place where nice things are supposed to happen. Not things like this.

"Sit down, I guess," Cheyenne says as she curls up in an armchair already draped with a blanket, a cup and crumb-dusted plate

on the table next to it. Grace and Rosina sit on the couch, and Erin takes the matching love seat with the arms just high enough Cheyenne won't notice her rubbing her hands.

"So how do you think you're going to help me?" Cheyenne says.

"That's up to you," Grace says. "At the very least, we can listen. You don't have to keep it all in."

Cheyenne looks at them, one by one. Erin studies her face as it softens. She can see the moment Cheyenne makes the decision to trust them.

"It happened on Saturday night," she says. "I got home early Sunday morning, before my parents woke up. They didn't even know I missed curfew. I slept almost all day yesterday, and when I woke up, I told my mom I have a fever. She let me stay home sick from school today."

"Your parents don't know?" Rosina says.

Cheyenne shakes her head. "I was going to tell someone," she says. "My mom, or the counselor at school or something. But I had no idea how to do it. I was waiting to feel like talking about it. But that never happened."

"Can you talk about it now?" Grace says. "With us?"

"Yeah," Rosina says. "Do you want to talk about something superintimate and scary with these weird girls you've never met in your life who just showed up at your door?"

"Honestly, I think it's actually easier," Cheyenne says. "Because I don't know you, I don't have to worry about your reaction. I don't have to worry about how it's going to affect you." Her eyes crinkle when she smiles. "Plus, you're the Nowhere Girls, right? So I know I can trust you."

"How'd you know?" Grace says.

"You've heard about us?" Rosina says.

"Of course I've heard about you," Cheyenne says. "Everyone's heard about you. You're like superheroes or something."

"Wow," Grace says, and Erin can tell she's trying not to smile.

"I don't even know their names," Cheyenne continues.

"We do," Rosina says.

"I don't want to know," Cheyenne says quickly. "Please don't tell me."

Erin wonders if Rosina was right—maybe they shouldn't be here. Maybe they shouldn't be pushing Cheyenne to talk. Maybe it's not always a good idea to talk about it. Everyone is always saying "Talk about it." But what if talking hurts? What if it does more harm than good? What if talking about it just makes you relive it over and over again? What if it just gives the pain more fuel?

Or what if talking about it burns it out? That's the theory, anyway. But has anyone scientifically proven it? Do memories have a half-life, like carbon? Do they shrink over time until they're minuscule, microscopic? Can you share something so much you give it all away?

Erin does not know the answers to any of these questions. She hates not knowing. She hates looking at this girl in pain and not knowing how to fix it, but also not knowing how to run away, not knowing how to stop caring. Erin is powerless. She hates being powerless.

She hates the feeling of the world crushing her. She hates metaphors being the only way to describe it.

Cheyenne takes a deep breath. "I was at a party. A girl in my math class invited me. I just moved here so I don't really know anyone that

well. I went because I thought it'd be a good way to meet people, to make friends." Her face scrunches up. "How ironic, right?

"There was this punch, and you couldn't even taste the alcohol, so I had no idea how much I was drinking. I was just standing there in the corner, not talking to anyone, holding that stupid plastic cup and drinking because I had nothing else to do. I was so embarrassed. And then these three really cute guys started talking to me, and I was so grateful, you know?"

"Do you remember what happened?" Rosina asks.

"Of course I remember," Cheyenne says. "I remember everything. I wasn't *that* drunk. I wish I was. Then I'd have an excuse."

"An excuse for what?" Grace says.

"For not doing anything," Cheyenne says. Her hands grip the arms of her chair. She squeezes her eyes shut as she pulls her blanket-covered knees close to her chest. "I could have fought back maybe. I could have screamed. But it was like I was frozen. I just laid there. I couldn't move. I saw everything. I felt *everything*."

Cheyenne is shaking now. Erin looks away and tries to focus on the rhythm of her own rocking body. She thinks she might be shaking too. She doesn't know which feelings are Cheyenne's and which are her own.

Erin thinks about Spot. She thinks about what he does when she's shaking, when Erin feels like Cheyenne must be feeling. Erin thinks of Spot resting his furry warm face on her hand. She thinks of the feeling of his breath on her fingers. She gets off her chair and walks across the living room. She kneels on the floor and puts her hand on Cheyenne's. Erin thinks of what she would have wanted to hear if someone had ever helped her.

"Just breathe," Erin says. And Cheyenne breathes. And Erin breathes with her. They wrap their fingers together. They hold hands. Erin knows she is breaking the rule of not touching her. They breathe in. They breathe out. Erin wonders how she can feel Cheyenne's tears on her cheeks, but then she realizes they're her own.

"It's not your fault," Erin says. "You didn't do anything wrong."

"But maybe I could have done something," Cheyenne says. "Maybe I could have stopped it. If I fought back. I didn't even fight back."

"You shouldn't have to," Rosina says. "We should never be put in a position where we have to fight someone off us."

"Shit," Cheyenne says, covering her face with her hands. "I can still feel them on top of me. The weight. They were so heavy. I can smell them. Their BO. The beer on their breath." She speaks between her fingers. "My neck got wet when they breathed." She puts a hand on her neck, as if she's trying to cover up the memory on her skin.

Erin leans into Cheyenne's leg. Her whole right side is touching another human being, and she is not freaking out. Erin is not thinking about herself at all.

Cheyenne lowers her hands to her lap. Her lips are closed tight and thin as she sits up a little straighter.

"I knew I was supposed to tell the cops right away," she says. "I know that's what they're always saying on those detective shows. But I was so tired. I just wanted to take a shower. I had to. There's no way to describe it. I didn't care about turning them in, or justice, or any of that. I didn't care about *them* at all. I just wanted to sleep. I just wanted it to be over. I just wanted to make it go away. I had

just dealt with it for the whole time it happened, I didn't want to deal with it any more." She looks up. "I'm sorry. I should have told someone. I shouldn't have waited this long."

"There's nothing to be sorry about," Grace says. "You didn't do anything wrong."

"They were so nice to me at the party," Cheyenne says, shaking her head. "They were asking me all sorts of questions about myself, like they really gave a shit. And then I realized I was drunk, and I said it. I remember. I said, 'Hey, I'm drunk,' and started laughing, and then they looked at each other, like they were giving each other a sign, like that's exactly what they were waiting for. I should have known then. I shouldn't have gone outside with them. God, I was so stupid. They said they were going to walk me to my car and drive me home because I wasn't fit to drive. I thought they were being so nice. I thought they were *helping* me.

"I didn't know something was wrong until it was too late. We were outside. I handed one of them the keys to my car. He opened the back door and told me to get in. He was older. He was the leader. His voice wasn't nice anymore. He told the others what to do."

"Do you need to take a break?" Grace says. "You don't need to tell all the details if you don't want to."

The way Cheyenne shakes her head reminds Erin of how her mother shakes out the kitchen rug. Like she's trying to beat it clean.

"Only two of them ended up doing it," Cheyenne says. "The third one ran off. I remember he had a goatee. I could hear him throwing up in the bushes while it was happening."

"Jesus," says Rosina.

"I haven't touched my car since I drove home that morning. I never want to go in that car again. God, there's probably still their fucking condoms on the floor. Who fucking does that? Who rapes someone with a condom and leaves it lying around like that? Either they're really fucking stupid or they're so delusional and arrogant they think they'll never get caught."

Cheyenne stops speaking abruptly. Her face turns pale, gray tinged. She covers her mouth, throws the blanket off her lap, and stands up. "Excuse me," she mumbles, and runs out of the living room into a room off the hall, closing the door behind her.

Erin moves off the floor and back to the love seat. She tries not to listen as Cheyenne throws up in the bathroom.

Erin's nerves are all on fire. It hurts so much she almost can't stand it—this caring, this remembering. This letting go. This letting the world back into the places she's worked so hard to shut it out of.

"You guys," Rosina whispers. "What are we doing here? What are we doing to this poor girl?"

"What do you mean?" Grace says. "We're helping her."

"She's so upset she's puking in the bathroom. How is that helping her?"

"She's choosing to talk to us, Rosina," Grace says. "We're not making her do anything."

"We don't know that. Maybe she was afraid to say no to us. Maybe she's in so much shock she's not thinking straight. We want to get these guys so bad maybe we're not thinking about what's best for Cheyenne. Maybe we're taking advantage of her."

"You're not taking advantage of me," Cheyenne says from the

hallway. "I want to talk." She walks to her chair and sits back down. "I want to get those guys as much as you do."

"Okay," Rosina says.

"My car is full of evidence," Cheyenne says. Something about her has changed. All of a sudden it's like she's leading a business meeting instead of talking about her own rape. "Fingerprints. The condoms. All kinds of DNA." She pauses. Swallows. "I have bruises."

No one says anything. Erin knows it's because there's too much to feel and no words for it. Disgust. Horror. But also the thrill of hope that Cheyenne may help them finally get these guys.

"Do you think you could identify them?" Grace says. "In a lineup or whatever?"

"Yes," Cheyenne says. "Definitely."

Erin unzips her backpack, pulls out the yearbook she brought, the one from last year that Mom insisted on buying even though Erin knew she'd never ask anyone to sign it. She opens to a page near the middle, an entire half page dedicated to Spencer, Eric, and Ennis, the three kings of Prescott High, arms around each other and smiling like they rule the world. Erin walks slowly, carefully, across the room, the book open in her hands like an offering, a gift.

Cheyenne flinches and looks away. "You can close it now."

"Is that them?" Grace says.

Cheyenne nods, looking down at her lap. She fiddles with a snag on her blanket.

Then all of a sudden she looks up, eyes wide. "Oh, shit," she says. "Are these the same guys who raped that girl last year?"

"Yes," Grace says.

"Of course they are," Cheyenne says. "Jesus, I can't believe that didn't even cross my mind until now. Isn't that sick?" She emits something like a laugh, but also the opposite of a laugh. "I just assumed it was entirely different guys. Like anyone could do this. Like it's that common."

"It is, though," Rosina says. "Way too fucking common."

"We have to stop them," Cheyenne says. "I have to stop them. I have to talk to the cops." She stands up. She pushes her hair behind her ears.

"Are you sure?" Rosina says. "Your life is going to totally change. People will find out. Your parents, your school. It'll probably be in the news."

"But what else am I going to do?" Cheyenne says. "Sit around here forever trying to forget about it? Keep it inside me for the rest of my life and not do anything to make it right? If I don't do anything, they're just going to keep raping other girls. Then I'll have to live with *that* the rest of my life. They need to go to jail."

"But there's a chance they won't," Rosina says. "There's a chance they'll get away with it, just like they did last time."

"I know," Cheyenne says. "But I have to at least try. I have to fight. I want to tell the police. Right now."

"We'll take you," Erin says, her voice so strange in this room that has barely heard it. "We'll stay with you as long as you need us."

"Thank you," Cheyenne says, holding Erin's gaze with her own. "Thank you."

ROSINA.

No one talks much on the way to the station. Grace asks Cheyenne if she wants to call her parents, but she says she doesn't want to involve them until after she tells the cops her story. Grace probably thinks this is crazy, but Rosina gets it. Cheyenne doesn't want her parents' fear to get in the way of her courage.

Erin's in the front with Grace. Rosina keeps peeking at Cheyenne out of the corner of her eye. She doesn't want her to know she's looking. Cheyenne is so still, so emotionless. They're driving through farmland, the land flat and empty until it reaches the mountain foothills so many miles in the distance. The sky has cleared and the light of the late afternoon sun warms Cheyenne's skin with an orange glow. Rosina wonders if she had met Cheyenne before what happened, would she notice now that something is different. She wonders if you can see rape on someone's face.

"Does anyone want to listen to some music?" Grace says.

"Nothing you have," Rosina says. "No offense." Grace has the

world's worst taste in music. She's almost seventeen and still listens to boy bands.

"Does Fir City even have its own police station?" Erin says.

"No," Cheyenne says with a flat voice. "We have to go to the county sheriff. There's a station down the road a couple of miles."

They drive in silence. Grace's hands are at a perfect ten and two on the steering wheel. Erin is straight backed, looking out the window, probably thinking about how this all used to be underwater, how there are shells and fish fossils under all this grass and cow shit.

"I'm not going to break down, you know," Cheyenne says suddenly. "I'm not like that other girl. I heard about how she went crazy and had to leave school and everything. I heard about how she lost it. I'm not going to be like that. I'm not going to let them ruin my life."

"Lucy didn't *let* them ruin her life," Rosina says. "They just *did*. It's not something she chose." It comes out sounding a lot meaner than Rosina intended.

"I know," Cheyenne says. "But I'm going to be strong. I'm not even going to cry anymore about it. I'm done. Those assholes can't have any more of me."

She is looking out the window. She is clenching her jaw so tight Rosina can see the muscles moving down her neck.

"I really appreciate you guys coming out here and helping me do this," Cheyenne says. "Don't get me wrong. But I don't think you can really have an opinion about how I'm supposed to feel right now. I mean, have any of *you* ever been raped?"

Erin's head snaps forward. "My research about how to best talk

to a rape victim states that those trying to help should not share their own experiences because it takes the focus from the victim and belittles her experience."

"That's bullshit," Cheyenne says. "This rape victim wants to know."

"I've never been raped," Grace says very quietly. Her knuckles are white on the steering wheel.

"Me neither," Rosina says.

Erin is silent. Rosina feels like she's been ejected from the car, like she's falling, like the air is being sucked out of her and she's trapped in a vacuum with nothing to inhale.

"Erin," Cheyenne says. "You have?"

Erin folds her arms over her chest. "I never cried about it either," Erin says. "I've spent the past three years not crying about it. In retrospect, I'm not sure that was the best approach."

"Oh, Erin," Grace says. Rosina can hear the tears already in her voice.

"Sometimes the not crying hurts worse than the crying," Erin says.

"What happened?" Grace says. Rosina knows her face is already drenched even though she can't see it from the backseat. Grace cries enough for all of them.

"You're not supposed to pressure the victim for details," Erin says. "And you're definitely not supposed to get more emotional than her."

"I can't help it!" Grace is full-on sobbing now. Rosina is grateful for Grace's display of emotion. It takes attention away from her; no

one sees her face twitching, her lips tightening into a thin line.

"Are you okay, Grace?" Cheyenne says. "Do you need to pull over?"

"Oh, Lord," Grace sniffles. "You're asking me how I am? I'm fine. How are *you*?"

"I don't want to talk about me right now," Cheyenne says. "I'm going to have to do a lot of that in a few minutes."

"I don't want to talk about me, either," Erin says.

"I'm sorry," Grace says. "I'm just so sorry."

Grace manages to pull herself together over the next couple of miles. "We're almost there," she says as a cluster of buildings becomes visible in the distance. "Are you ready, Cheyenne?"

"As ready as I'll ever be."

The Fir County sheriff's office is in a town even smaller than Fir City. Only a handful of buildings make up the main street area. Grace pulls into the almost-empty gravel parking lot. She turns off the car. Nobody moves.

"This is really happening," Cheyenne says. "I'm really doing this. Shit, you guys. I'm scared."

"You should be scared," Erin says, turning around to face Cheyenne. "This is going to be really hard."

"Um, Erin?" Grace says.

"You didn't let me finish," Erin says. "What I was going to say was this is going to be really hard, but nothing will ever be as hard as that night. You already survived that. You can survive anything now."

Someone besides Rosina might be full of love for her friend right now, might want to wrap her arms around Erin and never let

go. But Rosina doesn't do things like that. Instead, she looks out the window and rubs her nose, which is a little wet, but of course it's not from tears.

"Okay," Cheyenne says. "Let's do this."

The inside of the sheriff's station is almost identical to the Prescott police station—the same beige walls, the same handful of mostly empty desks behind a long counter in the front. "Hello, ladies," says the deputy behind the counter. "How can I help you?"

"Um," Cheyenne says. "Is there a female cop I can talk to?"

His face softens. "I'm sorry," he says, and he might actually mean it. "Unfortunately, we don't have any gals here right now." He pauses, smiles warmly. "How about you talk to the sheriff?" he says. "He's in his office right now. I promise, he's a real nice guy. Has twin daughters almost your age. They're twelve now, I think. He loves those girls more than life itself."

It is Erin who Cheyenne looks to now. Some kind of wordless message passes between them. Erin nods. Cheyenne takes a deep breath.

"Okay," Cheyenne says. "I'd like to talk to the sheriff."

"We'll stay here until you're done," Grace says.

"You don't have to do that," Cheyenne says.

"Yes, we do," says Rosina.

Erin, Grace, and Rosina sit for what seems like several hours but is only about forty-five minutes. In that time Erin finishes her homework, Rosina avoids several phone calls from her mother, and Grace spends most of the time in the bathroom to, Rosina suspects, spare the rest of them from her emotional meltdown.

"You know what?" Rosina says. "This may sound bad, but I can't help but think maybe it's a good thing Cheyenne just moved here. She wasn't here to see what happened to Lucy after she reported her rape. She has no reason to expect that she won't be believed."

"God, I hope she's right," Grace says. "I've been praying about it the whole time we've been in here."

So that's what Grace was doing in the bathroom. For once Rosina doesn't think she's nuts. Maybe she's gotten used to her weird God stuff. Or maybe Grace has been secretly trying to convert her this whole time, and breaking down Rosina's resistance is all a part of her plan.

Or maybe, deep down, Rosina wishes she believed in something. Maybe she wishes she had a god she could pray to right now, like Grace does.

"What if we're setting her up to be another Lucy?" Rosina says. "Once word gets out, is Cheyenne going to be crushed like she was? Are we going to screw up her life more than those bastards already did?"

"We're doing the right thing," Grace says. "Cheyenne is doing the right thing."

"Since when does that matter?" Rosina says.

"Since we made it matter," Erin says, looking up from her book.

God, please, Rosina thinks. *Please help her.*

Is thinking the same as praying?

Please help us.

The door to the sheriff's office opens. The girls stand as Cheyenne walks out. Her face is unreadable. She looks tired, but not broken. She

smiles weakly at her friends as a tall, broad-shouldered man follows her out of the office. He looks like a dad. A good one.

"When your mom gets here," he says gently, "we'll need to all sit down together and talk about next steps, but I figured you needed a little break from my office. I know I do." He smiles at Cheyenne warmly, how Rosina as a little girl used to imagine her father would smile at her if he was still alive. Something twists inside her.

"These are the friends who helped you today?" the sheriff says, looking at the girls. Rosina wonders if she should be worried. Is he going to talk to Chief Delaney? Is he going to tell them they're the secret leaders of the Nowhere Girls?

"Yeah," Cheyenne says. "I couldn't have done it without them."

"Those are good friends to have," he says, but Rosina's not sure she completely believes him, even after everything Cheyenne has said to assure them she wants to do this. Because every step they take forward takes them further away from the time before any of this happened.

Rosina catches Erin looking at her strangely. "What?" Rosina says.

"Don't worry," Erin says. "I can see you worrying."

Rosina laughs. "*You're* telling *me* not to worry. That's hilarious."

The front door swings open. An older version of Cheyenne walks in wearing nurse's scrubs, spots her daughter behind the front desk, and they rush into each other's arms. Rosina is embarrassed to witness this moment between them. Something so intimate, something so primal, as a mother rocking her wounded child.

Rosina's phone buzzes with another call from her mother.

Rosina wonders, what if this were her? What if Cheyenne's mom were replaced by her own? Would she be here holding her like this? Would this be her mother's first reaction to news that her daughter had been hurt? Would she hug Rosina like this, love her like this, before asking any questions, no matter what happened, no matter what the story? Could Rosina trust her own mother to love her?

But that doesn't matter right now. Cheyenne is looking at the girls from inside her mother's arms. She mouths, "Thank you." And for a brief moment Rosina has an unfamiliar sense, not quite a thought but not quite a feeling, a sudden burst of clarity, of certainty—it's going to be okay. Is this what Grace's faith feels like? Does she feel it all the time? Is this how she knows God exists?

Cheyenne's mother lets go. She follows the sheriff into his office without ever acknowledging the three girls sitting in the waiting area.

Cheyenne stays back a moment before going with them. "You can go home now," she says. "I think we've got it from here."

The girls don't move.

"Really, you guys," she says. "I'm going to be okay."

"You have our numbers," Grace says. "You'll call us?"

"Of course," she says. "And you'll call me."

"I won't call you," Erin says. "I don't like talking on the phone. But I will text you."

"Okay." Cheyenne smiles.

"Cheyenne," her mom calls from inside the office. "Honey, are you ready?"

Cheyenne waves at the girls, turns around, and closes the door behind her.

Rosina can hear Grace taking deep breaths next to her.

"Grace," Rosina snaps. "Stop breathing so loud."

"Sorry."

"I'm hungry," Erin says.

"I guess it's time to go home," Grace says. She and Erin start heading out the door, but Rosina can't move her feet. She can't stop staring at the office door. The feeling she had a moment ago disappeared as soon as the door closed behind Cheyenne, as soon as Rosina realized it was time to go back to her own life.

"She's going to be okay," Erin says, pulling at the hem of Rosina's shirt. "Let's go."

But it's not Cheyenne who Rosina is worried about.

US.

In the almost hour it takes to drive back to Prescott, no one speaks. Grace, Erin, and Rosina look out the windows, each of their views slightly different. The setting sun will be dipping into the ocean soon, a hundred miles or so to the west. The light fades from the sky without fanfare, as if it is any other evening.

It is dusk when they pull up in front of Erin's house. No one is surprised to see the police car parked in front.

"What are you going to tell them?" Rosina says. "We have to make sure our stories match."

"The truth," Erin says. "What else is there?"

Spot greets Erin as soon as she enters the house, circling her ankles, sniffing her, licking her fingertips, all of his usual magic tools of assessment. Mom is sitting on the couch, stunned and red eyed, across from a nervous cop who looks barely older than Erin. Mom jumps up and lunges forward, then stops herself just short of tackling her daughter in a full embrace. She knows she cannot hold her, cannot be held, so instead she breaks into tears. She stands there, an

arm's reach away from Erin, sobbing so hard her shoulders shake.

"What happened?" Mom cries. "I don't understand how this could happen. I thought things were getting better. I thought you were better." Spot leaves Erin's ankles and rubs up against her mother's. "I tried so hard to take care of you. I try so hard. But I failed you. I let this happen. If I had just—"

Erin reaches out and touches Mom's shoulder. "Don't be scared, Mom," she says. "I'm not."

As soon as Erin pulls her hand back, Mom reaches up to her own shoulder, touching the vacant space. She sniffles a few times, as if surprised by her sudden absence of tears.

"They want you to go to the station now," Mom says, wiping her eyes.

"Then let's go," Erin says.

"Shouldn't we wait for your dad to get home?"

"No," Erin says calmly. "We're fine without him. We've *been* fine without him."

"But—"

"Mom, we don't need him."

Erin does not meet her mother's eyes, but she doesn't have to. Mom studies the surprising stillness of her daughter's face, her own face a mix of alarm and confusion and fierce, unnamable love, as if she doesn't recognize the young woman standing in front of her, like she is seeing her, hearing her, for the first time.

"We don't need him," Erin says again.

Erin looks up and studies the tense shock on her mother's face, then the gradual softening as Mom seems to realize what Erin's say-

ing, as maybe she lets a little of it in, as she tastes the tiniest hint of something that could turn into freedom.

Meanwhile, in front of Rosina's house, the lights of the police car are spinning, painting the block in colors that almost seem festive. A handful of people from the neighborhood mill around, waiting for something to happen.

"Jesus," Rosina says. "I should charge admission."

"Are you going to be okay?" Grace asks.

"I don't know." All Rosina knows is, she can't spend the rest of her life avoiding her mother's phone calls. She can't keep running away from the inevitable. She can't stop time. Whatever ends up happening may not be fair. It may not be right, or just, or the way things should be, but it is reality. It is Rosina's reality. It will be her reality until she figures out how to change it. But one thing Rosina knows for sure is that running away is not change. She steps out of the car and braces for whatever is about to come.

When Grace gets home, a policewoman is sitting on the couch with her parents with a cup of coffee in her hand. "Gracie!" Mom says as Grace enters, but no one says more than that as she drops her schoolbag by the door and comes in to sit with them.

"Hi," Grace says to the policewoman.

"Grace, do you know why I'm here?"

"Yes."

"We'd like you to come into the station for questioning. You've been accused of some very serious crimes."

"Oh my lord," Mom says. Dad puts his arm around her. Grace cannot look at them, cannot risk seeing the heartbreak in their eyes.

"May I ask whom I've been accused by?" Grace asks. "And what the accusations are?"

The officer looks at the notes on her clipboard and reads without looking up. "A complaint has been filed by Regina Slatterly on behalf of the Prescott City School District. It says here theft, theft of proprietary information, cybertheft, hacking, harassment, conspiracy, contributing to the delinquency of a minor—golly, this is quite a list."

What is that strange feeling bubbling up inside of Grace? Why is she so calm? Why is she smiling?

"Does Grace need to ride with you in the police car?" Dad asks.

"No, sir," the officer says. "She's not being charged with anything yet. She can ride with you."

"But if she's not being charged with anything," Dad says, "then technically she doesn't have to come in, right? She can stay here. I think maybe I should call a lawyer. I don't know if I'm comfortable with my daughter—"

"Dad," Grace says. "It's okay. I'm ready to talk to them." Finally she looks up, looks each of her parents in the eye. "I have nothing to be ashamed of."

"Honey," Mom says as soon as they're all buckled in the car, Grace alone in the backseat. "What is going on?" Grace can hear the fear in her voice.

"This isn't you," Dad says. "You don't get in trouble with the law. I don't understand how this is possible."

"I can explain," Grace says. She pauses for a moment, closes her eyes, searches inside herself for the solid part of her, the place her true voice comes from. "I am one of the founders of the Nowhere Girls.

It was me and my friends Rosina and Erin. We started it because we wanted to help Lucy, the girl who got raped last year. We wanted to help all the girls. The group took on a life of its own as it got bigger."

Mom turns to face her, but Grace cannot see her eyes in the darkness. But she can somehow feel the love radiating from them.

"We may have broken a few rules, small rules, but we haven't hurt anyone," Grace says. "We've helped people. We have helped so many people." Her voice cracks. "Mom," Grace says. "This is the best thing I've ever done."

Grace hears Mom sigh, sees her parents look at each other the way they do when she knows they're reading each other's minds. No one speaks for the rest of the way to the station, but something has been decided. Some kind of peace has been silently declared. They trust her. They have always trusted her.

Rosina's mom's car is equally quiet, but the silence is charged, dense, as if it is on the verge of combusting at any moment, as if the car is a moving bomb. Rosina thinks she must have missed Mami's angry stage, because all she's seen since she got home is something much worse, something beyond angry—Mami is terrified. She has said virtually nothing, not a word to shame Rosina or even to intimidate the police officer in her living room. She sat there almost demurely as he explained that he'd like her to drive Rosina to the police station. "Yes, sir," was all she said. And now she drives with white knuckles, staring straight ahead, the tears on her cheeks reflecting the fleeting glow of streetlights.

Rosina is dying to get out of the car, but neither of them moves when they pull into the police station parking lot. Something must

be said. They could wait forever for the other to say it.

Rosina looks out the window and sees Erin walking tall into the police station, her mother following close behind, holding her purse to her chest. Despite the oppressive air of the car, Rosina can't help but smile at the sight of her friend—such a small, tidy movement of the lips to express something so huge inside, such a tiny gesture to reveal this bursting of love and pride.

"You scare me, hija," Mami finally says. Rosina turns and is surprised to see a middle-aged woman with smeared mascara and fried graying hair. She never quite thought of her mother as beautiful, but she definitely never thought of her as old.

"You're always fighting," Mami says, her pleading eyes burning into Rosina's. "You want to fight everything."

"That's not true," Rosina says, but softly, without conviction.

"Someday you're going to lose," Mami says. "You're going to get hurt."

"Maybe," Rosina says. "But when that happens, do you want to be the one hurting me?"

Something happens in the silence that follows Rosina's question. Weight on either side of the car seems to even out, become equal. Fear and rage dissipate and all that's left are two women, half lit by streetlights.

"I've only ever wanted to protect you," Mami whispers.

"I know," Rosina says, because, suddenly, she does.

After a few moments Rosina says, "We should go in."

"Are you scared?" Mami says. Not accusing, not judging. Just asking. Just wanting to know what her daughter is feeling.

"Terrified," Rosina says.

To anyone else, Mami's nod would be almost imperceptible, but to Rosina it is like a mountain moving. A small glimmer of gratitude pulses through her, like one single heartbeat, and it is more than enough. This is the scale of their love.

Erin is as calm and collected as Rosina's ever seen her. She's rubbing her hands together the way she does when she's nervous, but it's more excited than anxious, almost joyful. Her mother sits on the bench next to her, closer than Erin would normally allow. She seems more confused than angry or scared, as if this is all a terrible mistake, as if she can't even imagine that her daughter is capable of doing something that would bring them to the police station. She has no idea what her daughter is capable of.

Rosina stands next to Erin while Mami marches up to the front desk to get some answers. "They're waiting for Grace to get here," Erin tells Rosina. "They want to talk to us all together."

"Is my daughter being arrested?" Mami demands, her old fire returned. Rosina never thought she could possibly feel sorry for a police officer, but there's always a first for everything. She smiles at the sight of her tiny mother bullying the cop, sees a glimpse of herself, of her own courage, and it pushes out her fear, just a little.

The front door opens. Grace and her family walk in as a pack, as a single unit, connected. Rosina's mom turns around and a look passes between the two mothers, so brief and subtle Rosina almost doesn't catch it, and for a moment her mother is not cruel or angry or even scared; for a moment all Rosina sees is love.

The officer at the front desk makes a call. Chief Delaney

emerges from his office, wiping crumbs off his mouth with the back of his hand. "All right, ladies," he says. "Let's make this quick. Are you ready to talk to me?"

None of them says anything.

Delaney sighs. "Since you're minors, I guess I have to tell you that you're allowed to bring your parents in."

All three girls say no without hesitation.

They are nervous as they walk to Chief Delaney's office, but they are not scared. The world is so much bigger than this tiny place, and justice is so much more complicated than the whims of this small man. Their understanding of the judicial system is limited, but they are sure something is going to happen now. They know Delaney can't stop it. They know the county sheriff is on their side. They have evidence. They have truth. There are finally people—adults—who want to hear it. The girls know, in some small way, they have already won.

What they don't know is that at the same time their parents were driving them to the station, county deputies were also arriving at the homes of Spencer Klimpt, Eric Jordan, and Ennis Calhoun. Sirens alerted entire neighborhoods of their arrival. Neighbors lined the streets to watch the boys get taken away in handcuffs and shoved into the back of cop cars.

With the door closed to the chief's office, the girls have no idea what's happening in the rest of the police station. They don't know that as they attempt to tell the bored and only half listening police chief their side of the story, the county sheriff arrives. They don't know the sheriff's been trying to get ahold of Chief Delaney all

night, ever since he talked with Cheyenne. They don't know how Delaney has a habit of avoiding the sheriff's calls, how he resents him for trying to make his job harder by insisting on jurisdictional communication. The girls certainly don't know the sheriff already dislikes the chief almost as much as they do.

Do the girls know when the boys enter the building? On some level, can they feel their presence?

The boys are whisked away into separate rooms as they wait for their parents to arrive. If they were smart, they wouldn't talk. They'd wait for lawyers. They'd play the game. But maybe fear—maybe even something else—has clouded reason. Maybe one of the boys is already talking. Maybe, all this time, he has been desperate to purge his shame.

In two separate rooms, truth is being told. In two other rooms, boys hold on to silence like a life preserver.

Neither they nor the girls are aware of the waiting area slowly filling up with their classmates. Word spreads fast in small towns.

One after another, they arrive: Melissa Sanderson, ex-cheerleader and Rosina's love; Elise Powell, jock; Sam Robeson, drama club girl; Margot Dillard, student body president; Lisa Sutter, cheer squad captain; Serina Barlow, rehab girl; gossips Connie Lancaster and Allison Norman; Lucy's old friends Jenny and Lily; the multicolor-haired freshmen Krista and Trista. All these girls who would normally never mix. Others. More. Everyone.

The Nowhere Girls are here. They are everywhere.

When Rosina, Grace, and Erin emerge, blinking, from Chief Delaney's office, the station erupts in an explosion of sound. The three girls try to figure out where all the noise is coming from.

What is all that cheering? Girls' voices bounce off walls and ceiling and floor, gathering momentum, gaining speed, crashing into one another.

In the midst of the chaos, Rosina's eyes settle on the one small place of silence. In a corner of the waiting area, apart from the crowd's madness, stand her mother and Mrs. Salter, facing each other, eyes closed, holding hands. Praying. Searching for peace in their own way.

Someone's giddy voice breaks through: "Holy crap, you guys. There are a ton of news vans outside."

Then office doors open, one by one by one, perfectly timed: Spencer, Eric, Ennis. A silence even louder than cheers washes over the police station. It is the stillness at the edge of a cliff—so many eyes watching, so much breath being held—the moment before the fall.

As Spencer exits one office, he sees Ennis walking out of another across the room. "What did you tell them?" he snarls at his friend, breaking the silence.

Ennis's head is down. He does not look up, does not respond, does not acknowledge anything that is happening. He is deflated, empty. He has said things inside that room that he can never take back.

"What the fuck did you say?" Spencer screams, then the whole room flinches as he lunges toward Ennis.

But an officer grabs Spencer before he gets anywhere and effortlessly pulls his arms behind his back, fastens his wrists into handcuffs. "Ouch," Spencer says with a weak, high-pitched yelp. "You're hurting me." Who knew he was so easy to catch?

"Move it along," says the officer, kicking Spencer in the back

of the heel like chattel, causing Spencer to trip and fall flat on his face without his hands to catch him. No one moves to help him up. Tense giggles pepper the air as he squirms to pull himself upright. Spencer struggles, powerless, and the giggles turn into laughter, then into something else entirely, a sound without definition, something born out of so many weeks', months', years', so many lifetimes' worth of held breath finally expelled, so many clear voices restored, feeding one another, building and growing until the station explodes in cheers so loud there is nowhere left for silence to hide.

Eric Jordan stares out at the waiting area, his eyes blank, unreadable, gone. He sees a wall of young women, his classmates, the girls he has hit on and catcalled and demeaned for years. He sees them as he has never seen them—a group, solid and formidable, and so much bigger than him. Not just bodies, not just skin and softness, not toys or tamable creatures. He neither wants them nor hates them. He doesn't know what he feels. He has been raised with the privilege of not being accustomed to fear.

But in this moment a spark of knowledge wedges itself inside him, the sudden realization of a world turned over—these girls are going to define his life as much as he has already defined theirs.

The girls are packed in so tight there is barely room enough to breathe, and still more are coming. Cheers turn to screaming, shouting, crying. The sound is deafening, primal. It is every feeling, all at once. It is all the girls, all their voices, calling out as loud as they can.

They burn through darkness. They brand the night.

CHEYENNE.

Mom said Cheyenne could skip school today if she didn't feel ready, but Cheyenne is sick of staying at home. Even though she barely slept last night, even though everything feels tender—not just her skin, but her eyes, her mouth, her lungs. As if every piece of her is exhausted, as if every molecule has been twisted and kneaded and prodded for hours upon hours, days upon days.

But she is tired of her life being on hold. She is tired of hiding. And she is just the right amount of sleep deprived for adrenaline to kick in, just the right amount of foolish to be brave.

She has an idea of what's going to happen when she gets to school. She knows how small towns work. She knows how people talk, how information spreads, whether it's true or not. In just a night, a true story can turn into something else entirely. And its subject can become something completely different from a living, breathing human being.

It's been only a month and a half since Cheyenne started at this

new school, and she hasn't made any real friends yet. She figures she'll get through her day much the same as she did before, not really talking to anyone. Maybe people will stare a little. Maybe they'll whisper. But there's not a whole lot for her to lose.

Cheyenne's mom drives her to school and tries not to cry as she watches her daughter walk into the building, as she watches her disappear behind its doors, as Cheyenne enters a world where her mother can't protect her.

The halls are full of the usual noise. Cheyenne walks with her head down. All she wants is to make it to class without meeting anyone's eye, without having to absorb their pity, their curiosity, their scorn. But she hears the hush that envelops the hall. She feels the eyes piercing into her. She senses movement, but she tries not to think about it. *Just go forward,* she thinks. *Just make it past this.*

What she does not realize is the movement has a pattern. It has a focus. It has a destination. One by one, each girl in the hall moves toward Cheyenne. Like a school of fish, they communicate without speaking. They move together, falling into formation around her as she walks through the hall.

Finally Cheyenne looks up. She sees the girls surrounding her. She meets their eyes, and it is not pity she sees, not judgment, not scorn. What she sees is fire. What she sees is eyes full of flame.

She feels a tickle on her right fingers and realizes the girl next to her is holding her hand. She feels the heat of the bodies around her, shielding her from whatever might get in the way, holding her up,

driving her forward. They walk like that all the way to Cheyenne's first-period class. They take up the entire width of the hall. The sea of students parts to let the girls through.

Because the girls are unstoppable. They are a force. They are a single body.

LUCY.

In a town somewhere a girl named Lucy Moynihan knows her parents are talking to their lawyer again. She knows her rapists have been arrested and her case will finally go to trial. She knows her ghosts have been turned into news.

Of course, all this attention will die down as soon as there's another story to take its place. Everyone will forget about the Nowhere Girls and Prescott, Oregon, and the shocking crimes of three boys who almost got away with it. Because of her age, Lucy's name is protected in the media. But still, she knows people are talking about her. They are talking about a girl none of them knows.

Who knows what will actually end up happening? Who knows what justice even looks like? What punishment is equal to those boys' crime, equivalent to the permanence of what they did? Is there even such a thing as justice? Nothing can bring back the girl Lucy was. Nothing can undo what happened.

Lucy is trying not to get her hopes up. Despite all the good news, there was still that case a couple of months ago about that boy

who was caught raping a passed-out girl in his frat house's laundry room. Even with eyewitnesses, even with video evidence, he still only got three months. Because he was rich. Because he was white. Because when jurors and judge looked at him, they did not see someone who looked like he was supposed to go to prison. Lucy remembers reading a statistic somewhere that only three percent of rapists spend even a day in jail. Those are not good odds.

But maybe things are changing, Lucy thinks. Just a little, day after day, can add up to a lot after a while. The world is already a different place than it was last spring, when there was no way the Nowhere Girls could have existed. But now here they are, in the exact same impossible place she left, doing impossible things.

Lucy sits in the bedroom that's been hers for only a few months. She thinks about the desperate words she scratched in the walls of her old room, when she wanted to scream but couldn't, when crying wasn't enough. She wonders if anyone ever found them.

RESOURCES

National Sexual Assault Hotline:
800.656.HOPE and www.online.rainn.org
En Español: www.rainn.org/es

RAINN: www.rainn.org
RAINN (Rape, Abuse & Incest National Network) is the nation's largest anti–sexual violence organization. RAINN created and operates the National Sexual Assault Hotline in partnership with more than 1,000 local sexual assault service providers across the country. RAINN also carries out programs to prevent sexual violence, help victims, and ensure that perpetrators are brought to justice.

Planned Parenthood: www.plannedparenthood.org
America's most trusted provider of reproductive health care and a respected leader in educating Americans about reproductive and sexual health.

Our Bodies Ourselves: www.ourbodiesourselves.org
Our Bodies Ourselves (OBOS) is a global feminist organization that distills and disseminates health information from the best scientific research available as well as women's life experiences, so that the individuals and communities they reach can make informed decisions about health, reproduction, and sexuality.

Advocates for Youth: www.advocatesforyouth.org

Advocates for Youth partners with youth leaders, adult allies, and youth-serving organizations to advocate for policies and champion programs that recognize young people's rights to honest sexual health information; accessible, confidential, and affordable sexual health services; and the resources and opportunities necessary to create sexual health equity for all youth.

Stop Sexual Assault in Schools: www.ssais.org

SSAIS is spearheading the movement for awareness of sexual harassment and sexual assault in K–12 schools in order to prevent it, support victims, inform students about their rights, and empower them to protect their peers.

ACKNOWLEDGMENTS

First, as always, thank you to my tireless cheerleader and agent, Amy Tipton.

My editor at Simon Pulse, Liesa Abrams. You are this book's soul mate editor. I could not have gotten luckier. Your passion and devotion to this book were boundless. Thank you for believing in Grace, Rosina, and Erin. And me.

Everyone at Simon Pulse and Simon & Schuster who went above and beyond the call of duty to advocate and care for this book. I know I had a whole army fighting for *The Nowhere Girls*, and even though I don't know all your names, I am grateful for each and every one of you.

My foreign rights agent, Taryn Fagerness, for taking my girls across the pond.

The Weymouth Center for the Arts & Humanities Writer-in-Residence program, for giving me such a beautiful space to finish my first draft.

Trudy Hale at The Porches writing retreat in Virginia, for being my home away from home, and for the silence.

Thank you to my community in Asheville, North Carolina, for inspiring aspects of the resistance in this book. Readers may have heard of the event in September 2015 where the owners of Waking Life, one of my neighborhood coffee shops, were revealed to be behind a misogynist podcast series and Internet postings, including a graphic and degrading list of sexual conquests involving local women, which inspired the Real Men of Prescott blog posts in *The Nowhere Girls*. The people of Asheville immediately responded by boycotting the business, sending a clear message that the men's blatant sexism and abuse of women in our community would not be tolerated. Local businesses stopped carrying their products. Men and women stood together outside in protest. Within a couple of weeks, the

owners left town, disgraced. Asheville made it clear that it will stand up for women, that it will stand up to misogyny and sexism. I am proud of my mountain town.

Angélica Wind, Executive Director of Our VOICE, for reading an early draft of this book, and for the tireless work you do serving survivors of sexual assault and abuse in Western North Carolina.

Immense gratitude to my beta and sensitivity readers: Emily Cashwell, Jennie Eagle, Kimberly Egget, Stefanie Kalem, Alison Knowles, Constance Lombardo, Natalie Ortega, Meagan Rivera, Michelle Santamaria, Kaylee Spencer, Nana Twumasi, and Victoria Vertner. Very special thanks to Stephanie Kuehnert, plot-whisperer. You all helped breathe fire into this book.

Lyn Miller-Lachmann, for her wonderful book *Rogue*, and for steering me in the right direction. For invaluable insight about living with autism, and writing about life with autism, thank you to wrongplanet.net; L.C. Mawson's blog, lcmawson.com; Tania Marshall's blog, taniaannmarshall.wordpress.com; Samantha Craft's blogs, everydayaspergers.com and everydayaspie.wordpress.com; and disabilityinkidlit.com, especially posts by Corinne Duyvis and Elizabeth Bartmess.

My most profound and humble gratitude goes to Jen Wilde and Meredith McGhan, for the depth of their generosity in sharing their experiences with me, and for their honest (and sometimes hard to hear) feedback. You pushed me to be a better writer, and a better person. Everything I got right about Erin is due to the help of these fierce and brilliant women. Anything I got wrong is my fault alone.

Thank you to Brian, for being my home. And Elouise, for being my hope. You are my light in the darkness.

Always, more than anything, thank you to my readers and teens everywhere, who continue to inspire me with your courage and compassion. Keep resisting. Keep speaking your truth. The world needs your voices, now more than ever.

Turn the page for a look at
an unforgettable, surreal story from Amy Reed.

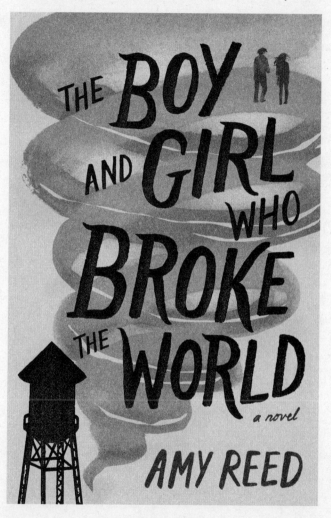

"Gritty, gutsy, and ferociously strange. Amy Reed offers us a surreal yet oddly
familiar world teetering on the edge of destruction and offers hopeful and
inventive ways to survive the pain and salvage our dreams. This story is powerful
and unique, and I envied its wild and irreverent vision to pieces."

—NOVA REN SUMA, #1 *New York Times*
bestselling author of *The Walls Around Us*

BILLY

THIS ISN'T ANY OLD FIRST DAY OF SCHOOL. FIRST OF ALL,
it's my first day of *senior year*, which is supposed to be some kind of
Big Deal, like a rite of passage or something, except I don't really see
myself or most of my classmates changing much anytime soon, and
isn't that what a rite of passage is supposed to make you do? As far
as I can tell, most people in Fog Harbor stay the same until they die,
except instead of being in high school, they're working at BigMart
or the prison. So senior year isn't so much about growing up as it
is about doing a bunch of illegal things before you can get a permanent police record. But I have no interest in drinking and doing
drugs, and I don't know any other, cleaner options that sound any
good. I'm not cool enough to be straight-edge, and I'm not smart
enough to be a nerd, so mostly I'm just sober out of fear, which is
my motivation for most things when I think about it. Grandma's
been telling me since before I can remember that addiction is in
my blood and I'm a junkie waiting to happen, and I figure going
through withdrawal once as a baby is more than enough. Plus, I've
heard enough horror stories watching the AA channel on TV that
drinking and doing drugs don't really seem worth the trouble.

The whole Big Deal of senior year pales in comparison to

the *Really* Big Deal: that the high schools of Carthage and Rome will be combined this year. Things are tense, to say the least. Even before my uncle got famous, even before Carthage's Unicorns vs. Dragons connection, Rome and Carthage have had a rivalry as long as anyone can remember. This is one of Grandma's favorite topics of conversation, in addition to "environmental terrorists" and "fake news." The rivalry started sometime in the early 1900s, with a sordid story involving opium-crazed mill workers and a serial killer named Hilliard Cod, who was also the first mayor of Rome and was supposedly into witchcraft and put a curse on both the towns right before he was executed. For years, the biggest night of the year for both towns has been the annual Carthage High versus Rome High football game, which has the highest official violent crime rate of any night all year. But since Carthage High is closed down due to dwindling enrollment numbers and being condemned for a rabid raccoon infestation and literally the whole thing being a giant, crumbling box of asbestos, that particular night won't be a problem anymore. But now the whole school year might.

Until just a few years ago, most people only knew about us for having the highest per capita heroin deaths in the state and the most foggy days per year of anywhere in America and one of the worst rates of unemployment after all the logging jobs disappeared. We're also known as West Coast Appalachia, which sounds kind of fancy to me but apparently is not a compliment because the one time I asked Grandma what it meant, she yelled and chased me around the

house (but slowly, due to her bum knee and arthritis and diabetes and a few dozen extra pounds) and threatened to smack my chin, even though these days, smacking chins is mostly considered child abuse, which she claims it wasn't back when her actual children— my mom (RIP) and uncle (estranged)—were kids. But look how they turned out (not good).

But Rome is famous now for something way bigger than fog and heroin and unemployment, and that big thing is my uncle, Caleb Sloat. The WELCOME TO ROME sign when you drive into town got replaced last year with a new sign that says WELCOME TO ROME—YOU CAN'T GO HOME AGAIN, which is the title of the song that catapulted Rainy Day Knife Fight (my uncle's band) into fame three years ago. If you ask me, it was a kind of hasty decision for Rome to make a whole new sign to commemorate a hometown hero, especially one who's only been famous for three years and isn't even dead yet, but I guess they were desperate for a hometown hero. The funny/tragic/ironic thing is that "You Can't Go Home Again" is basically a song about how much Caleb hated growing up in Rome, which is what most of his songs are about and pretty much all he ever talks about in interviews, and if you think about it, the sentiment that "you can't go home again" is maybe not the most welcoming thought to have on a town's welcome sign.

So that's what Rome, Washington, is famous for—my uncle Caleb, who I haven't seen in five years, back when I was twelve and he was a twenty-two-year-old starving musician busing tables

at Red Robin in Seattle and sharing a one-bedroom apartment with his bandmates. He came back to Rome for a couple of holidays but left both times screaming out the window of his junk car as he drove away, while Grandma stood at the front door screaming back, and I just sat in the house watching TV with the volume turned way up. Then Caleb got famous and stopped coming at all.

I feel weird even thinking about Caleb as my uncle these days. Sometimes I wonder if my real memories have been replaced by things I've seen on TV and online, and most of the things I think I know about him are based on stories he's told in interviews, which Grandma says are all lies. Then, of course, there's all the celebrity gossip about how he's a junkie and hasn't written a new song in two years, which I don't want to be true but I think probably is.

I don't know who to believe (Grandma and Caleb and celebrity gossip are all notoriously unreliable sources), so I try not to think about it too much. One thing I do know for sure is that old-timers like Grandma can't stop being nostalgic about a version of Rome none of the young people ever got a chance to live in. Not me. Not Caleb. Not my mom (RIP). None of us saw what it was like when, according to Grandma, our neighborhood was actually nice, back when everyone had good logging jobs. But then all the trees got cut down, and so did the people, and now our street is just one of many full of dilapidated houses with overgrown lawns and faded FOR SALE signs, in a part of town everyone calls "Criminal Fields."

But it's my home, so I have to love it. I love how everything is

green all year and never dries out. I love how the air is fresh because it's always getting cleaned out by the ocean. I love how most everyone who lives here has lived here forever, so you always know what people are up to. I love how I can walk everywhere I need to go. I don't know much, but one thing I'm sure of is that happiness is all a matter of perspective.

So, in my humble opinion, Rome and Carthage have plenty to be happy about. Rome has my uncle, and Carthage has Unicorns vs. Dragons, which, if you ask me, makes the towns about even, but I guess no one's ever satisfied with what they have, even if what they have is the most famous rock star in the world and/or the most successful teen book and movie series in the world. One thing that really didn't help the rivalry was when Rome High changed its mascot to the Unicorns right after the first Unicorns vs. Dragons book came out, even though everyone knows the books mostly take place in Carthage. The city of Carthage actually sued the city of Rome for that, but some judge threw it out. Carthage High had to settle for the Dragons being their mascot, which they never quite got over, but when you think about it, aren't dragons way tougher than unicorns? And isn't it cooler to breathe fire than ice? But I guess when you think someone stole something from you, it makes you want it even more.

With the school merger, the mascot of the new Fog Harbor High is changing to the Lumberjacks, so now nobody's happy.

Honestly, I'm feeling pretty relaxed about everything, though

Grandma suggested I bring a steak knife to school today "just in case." One perk of being a loser is that I'm not all that attached to things staying the same. Where else were the Carthage kids supposed to go? Plus, Rome High has plenty of room because the town's population is about one-third the size it was when the school was built, since everyone who can moves away. I figure this is an opportunity for things to change a little, maybe end the town rivalry once and for all. Grandma says that's ridiculous, but she is against change in general as a principle, so I'm not putting a whole lot of stock in her opinions on the matter.

Besides practicing gratitude, another useful thing I've learned from therapy talk shows is to keep my expectations low and my acceptance high. That way, I won't get too disappointed. So I'm trying not to get my hopes up too much about this whole school merger thing, but I can't help thinking that maybe this year I'll find someone to eat lunch with besides Mrs. Ambrose, who spent all last semester telling me about her college year abroad in Prague a million years ago and harassing me to start a Gay-Straight Alliance club, and I couldn't break it to her that I'm not gay because I was afraid she'd be disappointed, like maybe my fictional gayness was the only thing she actually liked about me, and if I broke the news to her that I'm straight, she wouldn't want me eating lunch in her classroom anymore, and she'd throw me into the hall to fend for myself, which I am notoriously not good at, and that would definitely increase my getting-shoved-in-lockers numbers for this year.

Who knows? Maybe this year will be an opportunity to meet some new people. Not that I necessarily need to meet new people. I'm grateful for the people I have: Mrs. Ambrose, even though she mostly talks about herself the whole time; Grandma, even though 97 percent of the time she talks to me, she's saying something mean or ordering me around; that homeschooled girl across the street from my house whose family's in a cult who I think is my age and I say hi to the rare times she's allowed outside, and sometimes I even get a whole sentence out before she runs back into her house, and that's kind of like a conversation. But maybe it would be nice to know someone I can say more than hi to. Maybe it'd be nice if someone said something back that was more than just telling me what to do, or getting mad at me for something that's probably not my fault, or pressuring me to start a Gay-Straight Alliance club, or making fun of me, or asking if they can meet my rock star uncle. Maybe it'd be nice if I could find someone who actually wanted to listen. Maybe then I could figure out what I wanted to say.

LYDIA

I WASN'T EXPECTING A WHOLE LOT FROM THE PEOPLE OF
Rome, but this is bad even for them. A handful of wrinkled old
ladies are standing outside the high school with handmade signs
that say GO BACK WHERE YOU CAME FROM and CARTHAGEANS NOT
WELCOME IN ROME and KEEP TRASH AWAY FROM OUR KIDS. Clever.
Someone painstakingly illustrated what appears to be a group of
dark-skinned dragons being smashed by a giant sparkling white uni-
corn hoof. Besides being incredibly racist, it is also incredibly bad
art. Someone's even holding up one of those PEOPLE BEFORE TREES!
signs everyone has in their front yards to protest the fact that there
are nearly a million acres of untouched old growth forest in Olympic
National Park being wasted on nature when it could be creating
jobs to cut them down. What that has to do with the school merger,
I'm not quite sure.

These people have never met me, and already they hate me. I'm
pretty sure they'd hate me after they met me too, but that's beside
the point. What sucks is the powerlessness of the whole thing, how
I have absolutely no choice about where I go to school, not to mention the fact that I don't even want to be here, but everyone still
hates me, as if I am purposely trying to make their lives difficult,

as if my very existence is an insult and threat to theirs. Plus, I'm brown, which has never been a particularly popular way to occupy space around here.

At least I'm getting to school early, before the explosion of arrivals officially starts. I recognize some Carthage kids on my way to the lunchroom, but they don't say hi. The unspoken rule about free breakfast is you do not talk about free breakfast, even though at least half of the kids in Fog Harbor are on some kind of reduced-price meal plan. There's also the fact that these people are all assholes and not my friends, and therefore not people I talk to.

A big banner says WELCOME, CARTHAGE STUDENTS! as I enter the lunchroom, but someone has already crossed out WELCOME and replaced it with FUCK YOU. I strap my skateboard to the back of my backpack and find my place at the end of the line to pick up today's offering of plastic-wrapped cinnamon roll, sugar cereal, and carton of chocolate milk. With free breakfasts like this, I'm pretty sure the government is purposely trying to kill poor kids with diabetes. My dad, Larry, said the King wants to get rid of food assistance programs altogether, so pretty soon all the poor kids will starve to death, which will be far more efficient. We already got kicked off of food stamps permanently four years ago because Larry accidentally ate a poppy seed muffin and the mandatory drug test everyone has to take tested positive for opiates. One more thing poor people can't do: eat poppy seed muffins.

I sit alone. I always sit alone. After three years at Carthage

High, three years at Carthage Middle, and six years at Carthage Elementary, it is just the most reasonable option. People in Carthage suck. By extension, I already know people in Rome suck. They are too close to be different. That's the big joke about the town rivalry that people around here refuse to recognize—Carthage and Rome are exactly the same. They're both washed-up old towns people either are desperately trying to escape or have resigned to stay trapped in, towns that no one cares about. The fame of Unicorns vs. Dragons and Rainy Day Knife Fight just adds insult to injury. Caleb Sloat got out. The author of those books has never even been here. Any interest people have in Carthage and Rome is for something imaginary.

What I'm not quite sure about is if this general suckiness of people is just a regional thing, or global. I wouldn't know, since I've never spent much time outside Fog Harbor. Apparently, there are rich kids who travel to places like Europe and the Caribbean on a semi-regular basis and go on African safaris. I've only been to Seattle three times that I can remember. My interactions with people there mostly involved restaurant staff, and those people were not promising. The majority of people are like restaurant staff when you think about it. If they're nice to you, it's probably fake and because they want something (like a good tip).

I have spent the last seventeen—almost eighteen—years perfecting my stay-away-from-me-or-you'll-get-stabbed look, but apparently this goofy-looking, mop-haired, skinny white boy currently taking a seat across from me is blind. I glare at him, and he just

grins like he's some bad actor in a toothpaste commercial, except his teeth belong nowhere near a toothpaste commercial. Not that I'm judging. I've never been to a dentist either.

"Hi, I'm Billy," he says.

"What do you want?" I say.

"Are you new? Do you need someone to show you around?"

"Billy is the name of a little boy."

"Or a pet goat."

"Did you mean to be funny?"

"No."

"Then that means I'm laughing at you, not with you."

"What's your name?" he says without a beat, as if he didn't even hear my obvious insult.

"Lydia."

"I've never met anyone named Lydia," he says.

"That's because we're usually chain-smoking old women."

"I know a lot of chain-smoking old women."

"Good for you."

"Are you Quillalish?" he says. Predictable. Everyone asks me that. Like inquiring about the source of someone's skin color is an appropriate way to start a conversation.

"No, I'm Martian," I say. "Are you?"

"No, I'm from Earth. Are you from Carthage?"

"Yes."

"Welcome!"

This kid Billy is a certifiable weirdo. Hypothetically, I might like

weirdos. But so far, I don't think I've ever met a real, true weirdo. Only the posers pretending to be weirdos because they think it's cool, those girls in pink sweatpants with fake rips and stains with that god-awful band's name printed on the butt from that god-awful Sizzling Subject store in the Fog Harbor Mall.

"What's your last name?" I say.

"Sloat."

"Your name is Billy Sloat?"

"Yep."

"What an unfortunate name. Do people ever call you—"

"Hey, Billy Goat!" shouts a large crew-cutted mouth breather as he slaps Billy hard on the back. The table shakes. Billy accidentally squeezes his juice box, and piss-colored apple juice erupts out of the straw.

"Hi, Grayson," says Billy as he mops up his spilled apple juice with a crumpled napkin. "How was your summer?"

"Whatever, doofus," the mouth breather grunts as he walks away. Then he shouts, "Unicorns rule!" and half of the lunchroom cheers.

"How long have you been putting up with that?" I say, surprised by a sudden, even-stronger-than-usual impulse to clobber the retreating baby-man.

"Pretty much since the day I was born," Billy says, attempting to clean apple juice off his shirt, but all he manages to do is spread ripped wads of napkin all over. He is some kind of rare alien species

that appears to not get embarrassed. He may be worthy of further study.

"What's your deal, Billy Goat?"

He pauses his sad attempts at cleaning his shirt, looks up at me, and blinks earnestly. "I have an artistic temperament with no particular artistic talent," he says with no hint of sarcasm.

"Tragic," I say.

He just shrugs.

"Stop what you're doing," I say, reaching over the table with a clean napkin. "Dab—don't wipe." I position the napkin on the wet stain on his shirt, just over his heart, and apply pressure. I can feel his heart beating in my fingers. For a few seconds, he seems to stop breathing. And for some reason the thought pops into my head—I wonder, when was the last time he was touched?—and a weird warmness spreads through me.

I lean back quickly, suddenly wanting to get as far away from him as possible.

"Thank you," he says with a wide-eyed look on his face, like he might start crying any second. What have I done? I can't think of anything snarky to say back. Only the first day of school and already I'm losing my edge.

A timely, empowering anthology of **#RESISTANCE**
that explores the diverse experiences
of growing up female in America.

OUR STORIES,
OUR VOICES

21 YA AUTHORS GET REAL ABOUT INJUSTICE,
EMPOWERMENT, AND GROWING UP FEMALE IN AMERICA

EDITED BY
AMY
REED

"Thoughtful, sharply voiced, and moving."
—*Booklist*